A Caper on CAROLINA BEACH

a Beach House Mystery

Seth Sjostrom

wolfprintMedia, LLC
Hernando Beach, FL 34607

This book is a work of fiction. Names, characters, places, and incidents are products of the author's imagination or are used fictitiously. Any resemblance to actual events or locales or persons living or dead is entirely coincidental.

Copyright ©2023 by Seth Sjostrom

All rights reserved, including the right to reproduce this book or any portion of the book in any form whatsoever.

For information, contact wolfprintMedia, LLC.

Trade Paperback
ISBN-13: 978-1-960501-09-7

1. Kate Harper (Fictitious character)-Fiction. 2. Nick Mason (Fictitious character)-Fiction. 3. Mystery-Thriller- Fiction. 3. Beach House Mysteries Series-Fiction 4. A Caper on Carolina Beach-Title.

First wolfprintMedia edition 2023.

wolfprintMedia is a trademark of wolfprint, LLC.

For information regarding bulk purchases, please contact wolfprintMedia, LLC at **wolfprint@hotmail.com.**

United States of America

A Caper on CAROLINA BEACH

Kathi, my eternal partner in crime (fighting).

My lifetime friends from Southport, Wilmington, Oak Island, University of North Carolina at Wilmington, South Brunswick High School.

My Hallmark and Great American Family friends.

A Caper on CAROLINA BEACH

One

Lightning fractured the sky, the brilliant blue light a brief respite from the storm-blackened night. The frothy waves of the Atlantic Ocean revealed for only a moment as the sky once more succumbed to inky darkness.

Wiping salty rainwater from desperate eyes, another flash of lightning allowed a stolen glance over a shoulder. The pursuer was closing the distance, the muzzle of a pistol dancing around their silhouette.

Not wanting to become an easy target, the man pushed himself to further the distance. Heart racing and breath labored, the rain-soaked man fought the wind in his face pushing him a half step backward with each stride he made. Each footfall in the soft sand felt like hands grasping at his feet, tugging at him as he fled.

A lightning bolt crashed into the sea followed by a percussive thunderclap scarcely a moment later. Unable to resist another glance at his pursuer, his foot snagged on a piece of driftwood, sending him headlong into the sand.

Spitting grains from his mouth, bits of sand sucking into his lungs as his chest heaved, the man spun onto his back. Kicking at the sand with his feet, he made a vain attempt to create distance. Desperate tears added to the rain stinging his eyes, "Why?"

The chase over, his pursuer slowed to a casual pace, their devilish demeanor revealed in another close flash of lightning. Taking measured steps, the figure closed the distance between them.

A grin swept across the pursuer's face, the tip of the gun shining in each burst of lightning. Menacing, the handgun aimed directly at the man on the ground.

The gunman's grin melted into a glare, captured in a jagged display of electricity lighting up the rain-soaked beach. "You shouldn't have come here."

"I belong here!" the man pushed with his feet, his bottom bulldozing a crude path in the soft sand.

The figure with the gun laughed, "Oh, you most certainly do not!"

A crack of lightning flashed so close that the hair on the fallen man's head rose from the electricity filling the air. Pulling the trigger to coincide with the inevitable roar of thunder, the crack of the gun was inaudible against the powerful rumble of the storm.

"You most certainly do not," the figure with the gun muttered, firing a second shot to ensure the chase was without a doubt over.

Two

The steel towers of the vertical-lift Cape Fear Memorial Bridge celebrated Kate Harper's arrival in the coastal North Carolina city of Wilmington. Once across the river, it was a short drive to the string of islands carved from the Intracoastal Waterway and the Atlantic Ocean.

The crest of Snow's Cut Bridge revealed sprawling sandy beaches of Pleasure Island, host to Carolina Beach and her southerly sister, Kure Beach. Both were quaint towns, each charmingly quiet when given back to the locals in the off-season. Summer would grow the population three-fold, a fact Kate's company was counting on.

Passing the iconic Carolina Beach Boardwalk, an enduring piece of nostalgia for visitors and locals alike, Kate spied the address she was looking for. "A short walk from the boardwalk, but far enough to feel tranquil. I'll have to stock some bikes and paddleboards," Kate scribed a note onto her phone.

Pulling into the short drive and under the tall stilts the house was built on, Kate studied the location. Nearing the imperceptible north-south line that separated Carolina Beach from Kure Beach, this area of the island was noticeably quieter than the spry nightlife of the boardwalk.

Stepping out of her luxury SUV, Kate noted how the night was silent save for the rhythmic percussion of ocean waves making their way onshore. A quick scan of neighboring houses, revealed homes painted in coastal pastels. Most were named by their owners and shared through artisan-crafted wood signs attached to their homes adorned with mermaids, dolphins or palm trees.

Appreciating the automatic lights that came on when she arrived, the setting sun cast shadows underneath the stilt house structure. Kate grabbed her purse and laptop bag, excited to investigate the house.

Fishing a key out of her pocket, she noted a memo into her phone to retrofit the entry to a modern electronic lock. Hearing the satisfying click of the tumblers lining into place, she turned the handle and shouldered her way through the door.

Unlike most of the beach houses managed by her company, the foyer in the Carolina Beach house did not offer a direct view of the ocean. Instead, a wall with an attractive prop surfboard greeted guests. Below the surfboard, a hall table with shells overturned to capture keys and a row of cubbies Kate assumed were to house sandy flip-flops made a homey statement.

Kate had to wander to the right to step into the hall which led the length of the house and spilled into a large open room highlighted by a wall of windows. Not wasting any time, Kate marched down the hall and flung open the first set of doors. Stepping out onto the back deck, testing the weather worn wood as she did so, Kate walked to the rail. Looking over a short dune separating the house from the Atlantic, she admired the sweeping vistas of Carolina Beach that ran north and south as far as her eyes could take her.

To the north, Kate could just see the outline of the Carolina Beach pier on the horizon. To the south, the larger hotels and condos gave way to smaller private homes sprinkling the coastline. It was the view directly behind the house that captured her attention. The constant rolling waves of the Atlantic Ocean spilling onto the sandy beach sang a song that filled Kate's heart.

Taking a deep breath of the salt-tinged scent of the sea, Kate enjoyed the moment. The beach was empty as the stars one by one replaced the pink and purple hues of the failing light. She marveled about the locations she was able to enjoy while getting paid to do it.

Lost in her thoughts, she jumped as a voice called up to her from below the deck. "Hellooo…?"

Kate took an instinctive step away from the rail as she tried to catch a glimpse of her intruder through the narrow spaces between the deck planks. Her heart raced as she tried to quickly discern the nighttime incursion.

"I knocked, but when you didn't hear me, I figured you'd be out back," the voice called up.

Kate grasped her chest as she let out her breath, "Nick Mason!"

"You said to come by…"

"I did. I just didn't expect you under my back patio," Kate gasped.

"I'll meet you at the front door," Nick called.

"Good idea," Kate grumbled, clutching her chest in an attempt to get her nerves called off high alert.

Marching through the house, Kate flung the front door open to reveal a grinning Nick Mason. The man stood, an odd mix of tidiness with a touch of chaos. His hair, while it somehow managed to be attractive, was wind tussled. His button-down tropical shirt was of good quality yet laced with wrinkles. Even his shoes, a pair of leather flip-flops. screamed juxtaposition.

Nick noticed Kate's wandering gaze and shrugged, "Florida chic."

Kate laughed, "You look great. A perfect postcard for beach vacation attire."

"And this seems like the perfect beach house," Nick said, his eyes trying to peer over Kate's shoulder and into the house.

"It will be, once we're done with it," Kate quipped. "Come on, I'll show you around. I have barely been able to give it a thorough inspection myself."

Welcoming Nick through, Kate nearly collided with him as he stopped abruptly. Looking at the entry wall, Nick craned his neck into the hallway that led into the house. "This is not Foo Young at all," Nick muttered as he tapped against the wall, listening to the sounds each rap of his knuckle made.

"I believe that is a Chinese egg dish. You mean *Feng Shui*, the principles of harmonizing your environment," Kate corrected.

Nick cocked his head at her, "I wonder if they have a good sushi place around here…"

"That's Japanese and I'm more than happy to treat you to dinner *after* our tour," Kate laughed.

"All right. Let's get to work," Nick said as he proceeded down the hallway.

Nick paid keen attention to the walls that made up the jog in the entry as they made their way into the open living area of the beach house. The views out of almost any angle were stunning, each capturing a stretch of quiet beach with the Atlantic Ocean relentlessly lapping soft waves onto the sand.

"This place is stunning," Nick admitted, his eyes covering every inch of the house. "Open it up a little over there, updated countertops, maybe redo the floors… this will be a million-dollar home."

"Pretty sure it already was," Kate said.

"Hmm," Nick absently nodded as he smoothed his hands over the frame of the bank of glass doors facing the ocean. "These aren't bad, but I'd upgrade to hurricane-rated glass and install shutters on the outside just to be safe. Protect that million-dollar investment."

"So, we've got some work to do," Kate said.

"We have options. A lot of nice to haves, not a ton of have to haves," Nick replied.

Kate looked thoughtfully around the beach house at the handyman's suggestions and nodded, "Let's get you checked into your place and I'll treat you to that dinner. We can write it all up then."

"Sounds good to me. I think I ate all of my road snacks," Nick said.

Kate frowned, "I thought I sent you an airline voucher."

"I know. I like the drive up the coast. Never know if you'll find a new surf spot," Nick replied. "Besides, I knew a guy who had a sailboat tied up just outside of Charleston. Made a great little stop along the way."

"Well, I think you'll like the spot I have you staying at," Kate said. "Let's go."

Kate shook her head as Nick pulled into the space next to her. Climbing out of her SUV, she looked at Nick, "You drove all the way up here in that thing?"

Nick let out a grin, "She's a solid ride. Barely over a hundred thousand miles. Gotta another two in her, at least. Besides, I was able to bring my tools, well, most of the important ones, anyway."

Turning her attention to the oceanfront bungalows, "What do you think? According to the locals, some of the best surf in Carolina Beach is right out your back door."

"Wow. You certainly have an eye for amazing properties," Nick admired.

"Let's check it out!" Kate grinned, a hop in her step as she tugged Nick toward his unit. A series of brightly painted townhomes stood in a line flanked by a shared pool and direct access to the beach beyond it.

"This is really spectacular," Nick exclaimed as he took in the waves crashing right behind the townhomes.

"This one is yours," Kate said, nodding towards an end unit.

Nick turned and stopped. His eyes squinted as they landed on a surfboard leaning next to the door.

"I had it delivered today. Was assuming you were flying in and might need a board," Kate said.

"I thought about bringing mine, but at seventy miles an hour it can get a little squirrelly up on the rack," Nick said. With a nudge, he asked, "Where's yours?"

Scrunching her nose, Kate shrugged, "We'll see."

"Let's check this place out," Nick said.

Kate pulled out her phone and scrolled to the confirmation for the rental, "I'm sending you the key code now. You can have it changed if you like."

Nick laughed, "I think you are trustworthy."

"We have clearly not spent enough time together," Kate laughed.

"Maybe we can work on that," Nick said, punching in the code to the door.

Swinging the door open, he walked into the bungalow. The open floor plan instantly welcomed a view of the Atlantic Ocean. The simple furnishings were placed to funnel all attention toward the glass doors facing the beach.

Light nautical touches were prevalent in nearly every piece of décor with coral, seagrass and seashells as tasteful elements in the fabric and scant artwork.

Opening the doors, their eyes swept over the sunken pool and beyond the light sand dunes to the breakers washing up on the shore. The rhythmic percussion played an atmospheric melody as the perfect soundtrack as evening set in over the eastern seaboard.

"This will do," Nick sighed, taking in the scene.

Standing shoulder to shoulder, Kate and Nick drank in the overwhelming power of the Atlantic's relentless push ashore. The energy between the two suddenly had an edge of awkward electricity.

As their eyes met, Kate took a slight step back. Almost in a whisper, she said, "I, uh, I promised dinner. I should make good on that."

"I could eat," Nick nodded, recognizing Kate's unspoken request for space.

"Any ideas?" Kate asked.

"I met a guy on the way in…" Nick started.

"Of course you did!" Kate laughed. "And?"

"There is this Tiki bar down the street that overlooks the water," Nick suggested.

"Sounds perfect," Kate smiled.

Nick and Kate settled around an oceanfront table. Both stared for several long moments at the Atlantic and its wisps of whitecaps as the breakwater kissed the sand.

"This life isn't half bad," Kate sighed. "Not bad at all."

Nick smiled, "I'll make you a beach bum after all."

"I'm already a beach bum," Kate laughed. "Just not so much a surf aficionado."

"There is more work to be done," Nick admitted.

A waitress stopped by and gathered some drink orders before whisking away and quickly returning with a glass of wine and a tropical cocktail.

Kate raised her wine glass, "To Carolina Beach!"

"To any beach!" Nick added.

"To any beach," Kate accepted, bringing her glass to her lips.

For a long moment, they allowed their beverages to flow through them as their attention bounced from glances at one another to the breaking ocean waves.

Each seemed to stumble over their words when focused on one another. Kate cleared her throat and asked, "So, the house. What do you think?"

Nick swung his attention directly toward Kate, "The place has great bones. There are a few awkward spots that will take a bit to address, and of course, it needs a fair share of updating, but I like it. It is a great piece of property. Uninhibited ocean view and backyard beach access, quiet yet walking distance to the pier and shops… I think your company hit a home run."

"That's what I thought. It lacks the luxuriousness of the Treasure Island house but carries a much more relaxed coastal feel," Kate said.

"I think you just wrote the beginning of your rental ad," Nick said.

"Couples looking for a quiet, private retreat can certainly have that. So can families looking for fun and adventure," Kate exclaimed.

"Anything outside of fundamentals you would like to add?" Nick asked.

"Well," Kate grinned. "I have learned that having some fun beach toys like surfboards and bodyboards can be good additions to the rentals."

"I saw this gorgeous wood rack design. It's almost like a natural sculpture," Nick said.

Kate craned her neck looking dubious, "Can the boards be locked down?"

"I can make it that way," Nick said.

"Done. I love it. I was curious how I could add toys and have my company still find the concept elegant," Kate said.

"I'll make it usefully elegant," Nick assured her.

"I know you will," Kate said.

Both heads slowly turned toward the ocean and got lost in its swells. Before they knew it, dinner arrived. As they neared dinner's end, Kate shifted in her seat.

Nick cocked his head deciphering what was running through her head.

"Look, just so that we are on the same page…" Kate began. Her eyes danced around the table, the sea and finally back to Nick.

"We, uh…" Kate stammered. "We kind of got caught up back on Treasure Island. I think… I think while working together, especially traveling for my company, we need to keep things professional. This is an important job in the company building their confidence in you. I hope you understand."

Kate turned alternating shades of white and red and back to pale white again as she fought to explain herself.

Nick fought how to respond and instead leaned forward flashing his trademark smile, "Of course. I promise. I will be a diligent employee and a perfect gentleman."

Kate's color returned, and her shoulders relaxed, "A surfer, a handyman… *and* a gentleman. You are quite the package, Mr. Mason."

Nick laughed as his gaze returned to the ocean, "Happy to help in any way that I can."

"I'm glad to hear that, Nick. I... I..." Kate was flustered.

Nick waved her off, "It's okay. We have work to do. This time we won't be afraid for our lives, hunkered down in the shadows. Laser focused."

"Thank you," Kate said, the color slowly returning to her cheeks.

Nick leaned forward, delivering a very serious look as his voice was steely, "That doesn't get you off the hook for additional surf lessons."

Kate flushed, "Fair enough."

Nick craned his neck around swirling his very empty glass, anxiously hoping for a refill.

The dinner talk dissolved into sharing their favorite beach towns. Nick's were driven by the quality of waves and flip-flop lifestyle. Kate's mirrored her properties with wide sandy beaches close to civilization but remote enough to feel private and tranquil.

When the check came, a stern glare from Kate-the-boss, a Nick-bestowed moniker that made Kate wince at least a little, encouraged Nick to retract his hand.

Kate pulled out her card and placed it in the folio with the bill. Looking up at Nick, she asked, "Are you... are you up for a nightcap?"

Nick's head tilted at the suggestion, "I probably shouldn't. Probably need to start early tomorrow and I've already seen the surf report."

"You are welcome to start after you have enjoyed your share of rides," Kate said.

"Still, I think I'll turn in early tonight," Nick insisted.

"Okay," Kate nodded.

As the waitress picked up the bill and returned for Kate to sign it, Nick and Kate pushed out their chairs and rose from the table.

"Thank you for dinner," Nick said.

"You're welcome," Kate acknowledged. "See you after surfing?"

"Coffee in hand, if that's still okay..." Nick's voice trailed.

Kate laughed, "It is more than okay. I do have a coffee maker and some delicious beans on their way, but they won't be there by tomorrow morning. And, I think I am going to need it."

"Then I will see you then," Nick said, "Good night, Kate."

"Good night, Nick," Kate said. She watched him walk out of the restaurant. She suddenly felt extremely awkward. She did not want to walk beside him as they made their way to their cars. She waited until the headlights of his pickup truck began to glow before heading to her own car.

Glad that she had waited long enough for Nick to have pulled out of the Tiki bar's parking lot before she reached her own car, she sighed. She enjoyed her time with Nick, and she hoped she didn't do too much damage to that.

Starting her SUV, Kate slipped it into gear and drove towards her beach house. Heading up the coastal road, she spied the Island Beverage shop still open. Wheeling into the parking lot, she walked into the store toward the long bank of coolers.

Turning the corner of the aisle, Kate made a beeline for what she was after. Lost in her own mind, she nearly collided with another customer laden with both hands clutching jangling beer bottles, nearly spilling them to the floor.

"I'm so sorry," Kate gasped. Looked up and shook her head, "Nick?"

Nick sheepishly danced as he resettled his wine store loot, "Fancy meeting you here."

Kate glanced at his sundry of wares, "A night cap after all..."

Nick glanced down at the six-packs of beer in his hands and flushed, "Yeah, I guess a beer on the beach sounded nice."

Kate looked at the refrigerated section of wine she was so focused on, "It kind of does, doesn't it? Sure you don't just want to join me? We could have a sip here. It has a great vibe."

"I don't know," Nick squirmed. Glancing at the crowd at the bar, he felt their eyes blazing in their direction. He thought better of it, "I don't want to put you in an awkward position with your company."

Kate glanced away, "Nick..."

"I am gunning for employee of the month," Nick spat and turned to pay for his beer.

Shaking her head, Kate couldn't help but laugh.

"I will see you tomorrow, Kate," Nick said, his voice resolute as he gave a nod and proceeded towards the check stand.

Once more, Kate was left to watch the handyman-surfer walk away. Resolute to her own request, she relented to select a bottle of Slo Down Wine that screamed "lonely night on the beach" and made her way to check out.

Instinctively, she scanned the parking lot, but Nick's truck was not there. Setting her bottle of wine in the foot well of the back seat, Kate climbed into her SUV and hit the start button.

The drive through the quiet streets added to the tranquil ambiance of Carolina Beach. Busy by day, particularly during tourist season succumbed to a peaceful hush only broken by the effervescent crashing waves. The moonlight swayed with the swells while the fronds of palm trees clacked in the evening breeze.

To most, those were the sights and sounds of a vacation paradise. To Kate, they were the sounds of home, even if temporary. She had lived life on the road traveling from beach town to beach town for what seemed like forever. When asked whether it bothered her to not have a place to call home other than a storage unit packed with stuff she barely missed, the answer was a fervent "no".

Getting out of her SUV in front of yet another new beach house, she drew in a deep breath. The smell of the salt air added to the clatter of the palm fronds and rhythmic rolling of the waves along Carolina Beach. No, she didn't miss having a home base. Living with whatever she could stuff into her SUV was a bit lonely at times. But, if she was honest, she sought that loneliness in the beginning.

Grabbing the bottle of wine from her back seat, she ascended the steps into the beach house. Shaking her head at the odd jog from the entry to the main hallway, she wasted no time walking to the back patio and flinging the doors open allowing the coastal air to move through the house.

Locating the wine tool she had stowed in one of the kitchen drawers, she went to work on the bottle. Freeing the cork with a satisfying pop, she poured a healthy glass and walked to the porch.

Stepping out to the rail, she looked out at the moonlight playing on the water as waves chased the light to the beach. Glancing up and down the beach, she caught a shiver. Kate's eyes narrowed in irritation as she realized the chill wasn't spawned by the cool air but by a memory.

Wanting to fight the feeling and be defiant, she couldn't resist the instinct to back away from the rail, her eyes making a final sweep before retreating into the house, quickly closing the doors and latching the locks.

With a sigh, she swallowed her wine in several gulps. Even inside the house, she backed away from the glass that separated her from the beach. Shaking her head, she grabbed the wine bottle and scooped up her laptop to settle in the third-floor master suite for the evening.

The master veranda, with the only access from the bedroom itself, was a safe enough solution to allow Kate to confidently open the doors and allow the full experience of the beach to enter her room.

Pouring another glass of wine, she sat in a chair placed directly in front of the open doors. Opening her laptop, she began making notes about her initial impressions and the brief walk-through with Nick.

As she typed Nick's name, she paused. She questioned how much her "talk" with Nick was about ensuring professionalism on behalf of her company versus ensuring she didn't allow herself to get too close to anyone. Taking a sip of her wine, she cursed herself for being so nervous and guarded, both with the house and with Nick.

Doing what she had done for the past two years, she resolved her consternation by burying herself in her work.

The hours whiled away, as did the contents of the wine bottle, until Kate finally succumbed to her exhaustion. Her wine glass lying on its side cast haphazardly to the floor, her laptop sliding inches from descending off her lap, Kate listed backward, asleep in the chair cooled by the evening ocean breezes.

Three

Kate had barely gotten herself ready for the day when a rap on the door nearly made her jump. Descending the steps as another set of knocks, progressively louder than the first rang through the beach house.

"I'm coming!" Kate called.

Smooshing her face against the door so that she could peer through the peep hole, she saw Nick shuffling on the front porch.

Undoing the locks, Kate pulled the door open, "I'm a little surprised to see you so early. Insufficient surf report this morning?"

"Just eager to get to work, boss!" Nick grinned, holding up a coffee for Kate, which she readily accepted.

"Well, come on in, and I'll show you my plans," Kate said, welcoming him in, flinching at being called 'boss.'

Following her into the kitchen, Nick set his own coffee cup on the counter and pulled out his clipboard.

Kate reviewed her work from the evening before. Spinning her laptop around, she said, "I received a copy of the architectural blueprints."

Nick leaned over the counter and studied the screen, "It doesn't look like there are any support beams in there, I think we are good to go for demo and open up that initial viewpoint as you walk in the house."

"Great!" Kate pumped her fists excitedly.

"I'll want to get the countertops and flooring ordered right away as there can be long lead times on those," Nick said. "I'll tackle the mold spots to make sure there isn't anything under the surface we aren't seeing. The rest of it is simple cosmetic stuff, besides the entry. This place really does have good bones."

Walking out to the deck, Nick began stomping on the boards and shot Kate a playful glance, "Decking looks good. You want to give it a go?"

Kate scowled and then laughed, "I *do* have a knack for finding the weak spots."

"I'll start grabbing my tools," Nick said.

"I'll start requesting samples and bids from the local countertop and flooring companies," Kate added.

Retreating to their respective duties, they worked through the morning. By the time Nick had set up his work areas with the necessary equipment, Kate had several appointments scheduled for the afternoon.

As Nick set down the last of his tools, Kate peeled around the corner.

"What do you say we grab some lunch real quick?" she asked.

Nick paused looking at the array of tools at his feet, "We just got set up."

"I know. I have granite and quartz guys coming all afternoon. Besides, we can fuel up and power through the day," Kate suggested.

"You're the boss," Nick said, inducing an immediate wince from Kate. "What do you have in mind?"

"How about we walk down to the boardwalk? I've been wanting to see what they have to offer down there for my information packet," Kate said.

"Sounds good to me," Nick said, placing his tools out of their path.

Locking up the house, they headed down the back walkway towards the beach. Kate paused to take her shoes off, holding the straps in her fingers. The sun was warming the sand, but it felt good underneath her feet.

Nick strayed closer to the water where his footsteps didn't sink as much on the harder, tide-compacted sand.

"How does this compare to beaches back at home?" Kate asked.

"Being on the Atlantic, there are definitely more waves. They look pretty enticing," Nick said.

"You can cut loose early if you want to get out there," Kate offered.

"Maybe tomorrow. I'd like to see how far I can get with demo," Nick said.

Kate quietly nodded as they shuffled down the beach.

"Man, it's like we have the beach to ourselves," Kate said.

"The Carolina coast has about everything. If you want quiet, you can find a lonely stretch of beach. If you want excitement, well, you can find that too," Nick said.

As they got closer to the pier and the boardwalk, the empty stretches of beach were increasingly dotted with beach goers.

Stepping up from the sand along a wooden walkway, they arrived at the Carolina Beach boardwalk.

"We're walking on what a magazine labeled as one of the top ten beach boardwalks in America," Nick shared.

"I'll put that in my write-up," Kate said.

Looking at the Ferris wheel looming overhead, she asked, "You up for a ride?"

"Maybe," Nick shrugged. His eyes scanned the ground as he shuffled a few steps.

Kate's eyes grew wide, "Are you afraid of heights?"

"Not really," Nick squirmed. "I'm not a huge fan of rides in general, especially those with nuts and bolts slathered in salt water."

"You're a surfer!" Kate exclaimed.

"Yeah, but if I don't like my ride on a wave, I get to hop off," Nick said defensively. "Here I'm at the mercy of the attendant and their disposition that day."

Kate stopped in her tracks and studied Nick, a wry smile crossing her lips, "If you go on a Ferris wheel ride with me, I'll go surfing with you."

Nick cocked his head at the proposition, "Alright. You're on!"

Kate grabbed Nick's hand and tugged him towards the amusement ride.

"Whoa, whoa… right now?" Nick protested, digging his heels against the wood planks of the boardwalk.

"Fine, lunch first. Ooh, maybe a nighttime ride!" Kate suggested.

"Let's eat, get some work done and determine whether our death-defying trip would be better in the light of day or not," Nick said.

"I thought *I* was the boss," Kate pouted.

Nick laughed, "Sure, toss *that* one around when it benefits you…"

Kate beamed as she studied their lunch options along the boardwalk. "Hamburgers, hotdogs, taffy, ice cream…"

"Classics," Nick nodded.

"Why don't we just grab something and sit on a bench and watch the waves?" Kate suggested excitedly.

Nick scoffed, "Didn't see you as a hot dog person."

"Didn't see you afraid of a Ferris wheel," Kate retorted.

"Touché. Dogs on the pier it is," Nick conceded.

Kate had hoped their walk and playful lunch would thaw some of the awkward chill. She was keen to note Nick's glib attitude reminded her of when they first met. Before they were swept up in the moment of the murder investigation that drew their pounding hearts closer together.

It was like the same Nick but with a guard up. As they rolled up their sleeves and got to work, Kate reasoned their focus on the job, as opposed to each other, would help put things back into perspective.

Nick didn't waste any time grabbing his tools and getting to work. Carefully peeling trim boards from the entryway walls, he inspected each before determining whether their usefulness would live on with the remodel or end up in the scrap pile.

Kate retreated to the kitchen. Using a quaint little nook, she set up her laptop and notes. Uploading photos she had taken of the house, she allowed the software to create a digital version of the beach house. Kate could add décor, paint walls and even envision what a straight-through entry would look like.

From the kitchen, she could hear Nick working down the hall. She admitted to herself that the sounds of nails squeaking as they pulled out of decades-long hold were odd music that gave her comfort.

She shook herself as her mind drifted into the events of the Florida beach house. She could still hear the shattering glass cascade to the floor and see the figures slipping into the shadows. Scowling, she focused on her laptop and the design work for the Carolina Beach house.

Pleased with her digital sketches, Kate leaned back to study them from a different perspective. Her software allowed her to change the position of the sunlight streaming into the home. As she cycled through the changes, Kate squinted. Tapping the edge of her laptop, she dialed through the hues, adjusting her paint ever so slightly to appeal in the evening light as much as the morning.

Down the hall, Nick's work graduated from careful prying to heavy demolition. After cutting through the sheetrock with a utility knife, he began removing whole panels revealing a framework with surprising depth.

Curiosity getting the best of Nick, he traded the clean, careful cuts of the utility knife and instead attacked the wall with his framing hammer. "Oh, sh…!" Nick exclaimed as he pedaled away from the wall, his hammer falling to the floor.

Kate's head shot up from her work, "Everything alright? You need a hand down there?"

"Uhm, nope. Got plenty of those!" Nick replied.

"What?" Kate frowned. Sliding away from the kitchen nook, Kate decided to investigate firsthand what problem Nick had found.

Kate wheeled around the corner into the hall to see Nick kneeling next to the hole he had created in the wall.

With a wry grin, Nick said, "I said this place had good bones."

Kate's eyes moved from Nick to the rubble on the floor. Amidst the pile of sheetrock was a hand, or what was left of it.

"Oh, my goodness!" Kate gasped as she cautiously moved closer. "Is that…?"

Her eyes followed the bony hand, tracing it up the humerus to the rib-lined torso. A despondent skull with its vacant eyes listed to the side.

Nick's eyes went wide, a smile across his lips that Kate found an oxymoron to the horrifying discovery, "Suppose there is treasure somewhere in these walls?"

Shaking her head, Kate was taken aback, "What?"

"Treasure!" Nick shrugged. "Come on. It's gotta be a pirate, right?"

Brushing off Nick's glib suggestion, Kate approached closer, flipping on the flashlight on her phone. Inspecting the discarded skeleton, tattered fragments of fabric still clinging to it, Kate shook her head, "Not a pirate, I'm afraid. But a victim, for sure."

"No… treasure?" Nick's voice fell.

Kate was lost in her examination of the bones.

Nick watched Kate squatting next to the dusty set of bones. He sighed to himself as he could see the wheels in Kate's head working overtime. She could not resist a mystery.

"Uh, oh. Here we go again," Nick muttered.

Four

The room full of police and forensics teams at one of her firm's beach houses had become an all too familiar scene for Kate. Remanded to the kitchen island while the detectives worked, Kate and Nick craned to see and listen to what was going on.

"How long do you suppose that has been in there?" Kate asked.

Nick shrugged, "Based on the building materials used, last decade… decade and a half."

Kate shuddered, scrutinizing her recall of the corpse's condition. With a frown, she turned to Nick, "Didn't it seem in really good condition to you?"

"There was an impermeable layer in there, the stuff you use on exterior walls, especially places like the coast to keep moisture and mold out," Nick said.

"Like wrapped in kitchen wrap!" Kate said.

"Sort of. Yeah," Nick nodded. "Probably an effort to keep the smell in check."

Kate cringed at the idea of a fragrant, rotting corpse before returning a thoughtful hand to her chin, "Hmm…"

Peering down the hallway, Kate watched as a woman strode through the house, the officers and investigators clearing a path for her. After stopping to study the hole in the wall and the remains, the woman's head snapped up. Seeing Kate's head poke around the corner, the woman's eyes narrowed.

Moving with great confidence, the woman made a beeline toward Kate and Nick. Giving both a deep consideration, she identified herself, "I'm Detective Pam Nixon. You two found the… body?"

Kate nodded with a glance toward Nick, "I'm Kate Harper. My company just bought this house. I get beach houses ready for families to rent."

The detective's eyes landed on Nick. She looked at him without flinching for a long moment.

"This is Nick. He's our…" Kate started.

"Nick Mason," Nick held his hand out for an unrequited handshake. "I'm the hired contractor."

"You licensed in the county?" the detective asked.

"I'm not for hire, just exclusive to the property management company," Nick said.

"All permitted work will be done by local, licensed contractors. Nick supervises and... does a little demo," Kate said.

The detective shrugged as though she didn't care about Kate's statement. Maintaining her attention on Nick, she asked, "I assume that is your handiwork in the hall?"

"It is," Nick nodded. "Definitely did not expect that."

"I'm sure you didn't," Detective Nixon said. With a deep breath, the detective said, "Suffice it to say your work here is postponed until the crime scene team has completed their work."

Kate was taken aback, "I hadn't even thought of that in all the excitement. I'm staying here."

"Not until we are done you're not," Detective Nixon said. "I'm sorry, Ms. Harper. You'll have to find someplace else to stay."

Kate nodded, "Sure. Of course. Not so sure I want to stay here with dead bodies falling out of the walls."

The detective's eyes swept over Kate as she considered the statement. "I'm sure there won't be *too* many more," Detective Nixon said.

Kate's eyes went wide.

For the first time since she entered the beach house, the detective cracked a slight grin.

Kate slumped, "You're teasing me."

Detective Nixon offered a tight-lipped response.

"Say, if there's treasure, she... I mean, her company, gets to keep it, right?" Nick asked.

"If there are items that lawfully belonged to the previous owner, I suppose," the detective said.

"Who owns pirate treasure?" Nick asked.

"Who'd the pirate steal it from?" Detective Nixon replied.

"Right," Nick nodded.

"Detective!" a voice called from down the hall.

"Excuse me," the detective said and spun.

Kate slipped from her seat at the kitchen island to follow.

Detective Nixon didn't even turn her head. A look toward uniformed officers was all she needed to have them step in behind her. Kate slammed on the brakes as she tried to see past the officers.

"This could be a while, ma'am. Why don't you make yourself comfortable?" one of the uniformed officers said.

"A body spilled out of the wall and onto the floor of the beach house I am staying in while I'm in charge of prepping it for my company. I'll find comfort in answers," Kate said, her head dodging and weaving to try and see what was going on down the hall.

"When Detective Nixon is ready, she'll share answers with you," the officer said.

Kate stopped trying to look past the officers and instead at them, "Have you seen things like this before? A body stuffed inside a wall?"

One officer frowned, "Under crawlspaces, in a garden shed… not inside the walls of a house."

"Any cold cases that would be… roughly ten to fifteen years old?" Kate asked.

"I'm not sure, ma'am. That would be information shared by Detective Nixon, if she felt it was something she wanted to share," the officer said.

The other officer chuckled, "She's not generally the sharing type."

"Get a lot of murders in Carolina Beach?" Kate asked.

"No one said this was a murder," the officer said.

Kate looked at the officer directly, "You think someone stuffed themselves in the wall and then put up drywall and paint from the inside?"

The other officer laughed.

"Well, I'm just saying, there are protocols…" the officer said.

"The officer is right. There are protocols," Detective Nixon said. "Ms. Harper, why don't you get your things? I will need your contact information and a good email. I'll need to request several documents regarding the purchase of the beach house."

Kate nodded, handing the detective one of her business cards.

Slipping it into her pocket, the detective looked at Nick, "I'll need your information, as well. Then, my officers will escort you out of the house. We'll let you know when you can come back."

Nick looked at Kate, who began heading up the steps to the upstairs master bedroom, "You need help?"

"No, I've got it. I really haven't taken time to unpack yet," Kate said as she disappeared up the stairs.

A few moments later, Nick heard a calamity of cases banging against doorjambs. Looking up the steps, Nick saw Kate with bags over both arms and two additional large bags being wheeled through the threshold.

"I don't mind you creating more trim and drywall work for me, but it is okay to ask for help," Nick said, ascending the steps and reaching his hand out for Kate to hand over the large bags. Grasping the handles, Nick dangled the luggage in front of him as he led the way to the main floor.

A pair of officers held their arms out, indicating they should exit out the back door to avoid the main hallway. Once they were outside, the officers closed the door behind them.

"Well, I guess that's it for our crazy evening," Kate said.

"Where are you going to go? I could move out to the living room, I believe the sofa pulls out into a bed," Nick suggested.

Kate scowled, "I'll find a place. Thank you."

Nick chuckled.

"What?" Kate asked.

"Another adventurous beach house, huh?" Nick said.

"Yeah. An adventure," Kate admitted softly. Kate pulled out her phone. Her fingers worked the digital keys in a frenzy. After a few moments, she let out a satisfied grunt.

Nick cocked his head in curiosity.

"It looks like I'm going to be your neighbor," Kate said.

"Might as well make the best of it. A little forced R and R. Could be worse," Nick said. His eyes brightened, "We should find you a surfboard after all!"

Nick studied Kate through the soft moonlight realizing that his playful jabs hadn't received the response he was hoping for. In fact, they didn't garner any response at all.

Kate stared out at the Atlantic, thoughtfully despondent. Realizing she had been ignoring Nick, she said, "I'm sorry. I just can't get the mystery of the bones out of my head."

"This time, the police are well in play before you get into trouble," Nick said. "At least the bones aren't going to get up and threaten your life."

"You're the one who disrupted their resting place. It's you they'll be after," Kate said.

Nick's expression fell, "That's not real comforting."

"But who do they belong to? Who put them there? Are they still around here?" Kate asked.

"Are they even still alive?" Nick added. Shaking himself from getting pulled into Kate's sleuthing trap, Nick said, "Nothing we can do with this one. This is all the police."

"I can look into the previous owners…" Kate said.

"Wasn't this place a rental before? Could have been anyone with a two-week window. Heck, I could have done it in a weekend," Nick said. Looking at Kate, he scrambled, "I mean, the drywall work."

Kate nodded. Her phone chimed. Glancing at the screen, she said, "There's my door code."

Punching the numbers into the pad, she shouldered the door open.

Nick helped her wheel the luggage into the condo. "Say, you want to grab a bite?"

"I think I'm going to order something for delivery. I want to do some digging into the beach house's mysterious past," Kate said, her voice tinged with a hint of excitement. "I can order you something too…"

"No. That's okay. I think I'll explore. See what Carolina Beach or Kure Beach or Wilmington have to offer," Nick said.

Kate nodded, "Okay."

"I'll see you…" Nick started and realized he didn't know when.

"Coffee. In the morning?" Kate asked.

"Yeah," Nick agreed.

"Check the surf report. Maybe you can get in some rides," Kate said.

Nick smiled, "I'll check it out. You should see about getting a board yourself."

"Solid maybe on that," Kate smiled back.

"See you in the morning, Kate," Nick said.

Kate watched as the surfer-handyman disappeared down toward the parking lot.

Five

Kate scoured the history of the beach house. Starting with her company paperwork, she used it to begin tracking back over the home's lifetime.

Digging through the available real estate sources, she began making a timeline and ownership tree. Pulling out a notebook, Kate worked furiously, matching owners to newspaper articles and obituaries.

Scanning social media files, Kate worked her way through the lives of the beach house's previous owners, compiling as much of a life sequence as she could put together.

Kate jumped when the softest rap at her door broke her attention. Clutching her chest, she took several breaths to center herself. Muttering a curse for allowing herself to be rattled, she pushed away from her work. Straightening her blouse, Kate opened the door.

Seeing Nick standing in front of her bungalow, she looked confused.

"When I came back from dinner, I found this outside your door," Nick said, holding up a bag of food. "Based on the temperature, I'd say it was delivered a while ago."

Kate blushed, "I must not have heard the delivery driver. Totally spaced out. Thank you."

"You might as well take a break and eat," Nick suggested.

Kate glanced at the bag of food. She hesitated as she leaned back toward her work and the relative safety of the bungalow.

Nick sensed her hesitation, "The bungalows have great outdoor seating… right there. Take a moment. Watch the waves crash. Your work will still be there."

Kate said, "You're right. It is lovely out here."

Nick placed the food bag on the patio table closest to the ocean. Turning towards his bungalow, he paused as Kate reached her hand out.

"You aren't going to stay with me?" Kate asked.

Looking unsure what to say, Nick said, "I was going to leave you be."

Kate looked at Nick, "Stay. Please."

Nick looked thoughtful and then nodded, "How about I grab a couple of beers?"

"That would be great," Kate smiled. "A marvelous pairing with cold fish tacos."

When Nick had returned to the table with two opened bottles, Kate had set out her spread. Her eyes were locked on the ocean and the streaks of the moon playing on the rolling waves.

For a long time, they said nothing. Kate took bites of her meal as she sat up at the table and watched the waves. Nick lounged in his chair, his legs stretched out, bringing his beer to his lips.

When Kate had eaten most of her food, she swung her attention from the Atlantic Ocean to Nick. Her eyes danced excitedly in the moonlight, "Want to hear what I found?"

Nick laughed, "Sure. Lay it on me."

Kate set her food tray aside and leaned in, her eyes wide, "So, the last owner, had the place for the last five years. They used the place as a rental but spent a few weeks out of the year as a family vacation spot. They are not likely a suspect because of the decay of the body, and from your experience, the materials were last generation."

"Any connection to the previous owner?" Nick asked.

"No, not that I can tell. But, I'll make a sleuth out of you yet. That is why I leave them on the list," Kate said. "Now, the owners before that, only had the house for two years. They didn't rent it out. They used it exclusively as a vacation home," Kate shared.

"So, that's seven years…" Nick prodded.

"Right. Before that, there were two more owners. Both overlapping in the era where that, uh, that material you said," Kate looked at Nick.

"The moisture barrier. Version two came out, and the industry nearly overnight moved to the superior model. So, fifteen years ago," Nick said.

"Right. Larry Simpson. He owned the house for nine years. The market took a steep upturn when they sold. It made sense," Kate said.

"And before that?" Nick asked.

"The family that bought the land and built the house?" Nick asked.

"The Hayes Family," Kate said.

"Why is that name familiar?" Nick asked.

"Because they are big name business owners, sponsor professional golfers, golf course designers and politicians," Kate said.

"Politicians?" Nick cocked his head back. "That puts them top of the list for me."

Kate laughed, "Yeah. Probably me, too."

"What else do we know about them?" Nick asked.

"Well, lots of philanthropic stuff. Golf tournaments and golf course designs," Kate said.

"Not exactly damning," Nick said.

"No. And it says nothing of all the people that have stayed here over the years," Kate said.

"Or worked on it,'" Nick suggested.

Kate pointed at Nick, "Right. I hadn't even thought of that. Good point."

Nick looked pleased to receive Kate's praise, especially in reference to the investigation.

"I won't be able to get the renters information unless I can get it from the previous owners or find out who the management companies were," Kate said.

"The police will have to use warrants for that, won't they?" Nick asked.

"Most likely, especially to get information from the management companies," Kate nodded.

Nick leaned back, his eyes swayed to the ocean. Taking a purposeful sip of his beer, he kept his eyes locked on the crashing waves.

Kate followed suit, eliciting a grin from Nick.

"What?" Kate asked.

Nick smiled, "Sometimes, when you have exhausted your questions or at least your options, you actually settle and relax."

"I can relax," Kate looked cross.

Nick raised his eyebrows.

"You have never known me without some sort of murder and mayhem hanging over me like an ominous cloud!" Kate said defensively.

With a laugh, Nick said, "Even your clouds are ominous."

"They don't have to be!" Kate snapped.

"Have you ever not been drawn in by the mystery or the drama?" Nick asked.

"Of course!" Kate frowned. "I mean, I don't *ask* for it."

"But you find it," Nick said.

Kate's frown deepened, "Sometimes, it finds me."

Nick nodded and stared out at the surf. Kate's eyes followed and they allowed themselves to be lost in the rhythm of the Atlantic Ocean meeting the Carolina Beach shore.

Six

Kate stepped out of her bungalow with the sun peeking above the rim of the Atlantic Ocean. It was unusual for her to sleep that late. With a sleepy yawn, she threw a robe on and shuffled out onto the veranda.

Bobbing in the swells directly out from the hotel, a surfer gleamed in the morning sunbeams as he waited for a rideable set. Kate leaned against the rail and smiled. Nick was a lot of things. But he was an honest man who enjoyed the most honest thing the earth had to throw at him– the power of the ocean.

Lifting her phone, she punched a few keys on her app and returned her gaze to the ocean. Nick spied a set of waves, resisting the first couple. He eyed the one that would give him the best ride. Diving onto his board, he thrust his arms into the water and with a few hearty strokes, found himself atop the wave. Hopping to his feet, he stretched his arms out and bent his knees, gliding across the water. With a kick of his right heel, he turned the board to follow the power of the wave.

Taking it as far as he could, Nick hopped off, spinning his board right as the wave broke hard against the shore. Waist-deep, he palmed his board. A glance toward the bungalows showed him he had a spectator. Pausing, he looked up. Seeing Kate peering over the rail he couldn't resist a quick wave of his hand.

With a deep breath, he tucked his board under his arm and marched out of the sea and onto the beach.

Seeing his towel on a lounge chair, Kate picked it up to meet him at the beach stairs.

"Thanks," Nick accepted the towel.

"How was it out there?" Kate asked.

"Surf was a bit light. But after searching for waves in the Gulf, this was easy," Nick said.

Kate frowned, "If you are so all about surfing, why end up on the Gulf side of Florida anyway?"

"It was the total package- the water, being able to find a quiet spot not dominated by towering hotels, the unbelievable wildlife. There isn't a day I don't see dolphins or manatees or rays or turtles. It's amazing. Every day," Nick said.

"That is a very romantic notion of life," Kate said.

"If it's there, why not take it?" Nick shrugged.

Kate looked at Nick as he rubbed his sea-soaked hair with the towel. "I just mean, why not find a better surf spot? There are tranquil places up the Carolina coast, along the Outer Banks…"

Nick's eyes cast out to the sea, "It just called to me. I think, there was a week where I hit some reasonable surf pushed up from a storm down in Mexico. I snorkeled with manatees. I swam with dolphins. I was surrounded by pelicans and anhingas and herons. It was magical. So, I stayed."

"Like I said, romantic. Just not the Valentine's style of romantic," Kate said.

"Oh, I don't know. Depends on who you ask," Nick smirked.

Kate smiled, "I suppose so."

Their attention was cut by a wandering voice walking up on deck.

Turning, they found a young man holding two large cups of coffee.

"Perfect!" Kate said, walking to greet the man.

Handing him several bills, she took the cups and held them up as she returned to Nick.

"Coffee?" Kate asked.

"Absolutely!" Nick accepted.

Both sipped their drinks as their eyes moved from each other to the breaking surf.

"This isn't bad," Kate sighed.

"Not at all," Nick said.

Leaning against the rail, they watched the set roll in as the sun climbed higher into the sky.

"I'm surprised you aren't at the beach house clamoring for answers," Nick said.

Kate laughed, "Thought about it. I stayed up a bit late. I guess the lullaby of the ocean made sure I got the sleep I needed."

"The ocean can do that," Nick admitted.

"How about you? You seemed up and at it early," Kate said.

Nick shrugged, "The moment the sun splashed over the horizon, I was up. The waves weren't great, but reasonable enough, I thought I'd see what I could do out there."

"Isn't it lonely?" Kate asked. "Surfing by yourself. There wasn't another soul around."

"The ocean, a few fish. Seagulls. A little shark, a thresher. And a pod of dolphins. I wasn't alone," Nick said.

"A shark? Threshers aren't small!" Kate squealed.

"No. But among threshers, this one wasn't particularly big," Nick said.

Kate frowned, "Couldn't there have been others, bigger, out there?"

"Probably," Nick shrugged. "We aren't food and I do my job right, I don't bother them. Doesn't mean accidents don't happen, but I guarantee, most people's morning commutes are way more dangerous."

Kate shook her head. "I don't know how to argue that. Still gives me the heeby jeebies."

"Does for most people. I have surfed, swam, dove, and snorkeled with hundreds of sharks. Not one has eaten me," Nick said.

"Yet," Kate quipped.

"If I gotta go, I'll take the ocean over some jerk in a hurry without a turn signal," Nick said.

"I'm all about reducing risk and ending up on a porch with a white rocking chair someday," Kate said.

"I like that idea," Nick said, hoisting his coffee cup in the air. "I'd one up with you an Adirondack looking over the ocean."

"Ooh, or maybe a hammock!" Kate grinned.

"Even better," Nick smiled.

Their eyes drifted from each other to the golden sun glistening against the Atlantic waves.

Kate had to admit to herself that she enjoyed these relaxed talks. There were times when Nick Mason could make her feel so comfortable. And then there were those times when he could make her feel decidedly uncomfortable.

Sipping her coffee, she forced her eyes to remain focused on the ocean.

In reflective silence, the pair enjoyed watching the birds playing along the sand, scurrying each time the frothy waves pushed ashore. As Kate's coffee cup became lighter, she began to shift in her seat, evermore restless with each sip.

Nick laughed, "You just can't handle it, can you?"

"No!" Kate let out an exasperated breath. "I need to know what is going on over there."

With a nod, Nick swirled his cup indicating he was about finished himself.

"I mean, my company will want an update," Kate said.

"Right. Your company," Nick said. "It has nothing to do with the burning curiosity of a new mystery landing squarely at your feet."

"Well, in my walls, but…yeah," Kate admitted.

"Get cleaned up and head over? See what we can see?" Nick asked.

"Maybe Detective Nixon will have some information," Kate suggested.

Nick raised a doubtful brow, "Yeah, she seemed like the sharing type."

"Well, still…" Kate shrugged.

Nick stood up from his chair on the oceanfront deck. Grabbing his coffee cup and his board, he said, "Meet you in fifteen?"

Kate winced. Despite her excitement to get to the beach house, she countered, "Twenty?"

"Twenty," Nick said.

Kate watched Nick walk to his bungalow, setting his surfboard next to his door.

With a slight bite of her lip, she bounced on her heels and headed for her own bungalow, eager to get some answers.

Seven

Kate drove south on U.S. 421 towards her beach house. Slowing, she found her driveway and the street immediately in front of her house, blocked by police vehicles. Pulling into a neighboring driveway, she hoped the for sale sign posted in front would buy her some leeway.

A uniformed officer posted sentry out front, carefully monitoring the investigation team entering the beach house. Kate flashed him a friendly smile. Seeing it unrequited, she slowed her approach.

"I'm Kate Harper. This is my house. I called in the, uh, discovery," Kate said.

Unmoved, the officer looked at Kate, past Kate to Nick and back to her again, "I'm sorry for your inconvenience, ma'am, but while this a crime scene investigation, you'll need to stay outside."

"I understand. If we could sneak in for just a minute, I need my…eyeglasses," Kate said, trying to think of something that might gain entry.

The officer shrugged, "I'm sorry. Without Detective Nixon's express consent, no one other than the forensics team can go inside."

"And my medicine!" Kate blurted. "It would just be for a second."

"I'm sorry, ma'am," the officer held firm.

With a slight pout, Kate considered her options, "Is there any news? Any idea of how long this will take?"

"If Detective Nixon has not reached out to you, it would mean there is nothing to report at this time," the officer said.

Kate sighed with a half-hearted nod, "All right. You are very good at your job."

"Thank you, ma'am," the officer straightened proudly.

With a slight roll of her eyes, she nodded to Nick to back away from the front entry. As they reached the end of the driveway, Kate eyed the house.

"What's the plan? I know you aren't finished here yet," Nick said.

"Do what we can, I guess. Sweep the outside and see if the police have taken an interest in any other spot in the house," Kate said.

Nick nudged her and offered a childish grin, "Like where the pirate treasure might be hidden. No wonder they won't let you in. They don't want to share."

"Well, we already know Detective Nixon isn't the 'sharing type'," Kate laughed.

Using the side yard of the house where Kate parked her car, they walked between the houses. From the side, there was nothing they could see. Continuing along, they walked toward the beach.

For a moment, they ignored the breathtaking view that the houses afforded and instead, their eyes swept along the back of Kate's beach house. Another uniformed officer held watch, ensuring no one approached from the beach.

Through the giant east-facing windows, they could see activity inside. Investigators used a table lined with bins to catalog evidence.

"What do you suppose they're looking for?" Kate asked.

"Fragments among the sheetrock? Hairs, fibers… anything that might have been accidentally left behind by whoever stashed the body in there. Nails, rough wood, mudding tape… there are all sorts of things that could capture some small hint of whoever built that wall," Nick said.

Kate stared at the house and considered the work being done inside. Scrutinizing the pile of drywall rubble for the tiniest of clues. Pursing her lips, she decided there was nothing else they could see from outside the house.

"What now?" Nick asked.

"I think we head to the station. See if we can get someone to tell us something. I mean, I am displaced from where I am supposed to be sleeping. They owe me some information," Kate said.

Nick wrinkled his nose, "They might have a different idea of what is owed or not."

"Well, you know what they say, squeaky wheels and all," Kate said.

Admiring her persistence, Nick smiled.

The scene at the Carolina Beach Police Station was as busy as Kate's beach house. Kate spied several state police vehicles in the parking lot, assuming murder, or at least unearthed corpses, lent toward the combined jurisdiction of state investigators.

A small crowd was gathered in the lobby, note pads, cameras and phones in hand, ready to note any crumb of interest. The desk officer seemed numb to the pool of reporters incessantly lobbying questions at her.

Seeing Kate and Nick emerge from the crowd, appearing different enough from the media to grab her attention. "Can I help you?" she asked, her eyes casting an irritated glance toward the reporters.

Kate nodded and with an appreciative look, she said in a low voice, "I'm the one with the beach house."

"Oh, I see," the desk officer said. Looking Kate and Nick over and then at the crowd of reporters, she waved them back, "Why don't you two come back with me, away from this circus?"

Allowing Kate and Nick through the barrier that led into the precinct, the desk officer found a spot in the hallway out of view of cameras and earshot of microphones. "You two wait here. I'll see who is available to talk to you."

Kate and Nick watched as law enforcement officers scurried back and forth. Kate's neck craned to see into a room that absorbed most of the activity. She had just laid eyes on a glass board with several photos from her beach house tacked to it when Detective Nixon walked up to the open door. Her eyes locked with Kate's and without a flicker of acknowledgment, she shut the door.

Slumping her shoulders, Kate leaned against the wall, her lips in a pout.

A large, confident man walked through the office, his eyes giving Kate and Nick a thorough sweep.

In what seemed fewer strides than it should have, he reached his hand out, "Harvey Banks, Chief of Police. You must be Kate Harper and… Nick Mason."

Kate and Nick nodded their heads.

"I'm not sure any of us can appreciate what it must be like to discover something like that," the Carolina Beach Police Chief said.

"It's pretty unnerving," Kate said.

Chief Banks looked at Nick, "You're the one doing the demo, who first exposed the... the remains?"

Nick nodded, "It was quite the surprise. I stopped as soon as I realized I had disturbed something, well, disturbing."

Kate winced at Nick's pun.

"We'll get to the bottom of it, rest assured," Chief Banks said.

"Thank you. That makes me feel better already," Kate gushed, holding her hands close to her chest. Cocking her head, Kate asked, "What happens now?"

"Our forensics team is combing through the house demo location to ensure no evidence was missed. The morgue and the lab are examining the remains to see if we can identify the body," the chief said.

"Any idea on the age of the victim or how long it had been in the wall there?" Kate asked.

Chief Banks shook his head, "We have guesses, but the stage of decay was thrown off by how the body was sealed up in that wall."

"It was carefully sealed with barrier wrap. That would throw off the amount of oxygen and humidity levels that would affect it, and of course, keep out any creepy crawlies too," Nick said.

The chief glanced at Nick, "Right. So, instead of guessing, we are leaving it up to the medical examiner and the lab. The bone dating will give us a clear indicator of age and help to resolve when the victim died. Hopefully, the medical examiner can hone in on the cause of death."

Nick's eyes danced at the words and he shot a look toward Kate.

"Are there any unsolved cases from the area that you think the remains could be from?" Kate asked.

Chief Banks swayed as he considered the question, "That's information we would need to keep quiet while the investigation pieces all of that together."

"Chief!" a firm voice called from a rapidly approaching figure. "I see you have met our witnesses."

"Ms. Harper and Mr. Mason have uncovered quite the find," Chief Banks said.

Levying her superior a disapproving gaze, Detective Nixon snapped, "Sir, we have yet to determine Ms. Harper's role in this case. Once we identify the bones, we need to reach out to the victim's family and then once we reach out to the press, I am sure Ms. Harper will have a fascinating read in the newsfeed. At which time, we will turn the keys of the house back over to Ms. Harper."

"Yes, of course. Ms. Harper, I am sorry for any trouble the investigation is causing you and your company," Chief Banks said. With a glance at his detective, his gaze returned to Kate and Nick. "I am sure we will complete the portion of the investigation at the beach house soon. Nice piece of property, that one, too."

"Thank you, Chief Banks," Kate said.

"How is the investigation going, Detective Nixon?" Nick asked. "Is there anything we can do to help?"

"You can stay out of the way," Detective Nixon snapped. Softening, she said, "Look, working a cold case is difficult enough. Doing it with a circus-like what we have in the lobby doesn't help. Once they print whatever it is they are going to print, they'll stir up a frenzy with the public. None of that will make my job easier and if there is some nefarious business that went on, it will give whoever was behind it ample time to slip away or bury any additional evidence."

Kate let out a cough, "The press *can* cause trouble."

The detective's head swiveled sharply at Kate as she considered the words, her eyes narrowed slightly.

"Now, if you will, I have a lot of work to do so that I can return your beach house safely back under your care," Detective Nixon said. Eyeing the press pool around the corner, she added, "You two might be better off if you went out the back. I'll have Officer Manly escort you."

The detective nodded toward an officer at a nearby desk.

"Thank you, Detective… Chief," Kate looked at the two law enforcement officers before spinning to follow the officer through the precinct to a door near the rear of the building. Detective Nixon paused at the door of the room with the crime board until the two had passed before swinging it open and disappearing inside.

When Kate and Nick were outside, they shared a look.

"Chief Banks is nice," Nick said.

"Detective Nixon sure shut him down quickly," Kate said.

Nick shrugged, "She's protecting her investigation. You can appreciate her concerns over information leaking out to the media. You really want a bunch of nosey people showing up at the beach house?"

"No," Kate said. "I've had enough of people creeping around my beach houses."

"The last time your picture was in the news, it nearly got you killed," Nick said.

Kate looked up at him, "I doubt there is much risk of that with an old case like this."

"I'd just as soon not take our chances," Nick said.

Kate nodded softly as her mind wandered. Nick was quick to recognize the look Kate wore when her mental machinery was spooling up. With a sigh, he asked, "You are going to poke around, aren't you?"

With a grin, Kate said, "I just want to stop by the library. Maybe find a good beach read."

"If a good murder mystery novel will satisfy you from tackling a real one, I'm all in," Nick said.

"Something like that," Kate said as she slid behind the wheel of her SUV.

Eight

Watching Kate slide behind one of the library research stations, Nick knew that a cozy beach read was not on the agenda.

"Nothing by Naigle, Higgins or Macomber?" Nick asked as he leaned against an adjacent terminal.

Kate looked up from her seat, "Maybe. I am just dying to find what cold case mysteries Carolina Beach has had over the past decade."

"That's just it. I'm not a fan of you *dying* to find out," Nick said.

"It's just research," Kate shrugged.

"I'm sure the police are all over it," Nick argued.

"I can at least find out who used to own the house," Kate said.

Nick wrinkled his nose, "Can't you find that out through your real estate connections?"

"Yes, but those won't have the stories behind the owners," Kate said.

Letting out a low grumble, Nick shifted restlessly.

Kate's fingers danced along the keyboard, "There are three-foot swells for the next two hours. Why don't you take my keys? Pick me up in a couple of hours or if I am done early, I'll catch a ride service."

Slapping her car keys on the table in front of Nick, Kate looked up at him.

Nick started to protest, "I'm not going to leave you stranded…"

"You are going to leave me stranded. I love libraries. You deserve a little fun while you're here. This is… *my* fun," Kate insisted.

Hesitating for a moment, Nick had no choice when Kate lofted her keys in the air and turned back to the screen in front of her. Snatching the keys out of the air, he turned and huffed, "I'm doing this in protest."

"Have fun surfing in protest," Kate called, her eyes fixed on the results of her initial search.

Walking slowly and with a long glance over his shoulder, Nick relented and left Kate to her research.

With a deep breath, Kate collected herself. Taking her mind off of the man walking out of the library, she focused on the screen in front of her. Beginning with real estate websites, she began walking back to the beach house from the time that her company purchased it to the time it was built.

Kate didn't know how long she had been scrolling through real estate logs and news clippings. Glancing at the two-inch tall pile of printouts, she knew she had collected a ton of data.

Sorting through it, she made separate piles. With a blue highlighter, she made a circle atop documents she knew she wanted to pay closer attention to.

When she was about halfway through the pile, she heard a soft whistle behind her.

Turning her head, she saw Nick standing in the entry to the research room.

"That's a lot of stuff," Nick said.

Kate cracked a wicked grin, "Some of its pretty juicy."

"Juicy, huh?" Nick asked. "Tell me about it."

Kate slapped her hand to her stomach as it emitted a growl. Her cheeks blushed. Wrinkling her nose, she said, "How about I tell you over lunch?"

Nick laughed, "Sounds good. Let me help you with all this."

Gathering the stack of printouts, Nick led Kate out of the research room.

"How was the surf?" Kate asked.

"Pretty good. The winds were still offshore. He had a few good rides," Nick said.

"I'm glad," Kate said.

Nick gave Kate a slight nudge, "You should have come with me."

"I was busy surfing the web," Kate said.

Nick winced, "I thought bad puns were my thing."

"Finding us a good restaurant is your thing. At least, right now," Kate said, a twinkle in her eye.

"I might know a place," Nick said.

Kate laughed, "I figured you would."

Allowing Nick to convey driving directions, Kate drove north. Passing protected Masonboro Island, she swung her SUV once more coastward. Crossing the Intracoastal Waterway and onto one of North Carolina's barrier islands.

Serving as the premier beachfront of the adjacent city of Wilmington, Wrightsville Beach was a postcard of North Carolina vacations. Miles-long beaches dotted with hotels and restaurants with the blue-green water of the Atlantic as an impressive backdrop for tourists and locals alike.

Pointing to a spot for Kate to pull into, Nick smiled. "One of the surfers this morning said to check this place out," he said.

Kate stepped out of her SUV and looked at the restaurant attached to a long pier that ran out past the surf and the rolling swells.

"You can eat right over the ocean," Nick said.

"It sounds magical," Kate said.

Following Nick up the stairs, they were greeted by a hostess and whisked through the restaurant and out onto the pier itself. A light afternoon breeze gently lofted Kate's hair in the air as they were seated at a table. Just as Nick had described, their table straddled the golden sand beach and the soft breakwater.

"This is amazing," Kate said as she panned around the outdoor seating area of the restaurant.

"Welcome to Crystal Pier," Nick said. "My surfer buddy said he comes up here sometimes as a surf spot. You can come up those stairs right there and grab a bite."

Kate smiled, "I could pinch myself, to see if this job of mine is real."

"Touring beach towns while living in homes with million-dollar views? Not a bad way of life," Nick admitted.

A waitress came and took their drink order. Kate's eyes never left the sweeping vista the vantage atop the pier afforded them.

"Nice find, as usual, Mr. Mason," Kate said.

"Just doing my job. Figure if I can help you sleuth out great gems on these trips. Maybe you'll keep hiring me as your handyman," Nick grinned.

"If the food is as good as the view, I just might," Kate admitted.

On cue, the waitress delivered their iced teas and took their lunch orders.

"I'll have the seasonal fish," Kate said.

Nick looked like he could barely contain himself, "I'll have the three item Calabash Platter."

Kate shot him a look.

With a shrug, Nick replied, "Surfing works up an appetite. If you're in southeastern North Carolina, Calabash is the grail of freshly caught seafood."

The sun sparkled, shimmering golden streaks across the ocean. The breeze, the rhythmic song of the Atlantic, the departure from crime scenes and murder mysteries was a much-needed respite. Kate dazed out at the water, lost in its powerful tranquility.

Across the table, Nick watched as he left her to soak it in, trying not to pay too much attention to her, and instead allowed the waves to lure him into a pleasant bliss until their food arrived and the human world pulled them back in.

Thanking the waitress, they looked at their plates. Kate's was clean and fresh, with herbs sprinkled over the top of her fish. Nick's was piled with shrimp, oysters and fish liberally seasoned with Old Bay. Neither of them could hold back a smile as their appetites were triggered by the bounty on their lunch table.

Without a word, they dug into their plates. A few bites in, Nick asked, a shrimp skewered on the end of his fork, "How's the sea bass?"

"Melt in your mouth. I don't think it would be more fresh unless we caught it outside the hotel and grilled it up right there," Kate said.

Nick's eyes flashed, "We should do that."

"What, fish?" Kate scrunched her forehead.

"Yes. Have you ever done it?" Nick asked.

"No."

Nick leaned in, "How do you make a living touring beach towns but not experience true roll up your sleeves beach town living?"

"Oh, so teaching me to surf wasn't enough?" Kate asked.

"Nope. Time to teach you to cast, crank and catch your meal," Nick said, his voice triumphant in his idea.

"Oh boy. Everything with you is an adventure, isn't it?" Kate asked.

Nick grinned, "Life is an adventure. But, me? You're the one with literal skeletons in your walls and a nasty habit of entangling yourself with murderers."

"Yeah, I suppose that's fair," Kate laughed. "Fine, since our project is temporarily grounded, we will have an evening adventure of catching our meal… or at least part of it."

"You supply the wine, I'll arrange everything else," Nick said.

Kate beamed across the table, "How could I turn down such an offer?"

"You don't," Nick shook his fork in a stern gesture.

"This was delicious. We have our work cut out for us this evening," Kate said, setting her fork down as she took her last bite.

"You'll see. As long as we actually catch something," Nick said.

Kate cocked her head.

With a shrug, Nick admitted, "It's not a given. But the experience is half of it anyway."

Kate lifted her iced tea glass, "To experiences, then."

Nick joined her by gently tapping his glass to hers.

When the waitress cleared their plates, Kate practically danced in her seat. Eyes wide, she asked, "Ready to hear what I found?"

Nick chuckled, "I'm ready. By the looks of it, I'm not sure my readiness quotient would contain you anyway."

Pulling out three sheets of paper, each marked with her blue highlighter, Kate fanned them out in front of Nick.

"The Hayes family built the house roughly fifteen years ago. The house was remodeled five years after that and then sold the following year to Larry Simpson. Simpson owned it for nine years, from what I could tell, primarily as a vacation rental," Kate said.

"Those are the owners during the suspected materials used to seal up the wall," Nick said, leaning back in his seat.

Kate nodded.

"What do we know about the owners? Hayes sounds familiar," Nick asked.

"Mark Hayes is a renowned golf course designer. He has been grooming his son, Sheffield Hayes, to take over the business. He, himself, has won a few awards for his designs," Kate said.

Nick scratched his chin and shrugged, "Must be it. I'm not exactly an aficionado of country clubs and golf courses."

"The other owner is a respected local. He's an executive at New Hanover Memorial Hospital and a board member and the University of North Carolina at Wilmington," Kate said.

"Nothing sinister in those profiles, but we have learned that doesn't mean much," Nick said.

"Other than these are people with something they don't want to lose," Kate said.

Nick nodded, "The fear of losing something can be greater than that of gaining."

"The news media has been pretty kind to both families as well. The Hayes' are known for their charitable ventures. They were big in bringing professional golf to Wilmington which, in turn, brings millions of dollars into the area annually for the tournaments while putting southeastern North Carolina on the map with serious golfers," Kate said.

"Serious golfers mean serious money," Nick pointed out.

"It does," Kate nodded. "Several high-end resorts have opened up over the past two decades, two with high acclaim. One of them owned by the Hayes family, the other by Hauer Investments."

"Hauer Investments…" Nick mused as he rubbed his chin.

"Electric cars, hotels, airplanes and golf courses, whatever they seem to want to play in, they sink investments in. More often than not, they're quite successful," Kate said.

"The other owner?" Nick pressed.

"Larry Simpson. Again, the news reports include him opening a new wing at the hospital, various fundraisers, especially in connection with children's healthcare and establishing scholarship programs at the local university," Kate said.

"Any black sheep in the families?" Nick asked.

"Honestly, not that I could tell," Kate admitted.

"Where do we go from here?" Nick asked.

Kate grinned, "From here? You're in for a little sleuthing?"

"Would you poke your nose on your own without me?" Nick asked.

"Yes," Kate laughed.

"Then, I am in," Nick said.

"I think we dig below the surface. People with that much power, that much money, squeaky clean across the generations? Really?" Kate scowled.

"That's a bit cynical," Nick said.

"It is," Kate conceded. "I'm not saying they aren't squeaky clean, just that we might want to poke past the immaculately manicured hedges to see if the rest of the family home is as pristine."

Nick looked out at the indigo sky that shrouded the Atlantic. Silver streaks of the moon played against the waves. Glancing back at Kate, he said, "Well, it sounds like it is going to be a busy day tomorrow."

"Yeah," Kate nodded. "Thank you for… finding another great spot. You have quite the knack for it."

"Hmm…adding official dining advisor to my list of attributes for you, I mean, your company. I could do that. What's it pay?" Nick asked.

Kate smiled back, "You keep selecting great meal locations and I'll keep picking up the tab."

"Just the kind of arrangement that could really attract a vagabond surfer," Nick said.

"Good. I need someone to help keep me out of trouble," Kate said.

Getting up from his seat as Kate flopped the signed bill down on the table, Nick grimaced, "That is a tall order I don't think anyone could commit too."

"All right," Kate pursed her lips. "Watch my back?"

"Now *that* I can do," Nick laughed.

Nine

With flat surf conditions, Nick stood at Kate's door, a wide smile across his face. Two cups of coffee were held up in front of him.

"For a surfer/handyman/dining advisor, you're pretty fantastic," Kate said, happily accepting one of the coffees. "You're earlier than I expected."

"Glassy surf but an otherwise gorgeous day. I figured we're going to get busy back to work on the house or if still barred, then you were going to put your sleuthing hat on," Nick said.

"And astute, too," Kate said. "Let me get my things."

Disappearing into her bungalow, Kate shoved papers into her bag along with her laptop. "Let's see what we've got to work with today."

Kate slowed as she neared the beach house. Traffic was unusually thick and moving slowly past as heads craned to see what the crime scene unit was finding as they crept by. A number of cars and vans were parked along the road. Cameramen and reporters with microphones held in front of them relayed what they were seeing.

Kate didn't even hunt for a place to park. Instead, she pressed the accelerator and roared away. "I'm in no rush to be part of a news report on a possible crime scene again," she explained as she glanced over at Nick.

Nick quickly scrolled through his phone, "Well, I guess it is official. Your company purchased a murder scene. Or at least a stashed body. John Doe is said to have been stashed in the house for nearly a decade. His age at the time of death… he was twenty-four years old."

Kate allowed Nick's report to sink in as she pulled into the Kure Beach Fishing Pier parking lot to turn around and head back into Carolina Beach. "That puts the Hayes family square in the cross hairs of this investigation," she said.

"Maybe not so squeaky clean after all," Nick said. "What do we do now?"

"See what the police will tell me. I owe a report to my boss, anyway," Kate said.

The Carolina Beach Police Station parking lot was nearly full. Nick and Kate walked past the crowd of reporters and onlookers. The desk sergeant saw them and quickly placed a call to the back.

Chief Banks waved them back. "As you can see, the word is out and the circus has officially begun," the police chief said.

"I know you have your hands full, Chief Banks. I was hoping I could get some sort of update to my employer," Kate said.

The chief nodded, "I understand, Ms. Harper. There is nothing I can say about the investigation other than what you can read in the news. As far as accessing the house, I can tell you that the forensics team should be wrapped up with it this afternoon."

"Have they found anything that my company needs to be aware of? Other bodies, evidence of the crime actually taking place there, who the murderer might have been?" Kate asked, barely able to contain herself.

"Ms. Harper, at this stage of the investigation, I wouldn't be able to share any of that. What I can tell you, is as soon as Detective Nixon gives the okay for you to return there, the house will be perfectly safe for you to continue your repairs and prepare to rent it out," Chief Banks said.

"Where is Detective Nixon now? Can I speak to her?" Kate asked.

The police chief shook his head, "She is working hard to get you your beach house back. I can tell you, that with this being such a cold case, you aren't in any imminent danger."

"And we'd like to keep it that way," a curt voice called from behind them.

Turning, they saw Detective Nixon, arms laden with a box marked *evidence*.

"Is that from the beach house? What have you found? Who is the victim? Was the Hayes family involved?" Kate asked.

The detective's perma-frown turned into a bona fide scowl, "Ms. Harper, I will tell you what you need to know at the appropriate time. For now, I can tell you that we have almost concluded our analysis at your beach home."

"We certainly understand your curiosity, but we need to make sure that information isn't leaked that can compromise the investigation," Chief Banks added.

"I have your cell phone. As soon as I am confident we have what we need from your beach house and it is safe for you to return, I will let you know," Detective Nixon said.

"Yes, of course," Kate said, her eyes never leaving the box the detective held.

"If you'll excuse me, I need to get this processed and get the scene cleaned up so that you can be allowed back in," the detective said, brushing by and casting a wary glance at Kate.

The chief let out a sigh and, with his hand pointing toward the back door, said, "Well, that is about the lot of it, for now. As Detective Nixon said, the moment the scene is cleared, we'll let you know."

Kate watched Nixon disappear behind a locked door.

"We'll call you as soon as we share anything," Chief Banks said, his tone more assertive.

Nick placed a hand on Kate's arm to guide her toward the exit while Kate gave an absent nod, her wheels clearly turning.

Pushing open the door, they slipped out the back as they had the previous day to avoid the throngs of reporters.

"What are you thinking?" Nick asked.

"We need to learn more about the Hayes family," Kate said.

Nick studied Kate, "And how are we going to do that?"

"How do you feel about a round of golf?" Kate asked.

"We'll learn exactly how bad I am at golf, but I don't know how much light that will shed on this investigation," Nick said.

"Okay, how about lunch at a luxurious country club?" Kate asked.

"I could eat. Might lose my job as dining advisor, though," Nick laughed.

Kate eyed Nick for a moment, "I wouldn't worry about that. We might need to find you some fresh clothes more appropriate for the resort sleuthing lifestyle."

Nick frowned, pressing out the wrinkles of his linen shirt with his hands, "What do you mean?"

"Come on," Kate beckoned as she opened her driver's door.

After a whirlwind romp through Lumina Station, Nick was appropriately attired with a few days' worth of backup wear for rubbing elbows with Wilmington's finest. Kate grinned from ear to ear while Nick tugged at his collar, desperately trying to make additional room for his neck.

With a grimace, he said, "This is why I left the corporate world."

"Suits?" Kate laughed.

"Ties!" Nick said. With a hooked finger, he slipped the tie free and undid a button on his shirt.

Kate pouted, "You looked nice!"

Striding toward Nick, one of his arms laden with garment bags and handled craft bags, Kate paused. Fixing his collar that had become lopsided while slipping out the tie, she smiled, "You still look great, even without the tie. Like someone important enough in station you don't need a stinkin' tie."

"I like that station," Nick admitted. "Can we go now?"

"Not a big shopper?" Kate asked.

"I kind of liked the beach lifestyle store," Nick said. "But, no. If I can grab my clothes and shoes in the same place I get surfboard wax, I'm pretty happy."

"I see," Kate said as Nick placed his new wardrobe in the back seat of her SUV. "Well, Mr. Mason, I think you look rather dapper. Ready to investigate Wilmington's upper crust?"

Nick shrugged his response as Kate started the vehicle.

Ten

The massive antebellum main lodge came into view squeezed between large oaks draped with Spanish moss. As the oaks gave way, colorful magnolias took over.

Azaleas lined the walk from the parking lot to the lodge. Nick's eyes swept over the expensive vehicles neatly parked, especially those in the separate valet lot.

"Aston, Porsche, Maserati..." Nick mumbled as they walked.

Kate cocked her head, "What?"

"Oh, the cars in the parking lot. They are all high-end," Nick said, his head nodding toward the separate lot. A line of cars backed into spaces along the building was of particular note. "Bentleys, a Rolls, a Maybach... these guys aren't playing around. Except for maybe that one."

Kate followed Nick's eyes.

"You don't often see an Aston Martin with surfboard racks on it," Nick said.

"Welcome to Wilmington," Kate said.

"I guess if I had to endure being rich, this would be a pretty good place to do it," Nick said.

As they approached, the large double doors of the large country club's main house parted. Nick offered a nod of thanks as they were ushered in.

The clubhouse was grand in almost every way. Plantation-style furnishings and décor gave the posh building an atmosphere of being transported back in time. Giant ceiling fans spun lazily overhead while light fixtures provided almost amber light through the main corridor.

Guests ambled about with mint juleps and tropical mimosas while attentive staff ensured they were topped off promptly. Golfers dashed through intent on making their tee times or starting their play through with something from the sunlit bar that overlooked the rolling greens of the course.

Nick straightened his suit. Even with the high-end duds, he felt somewhat out of place. Kate recognized the strained look and slipped her arm into his in an attempt to give him confidence.

With a smile that brought the sparkle back in his eye, Nick whispered, "Thank you."

"You've got this. Your wardrobe might cost…a *lot* less than what they are wearing, but none of them have your charisma," Kate said.

Fueled with encouragement, Nick asked, "So, where do we go from here?"

"Where is the best place to casually observe without seeming like we are clearly out of place?" Kate asked.

Nick smiled, "May I buy you a drink, milady?"

"You may, good sir," Kate grinned.

Nick led them to the bar. Finding a seat that afforded a view of the course, the bar and a peek down the main corridor of the clubhouse, he pulled out Kate's chair for her. With a nod to the bartender, he ordered a couple of drinks.

Kate eyed the mimosa placed in front of her and the bloody Mary that Nick raised for her to toast.

Nick shrugged, "Resort breakfast."

With a laugh, Kate offered him a cheers as their glasses met.

Leaning back in their chairs as though they were in full relaxation mode, their eyes swept the landscape. Their attention wasn't on the guests or the golfers, but on the executive staff that would occasionally meander by.

Kate eyed a man followed by a small entourage. He seemed to point out a few things around the country club, receiving hearty nods. His photo didn't match any of the Hayes family members Kate had studied, but he was clearly a figure of great importance at the resort.

"I wonder where he's going?" Kate mouthed.

Nick shot her a curious look.

"Ultimately, he will lead me to the executive offices. Our best bet at laying eyes on the Hayes family," Kate said.

Grabbing her mimosa, she placed a hand on Nick's arm, "I'm going to wander. I'll be back."

Slipping out of her seat, Kate sauntered toward the bar. Casually walking in the direction she had seen the man with the entourage head, she found herself walking down a secondary corridor. Lined along the walls was a series of photos. Professional golfers and celebrities, either in action shots on the course, regaling an audience at the bar, or flanked by members of the Hayes family, made up an impressive collection.

Hearing the cacophony of footsteps ascending stairs at the end of the corridor, Kate paused until the echoes changed, an indication she hoped meant that they had rounded the corner. Kate pressed forward, taking soft steps on the stairs.

Pausing again, she could hear final orders being handed out before the entourage dispersed in various directions. As one employee brushed by, intent on their mission, Kate strode forward confidently. The attendant scarcely paid her attention as they disappeared toward the main floor.

Setting her mimosa down on a table that sat between a pair of chairs just outside the executive offices, she took a breath and leaned her shoulder against the door. Listening for a moment, she gently turned the handle and pushed the door open. Seeing the lavishly furnished foyer empty, Kate scanned the room.

More intimate photos, mostly of the Hayes family at the country club. A few older photos of people she didn't recognize caught her attention. Leaning closer, she studied them. All of the photos she had seen were black and white. These had a different patina, an almost hazy sepia tone quality to them.

Elements of the landscape were familiar, but the scenery didn't match the country club's rolling greens. The faces did not match any of the images Kate had searched online, but there was a familiarity to them just the same.

Snapping a few quick pictures with her cellphone, she followed the shelves of the room, admiring the décor and the photos.

Voices from the suite of offices caught Kate's attention. As the voices elevated in volume and in tone, Kate edged closer, cocking her head so that she could hear better.

"What do you mean Hauer has pitched an alternate Tidewater project? How did they know about it in the first place?" an irate voice asked.

"I don't know. I never held meetings in Wilmington. Our non-disclosure agreement is ironclad," another voice answered.

"You sure there wasn't bar talk involved at any point?" the first voice asked.

After a pause that Kate could imagine in her mind as a scowl, the second voice said, "From *me*, Dad? You know that isn't my thing."

"You don't think Robert...?"

"No. He knows I have something brewing that I want his help with, but I haven't shared any details to this point. He knows we need this win as much as you and I do."

"You think we need to press Cape Fear Development on whether they broke our NDA?"

"No. They called *me* and told me about Hauer's meeting. They also told me that Hauer has shaped a similar deal but gave them a twenty-five percent stake and have a major golf pro as a course consultant."

"That's not good. Can we match that?"

"We have Robert, of course. He's going to want a royalty. We don't have the cash reserves that Hauer does. Not after..."

"I know," the first voice snapped. "We *need* this, Sheffield."

"I know, Dad."

Kate was so enthralled in the conversation between who was clearly Mark Hayes and his son Sheffield that she didn't hear the executive suite door open.

"Can I help you, ma'am? You aren't supposed to be in here, unless you have an appointment," a curt voice snapped from behind Kate.

Kate turned from her listening post outside the inner offices. With slightly distant affect, she swiped at a signed club on display. "Is that the real thing?"

The woman who entered the office placed her hands on her hips in a huff, "Robert Grant's driver from his first PGA win. He considered it lucky but bent the shaft in his very next tournament. The Hayeses have been huge supporters of Robert, so he gave the club to the family."

"That is so cool," Kate drawled.

"Yes, it is. Now, if you tell me what you are doing in here snooping, I have security on the way," the woman snapped.

"I, uh, this isn't the restroom…" Kate said, adding a slight slur to her voice. With a staggered step, she moved toward the door.

The woman blocked her, a fierce scowl across her face.

Nick rather liked his job. Sit at the bar and observe.

While fiddling with his drink, his eyes cast just above the rim of the glass, watching the golfers, guests, and attendants flitter about the country club. Nick found the crowd mixed. Many guests walked around with an air of undue importance, their manner filtering to how they ordered the staff around as though they were servants. Others had a bit more grace to them, equal in fine attire and gleaming jewelry, but their conduct was kinder and more appreciative.

His attention was snapped as a confident voice asked, "Buy a lady a drink?"

Nick was taken aback at how the woman had managed to slide in next to him without him noticing. Turning his head to greet her, he was even more surprised that the woman was stunning. Strawberry blonde hair cascaded down over the straps of a blue dress. She cracked a smile through lips that had a slight permanent purse to them. Her eyes seemed to smile too as they gleamed, taking in the man she had slithered beside him.

"Uhm, yeah, sure. Bartender…" Nick called.

The bartender stopped polishing the champagne flute he was holding after the woman next to Nick nodded.

"You seem to fit in this place about as much as I do," the woman said.

Nick scanned the country club with his eyes, "Not a golf aficionado?"

The woman laughed, "Oh, no. I seem to be indentured to the golf course life, but I would rather spend my time on a boat or a private beach somewhere."

The bartender sat a glass of bourbon down in front of the woman.

Nick cocked his head at the woman.

With a sly smile, she shrugged, "It's gotta be noon somewhere, right?"

Nick offered an unsure frown and tilted his glass, "Cheers?"

The woman laughed, "Cheers."

Looking deep into his glass for some sort of answer to an unasked question, Nick took a drink.

The woman laughed, "What brings a man as out of place as I am to a stuffy golf course bar?"

Nick glanced around, "This place is nice."

"Ha! It's full of old men plotting to cheat on their wives and how to grow their already inflated bank accounts. Though, I will admit, watching the ones trying to play the part when they really can't afford it, that can be a bit fun," the woman said.

Nick studied the woman who took a solid swig of her bourbon.

"Don't try to figure me out. Those that have tried haven't faired so well," the woman said, motioning for the bartender to refill her glass. "Drinks are on me, by the way. I'm Sophia Hayes. My family kinda owns this place."

Following the theatrical wave of her hand, Nick settled back on her crystal blue eyes. His head reeled as he realized who he had been speaking with. Pulling himself together, he straightened. With an extended hand, he offered, "Nick Mason."

"So… what brings you to this elegantly decorated façade? It can't be the drinks, Barney's been known to hold back a bit on the pour," Sophia said as she shot the bartender a playful smile.

"I'm working on a house over on Carolina Beach. You might know it. It has been in the news, I'm afraid," Nick said.

Sophia's eyes widened, "You're the guy who found the bones. What an awful thing."

The woman's eyes looked distant for a moment as they fixed on a point across the bar.

"The owner said your family used to own the house," Nick said.

"Did we? Probably. We have and have had real estate all over North and South Carolina," Sophia shrugged, cupping her glass.

"It's a great place. You can't beat the view," Nick said.

Sophia nodded, "I should go stay at one of our beach houses for a while. We have a couple in the Outer Banks. During off-season, it feels like you're all alone in the world. Just you and the ocean."

"Why don't you? There is nothing better than a beach vacation reset," Nick said.

"There's a lot going on. Daddy seems to think I am somehow integral to the business. I think he likes that I am a pleasant distraction," Sophia said, adjusting her dress to be ever so slightly more revealing. "So, what's your story? You still haven't told me what you're doing at a golf course bar when you aren't a golfer."

"I was told the country club was a good example of antebellum architecture. I thought I'd check it out. Seems less weird studying building details from a seat at the bar versus wandering around staring at ceiling joists," Nick said.

Sophia offered a suggestive smirk, "I could show you around. Give you a personal tour."

"I'd like that," Nick said. He was almost grateful for the buzzing in his pocket as the woman had an intoxicating effect, almost like reeling him into a swirling whirlpool. "Forgive me."

Pulling out his phone, he glanced at the message, *911, executive office.*

Looking up from the screen, he stammered, "I...I have to go."

"Architectural emergency?" Sophia asked.

"Something like that," Nick winced.

"It's okay. I've got this," Sophia smiled. "When you are ready for that tour, you know where to find me."

"Thank you," Nick nodded. Sliding out his chair, he moved quickly toward the sign for the executive offices.

"Woo, those mimosas were flowing. You know what that's like, right?" Kate stumbled forward, placing a hand on the woman's shoulders.

The woman glared at Kate and turned away from the contact.

"I'll just… go," Kate said, taking another step toward the door.

"I think it would be best if security escorted you out," the woman said.

Pointing a finger oddly close to the woman's ear, Kate said, "Are those real? They are gorgeous!"

The woman instinctively reached for her earrings, "Yes. They were a gift."

The door opened, and both women turned, expecting to see a security guard. Instead, they found a perturbed Nick Mason, "Honey, I said two doors down on the right on the *first* floor."

Without waiting for a response, he strode forward, sliding an arm around Kate. Flashing his signature Nick Mason smile, he said, "I'm sorry. The doctor warned us that alcohol might have a stronger effect with her medication."

His response was met with a silent scowl.

Steering Kate with his arm around her, he opened the door with the woman on his heels to ensure they did in fact exit. A security guard hustling down the hall saw the situation. When he received a nod from the woman, he paused and watched as it appeared Nick had the disturbance under control.

Kate looked up at Nick offering a wild grin, "Thanks, *honey*."

"We should probably go," Nick said with a roll of his eyes.

"Yeah, we should," Kate nodded as she stole a glance at the woman and security guard watching them from down the hall.

Passing the table and chairs, Kate veered from Nick's side, "Ooh, my Mimosa!"

With a sturdy arm, Nick steered her back close to his side, "I'll get you another one."

Eleven

Nick ushered Kate through the main foyer of the country club and out into the parking lot.

"Well, that was fun," Nick said as he opened Kate's door for her.

"Thank you for the rescue," Kate offered a meek smile.

"Anytime. You know I have your back," Nick said.

Kate winced, "You saw how my excursion went. Anything interesting on the main floor?"

Nick laughed as he slid into the passenger seat, "I met Sophia Hayes."

"You did?" Kate exclaimed, turning in her seat to give Nick her full attention.

Frowning, Nick nodded, "I think she may have invited me to a private tour of the country club."

"Just how private of a tour are we talking?" Kate was taken aback.

"The kind of private where you would not be invited," Nick said.

"Is she pretty? I mean… just, did she match the photos of her online?" Kate grimaced at her line of questioning.

A mischievous smile crossed Nick's lips, "She was pretty. Just like online."

"I see," Kate twisted to face the windshield as she started her SUV.

"She seemed- unhappy," Nick shared.

"Oh, how so?"

"Well, for one, she drinks bourbon for breakfast. She referred to her life as indentured to the family. It seemed the country club life wasn't agreeing with her," Nick said.

"Then why stay? She's an adult," Kate asked, putting the vehicle into gear and pulling down the long vibrant green lawn drive of the country club.

"She said something about the family business and how her father felt as though she were an important -no- *integral* part of it," Nick replied.

"I'd assume the Jaguar convertible and access to a home on Figure Eight Island has a little something to do with it," Kate said.

Nick looked thoughtful as the Wilmington landscape moved by the window, "I'll take the surfboard, decade-old pickup truck and shack near the beach lifestyle and not be beholden to anyone any day."

"One lives in opulence and is miserable. The other in relative meagerness but is content? The makings of a fable," Kate said.

"How about you? Other than angering a staff member and getting stink eye from security, did you come up with anything?" Nick asked.

Kate wrinkled her nose as she drove over the bridge toward Carolina Beach, "The family has a connection to the land long before it was a country club, at least according to the photographs in the office. I'm not sure business is going very well. Before I got tossed out, I overheard two voices. I determined them to be Mark Hayes and his son, Sheffield. They were talking about a big deal in 'Tidewater'. It sounds like a rival might have swooped in. They weren't too happy about it, to the point there were accusations of leaking information about the deal."

"Family business drama. Maybe Sophia has a reason to want out," Nick said.

Kate shot a quick look toward Nick before returning her attention to the road ahead, "The conversation was heated. Mark was adamant 'they needed a win'."

"How much money does one family need to make to feel like they 'won'?" Nick scoffed.

"I don't know. The tone was serious," Kate said, slowing and craning her neck as she passed the beach house.

Crime scene investigators were loading gear into vans and trucks. Uniformed patrol officers managed traffic and held a slew of reporters at bay. Detective Nixon stood in front of the cameras and microphones looking very cross. The detective's sour expression made Kate giggle.

"Good news, they are packing up. Bad news, they are clearly not quite done yet, and I am in no hurry to be part of the news broadcast regarding a murder again any time soon," Kate said.

"Other good news, it means our afternoon is free. It would be great to try our hands at catching dinner," Nick said.

Kate pulled into an empty driveway to turn around. Looking at Nick, she considered the suggestion, "I'd really like to do a little more digging since I can't work on the house."

"How about this? You do some research, somewhere safe, like the library, and I will gather up all the gear and supplies we'll need for beach fishing," Nick suggested.

"All right. Bring the receipts. We'll put together a package for future renters. I'll have the company pick up the tab in my entertainment supplies budget," Kate said.

"Sounds good to me," Nick agreed.

Kate dropped Nick off at his truck and drove to the Carolina Beach Library. Nodding to the now-familiar librarian, Kate disappeared into the research room.

With the heated discussion between Mark Hayes and his son, Sheffield, Kate wanted to get a better picture of the family's business. The family's land development roots went deep, back several generations. Mark Hayes' father and grandfather developed swaths of valuable Cape Fear River footage properties key for shipping and trade while Wilmington was a valuable upcoming seaport.

The money from riverfront development turned into key beach properties, including one of the first multi-floor hotels serving Wrightsville Beach. They helped fund the bridge that crossed the Intracoastal Waterway leading to years of tax benefits and government repayment with a healthy percentage of return.

Mark Hayes took the family business in a different direction from industrial to high-end projects- at a time when affluence began replacing affordable real estate in the region.

Kate sat back and whistled, "These guys strike gold all the time."

Tapping her pen rapidly against the table as she thought, she squinted, "What is upsetting their very successful apple cart?"

Scrolling through the clips, she found articles on their most recent development, a massive project built around Albemarle Sound in Edenton Point. The result was a stunning property with two PGA golf courses and exclusive gated housing as well as a marina for large boats. Despite massive investment and a slew of celebrity endorsements, the project ran into issues as environmental and historical archeological issues halted and threatened to kill the project multiple times.

"I guess when you dig for gold long enough, you're going to find a pit of rattlesnakes," Kate muttered as she continued progressing through news clips of the project. "To move the project forward required a massive injection of additional funds and a sudden reversal from the county on a key ruling. The project was finally completed, but way over budget."

Kate pursed her lips. One rather harshly written article painted the Hayes family and their business dealings in a very negative light. From the mysterious reversal at Edenton Point all the way back to the development of the first country club in Wilmington, there were allegations of shady dealings. The article questioned the family's right to the land dating from their very first land sale along the Cape Fear River.

An old article from when the Hayes' resort was groundbreaking told about a contrarian tale to their family's link to the land. One that was quickly scuttled by an area judge at the time. This piqued Kate's interest.

Scrolling through the news clips, she emailed articles of interest to herself. Scribbling in her notes, she wrote about the Hauer family as a key rival. Following the Hayes' lead, they also began developing pro golf courses using celebrities as their named partners and designers. The two companies had one-upped each other on multiple successive deals over the past decade.

A particular photo of Thomas Hauer caught her interest. The attractive man had his arm slung around Sophia Hayes. Pro-golfer and machismo model Robert Grant stood in the background. The image caught a very unhappy look on the golfer's face. The article caption captured the moment as Sophia Hayes' ex-fiancé looked on as she cozied up to her family's rival.

Twelve

Kate stood on the deck of the bungalows looking out at the beach. Just where the sand escaped the tide and remained, a pair of chairs sat on either side of a cooler. Nick stood fiddling with the line of a fishing pole.

As though he felt he was being watched, Nick turned his head toward the bungalows. Seeing Kate, he gave an excited wave. With a laugh at his childlike exuberance, Kate walked down the steps to join him.

"You've been busy," Kate said, observing the sundry of buckets and gear at Nick's feet along, with the pair of poles he had planted in the sand.

"Labor of love. I even got fishing licenses for us, so we don't give Detective Nixon another reason to toss you in the clink," Nick said. "Here. I just finished rigging yours."

Kate reluctantly accepted the pole. Staring down its shaft and playing with the gleaming blue reel, she bit her lip, "Where do we start?"

"Like any good fishing trip," Nick said, reaching into the cooler, "It starts with a little refreshment."

Popping the top of a beer, he handed it to Kate.

With a shrug, Kate took a swig. She had to admit, the cool liquid went down well with the late afternoon sun still casting its powerful glow over them.

"And then, you're going to need this. Here, I'll help you," Nick said. Stepping close to Kate, their eyes caught for just a moment.

Their breathing stilled until Kate saw what was in Nick's hand, "Ew!"

Kate staggered back a step.

Nick laughed, "It's okay. We're using dead bait today."

"You use live bait?" Kate looked horrified.

"Depending on what you want to catch, yeah," Nick shrugged. "Here."

Nick placed the mullet on the hook strung to Kate's pole.

Kate offered her unfortunate friend a disapproving look, "I have had my fill of corpses."

"Come on, now. That is your buddy. He wants you to have a tasty dinner tonight, I promise," Nick said.

Kate's wary lips remained pursed.

"All right. Here's what we do," Nick closed in around Kate. With his fingers over hers, he said, "Place your thumb on top... Yeah, right there. Wrap your fingers so that they are at the base of the reel. Make sure your drag is set. Hold the line with your index finger... Yes. Just like that."

Reaching completely around Kate as though he were hugging her from behind, Nick placed his left hand around Kate's. Rocking back and forth, he moved her with him in a close sort of dance. "We want to move directly overhead. Look behind you to make sure you are clear and... fire away!"

As Kate flipped the line overhead, Nick lifted her pressure off the line and allowed the weights to pull the hook and the bait twenty yards into the surf.

"There you go. Great job," Nick said, releasing Kate.

Kate's head swiveled, "Now what do I do?"

"You wait. See if there is someone out there who would like a snack. Accept your invitation to dinner," Nick grinned, picking up his own pole.

With a quick swing, his cast flew out past hers.

"Oh, sure. Show me up," Kate scoffed.

"You'll get there. It is all about timing and angles. You want to release at about forty-five degrees. With me guiding you, we were probably a little late. Still pretty good, though," Nick said.

"Should I try again?" Kate asked.

Nick shrugged, "You can. Or, you can let it bob around there. Just relax."

Planting his rod in the sand, he walked over and grabbed Kate's beer and handed it to her. Grabbing his own, he spun the top. Clinking his glass against hers, he let out a breathy, "Cheers."

"Cheers," Kate said bringing the beer to her lips. Moving her eyes from Nick to the surf where her line was cast, she fell into the motion of the sea.

Letting out her own sigh, she admitted, "This is kind of relaxing."

"I think that's the secret. With your line in, there's nothing to do but wait. That is your *job*," Nick said. "Sure, there's the excitement of the catch, but that doesn't explain the people who go out every day, even when they know they aren't likely to catch anything. Enjoy the moment to do…nothing."

"I can handle that. It's like being obliged to be still for a bit," Kate said.

"Exactly," Nick nodded, sipping his beer.

For several long minutes, they stood with their attentions out at the sea. The rolling waves made their relentless though gentle roll toward shore. The sun tilted from overhead to slowly sink toward the horizon.

As they each recast their lines, Kate rolled through her research, "The Hayes' family leveraged a ton of money, nearly their entire net worth on a project up north. They stand to make a lot of money if they can withstand long enough for the pay off."

"Explains the 'need a win' talk," Nick said, gently playing the line in the water.

"It turns out, the family has been enveloped in allegations of suspicious dealings for generations, leading back to their very first development projects," Kate said.

Nick looked over, "Oh? How so?"

"There's some doubt whether they had claim to all the land they sold. Even the country club's exact ownership history is a little dubious. Ultimately, they clearly got the approvals they needed. The scuttlebutt is they greased a few palms to make that happen," Kate said.

"Welcome to big money and politics," Nick scoffed.

"Your new friend, it seems, likes to play Juliet. She dated the family's main rival for a while, Thomas Hauer," Kate said.

"That's juicy," Nick said.

"And, it was around the time of the new addition at the beach house," Kate said. "I guess she was engaged to Robert Grant, the golfer that's on the golf course brochures for the Hayes' country club."

"Let me guess, also around the time that our buddy was stashed in the walls of the house?" Nick asked.

Kate screwed her face, "Don't put it like that. Our victim, yes."

"Sorry, that was irreverent," Nick conceded. "Any idea on who our unfortunate friend is?"

"No. I'm hoping the police were able to get that from forensics," Kate said.

Nick nodded slowly, looking out at the horizon. The sun was behind them, but it didn't stop the sky from being a colorful display of reds, pinks and oranges. The moon appeared almost as a watermark in the sky, leaving its brand on their fishing adventure.

The peaceful drift of Nick's mind was cut short as Kate's line snapped taut. Her eyes went wide, "What do I do?"

Nick grinned, "We have dinner!"

Gone from Kate was the look of pondering the case. Her pulse raced as her rod wriggled wildly in her hands. Nick planted his pole in the sand and wrapped his arms back around her using his fingers in a dance with hers to manipulate the reel.

"All right! Let's land this and see what we've got," Nick said. "Take your fingers and wind the reel so the line is tight. Give a gentle pull back on the rod… that's it. When you feel slack, reel it in, pull back. Reel, reel, reel…"

Getting the feel of the process, Kate was released from Nick's supportive arms. She was on her own to land her first fish. It danced across the water as it neared the beach until it was dangling from her pole.

Heart still racing, eyes wide and an inexplicable grin on her face, she looked at Nick, "Now what?"

Helping her remove the fish from the hook, he dropped it in a bucket. Kate leaned over to take a peek, both exhilarated and a little soft-hearted for the fish removed from its ocean home.

"That's a blue. It will make a good dinner. It'll be all right. The world has a balance to it as long as no one gets greedy," Nick assured her, seeing the contemplation on Kate's face.

Kate didn't have much time to dwell. Movement caught her eye, pointing, she called, "Ooh, your line!"

Nick raced over plucking his pole from its sandy perch. Simultaneously snapping the line back and reeling in the slack, he quickly brought the fish to shore. "Two blues!" he exclaimed, adding the second fish to the bucket.

"This is easier than I thought it was going to be," Kate said.

Nick laughed, "Yeah. Works like that every time. You just cast and reel in dinner. Just like that."

Kate scowled, "You're teasing me. "

"I am," Nick nodded.

Kate pouted as she peered into their bucket.

"Come on," Nick said. "We have fish to grill."

Back at the bungalows, Nick brought the fish to the cleaning station while Kate disappeared to wrangle vegetables. By the time she returned to the oceanfront deck with two glasses and a bottle of wine, Nick had the fish on a grill.

"This is going to be good," Nick said as he squeezed lime on the fillets he had on the grill.

Kate joined him, handing him a glass of wine. They clinked their glasses just as the sun had all but disappeared, leaving a gorgeous Atlantic glisten.

"Not a bad day at all," Kate breathed, staring out at the ocean.

Nick nodded as he sipped his wine, "Yeah."

Turning his attention to the fish, he scooped the filets and placed them on a plate. "Dinner is ready."

Kate led Nick to a table she had prepared for them. Settling into deck chairs with a beautiful dinner in front of them, Kate shot a look toward Nick.

"That was fun," Kate said. "Thank you."

"I'm telling you, fully embracing the beach life is a good thing," Nick said dishing the prettiest of the fillets onto Kate's plate.

"I can see that. I've been missing out. I witness incredible views, but that's clearly only a tiny bit of the story," Kate said. "Thank you for sharing that with me."

"My pleasure," Nick said. "Surfing, fishing… we'll have to see what is next."

Kate dug in with a forkful of bluefish, "This is delicious. Even better than the restaurant's, and that is saying something."

"You can't beat fresh caught, no matter how talented the chef," Nick said, digging in for his first bite.

"Well, clearly, we got the best of both worlds. Ocean fresh fish *and* a talented chef," Kate said.

"I know my way around a grill," Nick said.

Kate cocked her head, another bite raised on her fork, "I admire your confidence in what you do."

Putting his fork down, Nick looked across the table at Kate. Candlelight danced in her eyes and cast a warm glow over her face. "Not everything," Nick said.

Kate shifted in her seat. Her eyes darted away as she sought desperately to lock them onto something other than her dinner date. Realizing she was still holding a forkful of fish, she took a bite. "Delicious…" she said, her voice drifting.

Snapping into a different mode, she said, "While you were preparing the fish, I got a call from Detective Nixon. We can start back up at the house tomorrow. Ready to get back to work?"

"Yeah. Hopefully no more dead bodies. A chest full of gold, maybe or at least a treasure map," Nick suggested.

Kate laughed, "You are relentless."

Nick shot her a look, "*You* calling *me* relentless…"

"Yeah," Kate shrugged. "I guess both the pot and the kettle are black, in our own ways."

Settling back in her chair with a glass of wine in hand, Kate breathed deeply, "If I have to have a project delayed, this is the way to do it."

"It sure is," Nick said, tilting his glass slightly toward Kate, "To the beach life."

"To the beach life."

Thirteen

Kate sipped her coffee, watching sandpipers play along the waterline. The sky was painted in brushstrokes of pinks and soft peachy oranges against a Carolina blue backdrop.

A tiny silhouette a few hundred yards down shore stood atop a wave. Dropping from the lip into the pocket, the surfer allowed the wave to move them both laterally along the beach as well as toward the shore itself. Losing energy at the break, the rider stepped off the board into the whitewater.

Kate took a deep breath as she hugged her coffee cup. A Carolina Beach morning was a spectacular way to start a day. A part of her considered being out there trying her hand at the Atlantic Ocean waves. Instead, she retreated into her bungalow. The work delays had piled up, and she had a schedule to get back on track.

Stopping at Nick's door, she placed a coffee and breakfast sandwich wrapped in a white bag for him when he returned from surfing. Disappearing into her rental unit, she readied herself for the day.

Nick was waiting in front of the bungalows when Kate appeared, her work bag slung over her shoulder. Offering Nick a smile, she asked, "Ready to finally get going on the beach house?"

"I am," Nick nodded. He pulled his eyes from the beachcombers that had replaced the sandpipers. Heads bowed down, they scanned for shells and sand dollars. The image spurred Nick to reach into his pocket. "For you."

Kate gently held the item in her fingers and held it up, "It's perfect." The little white disc had a unique star-shaped pattern embossed on its shell. "They are so beautiful and delicate."

"We can find a pile of them and place them in a little jar for the guest bedroom," Nick suggested.

"You taking over the interior decorating?" Kate laughed.

Nick shrugged, "If you want to start swinging a hammer."

"I'll leave you to the hammering. I may well take you up on your advice, though. If nothing else, it might be fun looking," Kate said.

"Thank you for breakfast, by the way," Nick said. "I thought about knocking on your door to see if you wanted to hit the waves, but I didn't know if you were up. Had an early start."

"I probably wasn't long after you. Sunrise was gorgeous," Kate said.

Nick studied Kate for a moment, bathed in the soft glow of the still-rising sun, "It is."

Kate shuffled slightly, turning her head, and she began striding for the parking lot, "You're welcome for breakfast."

Pausing a moment before following, Nick bit his lip.

Detective Nixon leaned against her unmarked police cruiser waiting for them. Her eyes were hidden under dark aviator sunglasses, and her flat expression hid whatever mood she was in. Kate and Nick had learned very quickly that it was best to assume sour.

Kate got out of her SUV. A spare coffee that was a little better than lukewarm in her hand. "Good morning!" Kate called cheerily.

Nixon remained expressionless.

"Beautiful day," Nick added as he joined Kate in front of the detective.

Nixon held out the keys to the beach house. The "crime scene" tape and the warning notice which had been taped to the door were removed. Any evidence of a forensics team had been scrubbed.

"My team cleaned up the hallway. The drywall, insulation and membrane liner were removed from stud to stud in a six-foot span. No other parts of the house were affected," the detective said. "You may find spots along the walls or flooring where the clean-up team might have missed. The lidar equipment can leave marks where the rubber wheels went over them. They should be superficial."

The detective pushed up from the hood of her vehicle and placed the keys in Kate's palm.

Kate scowled as the detective started to walk away, "Detective, I have questions."

"I'm sure you do," Nixon said, unmoved by the statement as she opened her driver's door.

"Do you know who the victim was?" Kate pressed.

"It is an ongoing investigation. We have to complete our portion of the investigation. We need to inform any family members, and then we will speak to the press at which time. You will get whatever answers are made available at that time," Detective Nixon said. Her statement sounded as though it was a familiar speech.

"But this is my house. Or my company's house. I'm supposed to be staying in there," Kate said.

"So, stay in there. There is no evidence that this very old case presents any danger to you or your future occupants," Detective Nixon said. "Provided you keep your nose to yourself, of course, Ms. Harper."

Kate's face fell.

"I spoke to Detective Connolly in St. Petersburg. The case he was working in Treasure Island was high profile, and he said he tripped over you throughout the course of the investigation. I can tell you that I will not tolerate any interference with my investigation. At all. Am I clear?" the detective sounded like a mother scolding her precocious child.

"Clear, Detective Nixon," Kate affirmed.

Nixon gave Kate a deep look and a shot at Nick before turning to retreat to her car.

"Oh, but what if I *do* find something? Like in the course of the remodel, for example," Kate asked.

"You report it to me immediately. And leave it alone. *Period*. If I uncover that you do not share what you know as it pertains to this case, I will haul you in on obstruction," Detective Nixon said.

"What about legal ramifications for my company? Having answers may erase some bad press. I mean, who wants to rent a murder house?" Kate asked.

"I'm sure there is a type that might find that a unique property feature," the detective said starting her police cruiser. "I'm sorry, Ms. Harper. That is all I have for you at this time."

Kate stood still as the detective closed her door and backed out of the driveway. Even as the taillights of the unmarked police car vanished down Highway 421, her head swiveled to Nick, who shrugged.

"She's nice," Kate scowled.

"Best to let me handle dealing with Detective Happy," Nick said.

"Yeah. That might be best," Kate nodded. Spinning, she opened the door, "Let's see what we've got to deal with."

"Nothing to do but get to work on the house, right?" Nick said, a questioning tone in his voice as he watched the wheels spin in Kate's head.

"Yeah, work," Kate muttered leading Nick into the house.

The house was, as the detective had said, largely cleaned up. The hole in the wall had been torn down for a span of four studs. Nick inspected the area while Kate seemed to avoid the spot where the skeleton had spilled out of the wall and onto the floor.

Eyeing rows of streaks that Detective Nixon had warned them about, Kate ran her hands along the affected drywall with curiosity.

Nick slumped.

"What?" Kate asked, concerned the damage was worse than it looked.

"If they searched the house with lidar, that probably means no hidden treasure," Nick pouted.

"Would lidar be sensitive enough to see papers?" Kate asked.

"No, I don't think so," Nick said. His eyes went wide, "Or a treasure map! There's still a chance."

Kate laughed, rolling her eyes almost as much at herself offering the suggestion to Nick. "Well, I guess I can get back to work."

Kate nodded. "I've got a lot to catch up on as well."

Walking the house, Kate tried to regain her bearings. Her property management hat seemed to fit in place as she reimagined the space with fresh eyes and made furious notes as she wandered the house.

"Maybe we need one of those fish cleaning stations out back!" she called out as much to herself as to Nick.

"Easy enough to do," Nick said as he had already gotten to work dismantling the remaining drywall from the faux wall.

When she was done with her freshened tour, Kate settled down behind her laptop to tweak her plans based on the notes she had jotted down. By the time she had gotten to the point of scanning through a thousand shades of coastal hues for bathroom colors, her mind began to drift.

The thought of a dead body buried in the walls behind her gave her a shiver. Her curiosity became anger as she was determined to get answers. She *needed* answers. Who was in her walls?

Pulling open a new tab in her browser, she started a search.

Nick had the entire faux wall cleared and was working on removing the studs when Kate brushed by, her work bag strewn over her shoulder.

Recognizing the look on Kate's face, Nick asked, "Where are you off to? A flooring or tile store, I hope."

"I, uh, I have an appointment," Kate said.

"Kate…" Nick pressed.

"I just have a few questions. I'll be back with lunch in hand," Kate assured.

"I don't think batting your eyes at Detective Nixon is going to be as effective as it was for Detective Connolly. He had a certain… affection for you," Nick warned.

"I guess you'll have to be the official eye batter this time around," Kate grinned and wheeled out the door before Nick could object any further.

"Oh, boy!" Nick sighed to himself as he stared at the closed door in Kate's wake.

With a shake of his head, he focused back on his work.

Fourteen

Kate drove from Carolina Beach to the busy stretch of College Road, not far from where the edge of Wilmington ended and Interstate Forty began. Nestled under tall stands of Carolina pines with their long needles was a scattering of colonial-style brick buildings, bold, white columns elevating the front of the buildings. Their Georgian architecture was a trademark of the people it served.

Kate found the main entrance. Long brick gates marked the University of North Carolina at Wilmington. A large swooping sculpture of the school's Seahawk mascot welcomed guests as they drove into the park-like campus.

Grateful for her car's map, Kate didn't have to navigate the maze of buildings on her own. Finding a parking space, she spied her target destination and meandered the concrete sidewalks of campus toward it. Walking past students enjoying that snapshot of their lives, she couldn't help but crack a smile. On the lawn or perched up against one of the giant pines, students read, played music or laughed together. Young love was markedly present as sweet expressions covered nervousness.

Seeing the sign for Bear Hall, Kate took the intersecting sidewalk. In the corner of her eye, she saw a projectile heading straight for her. Spinning, her bag nearly flying off her shoulder, she struck her hand out. More out of instinct than skill, her finger closed around the object just before it hit her square in the head.

A young man raced toward her, panting, an apologetic look strewn across his face, "I am so sorry, ma'am. That one got away from me. We kinda take Ultimate pretty seriously around here."

"Ultimate?" Kate frowned, handing the disc back to the college student.

"Frisbee. Ultimate Frisbee. Kind of like football but beach style," the young man grinned. "Thanks."

Rushing off, the young man returned to his group of friends, who seemed to be having a good laugh at his expense.

Kate turned and scoffed as she headed for the building, "Ma'am... I'm not *that* much older..."

Entering Bear Hall, Kate was hit with a blast of air conditioning. Students clutching stacks of books to their chests chattered as they walked the halls. Finding a directory, Kate followed the instructions up the stairs until she found a door marked "Criminal Justice Sciences".

Pushing into the suite of offices, Kate was promptly met by a young lady manning the desk. "Can I help you?"

"I have an appointment with Dr. Granger," Kate said.

The young woman's eyes went wide as she studied Kate, "You found the bones?"

Kate cocked her head.

"I saw it on the news and then we talked about it in class. Dr. Granger didn't list what the appointment was for, but one of the news stations had a photo of you and a rather attractive man in front of the house on Carolina Beach," the girl said.

Kate shut her eyes tight for a moment. The thought of being identified as any part of a murder news story did not sit well with her, "Yes, that was me. Are you a Criminal Justice major?"

"I am," the girl nodded. "Double major with Psychology. I want to be a forensic psychologist."

Kate nodded, "Good for you. I have no doubt you'll be great at it."

Getting up from behind the desk, she said, "Dr. Granger is finishing up with someone, but I'll let him know you are here. Have a seat or feel free to poke around some of the photos on the wall while you wait."

"Thank you," Kate said, obliging the offer to peruse the photos.

Most of the photographs were of student classes. Some had the students mixed with professors working on assignments. A number of law enforcement officers and even a judge had a spot on the wall.

"He'll be right out," the young lady said, returning to her seat. "You here to talk about the bones?"

Kate wasn't sure why she hesitated, but she did before nodding her head, "I am."

"Must have been kind of cool… and unsettling at the same time," the girl said.

"It was. Both," Kate admitted.

"Do the police know who it was?" the girl asked.

Kate shook her head, "If they do, they won't tell me. Said I had to see it on the news like everyone else."

"That's hardly fair," the girl frowned.

"Right?" Kate smiled. Walking over to the desk, Kate held her hand out, "I'm Kate, by the way."

"I know," the girl glanced down at the department chair's calendar. "I'm Sandy."

"Pleasure to meet you, Sandy," Kate said.

"Pleasure to meet you, too," Sandy perked up. "This is the first time I ever met a witness to a murder scene."

Kate laughed, "Well, I was about a decade late to the scene, but I suppose so."

Voices came down the hallway as two men made their way to the Criminal Justice suite foyer.

One of the men glanced at Kate before turning to a man in a suit and tie, thanking him for his time. Another glance at Kate and the man scurried out of the office. Kate couldn't help but feel a bit studied by the glances. Returning the favor, she made a mental note of the man's tan jacket and tattered leather notebook he clutched in his hands.

"Ms. Harper, come on back," Dr. Granger said with an arm spread down the hallway. "Thank you, Sandy."

Escorting Kate into the department offices, Dr. Granger said, "Popular topic today."

Kate stopped, "That gentleman was asking about the case as well?"

"Well, sort of, yes. He is doing an article on cold cases. They happen to coincide with the era that you are interested in," Dr. Granger said leading Kate into his office. Offering her a seat, the Criminal Justice professor slid behind his desk. Touching his fingertips together, he leaned back into his thickly padded leather chair, "So, you would like to know about cases of men in their early twenties who disappeared ten years ago with a five-year margin?"

"Yes, that's right," Kate nodded.

The professor smiled, "That is very specific."

Kate wrinkled her nose, "It kind of fits the profile."

"Of the victim's bones that were found in the beach house you are remodeling," Granger said.

"Yes," Kate admitted. She wasn't very happy with how obvious her situation was to the world.

Dr. Granger laughed, "It's not *that* big of a community, and a case like that, especially to a Criminal Justice Department, garners a fair amount of interest. I have already graded three papers with that case as the subject. None of them dialed in the criteria for cold cases quite as well as you have."

"Yeah, I would like to know who was in my wall. Or at least, get a good idea of it, anyway," Kate said.

"The police are being tight-lipped? I know Detective Nixon quite well. You won't get anything from her. Not until she feels all stones have been turned over," Granger admitted.

"So I have learned," Kate laughed.

Flipping a file of printer copies around, Kate found her name on a sticky note atop the manila folder.

"I found three cold cases involving males who disappeared during that general time frame that pointed toward suspected foul play," Dr. Granger began. "The first case is Jeffrey Marlett, a salesman traveling through Wilmington. He didn't stay at any of the beaches, but according to reports, he did spend a fair amount of time at the beach bars. He was a bit of a scoundrel with the ladies and despite his meager income, had a penchant to waste it on gambling."

"What happened to him?" Kate asked. "How was he found to be missing?"

"The motel he was staying at opened up his room after his checkout. His room had all of his things in it, but he never returned. The police followed his sales route. Never found him or his car," Dr. Granger said.

"Did he have family?" Kate asked. "That would be so horrible, scoundrel or otherwise."

"No family, at least no wife and kids," the professor said. Leaning forward, he shared, "This is an interesting one. Collin Royce-a professional golfer who was on the rise. He won a couple tournaments and landed multiple endorsements. He was a regular here in Wilmington. Played all of our nicest courses."

"Like the Hayes resort," Kate said.

"Well, yes. But he played all of them," the professor said. "He was playing in a tournament when he disappeared. He was one stroke off from the lead heading into the final day of the tournament. Never showed up for the final round. He just vanished."

Kate frowned, "How does a famous golfer 'just vanish'? You would think he would have an entourage."

"Golfers, especially heading into the final day of a tourney with a shot at winning it, sometimes just want to stay in their own heads and not be distracted by others," Dr. Granger said. With a laugh, he added, "Now the golfers without a shot at the lead, they on the other hand, have a pretty good time the night before closing out a tournament. Sadly, frivolity leads to pretty unreliable witnesses."

Kate nodded absently, picturing the scene.

"Lastly, we have Rufus Westerfield, the only Wilmingtonian of the bunch. He was every bit the salty fisherman. Sold to a few restaurants. Had a few tussles, including one where he was arrested for stealing crab pots– a serious no, no in these parts, akin to horse stealing in the old west. He went out one night. The Coast Guard found his boat but no Rufus," Dr. Granger said.

"Each disappeared without a trace. Each with at least the potential for motives lined up against them," Kate said.

Dr. Granger nodded, "That's pretty much it. Around here, with the ocean, the swamps, the Cape Fear River…"

"The remodeled beach houses…" Kate chimed in.

"Right," the professor laughed. "Aside from an Edgar Allan Poe story, I haven't come across too many cases like that. Attics, basements, storage sheds… even wells. But not an interior wall of an otherwise beautiful house. At any rate, there's no shortage of ways to disappear, by accident or otherwise."

Kate clutched the folder as she pondered the information she had been given.

"That was a quick print to give you a profile of the cold cases. You're welcome to peruse the Randall Hall Library on campus. It'll give you access to a lot more information," Dr. Granger said.

"Thank you, I think I will. Thank you again for taking the time to meet with me," Kate said.

"My pleasure," Dr. Granger said, getting out of his seat and shaking her hand. "I can walk you out."

"I think I can find my way, but thank you," Kate said.

"Of course," Dr. Granger nodded. With a pause, he said, "You wouldn't mind asking Sandy to come back as you walk out, would you? I have a professor running late, and I need her to greet their class."

"Be happy to," Kate said as she exited the office.

Walking up to Sandy's desk, Kate began to speak.

"Dr. Granger needs me to kick start Professor Daniels' class again. I've been fielding calls," the young woman said.

"Sounds like it," Kate nodded.

Sandy shot up and jogged down the hall to confirm with the department head that she would handle it.

Still holding the file folder, Kate paused at the desk. With a glance at the vacant hallway as Sandy conferred with Dr. Granger, Kate spied the appointment book. Leaning over the desk, she spun the calendar toward her. "Dennis Jones" was scribbled in the appointment slot preceding hers.

Spinning the appointment book back into position, Kate left the office and headed for the university library to deep dive into her list of possible victims who were sharing her beach house with her.

Fifteen

Kate made do on her promise, stopping at Merritt's Burger House to grab lunch on her way back to the beach house. The line for the iconic burger restaurant was long. Nick had told her it was a local favorite. Another one of his "I know a place…" referrals. The thought made her laugh out loud so that heads swiveled her way. She bowed her head and smiled behind her sunglasses. When she reached the front of the line, she ordered her "All the Way" sandwiches.

As she pulled into the beach house driveway, a car pulled away from the curb. Stepping out of her SUV, Kate eyed the vehicle as it sped down the street. A glance at the driver's side mirror, she thought she recognized the face captured in the moment.

Hearing the car pull up, Nick opened the front door to greet Kate. Seeing her staring down the street, her car door still open, he asked, "Everything okay?"

Kate turned toward Nick and nodded slowly, "Yeah. Fine. I think I saw that guy at the university."

"What guy? What university?" Nick frowned, his body subconsciously stiffening.

"Help me grab our lunch and I'll tell you about it," Kate said.

"Sounds like a fair deal," Nick said descending the steps to give Kate a hand.

Grabbing her notes and their drinks while Nick grabbed the bags of burgers, Kate glanced over her shoulder to where the vehicle had sped away.

Nick caught the look. "Kate…"

"I'm sure it's nothing," Kate assured him as she marched into the house. Seeing Nick's progress, she applauded, "This is coming along great! I love that the flooring extends into the covered section."

"We'll want to take a look at it and see if we can't save it. After years of UV and heavy traffic, I'm worried the portion that has been sealed off will be an obvious shade or two off," Nick said following Kate to the table overlooking the beach.

Setting the bags of food down, Nick smiled, "You found Merritt's."

"I did," Kate said. "You said you knew a guy who knew a place."

Nick laughed, "I did. Didn't I?"

"You should be on a food channel show, traveling to all the places referred to you by a guy you knew," Kate said as she opened up her lunch.

"Well, it can air right after your stunning beach house transformations on the home network," Nick countered.

"Or," Kate said in between bites of burger, "we can keep some of these secrets to ourselves."

"That wouldn't be selfish?" Nick asked.

Kate squinted, "Call it preservation."

"Oh, that sounds way more altruistic," Nick said.

"This is amazing, by the way. Your 'guy' was right, yet again," Kate said.

Nick nodded in agreement as he took a bite of his sandwich and stared off at the Atlantic Ocean, rolling softly onto the beach. Sandpipers and gulls chased the waves as tiny crabs appeared and disappeared into holes as the water stretched toward the sand and then receded again.

Turning toward Kate, he asked, "So, tell me about this guy from the university."

"I went to speak to the head of the Criminal Justice Department to see if I could gather insight into possible disappearances around the time of… of the remodel. As I was entering, a guy was leaving," Kate said, waving her fork in the air as she spoke. Her eyes gleamed, "I got his name. As I was leaving, I stole a peek at the appointment book for the office."

"Super sleuth back at work," Nick said in mixed admiration and concern.

"It may be nothing, but the glimpse I saw looked like him," Kate said. "I think I saw him at the library, too."

"Library?" Nick asked.

"Professor Granger, that's who I met, suggested I visit the university to learn a little more about the cases that he introduced me to. It is possible he gave the same advice to the visitor before me," Kate said.

"Why would he do that?" Nick frowned.

"Because the visitor was there for the same reason," Kate said.

Nick set his fork down and straightened in his seat, "Kate, this is starting to sound real familiar."

"This is nothing like what happened in Treasure Island," Kate said defensively. "This is a decades-old cold case. Not something I witnessed out my back door."

"A decades-old case that I am sure someone would like to remain a cold case," Nick said, his voice stern.

Kate grinned, "Good thing I have my partner in crime… fighting to keep me safe."

Nick rolled his eyes, "Is it a waste of breath to ask you to be careful?"

"No, it isn't a waste. I'll be careful," Kate said as their eyes locked. It wasn't often that Nick's playful expression turned stone serious. The moments impacted her in a way she didn't care to admit. "I'll be careful. Promise."

"Hmm," Nick grunted. His eyes widened and his child-like affect made an immediate return. Pointing past the swells, he called with excitement in his tone, "Dolphin!"

Kate's eyes followed his finger out into the water. "I don't... There he is! There's two...three!"

"I can spend every day on the beach and seeing them never gets old," Nick said.

Settling back into her seat, Kate smiled quietly watching pure glee wash over Nick as he watched dolphins dart in and out of the waves. Sucking in a deep breath, she shifted in her seat and played her fork through her food.

When the dolphins had swum away, the lunch table was cleared. Kate excused herself as her phone lit up with calls from her boss. "I had better..." Kate started.

Nick nodded, "I've got plenty to keep me busy."

Disappearing up the beach house stairs to the master suite, Kate hit the answer button, "Hi, Merilu!"

"Hi Merliu? Kate, we are nearly a week off schedule and have a house that is going to end up on one of those unsolved mystery shows or worse, be overrun by ghost hunters and mediums," Kate's boss called into the phone.

"Well, it is a burgeoning niche of traveling clientele," Kate said.

"This isn't funny, Kate. I can't have a seven-figure property dry up on me like that set of disgusting bones you found. You'd think that would be in the real estate disclosures," Merilu said. Even over the phone, Kate could sense Merilu's complexion turning pale, "Oh, my. *We* may have to disclose this in the future!"

"I'm sure that isn't the case. Here's what I can tell you. The police working the case assure me that there is no danger to anyone here at the beach house. It is an *amazing* property, Merilu. The views are stunning. We saw dolphins swim by while we were eating lunch. You buy million-dollar view properties, and this one is a bargain. Carolina Beach is gorgeous, family friendly. The beaches are peaceful, and the boardwalk is fun. It's a vacationer's dream," Kate said.

Merilu laughed, "You certainly can sell a vacation property. Tell me about your schedule?"

"We were shut down for a few days, but Nick is back on it and is confident we can catch up," Kate said.

Merilu's tenor dropped yet again, "Kate... as your boss, no as your *friend*, I hear your voice change every time you mention his name. You say 'we' like a married couple. What is going on with you and your surfer-handyman?"

"Nothing!" Kate gasped out a hoarse laugh. "Strictly professional, I mean, we're friendly... We're friends."

"Oh, my goodness, Kate! You are smitten," Merliu said.

"Merilu, you trusted me to hire Nick. I am not going to betray that trust by making it personal," Kate assured her.

"I'm just concerned about you. I want you safe. How well do you know this vagabond anyway? Didn't you meet him trespassing on the Treasure Island property?" Merilu asked.

"He, uh, he noticed some safety issues with the back deck, and I gave him a trial run. You saw the way the house turned out. It was spectacular. He does good work. That is why I hired him for this job," Kate said.

Merilu laughed, "You don't need to sell me. You need to be careful, protect yourself and protect my investment."

"And I will. I promise," Kate said.

"I know you will. Keep me up to date… on all fronts," Merilu pressed her.

"*Merilu…*" Kate scowled through the phone.

"Take care, Kate," Merilu said before hanging up the phone.

Kate looked at her phone for a moment before swinging the master door open. She was surprised to see Nick standing there, a hand raised, ready to rap on the door.

Flustered, Kate took a slight step back, "Nick, you surprised me!"

"I'm sorry, I was just excited. I wanted to show you something, if you weren't busy," Nick said.

Kate studied Nick for a moment as if to determine how much of the conversation with Merilu he might have heard. Seemingly unaffected, she hoped the exchange was just between her and her boss.

"Yeah, sure. Show me," Kate nodded.

Following Nick down the steps, he spread his arms wide to reveal the hallway in its original structural form. "What do you think?"

Kate kneeled to study the space in various lighting.

"I cleaned it all up. Buffed the floor, a few times. I think we might be okay," Nick said.

Kate eyed the flooring, paying close attention to where the faux wall had covered a portion of it. "I think you're right. That saves us a ton of time and money. Merilu will be happy about that."

"Hmm," Nick nodded, his eyes glancing sideways at Kate before returning to the construction. "Some fresh paint, new molding pieces… What do you think about mounting some wall sconces? The direct path to the beachfront windows let in a ton of light in the daytime, but I think at night, it would make a more welcoming entrance."

"Yeah, I think you're right. I'll pick some out," Kate said. "Great work, Nick."

Nick winced slightly at Kate's tone which sounded professionally forced.

Kate sensed the uncomfortable air in the room, "Why don't you come with me? I could use some advice to make sure I choose the right kind of fixtures."

"Sure. I want to pick up some protectant for the floor anyway. To get it to match, I basically stripped away a few layers," Nick said.

"Good. We'll head out whenever you are ready," Kate said.

"I'll make a few measurements and we can go," Nick said. He eyed Kate as she appeared fumbly and nervous after her phone call. "Everything go okay with your boss?"

Kate looked shocked, "Yeah. Why? I mean she's not thrilled to have had bones spill out of its walls, but I assured her that you and I would get this place in shipshape."

"All right," Nick didn't press though he sensed something was off.

Pulling the tape measure off his belt, Nick scribbled a few notes. "I'm ready.'

Sixteen

Kate didn't really need Nick's help at the lighting store, but she did appreciate his company. She felt bad about the awkwardness that had been inserted into their relationship. Feeling a mess with any romantic notions, she enjoyed their friendship.

Spending time focused on tasks together brought out the lighthearted silliness in them. Nick's loving life to the fullest was infectious and brought out a playfulness in Kate that she had tucked away in a closet full of professional skirts and blouses.

Finding the switch panel, Nick played with the dials, briefly turning the lighting store into a techno concert before an irate store manager caught him. Freezing, with his hands hovering over the massive switchboard, Nick offered a boyish smile. Fortunately, Kate had already whipped out the corporate credit card and was filling a healthy order list buying Nick a reprieve from store banishment.

At the hardware store, Nick grabbed a flatbed cart. "Get on," he nodded toward the cart.

"What?" Kate was incredulous.

"I'm merely offering a lesson in surfing. Surfing 102. Come on. When you think about it, it is really being efficient with our time. Multitasking. Shopping for floor finish while upping your surfing game," Nick suggested.

Kate shook her head, "I'm not riding the store cart, Nick."

"Suit yourself," Nick shrugged. With little warning, he gave the cart a push and hopped on. Spreading his arms out and bending softly at his knees, he and the cart flew down the aisle. Heading precariously toward an aisle display of paint brushes. Pushing down on his heels, he steered the reluctant cart just avoiding the cardboard stand.

Near the end of the aisle, he lost momentum and hopped off. With a grin, he looked at Kate, "Huh? You want on now, right?"

"No. I still don't want on. We nearly bought a hundred or so marginal quality paint brushes," Kate scowled.

"The cart's handling is a little off, but I made it," Nick said.

"Let's get the shopping done before we're banned from every home improvement store in New Hanover County," Kate said as a man in a store apron stood in the main aisle, arms crossed shooting disapproving looks their way.

"I get it. All work, no play," Nick pouted.

Kate's eyes grew as she suddenly understood Nick's shopping behaviors. "It doesn't have to be *all* work. We can still have fun. Let's go downtown for dinner tonight. See more of what Wilmington has to offer," she suggested.

"That Merritt's burger did me good, but I think it could work up an appetite," Nick said. With a grin and a motion toward the flatbed, he added, "Maybe with a little more surfing!"

Kate's arm lashed out grabbing a fistful of Nick's shirt, "*Without* the shopping cart surfing."

"Fine," Nick's head dropped. Eyeing tubes of foam insulation the perfect size for a sword fight, Nick smiled.

"No!" Kate said firmly.

"Chicken," Nick said and quickened his pace toward the flooring aisle.

Kate slipped one of the tubes out of its container and lashed out swatting Nick on the back of the head.

Spinning in shock, Nick eyed Kate as she grinned and nonchalantly flipped the insulation tube over her shoulder like a baseball player who had just hit a no-doubt home run.

Their shopping adventures complete and supplies dropped off at the beach house, Kate and Nick exited their bungalows, showered and freshly attired. The sun had all but set, leaving the sky streaked with pink that quickly faded into a palette of ever-deepening blues.

Nick wore linen pants and a linen shirt with sleeves rolled up. Kate studied his balance of beach casual with just enough air of elegance. His five o'clock shadow provided the bridge. His confident smile was the element that made it all work. A factor that was not lost on Kate.

"You look… You look nice," Kate said.

"As do you, though I think that can always be said," Nick replied.

Through lightly blushed cheeks, Kate asked, "Any ideas on where we should go?"

"I know a place," Nick nodded. "I met a guy at the bait shop."

"Of course, you did," Kate laughed. "I'll drive. You get to navigate."

Nick navigated Kate off the island and north toward Wilmington. Driving along the riverfront over the historic cobblestones, they found a place to park. The line outside the popular Elijah's restaurant and oyster bar said it all.

"Busy place," Kate said. Putting their name on a list, the hostess suggested they would have a table before long. Looking up at Nick, she asked, "Wander for a bit?"

"You know me and wandering," Nick said, holding his arm out for Kate to lace hers through.

Accepting the gesture, they found the wood boardwalk that lined the Wilmington riverfront. Across the Cape Fear River, the iconic bridge hung overhead to the south. The spotlighted *U.S.S. North Carolina* sat in its permanent berth on the opposite side of the river.

Kate spied a sign posted on the rail of the boardwalk. *Warning: Alligators.* "There are alligators up here?"

Nick nodded, "Yes. They like it up here. They stretch about as far north as the Green Swamp, but a few have been seen as far north as the Virginia border."

"Hmm," Kate seemed dismayed by the news.

"Planning on swimming in the Cape Fear?" Nick asked.

"Not planning on it, but I assume they don't stay in there," Kate said, her face screwed with concern.

"Ah, you'll be fine," Nick said as Kate instinctively pressed closer as they strolled.

The lit walkway with the shops and businesses on one side and the Cape Fear River on the other was a popular place for couples. Kate and Nick passed several holding hands.

"It's nice out here," Kate said after a deep breath.

Finding a quiet spot, Nick walked to the rail and leaned against it. The thought of alligators ten feet below them made Kate a bit cautious as she joined him. "You'll face down a murderer, but you're worried about an alligator making an Olympic high jump effort to… eat you?"

"I don't think it's going to eat me. Maybe just a taste," Kate said, giving in to the teasing.

"This place. You almost feel caught between two worlds. The past and the present," Nick said.

Kate looked at him, "It does. I can picture steamboats and hoopskirts and petticoats."

"I like the nostalgia of history. Simpler times, though not always better times," Nick said.

"You have to take the good history and mix it with the bad history to form a better future. You can't ignore the stains, but when you make something even better from it you are left with…" Kate began.

"Something beautiful," Nick finished.

"Yeah," Kate breathed.

For a moment, the pair looked at each other. Their eyes searched for answers to questions that hadn't properly formed. A chime at Kate's side made her jump. Glancing at her phone, she said, "Our table is ready."

"Shall we?" Nick asked, his arm out.

Kate smiled as she hooked her arm in his, "Let's go!"

The restaurant was split into two sides. A candlelit main dining room was dark and elegant. A bank of windows looked out onto the Cape Fear River. Up a few steps, the more casual, at times, more raucous oyster bar spilled out onto a massive wooden deck stretching out over the water's edge. Kate chose the outdoor seating as it seemed more like an extension of their evening walk through Wilmington's waterfront.

Taking their seats directly against the rail overlooking the water, they settled in, studying their menus.

"What do you think? Did your bait shop guy go as far as to offer recommendations?" Kate asked.

"He did, in fact," Nick nodded. As the waiter stopped by their table to take their drink orders, Nick added, "A dozen oysters on the half-shell and an order of crab dip, please."

With a nod, the waiter whisked away.

"Oysters on the half-shell… like raw?" Kate winced.

Nick laughed, "Yes. Don't knock it until you try it. If you don't like it, no one says you need to have it again."

Kate pursed her lips into a wary frown.

A glass of Pinot Grigio was set in front of Kate while a frothy beer made its way to Nick. Raising his glass, Nick offered, "To playful afternoons, pleasant evenings and adventurous appetizers."

Raising her glass of wine, Kate asked, "Are those options or do I have to take them all?"

"It is a package deal," Nick said.

"Fine," Kate's glass delicately clinked against Nick's.

Kate didn't have long to fret as a stainless-steel tray of oysters sitting on a bed of ice landed on their table. She stared at the globs of delicacy resting in their roofless homes.

Nick offered an encouraging smile, "Go ahead. Like this." Nick lifted a shell and holding it to his lips, drank in the oyster. "Or if you prefer, take a dab of the cocktail sauce. I like mine with plenty of horseradish."

Kate observed another shellfish enjoyed by Nick.

With pursed lips, her fingers played along the edge of one of the shells. With an unhappy sigh, she picked up the oyster. Staring at it just for a moment, she kicked her head back and let the oyster slide into her mouth.

With a wincing swallow, she set the oyster shell back down in its little ice trough on the tray.

"Well?" Nick asked expectantly.

Kate shook her head thoughtfully, "I'm going to say 'no'."

Nick dropped his head in disappointment, "That's all right. It's kind of a rite of passage. You prevailed."

"Shooters, maybe when they are all crammed with other goodness, taking away from the slimy, globby blob. Otherwise, I have to say no," Kate dabbed at her lips with her green cloth napkin.

"Well, this you will enjoy," Nick's eyes brightened as the server slid a plate onto the table.

Kate eyed the circle of baked toast points ringing a baking dish filled with crab and cream straight from the broiler. Taking a knife, she spread the crab onto a piece of toast and took a bite. The satisfying crunch was followed by a broad grin, "This is delicious. You can have the oysters. This is mine!"

Pulling the plate of hot crab dip further from Nick's reach, Kate did her best to horde the appetizer. Polishing off another oyster, Nick nodded for the server to take the tray away.

Looking across the table at Kate, Nick was rewarded with a piece of toast covered in crab dip. "Man, the guy at the bait shop wasn't wrong. This is great," Nick studied the concoction attempting to discern the ingredients for his own kitchen experiments.

Ordering their meals, they leaned back with freshened beverages.

"Well, this is fun. Culinary experiments and all," Kate said. "Great job as usual."

"Just good at receiving advice from the people who know," Nick shrugged.

As they waited for the orders, Kate leaned in, "You never asked me about my research."

Nick laughed, "I am surprised you held out this long."

Kate feigned a hurt expression before launching into what she learned about the missing persons cases that aligned with the time frame matching the building materials used to seal up the wall.

"A philandering salesman with a gambling problem, an aspiring golfer on the cusp of winning a major tournament worth a load of cash and a salty fisherman with a reputation for violating the fisherman equivalent of horse theft. Quite the cast of characters," Nick said.

"Right?" Kate said. "They all line up to provide motive to a devious murderer."

"I don't know. Killing a guy in order to win a golf tournament, taking out a crab pot thief... those seem a bit weak. The philandering gambler... that's my person of interest," Nick said as he rubbed his chin. Pausing, he asked, "Collin Royce. Why is that name standing out? Other than seeing him on ESPN, I mean."

"I had the same thought," Kate said. "I don't know."

"The crab pot guy... let's assume that was only one of his many annoying flaws. He could have been one of those local thorns that someone finally had enough of. I changed my mind. They are all candidates for beach house stowaways," Nick said, pulling back from the table as their food arrived.

"Unless we uncover more evidence, I don't know where we go. I keep researching, I guess," Kate shrugged. Stopping mid-bite, Kate slowly looked up as a figure stood in front of their table.

"I thought that was you, Nick Mason," Sophia Hayes smiled. Her flowy white sundress played softly in the evening breeze as she took a step back to acknowledge Kate. "I'm sorry, y'all. I didn't realize you were on a *date*."

Kate immediately found the stunningly attractive woman's sultry confidence annoying.

"Oh, we aren't dating," Nick said.

Kate paled as Sophia broke into a wicked grin, all of her southern belle charming streaming out, "Well, in that case, you should come by the country club tomorrow. My treat. I owe you a tour, don't I?"

Kate grimaced as Nick nodded, "That would be lovely."

"It's a *date*, then," Sophia said and whisked away after trailing, "Goodnight, y'all."

Kate forced her face to fall nonchalant as Nick's gaze swung back toward her.

"Well, that was fortuitous," Nick said.

Kate's scowl returned, "Fortuitous?"

"Yeah. We wanted to learn more about the Hayes family. This is a great opportunity," Nick said.

"Oh, she wants to take advantage of an opportunity all right," Kate said.

Nick's eyes narrowed, "Does that make you uncomfortable?"

"Why would that make me uncomfortable?" Kate snapped.

"I don't have to go…" Nick said.

"What reason would you have to not go?" Kate asked, her voice just shy of an angry growl.

Nick tilted his head, "If you don't want me to. I'd solely be going for the case."

"For someone who tries to stay out of sleuthing, you suddenly seem a bit eager," Kate said.

Nick choked a laugh, setting his napkin on his plate, "Come on. Let's enjoy the beautiful evening. We can walk along the river for a bit."

"No. Tomorrow seems like it's going to be a very busy day. Even busier now," Kate said, pulling her company card out for the check.

The ride back to Carolina Beach was a quiet one. Kate kept focused on the road ahead, only offering vague grunts to Nick's attempts at a conversation.

When they got back to the bungalows, Kate hopped out, cast a "Goodnight" to Nick and disappeared inside her unit before a beachfront nightcap could even be suggested.

Slamming her back into the closed bungalow door, Kate seethed. Not at the elegant southern belle Sophia and Nick meeting her, but for her own childish outburst of jealousy that she struggled to keep contained.

Hearing the neighboring bungalow door open and close and then open again, Kate couldn't resist. Carefully fingering the curtains aside just enough where an eyeball could peer out onto the back patio, she watched Nick walk slowly out toward the rail overlooking the beach. Opening a bottle of beer, he slid the cap into his pocket and took a big sip before leaning against the rail to watch the waves.

Kate slumped. A part of her wanted to join him, but she was so embarrassed of her actions after Sophia visited their table. With a sigh, she let the curtains fall closed.

Unaware as she relented to get ready to turn in, Nick pivoted from watching the waves to peer at her bungalow. After Kate's bungalow lights went dark, he returned his lonely gaze toward the moonlit Atlantic.

Seventeen

With low surf and a schedule to catch up on, Nick got an early start. By the time Kate arrived at the beach house, he had nearly finished the hallway floor treatment. Working on his hands and knees he scanned the hall to ensure he had applied an even coating.

Freezing in the doorway, Kate called down the hallway, "Should I come in the back?"

Looking up, Nick pulled earbuds out from his ears, "Good morning! Yeah, the back porch is unlocked. I was hoping to get it done before you got here, but it might take a little while longer to set."

Kate nodded and wheeled back down the front steps and around to the back steps that intersected with their private boardwalk to the beach. Pausing at the intersection, she glanced over the slowly waving seagrass, listening to the waves crash, feeling the coastal breeze kiss her cheeks. It was a glorious feeling. Her chest swelled as her spirit lifted with the power of the coast.

Invigorated, she marched up the steps and slipped through the beach house's glass doors and into the house. Setting two cups of coffee on the counter and her things on the dining table, she pulled out her list of to-do items.

The early part of the morning was spent pulling nails and patching tiny holes throughout the house for the painters to come through. By the time she reached the hall, Nick had given her the okay to walk on the wood while he began pulling fixtures and electrical covers.

Kate paused to admire the floor that Nick had just finished. The front and back doors, which now offered a direct view through the house, were open to allow maximum air flow. Kate kneeled, using the light to study the floor. She was amazed at how good it looked. There was no sign that a portion of it had been covered for over a decade while the other was hit by UV light and foot traffic. It looked brand new.

"The floor looks great!" Kate called through the house. Not met with a response, Kate assumed Nick still had his earbuds in.

With a shrug, she started to push back up to her feet. A shadow in the open doorway made her freeze. Heart racing, she braced herself. In a sudden spin, she leaped to her feet to face a figure staring in at her.

Both she and the figure jumped back slightly, Kate catching her chest. After recognizing the person, her eyes scanned her peripheral vision desperately hoping to find Nick behind her.

"I'm sorry for the intrusion. I didn't mean to startle you," the man said, a sideways smile across his face.

Studying the man, Kate said, "You were at the university yesterday. And at my house. What do you want from me, Mr. Jones?"

The smile turned into a grin, "You've done your homework. Should have figured after what I read about you in Treasure Island. I did my homework, too, Ms. Harper."

Kate fought to keep her cool and not appear rattled.

"Mind if I come in?" Jones asked.

Kate looked at the floor and her shoeless feet, "We just finished the floor. It's still a bit delicate."

"I see that. It looks great. Some real quality work," Jones said.

"Well, in about a month, you can rent it. It is a beautiful property," Kate said, her voice even.

"It sure is. But that's not what I'm here for. I'm a reporter. I just wanted some information. You and your handyman found the body. Do you have any indication of who the body is? I assume the police haven't told you and that's why you were visiting the

Criminal Justice Department at the university," Jones said.

"Just like you were," Kate said.

Jones nodded, "That's right. Call me Dennis. It is clear the victim was murdered."

"Well, they didn't crawl inside the wall themselves, I would bet," a stern voice said from behind the reporter.

Kate's entire body relaxed as Nick's full-frame shouldered between the reporter and Kate.

"No, I suppose they didn't," the reporter snorted an uncomfortable laugh. "Look, I think we both want answers to the same questions. I just thought we'd compare notes. See what each other knows. I'd keep your names out of it. We all know what sort of problems that created for you down in Florida."

The insinuation at leverage made Nick bristle. Through narrowed brows, he leaned close to the reporter, "You don't want to make trouble for Kate."

"No trouble. Just a friendly agreement," the reporter did his best to create space between Nick and himself.

"Dennis Jones, leave these people alone," a voice with even more edge than Nick's called from the bottom of the steps.

The reporter turned to see Detective Nixon looking up at them.

"Detective, good, I've got some questions for you, too," Jones said.

"And the department liaison officer will provide an update at the scheduled afternoon briefing," Detective Nixon said. Seeing that Jones was not moved, she snarled, "Goodbye, Mr. Jones."

Jones looked at Kate and then at Nick before nodding. Pulling out a card, he tried to hand it to Nick who stood with crossed arms, "Right." Spinning toward Kate, he held the card out, "If you feel like sharing or comparing notes, this is a deeper thing than just a pile of bones. You should know that."

Kate's expression changed at the reporter's revelation.

"Goodbye, Dennis," Nixon pressed.

Reluctantly descending the steps, the reporter cast a quick glance. His eyes narrowed seemingly noting Kate's interest in his last statement. Climbing into his car, he drove away.

"Thank you, Detective," Nick said as Nixon walked up the steps.

With a quick nod, the detective said, "I wanted to check in on you- make sure you weren't being harassed. I guess my instincts were solid."

"You *are* a detective," Nick said, his eyes falling as he realized his words came across as condescending.

The detective's glare was like a telekinetic beam moving him aside. "Are you moving back in, Ms. Harper?"

"I've been thinking about it," Kate shrugged. "We have painters coming and the floor is curing. I'll at least hold off until all that is finished."

Detective Nixon nodded, "You know how to reach the department. Let us know if you need anything or if reporters or curious locals give you a problem."

"I will. Thank you," Kate nodded. Her hands reached out in the air as the detective began to turn around, "It would make me feel a lot better if I knew what was going on. Rest my fears that I am not in any danger… once I decide to move back in."

"If I thought you were in danger, Ms. Harper, I wouldn't have let you back in," the detective snapped.

Kate's mind reeled through the list of missing persons she had received from the Criminal Justice professor, "Jeffrey Marlett, Collin Royce, Rufus Westerfield…"

"What?" the detective snarled.

"The body in the wall. It was one of them, wasn't it?" Kate asked.

"Listen to me very closely, this is an on-going investigation. When I choose to share information or not share it is because it impacts that very investigation. I strongly encourage you to focus on the house. I will focus on the victim and getting to the bottom of it.

That is the best way that I can ensure *everyone's* safety," Detective Nixon said.

"You think Kate might not be safe?" Nick asked.

"That isn't what I said, Mr. Mason. We combed the beach house meticulously. There is nothing for the… uh… whoever may have been involved to come back for, other to raise suspicion on themselves," Detective Nixon said.

Kate frowned, "Isn't there a thing about criminals returning to the scene of the crime?"

"You read too many mystery novels, Ms. Harper," Nixon snapped. "Now, I need to get back to solving this case."

Without another word, Detective Nixon marched down the steps. Despite her dark sunglasses shielding her eyes, Kate and Nick could feel her staring at them as she slipped behind the wheel of her police cruiser.

Watching the detective drive away, Nick glanced at his watch, "I've got to get cleaned up."

"That's right," Kate grinned a sour grin, "Your date."

"It's not a date," Nick argued.

"She called it a date," Kate said.

"I don't have to go," Nick said. "Especially with…" his hand waved to where the reporter had parked.

"I'll be fine. You… you go have fun," Kate said.

Nick eyed her warily, questioning the sincerity in her smile, "It's for the case."

"Uhm, hmm," Kate hummed.

"It *is*," Nick's voice trailed off as he descended the steps toward his truck.

Kate watched from the front porch as Nick backed his truck out of the driveway and started down the street. She was left with an inexplicable lump in her stomach as his taillights disappeared.

Eighteen

Nick found a lonely spot in the far reaches of the country club parking lot. His work truck was definitely out of place among the high-end vehicles being cycled through valet. He absent-mindedly pressed out any wrinkles in his linen suit that creased while driving.

He tugged at his unbuttoned collar trying to ward off the strange nervousness and anxiety that washed over him. Slipping on his sunglasses and straightening his posture, he strode with confidence, resolute that this was a sleuthing mission and nothing else.

Entering the country club, he whipped off his sunglasses and stuffed them into his pocket as his eyes adjusted to the change in light. Whatever confidence he had mustered instantly eroded. Sophia Hayes sat in the foyer, her bare legs crossed as they protruded from an impeccably fitted red dress. Its deep V shape dove well past the level Nick's eyes were comfortable taking in.

He snapped his attention on her sea-green eyes instead.

"Hello, Nick," Sophia smiled from her position in the overstuffed chair.

Nick offered a tempered smile, "Sophia. Thank you for inviting me to take a tour."

Sophia rose from her seat. The full form-revealing nature of her dress was proudly declared, "I hope you like what I have to show you."

"I'm sure…" Nick croaked. Stifling a hard swallow, he said, "I'm sure I will. This is an amazing place."

"It can be," Sophia said, holding her arm out for Nick to take it.

Obliging, Nick followed her to the bar where they first met. The bartender placed two drinks on the bar for them. Nick nodded a thank you as Sophia turned to cheers Nick's glass. The nearly clear Mimosa was essentially champagne with a splash of orange juice for color.

"To new adventures," Sophia said.

"To new adventures," Nick repeated, studying the sultry Hayes daughter as she took a long sip of her drink that the bartender promptly refilled.

Sophia laughed, "You seem tense. If the champagne doesn't loosen you up, I'll have to recommend a couple's massage."

Nick nearly spit his sip of Mimosa out.

"I'm kidding," Sophia laughed, placing a reassuring hand on Nick's arm. As relief began to seep into his expression, Sophia shrugged, "Unless you're down for one, that is."

"No, champagne is fine. Thank you," Nick said.

Sophia grinned, clearly enjoying toying with the man so clearly out of his element. "Come on, I'll make good on my invitation and show you around."

Parading Nick around the country club, Sophia seemed to relish showing him off. He stood out from the members and guests. Nick's attire, well put together by his standards, was not as polished as the others. His wardrobe put together by Kate was quality, but not the Italian labels worn by many. His slightly wind-tussled hair, near permanent five o'clock shadow and carpenter's hands were subtle but definitive clues he was not from the mold.

The bright, almost bouncy nature Sophia exuded as they wandered the buildings and the grounds told Nick that she was acutely aware and savored the square peg of a man she was purposely slamming into the round holes. The experience was only the more evident when she tugged him along into the executive office suite.

Two men that Nick recognized as Mark and Sheffield Hayes stopped mid-conversation with another man who was familiar but not placeable to Nick. The rolls of the eyes from the men told Nick that the disruption from Sophia and one of her toys was not an uncommon one.

"Robbie, I didn't know you were going to be here today," Sophia cooed.

"Yes, you did, Sophia. I asked if you wanted to grab lunch before the press event," the attractive, athletically built man conversing with the Hayes' said.

Suddenly, Nick recognized him as Robert Grant, the professional golfer and personality.

"Sorry, I forgot," Sophia said without a trace of remorse.

"Sophia, do you mind? The grown-ups have work to do," the younger Hayes snapped at his sister.

"Sheffield, let's have manners," Mark Hayes, the family patriarch, strode forward to Nick. "Mark Sheffield."

Nick shook his hand, "Nick Mason. I am doing some restoration work, and I like to match the spirit of the architecture. Your club is the perfect example of neo-classical North Carolina with a livable modern twist. Sophia offered to show me around."

"Well, I'm sure you are in good hands with Sophia. You may know of Robert Grant. He is a longtime friend of the family and one of the fastest-rising stars on the PGA circuit," Mark said.

Nick reached out to a perturbed and reluctant Robert Grant, "Pleasure."

Grant offered a nod before returning his gaze toward Sophia.

"This is my son, the future of Hayes Properties, Sheffield," Mark held his hand out toward his son.

Sheffield's response was even cooler than Grant's. Giving Nick a quick once over and casting him as a non-fit, he said, "Always good to have fresh eyes around the club. I could schedule time with our head of the grounds. He could give you actual insight beyond the lens of a Mimosa glass. You two would probably get along."

Grant choked a laugh at his friend's inference.

"Well, we do really need to get along. Robert is doing a spread for Golf Monthly on the ninth hole. We were just going to grab a bite before we headed out. You are welcome to join us," the Sheffield patriarch said, his tone refuting his own offer.

Sophia wrinkled her nose, "I think I've got things well in hand."

Sheffield and Robert shared a grunt as Mark ushered them out of the office suite.

For a moment, Sophia looked at the door as the room emptied. Nick could see she was angry and embarrassed by the interactions, particularly with her brother.

Taking in a deep breath, she pivoted to Nick. Through the broken and almost sympathy-inducing face, Sophia's wickedly sultry attitude made an effervescent return. "Shall we?"

Nick cocked his head, his senses and morality on full alert.

"Finish our tour," Sophia said, seeing the tension in Nick. She practically purred, "The massage is still on the table, if you'll forgive the unintended pun."

"I wanted to ask you about the house I'm working on," Nick said.

"An invitation to visit?" Sophia asked with a mischievous glisten of hope in her eyes.

Nick shook the notion off, "No. The house on Carolina Beach. The one your family used to own."

"Right. So disturbing, someone stuffing a body into the wall. I couldn't believe it. The police even asked my family a bunch of questions, but our lawyer stepped in," Sophia said. Her brows furrowed, "You're the one who found the bones."

"Kate and I," Nick nodded.

"Kate. Your non-date," Sophia studied Nick, her mouth slipping into a wicked smile. She circled Nick, making him feel as uncomfortable as he had ever felt. "She's pretty. Seems smart. You *like* her. I *know* she likes you. The way her face fell when you said you weren't dating. It was precious."

Nick's face screwed into a perplexed expression, "That's… I don't know, Kate and I are complicated. That's not the point."

"The beach house. I don't know what to tell you," Sophia shrugged.

"Why was your lawyer called in?" Nick asked.

Sophie laughed, "With our family, the lawyer is always around the next corner. Gotta protect the family image, right? How about you? What is your interest in the beach house?"

"I'm sort of in real estate," Nick said.

"Aren't we all? Supposed to be a good asset, unless you find a literal skeleton in the closet. I think we sold that one quickly. Unusual for us not to get top dollar and soak every dime from an investment," Sophia said.

Nick looked at her.

"Sure, I mean, just put our name on something and the value goes up. The attachment to the golf tournaments puts us in country club royalty, I suppose," Sophia waved a dismissive hand in the air.

"You don't seem so thrilled with it," Nick said.

"Don't get me wrong. Life is good. *Really* good. It's just… it feels a bit veiled sometimes. Some false veneer on reality. Sometimes, I like something a bit more *raw*. Look at you. You don't have that stuffy country club vibe. But I do think I saw you at the pro shop yesterday. I didn't think you were a golfer?"

"Not really, no," Nick admitted. "I'm more of a water sports guy."

"You're a surfer," Sophie nodded slowly. "Of course, you are. Why do I need to be attracted to the type?"

"Sorry if that offends you," Nick said.

"No. I'm sorry. I just… have experience with a surfer or two in my dating portfolio. They really didn't end well. Then again, neither did the golfer, polo player, or the yacht racer. Though I did appreciate the sailboat. I think I just want a normal life but keep the houses, cars and wardrobe budget, if I could manage it."

"Has your family always been in the golf course business?" Nick asked.

"Daddy was a real estate developer. He liked to fancy himself part of the country club set. He pulled together some partners and set out to create a course and club that would attract the national tour. He was pretty good at it. Now my brother has a hand in it. He must be pretty good, because he has won some awards for his designs. How about you? Surfing and dabbling in real estate. Must be quite the dabbler to live the beach lifestyle," Sophia said.

"I'm more or less in early retirement. I still like to swing a hammer once in a while. Makes me feel more connected to the projects," Nick said.

Sophia laughed, "I can't see Sheffield or Daddy lifting a finger to *actually* build out a course."

"I suppose not," Nick said. "Their expertise is in the design and money aspects of the project."

"So, what *is* the deal with the woman you were with at the restaurant last night? She didn't seem too keen on us having lunch together," Sophia asked.

"It's complicated," Nick said.

"I see. I've had a few of those. Robbie and I, for one. Though I prefer uncomplicated. Life can be complicated enough. I prefer my relationships to be a bit… more fun. Relaxed." Sophia gave Nick an alluring look. "Have you seen our penthouse suites? I could order up some champagne and…"

"That," Nick's face reddened, and he cocked his head slightly, "Sounds like a lovely way to spend an afternoon, but I'm meeting a contractor back at the beach house."

Sophie almost looked shocked at the rejection, "Not even for one… quick… glass?"

"I, uh, no. I really should get going. This was nice. Thank you for the tour," Nick said, taking a purposeful step toward the door.

Sophia studied him, trying to understand the man. "The offer stands. If you manage to free up your time."

Nick nodded and scampered out of the executive suite. He tugged on his collar, which seemed to suddenly be restrictive as his body temperature spiked.

Nineteen

Kate paced around the beach house. She would find herself drawn to the window at the front of the house every time she thought she heard a car pull up.

"This is ridiculous," she cursed at herself.

Pulling out her laptop, Kate began sorting through her case notes. It was an absorbing distraction. In a fury of energy and acuity, she began assembling a who's who attached to the house and the possible victims. Setting up her printer, she made labels, timelines and photos of each of the potential victims and possible suspects.

Pinning them to a wall in a spare bedroom, she stood back, getting a larger picture of the facts and players that all seemed very disconnected. Turning her attention to the potential victims, she spliced the overall picture into a subset. Deep diving each, she printed out the pros and cons of why it could be any one of the three.

She circled the Hayes family because they owned the house during the most likely timeline. Posting a note, she added that rental logs would need to be considered for the beach house as well. Narrowing her eyes, she shook her head. "I would think a beach house owner would notice if a renter put up a wall. Unless they barely went there themselves," Kate tapped her pen against her lip as she thought.

Sitting in front of her laptop, she began searching for the Hayes family. Beginning with news reports, the Hayes family was largely regaled as heroes of the community. They were generous, involved smiling in an exhaustive collection of photos with political leaders, school children and philanthropic organizations.

On the verge of being discouraged, she leaned in closer as the polished family image began to take on a patina of tarnish. Buried underneath all of the good deeds and positive photo ops were unsanctioned editorials that called their connection to the land in question. Following that string, Kate found that claim popped up multiple times throughout history. The questions led to a court ruling that seemed mired at best granting the Hayes family the land that the country club now sat on.

Sitting up straight, Kate printed out the article and pinned it on her wall with a big red exclamation point painted across the page. "I think a near billion-dollar country club would be motive to murder if the family stood to lose it," Kate surmised as she leaned back in her chair.

The beach house doorbell nearly made her leap out of her chair. The now familiar feeling of her chest pounding, pumping blood through her body to be ready for action, was a frustrating, lasting side effect of the ordeal she had gone through in her last assignment.

Pressing her palm to her chest and taking a deep, calming breath, she swung the front door open. She found Nick on the porch steps, looking a bit like a lost puppy.

"Deadbolt was locked," he said. His linen suit had been traded out for his work clothes. He waited for Kate's response.

Glancing at her watch, Kate said, "Long lunch."

"An interesting one, if you care to hear it," Nick promised.

"You can leave out any juicy parts," Kate said, turning on her heel and leaving Nick to follow.

"You're jealous," Nick observed, his head cocked slightly.

"I'm not jealous! Why would I be jealous?" Kate nearly stomped on the ground as she turned to face Nick.

"Clearly," Nick struggled to stifle a laugh making Kate only the more irate.

Kate spun in a huff, marching down the hall.

"Okay, okay, you're not jealous," Nick said, his voice ringing with disbelief.

Kate continued to walk away.

"All right. I'll keep it to myself," Nick called.

Kate whirled, her eyes narrowed, "Fine. Tell me all about your date."

"It wasn't a date," Nick rolled his eyes. Taking a breath, he clamped his hands together, "So, Sophie is a bit of a wild one."

"You don't say," Kate snapped.

"She's a bit of the black sheep of the family. She embraces the lifestyle and the money, but not the pomp and circumstance. Her father built an empire with real estate and gathered a consortium to build a tournament worthy golf course. Clearly, he was successful. Enough so, he and his son have been commissioned to build several courses over the years. The course here in Wilmington has always been their flagship, though," Nick said.

"I could have gotten all of that off the internet without eyes batted at me from across the table," Kate said.

Ignoring the comment, Nick continued, "Sophia said they sold the beach house quickly. She felt it was undervalued."

Kate leaned in with interest, "I can pull up historical comps and take a peek at it."

Pacing around the room, Kate mused out loud, "Now, why would a successful real estate family flip a beachfront house undervalue?"

"Cause they stuffed a dead body in the wall?" Nick said.

"Maybe. All right. *That's* interesting," Kate asked. "Anything else?"

Nick pulled at his collar uncomfortably, "No. That was pretty much it. She gave me the tour, and I left. Right after we ran into her father, her brother and Robert Grant."

"Already meeting the family. You move quick," Kate teased.

"It was really contentious. Sheffield, her brother, does not seem to appreciate his sister's antics… at all. Her father is a bit more protective and coddling. There seemed to be history with Robert Grant," Nick shared.

"Robert Grant…" Kate sorted the names in her head.

"Pro golfer. Television personality. I think he and Sophia were an item," Nick said.

"Seems like Sophia is an 'item' with everyone," Kate spat.

Nick nodded, "That doesn't seem far from the truth. I kind of felt like a pawn. An intentional foil to the country clubbers."

"Grant isn't the first famous golfer that Sophia has had a relationship with," Nick said.

"Oh?" Kate asked.

"She didn't say as much, but there were photos of her by Collin Royce's side all over the place. When she wasn't in the photo, it was Mark or Sheffield," Nick said.

Kate's eyes went wide, "Yes! That's why he is so familiar. He was all over the country club executive office. Even a signed tournament-winning club."

Kate and Nick stared at each other for a moment, considering the avalanche of information. For a moment, Kate eyed Nick wondering if there was anything left out of the story. His afternoon with the alluring Sophia Hayes.

"How about you? Spend the afternoon preparing for staging the house?" Nick asked.

Kate brightened, a bounce returning to her step, "Come on. I'll show you."

Leading Nick to the space she was using as an office, Kate pointed at the wall.

Nick's eyes swept across the scene Kate had created, "You made a crime wall."

"I'm dialing in on who our mysterious occupant was," Kate shrugged, "Just lining my thoughts out."

"Any epiphanies?"

"I sorted through the missing persons cases for the time frame the wall materials were used. I did more research on each of our candidates, focusing in on their disappearance. Our philandering salesman *did* eventually turn up. Dead in a hotel room in Myrtle Beach. It was three years later and the news reports didn't make the connection. One of Dr. Granger's teaching assistants made the leap. He made reviewing the cases a class assignment after my visit," Kate said. Triumphantly, she walked up to the board and placed a large red letter X over the printed photo of Jeffery Marlett.

"That leaves two," Nick said.

Kate nodded, "But think about it. If you wanted to kill a small-time fisherman, pain in the tail or not, why go through the trouble of burying him in a wall?"

"You'd be just as well toss him into the Cape Fear, the intracoastal or the Atlantic. Between tides, alligators and ocean critters, he might never be seen again. And if his body was found, it would be pretty reasonable to write it off as an unfortunate boating accident," Nick said.

Kate nodded, "And Rufus Westerfield didn't really mix with the expensive beach house crowd. Owners or renters."

"That leaves…" Nick began.

Circling a photo in a fat, red circle, Kate gleamed, "Collin Royce. Collin Royce was the body we found in the wall."

Twenty

Kate and Nick worked together, ensuring the house was ready for the painters to finish the interior. As they patched holes and removed hardware, they tossed theories back and forth regarding the case.

"So, we think Collin Royce, an up-and-coming golfer a decade ago, was murdered and sealed up in the walls of the beach house owned by the Hayes family," Nick said. "Where does that leave us?"

"Well, it puts the bullseye squarely on your new girlfriend and her family," Kate said. Receiving a glare from Nick, she conceded, "All right, I'll stop."

"In the family, we have Mark Sheffield, the king of the empire," Nick said.

"Inherited king. His father and grandfather were in the game when steamboats patrolled the Cape Fear River," Kate said. "We have his son, Sheffield. By all accounts, a goody-two shoes who has even dabbled in politics."

"That alone puts him at the top of *my* suspect list," Nick said.

"And we have dear Sophia," Kate said.

"You really think Sophia is capable of killing an athlete and building an entire wall to case him in it?" Nick asked.

"You think either Mark or Sheffield Hayes are capable of it?" Kate scoffed.

Nick chuckled, "No, I suppose not."

"But any of them could have *paid* someone to do it," Kate said.

"It would be nearly impossible to find out," Nick said.

Kate studied Nick, a putty-tinged finger in the air, "Not if you had a warrant to look at bank records. I would imagine paying for a murder and a coverup is a notable expense."

Nick shook his head and frowned, "We can't get warrants."

"Detective Nixon can," Kate said.

"Detective Smiley?" Nick laughed. "You aren't thinking… I mean, we can ask."

"Let's go. We're almost finished here," Kate said.

Pulling into the police station, Kate and Nick were glad to see the throng of reporters had dissipated. "I guess the excitement over the bones has passed," Kate said.

"It looks that way," Nick said.

For the first time since they found the bones, they were able to enter the police station unaccosted. The front desk clerk greeted them.

"We may have some information on the John Doe at the beach house," Kate said. "May we speak with Detective Nixon?"

"I'm afraid Detective Nixon is out on a call. She won't be back for some time," the clerk said.

"Is Chief Banks in?" Kate asked.

"I'm sorry, he is out, too. There was a body pulled out of Nixon Channel," the officer said.

Kate squinted, "Where is that?"

"Just off Figure-Eight Island," the desk officer replied.

Eyes wide, Kate shot a glance at Nick.

"Drowning?" Nick asked.

"I can't say," the desk officer replied. "But, a drowning usually doesn't pull the detective and the chief."

Kate and Nick looked at each other.

"I'm sure Detective Nixon has her hands full. Could you have her give me a call when she has a moment? I may know who John Doe is," Kate said.

"I'll let her know. I have to warn you- a cold case will take a back seat to a new investigation," the officer said.

Kate nodded as she and Nick pivoted and left the police station.

"They think someone was murdered," Kate said. "I wonder if there's a connection."

"That's quite the leap," Nick said.

"It is," Kate admitted. "But it also means we are going to have to solve the mystery of our friend in the wall on our own."

Nick looked at Kate, "Why did you take note of the location of the body? Nixon Channel… Where's that?"

"Right off the island where the Hayes family calls home," Kate said. With a gleam in her eye, Kate dangled her keys, "Let's see what we can find out."

Nick winced, "Are you so sure that is a good idea?"

"No," Kate admitted.

"But we're going to do it anyway," Nick muttered, sliding into the passenger seat.

The grin from the driver's seat answered his question.

The scene at the Porters Neck Boat Ramp was chaotic. The number of police cars, emergency vehicles, and, of course, the rapidly descending press corps hit Kate with horrifying memories from the last time her instincts were correct.

Parking along the side of the road with a growing line of cars from curious residents, Kate and Nick surveyed the scene. Wilmington Police, New Hanover County Sheriff's Office, and North Carolina State Troopers held the crowd at bay as a Coast Guard Boat flanked by a pair of Sheriff's boats along with a Fish and Wildlife boat cruised toward the shore. The Coast Guard rigid hull boat slid alongside the dock while the other boats idled offshore keeping civilian boats at bay.

A group of men in suits stood just between the crowd and the law enforcement officials.

"Feds? They got here quickly," Nick noted.

The county coroner walked toward the dock surrounded by an entourage of law enforcement officials, including Detective Nixon and Chief Banks. The wall of bodies concealed the hoisting of the victim from the boat to the dock. The black body bag was quickly put to use, shielding the horrid view from the public and anyone onshore. Only the Coast Guard and news helicopters clattering overhead could see the victim being pulled ashore.

"This is terrible," Kate said.

"It is," Nick nodded, his voice soft.

Casting Kate a glance, Nick could see the conflict on her face. She was so eager to solve the mystery, but the scene at the boat dock was a cutting reminder that real people were at the core of the cases. Lives were lost. Families, somewhere, lost a loved one.

Swallowing hard, Kate pivoted, "Let's go. We don't need to be part of the problem here."

Nick followed, "It isn't sick curiosity. Some of these people are affected. This is their home. It is natural, almost right that they want to know what is happening outside their neighborhoods. Knowing is how they protect their families, themselves."

"Maybe it's wrong that I stick my nose into things," Kate said slipping behind the wheel of her SUV.

"You found a body in *your* walls. Trying to understand it so that you know your renters will be safe, so that *you* will be safe is not wrong," Nick said.

Kate offered a thin smile, "Thanks."

Starting the vehicle, Kate pulled out of her parking spot and turned the wheel hard, directing them back toward Carolina Beach.

The ride back to Carolina Beach was a quiet one. Both Kate and Nick remained within their own thoughts. Pulling into the beach house driveway, Kate glanced at the time. "The painters will be here soon. You can take off. Enjoy your evening," she said.

Nick looked at Kate, "I'm not going to leave you alone. If that's all right."

Kate nodded, "It's all right. In fact, if I was honest, I would prefer it."

Together, they got out of the SUV and walked into the beach house. Both scanned the house, not knowing what to do. They didn't have long to wait before a knock on the door was met with a man in rainbow-streaked coveralls that were once white.

Confirming the painting crew had what they needed, Kate and Nick left them to their work. Standing at each of their driver's doors, they looked at each other.

"Got dinner plans?" Nick asked.

"Not really. Rather not be alone, though," Kate said.

Nick offered a reassuring grin, "I know a place. I'll meet you at the bungalows and we can go together."

Kate nodded and climbed into her SUV. Driving on auto pilot, she parked in front of their rental units. With her mind far from the task of driving, she was relieved to have Nick with her.

Expecting to get into his truck, she was confused when he started walking toward the beach.

Following, she hopped, slipping off her heels and holding them by their straps. Nick cast off his loafers and tossed them under the bungalow deck steps.

"Uhm, we don't have our poles, and honestly, I'm not dressed for fishing," Kate said.

Nick smiled, "I know a place."

"Of course you do," Kate said.

Realizing they were heading toward the boardwalk, she nodded.

"Besides," Nick said. "I owe you a Ferris wheel ride."

"That you do," Kate laughed.

"Eat first or ride first?" Nick asked.

"How unhappy with Ferris wheels are you?" Kate asked.

Nick nodded, "Fair enough. Ride first."

Taking the lead, Nick marched along with triumphant strides until the flashing lights, spinning rides and overwhelming aromas of carnival food permeated his senses.

Kate took his hand and laughed, "Come on!"

Having to tug with some force, Kate drug Nick to the booth where they purchased their tickets and then again to wait for their turn boarding the Ferris wheel.

The salt air-battered steel groaned. The wheel groaned. The door holding the riders in place groaned. The toothy-grinning attendant seemed to groan as he loaded another group of passengers which had to be a monotonously numerous time for the day.

With a forced nod of appreciation, Nick settled into his seat next to Kate. The metal door slammed shut. Nick tested the latch even after the dutiful attendant had. Nick's eyes scanned the ride and the entire boardwalk calculating every possible thing that could go wrong as the wheel began to turn and lift them into the air.

Kate reached out and collapsed her fingers over his that gripped the steel bar in front of him. Forcing his fingers to let go of the metal and accept hers, she smiled at him.

Nick glanced over, clearly unhappy with his moment of weakness.

"We'll be fine," Kate assured him.

"Mm, hmm," Nick bit his lip. "I don't mind the height. It is the lack of trust in perpetually corroding materials and human incompetence when it comes to checking redundant tasks."

"Now that you're on the ride, how much of that can you control?" Kate asked, her voice soft and reassuring.

"None. None of it," Nick said.

Kate smiled, gripping his hand warmly, "Then enjoy the ride. Look at this, it is… stunning."

The cool Carolina coastal breeze tussled her hair. The fading light cast the sky in a blur of blues and pinks and oranges. The frothy waves below dazzled with the colors in the sky.

Nick drank it alongside Kate. His concerns abating, he turned toward Kate, "It is beautiful."

For a few moments, they rode in silence. Their minds were far from overwhelmed with terrible beach house discoveries, murder victims floating in coastal waters or potential flaws in impeccably serviced and inspected equipment.

Forgetting they were sitting in a creaky chair that rocked back and forth amidst rows of bright flashing lights, instead, they were floating above the ocean. Joining the seagulls and sandpipers, they soared over the beach, racing the waves as they rolled back and forth up the sand.

They almost forgot they were holding hands when their chair stopped at the bottom of the platform. Kate blushed slightly as they each squeezed before separating.

"That wasn't so bad, was it?" Kate asked.

Nick considered the woman next to him. Leaning toward the attendant, Nick whispered to Kate as he held out a bill, "Go again?"

The attendant glanced at the lull in the line, pocketed the twenty-dollar bill and pulled back on the lever that lofted them back into the air.

"I think this is just what I needed," Kate said.

"I think it is what we *both* needed," Nick agreed.

During their second run-through, they were cast into indigo skies. Even through the carnival-style lights of the boardwalk amusement park, stars shone in each other's eyes as they stole quick glances before returning to what was truly a breathtaking view of Carolina Beach.

When their second ride came to an end, Kate and Nick thanked the attendant. Without realizing it, they walked closer to each other than they had the entire trip. In almost a dance, they staggered through the amusements.

Spying the stacked milk bottles, Nick pulled away and ran up to the booth. As Kate caught up, she tugged on his arm and whispered, "You know these are rigged, right?"

Ignoring the warning, Nick handed over cash in exchange for a baseball. Tossing the ball in the air above his palm, Nick winced, noting the ball was lightweight. The attendant who handed him the ball grinned.

With a quick glance toward Kate, Nick whipped his arm across his body. Ending his follow through, his hand extending right at the base of the milk bottles. The ball followed his aim, slamming into the middle of the bottom row. The bottles danced, reluctantly wobbling from their comfortable perch.

One by one, they flipped in the air, landing in a resounding clatter at the attendant's feet. Forcing a smile through his initial scowl, the attendant cheered. Losing to the surfer-handyman, the attendant's marketing kicked in, "It's just that easy, folks. Step up and win a prize, just like this man did!"

Looking at Nick, the attendant shrugged, "All right, Bub. What'll it be?"

Nick looked at Kate, her eyes wide, and with almost a giggle, she pointed toward the large stuffed dolphin hanging from the booth rafters. Accepting the plush toy, they walked away from the booth.

"How did you do that?" Kate asked.

Nick rotated his shoulder, which he refused to admit was sore after a hard throw ages since the last. "I used to play baseball. Was pretty good, too. I know the bottles are weighted. The ball is filled with cork making it light and delivering a softened blow. You have to hit the stack just right, and even then, you can barely get them to topple over."

Grinning, Kate hugged her dolphin, "Thanks!" She bounced happily next to Nick as they wandered the little midway. Taking in a deep breath, she said, "This is so much fun. The sights, the sounds, the lights, the smells- they all mixed into a memory locked away from childhood and coaxed out on a starry night. With a heroic hurler and my prize!"

Nick smiled. He enjoyed the lighter side of Kate rising to the surface. "You should draw inspiration from your little friend for one of the guest rooms. Make it dolphin-themed," he suggested.

Kate held her dolphin in front of her, studying it. Looking up, she grinned, "I just might!"

Twenty One

Kate assumed the knock at the door of the bungalow was Nick. "I hope you have coffee!" she called.
Opening the door, she found the permanently grim Detective Nixon standing outside her door. "I don't have coffee, I'm afraid. I did come to bring you news, Ms. Harper," the detective said.
Nick stepped out of his neighboring bungalow.
The detective offered a nod toward the handyman.
Kate stepped all the way out of her rental and closed the door behind her. Her interest and senses were buzzing with the detective's early morning visit.
"I don't normally share information before it is released to the news, but I wanted you to hear it from me instead of the morning issues," the detective said. "The body we pulled out of the channel yesterday- it was Dennis Jones."
The color drained from Kate's face.

"He drowned?" Nick asked, a hand on Kate's shoulder to hold her steady as she absorbed the news.

"I am pretty certain the gunshot to the head had something to do with his death, but the medical examiner's official report is not filed yet," Detective Nixon said.

"He was murdered!" Kate exclaimed. She took a stunned whirl before readdressing the detective in gasps, "He was at the beach house. At the university. I saw him."

"I know, Ms. Harper," the detective nodded, her voice steady. Her face fell, "Wait, you saw him at the university?"

"UNCW. He was coming out of the Criminal Justice Department as I was walking in," Kate said.

Detective Nixon scowled, "What were you doing at the Criminal Justice Department?"

Kate looked sheepish, "I was reviewing cold cases during the time frame that body was most likely sealed up in the beach house."

"That is why you came by the station yesterday. The desk office gave me a note that you had information on that case," Detective Nixon said. Her voice declared her disapproval of Kate's sleuthing.

Kate nodded, "I had three disappearances in mind. Jeffrey Marlett, Collin Royce and Rufus Westerfield. I figured out it was Collin Royce."

Nixon cocked her head, "Forensics just confirmed that last night."

"I knew it!" Kate danced a victory jig. Looking at the irate detective, she added, "I mean, piecing together deductions isn't proof."

"No, that would be *my* job. Uncovering real evidence that can be presented in front of a jury. The state of North Carolina and the city of Carolina Beach approved me and pay me to do that."

Kate leaned in, "This has to be connected to the discovery of the bones."

"It doesn't *have* to be anything. It *may* be connected. We will see where the evidence leads us," Detective Nixon said, her eyes sweeping over Kate and Nick. "I need you two to notify me if you see anything. Anything out of sorts."

"Like?" Nick cocked his head.

"People taking an unusual interest in the beach house. In you two," the detective said.

Nick's face fell concerned, "Why us?"

"Because you found the body," Detective Nixon said. Her eyes narrowed, "Because Ms. Harper was poking around the same places the reporter was before he was shot in the head."

Kate's mind was wandering as she strayed from the conversation, "I was right. It *was* Royce!"

"Reel it in, Ms. Harper. While your fishing expedition landed one right answer, interfering with my investigation will land you in jail, or worse. Just ask Dennis Jones. Oh, but you can't," the detective's tone was cross. Shooting a glance at Nick, Detective Nixon said, "I'm going to hold you accountable for Ms. Harper's actions, too, Mr. Mason."

Nick soured at the detective's warning. His eyes swept over Kate's resolute expression. There was no way she was backing down.

"You see, hear, *learn* anything, you bring it to me immediately. Am I clear? I want to keep you safe and get to the bottom of all this," Detective Nixon said.

Kate and Nick nodded their heads. The detective spun on a heel and marched away without another word.

Like a child focused on what they wanted instead of their parent's message, Kate said, "I was right! It was Collin Royce."

"The other person closing in on the fact was found floating in the Intracoastal Waterway yesterday," Nick said.

Kate offered a shrewd look, "We don't know *why* he was shot. He was clearly close to uncovering *something*."

"I think this time, we need to heed the authority's advice and let them handle it," Nick said, not having confidence his words would have any real impact.

"Interesting Detective Nixon came to tell us the news in person. It is counter to everything she has said and done up to the point," Kate said.

"She wanted to share the news with us so that she could watch our reaction," Nick said.

Kate shot him a curious glance.

"Dennis Jones was on your doorstep being pushy when the detective showed up the other day. You having 'news' on the case and us being literally the closest to the discovered body, she wanted to see how we would react to the identification of the Jones' body," Nick said.

"We're suspects?" Kate gasped.

"By default. I think Nixon is coming to terms with you being more of a pain than a killer," Nick laughed.

Kate squinted her eyes at him.

She didn't respond. Her mind was whirring up to full speed, "Confirmation on Royce changes everything."

Nick frowned, "Huh?"

"How we attack this case!" Kate said, dashing into her bungalow.

"You mean the detective's case…" Nick called out to no avail.

Too distracted to work on the house until she had her mind clear, Kate had a spread of croissants, orange juice and coffee on a table in the room where she had created her crime wall.

Eager to get back to work, Nick humored her as she wheeled around the room. Removing Marlett and Westerfield from the victim board and the motives against them, she focused on the connections with Collin Royce.

"I remember reading there were a lot of reports about him suddenly dropping off the tour and vanishing. Some thought he succumbed to his party lifestyle in Thailand or something," Kate said.

"Right before a tour win? Right *after* maybe," Nick said.

Kate considered the background, "Some thought he caved to the pressure. Went on a bender and was too embarrassed to return to the sport."

"Or anywhere, since he was never seen again. And now we know why," Nick said.

"Who won that tournament?" Kate asked.

Scrolling through his phone, Nick looked up, "Uhm… Robert Grant. The two had been sparring for the PGA championship that year."

"And most likely the Hayes' high-dollar sponsorship," Kate added.

"More than that," Nick said.

Kate shot Nick a curious look.

"The affections of Sophia Hayes," Nick replied.

"Now, why does that not surprise me?" Kate scoffed.

Nick plucked the photo of Robert Grant and moved it to the top of the board, "My primary suspect."

"He would have to have been the police's primary suspect too," Kate said.

"Who else do we have?" Nick asked.

"I don't know. Grant sets up so well. Tournament, championship, a lucrative contract, the, admittedly, stunningly gorgeous Sophia Hayes... those are a lot of reasons to want Collin Royce out of the way," Kate said. "We need to learn more about Robert Grant."

Nick scratched his chin.

Kate pressed, "If only we knew someone who knew Grant..."

Nick's head dropped, "You can't be serious. It is like hand feeding a tiger."

"Give her a call, Nick. For the good of the case," Kate said.

"What about you?" Nick asked.

"I think I need to visit the Criminal Justice Department again. I want to learn about the investigation into Robert Grant ten years ago," Kate said.

"Thank you for meeting me again," Kate said, as she settled at a picnic table on the University of North Carolina at Wilmington grounds.

"Happy to. You were instrumental to updating our knowledge on the unfortunate end to Jeffrey Marlett. His unsavory vices ultimately led to his death. It appears he disappeared from his hotel to escape a debt that had come due. That move extended his life, but his life decisions eventually caught up to him anyway," Professor Granger said.

"Your teaching assistant did a great job. It helped me narrow down the identity of the body sealed up in my beach house walls... Collin Royce," Kate said, proud that her deduction had turned out to be accurate.

The criminal justice professor nodded, "Royce was top of my list, too. He had a lot going for him and then suddenly... gone."

"The reporter who visited you right before me, Dennis Jones... did you share anything different with him than you did with me?" Kate asked.

Professor Granger looked thoughtful, "Terrible news about him. The report didn't reveal the cause of death, but one can't help but wonder- at least when you teach about crime all day. We had a similar conversation. He was very focused on the Hayes family. But for me, they had a lot to lose from Royce's disappearance."

Kate's mind danced around the Hayeses and their connections to the victims and the suspects, "What about Robert Grant? He is an obvious suspect. Had to be for the police back then, too."

"He was," Professor Granger nodded. "They investigated him thoroughly, but ultimately walked away without anything concrete. Now that there is a body, all that might change."

"Oh?" Kate frowned.

"A missing persons case, no body. No evidence of foul play. The possibility of the person in question disappearing of their own volition leaves a lot of holes in investigating. There is the suspicion of a crime but no actual crime. A murder? That is a whole new can of worms. Warrants can be issued. Suspects can be called for questioning. It changes everything," Professor Granger said.

"The killer's world must be turned upside down right now," Kate said.

"That makes them extremely dangerous," the professor said.

"Do you think that is why Dennis Jones was killed? He got too close to the original crime?" Kate asked.

The professor tilted his head, "That is as strong a motive for murder as a golf bag full of money or the hand of a beautiful woman."

"Was there anything turned up on Robert Grant? Back then, I mean?" Kate pressed.

"Aside from a well-publicized rivalry? All we could discern from the police investigation is that they questioned Grant several times and didn't get anywhere with him," the professor said. "The next season, Grant was signed to the Hayes' golf resort as their signature golfer. He has even worked with them to design a course with his name on it."

"Wow. He really did benefit from Collin Royce disappearing," Kate said.

"Whoever it was, Robert Grant or otherwise, they can't be happy his body was found," Professor Granger said.

"Dennis Jones is evidence of that," Kate said.

The professor's eyes steadied on Kate's, "Perhaps. That is the most logical conclusion, but you can't allow yourself, as an investigator, to be blinded by it. Follow the facts and the evidence. Let your hunches lead you to those facts, not a quagmire of assumed conclusions."

Kate laughed, "Good advice, Professor. Thank you."

"Any time," Professor Granger shook Kate's hand. "Good luck to you. And be safe, Ms. Harper."

Kate nodded as she walked away from the picnic table. She couldn't help but feel the sensation of being watched. Glancing from both shoulders, she saw the usual students carrying books to and from class. The tall pines made for easy cover. She couldn't tell if the shadows weaving between them were real or in her imagination.

Instinctively, Kate picked up the pace. Reaching her SUV, she spun, scanning the parking lot for someone walking in her direction, looking her way.

Not seeing anyone or anything out of sorts, Kate dismissed her concern as nerves. The reporter's death in the wake of following the same trail as Kate was unsettling. If the case in Treasure Island taught her anything, taking control of the situation instead of letting it have the advantage over her was the best way for her to find comfort.

Answers were the key to her peace of mind, and her safety. Answers were what she was determined to get.

Twenty Two

Nick realized he would rather be in cargo pants and a t-shirt swinging a hammer than a summer weight suit once more invading the world of the golfers and country clubbers. Yet, here he was again, his head slightly dipped as he was the best bet to infiltrate and secure some answers.

While on a mission, Nick hadn't considered his approach. Other than staring at Sophia's number, his thumb hovering over the call button and sliding the phone back into his pocket, he decided to jump in the water and see where the currents took him.

As he walked up to the entrance of the resort's main entrance, Nick watched as a pair of the country club's security detail reacted at the same time and strode quickly through the building. Curious, Nick followed.

Hurrying up the stairs and down the hall toward the executive offices, they stood out front. Opening the door to the office suite, they made their presence known but held their ground. Planting his back to the corner closest to the corridor, Nick listened as raised voices carried down the hall.

"You know damn well we had a bid on the property. The question I have is how you knew about it?" Mark Hayes' angry voice was clearly heard.

"And stop trying to poach Robert. It's childish and he's not going anywhere. He's like family," Sheffield spat.

A voice Nick didn't recognize didn't share the anger,. The man was almost jovial, "It's just business, gentleman. Like golfers on the course, let the best of the weekend win. There's winners and losers. It sounds like, as of late, you guys have had your share of losses."

The sound of a tussle caused Nick to peer around the corner as security grappled to pull two men apart. One was Sheffield Hayes. The other man looked vaguely familiar, but Nick couldn't place him.

"That's enough, Sheffield," Mark said, his voice evening out.

"Look, I'm trying to help you guys out. I know you are leveraged to the hilt. I'm merely suggesting I lessen that load for you. You can't win the deal outright. But I can buy your land rights and you… you can start again. Somewhere else," the man Sheffield had been separated from said.

"We'll let our attorneys sort this one out, Thomas," Mark Hayes said.

"Very well. That will only delay the inevitable. I don't think any of us want this drawn out," the man said. As he began to walk out of the office, he turned with a smirk, "Say hello to Sophia for me, will you?"

One of the security guards was quick to step in front of Sheffield as the man began walking down the hallway.

As Nick curled his head back around the corner he was using as cover, he nearly jumped when a voice very close to him said, "That's a good spot. I spent a fair amount of time on that very corner deciding whether I wanted any part of what was going on down that hall."

Nick turned to see Sophia Hayes standing next to him. Despite hearing footsteps coming in their direction, she offered a calm smile, "Have to decide quickly whether you act like you were merely approaching with bad timing or you elect to pivot and disappear before anyone realizes you were there."

As the footsteps closed in, Nick looked at Sophia. Her calm sultry smile was undeterred, "I'm thinking disappear."

Holding out her hand for Nick, she tugged him down the hall. Her dress flowed as she glided across the floor and down the corridor. Waving her palm at a door lock, it unlatched, and she pulled Nick in just before the man turned the corner from the executive suite hallway.

Her hands still gripped around the lapels of Nick's jacket, Sophia gave a breathy smile, "So, what brings you here, Nick? You didn't call."

"I thought about it. Less of a social call," Nick said, his head backed against the door as Sophia's lips danced mere inches from his.

Frowning, she dropped his lapels, "Well, that's disappointing."

Nick offered a sheepish grin, "I was going to take your father up on his suggestion to meet with his head groundsman but then I came up against them arguing. Who was that?"

"Thomas Hauer. Every sport has its rivals. So does business. Thomas was a country club brat. His daddy is in commercial real estate or some such big money thing. Thomas took a keen interest in how my family built a beautiful golf course and country club for rich people instead of his daddy's warehouses and chemical plants," Sophia said.

"And he started honing in your family's business?" Nick asked.

"His graduation present was a chunk of land across town and blank check to launch his first golf course. The second tournament course to be built in the coastal Carolina marketplace," Sophia said.

Nick eyed her, "You seem to have a solid grasp of the history."

"Let's just say… Sheffield isn't the only one in the family who has tussled with Thomas," Sophia said.

"I see," Nick said.

Sophia's head dropped. With a deep sigh, she took a step back from Nick, "Look, I know how I must appear. Some rich, socialite turned harlot because I have too much money and time on my hands. I wasn't always this way."

Nick was surprised to see the softer side of Sophia spill out. His stance softened along with hers.

"I was in love once. True, heart-gripping, overwhelming love. And then… I lost it. It wrecked my world. I suppose chasing rich boys across the country club is my way of acting out. It has the added benefit of driving my family crazy which is one of my few forms of entertainment," Sophia said.

"I'm sorry about your lost love. That must have hurt," Nick said.

Sophia nodded, looking away she fought a tear from welling in her eye, "It's the lack of closure that messed me up the most."

Nick offered a sympathetic hand on her shoulder.

Sophia turned away, "I don't know why I am telling you any of these things."

"I'm happy to listen," Nick said, his voice firm yet soft.

Squaring up to face Nick directly, she cast a discerning eye, "It's because you are the first guy to come along that doesn't want anything from me."

Nick looked at Sophia curiously.

"For one, you are in love with that girl at dinner the other night. You looked at her eyes with every point of our conversation. You were more worried about her feelings than anything I had to say," Sophia grinned. "Everyone else, they want something. The tabloid conquest of the Hayes debutante, our money… information."

Nick stiffened at the word "information". At first, he felt guilty, but then he quickly realized she wasn't talking about him.

"Thomas… that slimy little worm," Sophia breathed.

"What happened?" Nick asked.

"Let's just say, he caught me in a down moment. I may have been in a condition that I let something slip. Something that likely led directly to arguments down the hall and to an impending land war," Sophia said. Looking distant for a moment, she returned to Nick. "I'm sorry. I'm talking your ear off. What was it you came here for?"

Nick looked sheepish. He felt sorry for Sophia Hayes, a more hurting and complex woman than her airy persona would suggest, "It doesn't matter. I can come back another day."

"No. You're here. Come on, I'll take you to Daddy," Sophia said grabbing his hand and flinging the door open.

Pulling Nick into the hallway, they nearly collided with a country club member. Sophia flashed a seductive smile and straightened her blouse.

Nick's cheeks reddened.

"Come on, I have to give them *something* to talk about," Sophia smirked as she led Nick toward the executive offices.

The scene in the office suite had calmed down as Mark and Sheffield Hayes seemed to be conferring calmly in the wake of the meeting with Thomas Hauer.

"We'll let the lawyers sort it out. In the meantime, be on the lookout for other opportunities," Mark told his son.

"You think we're going to lose this one," Sheffield said.

"I think we can't afford to lose it or have it tied up in court while we are bled dry," Mark said.

Sheffield nodded and scurried toward his office.

"Daddy," Sophia announced their presence in the office.

"Sophia," Mark said eyeing his daughter. Seeing Nick at her heels, he squinted as he dipped into his recall, "Nick. Interested in southern architecture."

"Coastal Carolina architecture, specifically," Nick nodded.

Sophia smiled, "I found him wandering the halls. You mentioned something about groundskeeping."

"Ah, yes. Arturo. I can see if he's free. Have a seat, Nick. Sophia, get our guest something to drink," Mark said as he turned to head out to his office.

Sophia looked at Nick as she opened a cabinet revealing a fully stocked bar, "What's your pleasure, Nick?"

"I'm fine. Thank you," Nick said.

With a shrug, Sophia poured herself a glass, ice popping as the liquid splashed over the cubes. "Coastal Carolina architecture?"

"The beach house," Nick nodded.

Sophia eyed him as she swirled her drink, her face paling slightly, "That's... that's horrible what happened to Collin. I can't believe it."

"Are there records or anything to show who it was rented to at the time? It might give some clues as to the wall that was built," Nick asked.

Swallowing hard, Sophia slammed the entire amount of liquid her glass held down her throat. "We don't need the records. It was Collin. Collin Royce. We blocked out time when he was in town for the tournament. Staying by the ocean helped him focus on the tournament and away from... away from trouble."

Sophia's voice trailed, and she choked, "I'm sorry. I need to go. Take care of yourself, Nick."

In a flash of sundress blowing in her wake, Sophia left the executive office suite, leaving Nick to stare at the door while her father came down the hall with a card.

"I spoke with Arturo. He can't meet with you right now, but you can call and set up an appointment. He knows everything about our buildings. Not just here, but all of our properties. He's the best. He brings the visions Sheffield and I conjure up in our heads to life. He helped build all of this, our first golf course resort property," Mark Hayes lauded.

"Well, that is quite the endorsement," Nick said, receiving the card. "Thank you."

"Good luck with Arturo. If you can pin him down, he will give you what you need," the Hayes patriarch said. With a dismissive wave of his hand, he turned, "Sorry, have a few fires to put out."

Nick let himself out of the office suite flicking the card with his fingers. He suddenly felt very fortunate to be a beach bum surfer living with meager but comfortable means.

"Mr. Mason!" a curt voice snapped him out of his thoughts.

Looking up, he stuffed the card in his pocket, "Detective Nixon. What brings you here?"

The detective scowled, "I am doing my job. The question is, what are *you* doing here?"

"Architecture," Nick replied.

Detective Nixon's scowl did not diminish.

"This property is a perfect example of coastal neo-classical..." Nick started before being waved off by the detective.

With a shake of her head, the detective stormed off in the direction of the executive offices. Nick stared after her, wondering what led her to the Hayes family and whether her visit had to do with the reporter Dennis Jones, the missing golfer, Collin Royce, or both.

Twenty Three

"How did you find this place?" Kate asked as she slid into her seat at the picnic table. Scanning the outdoor seating area, they grabbed the last spot at the busy Wilmington restaurant.

"I met a guy at the country club. I asked where to go when I wanted to trade my cloth napkin for an honest meal where you can roll up your sleeves. He nodded and, without hesitation, said Winnie's Tavern," Nick said.

Kate laughed as she looked over the menu, "It looks like we are in for a treat and will need a whole bunch of paper napkins."

"Pickles or okra?" Nick asked.

With a wrinkled nose, Kate asked, "Why?"

"He said we had to have either the spicy fried pickles or the southern fried okra," Nick said over his menu.

"Pickles all the way!" Kate said.

With a nod, Nick went to place their order.

Glancing past the life preserver decorated wooden fence that made up the back wall of the eating area, Kate saw a face peel back around the fence as her gaze turned that way. Curious, Kate got up from her seat and walked to the edge of the fence line. Looking up and down the street, she didn't see anyone.

As she started to walk toward an area of concealment, Nick's voice made her jump, "Everything all right?"

Kate spun, slapping her hand to her chest and nodding, "Yeah. Fine. I just thought I saw someone. Probably just peripheral vision messing with me."

Nick leaned out past the fence and scanned the area, "Maybe. I don't see anyone."

With their food ready, they settled back in their seats.

Leaning forward, Kate asked, "Well… how was Sophia?"

"The hot mess that she seemed to be. With a bit more soul in her core than she initially let on," Nick said. He went on to share their moment as they avoided being detected.

"Wow. You could have a new calling. Therapist for troubled wealthy people. The 'Rich Girl Whisperer'," Kate teased.

Nick winced, "Yeah, I don't think that one's going to stick. But it is a sentiment that money does indeed *not* buy happiness."

"I suppose not," Kate said.

"She seemed suddenly overwhelmed. I couldn't help but wonder what happened to her?" Nick said.

"Collin Royce. She was in love with Collin Royce. Why else would she get so emotional when you talked about him?" Kate asked.

"That must be it," Nick nodded. "He goes missing, her one chance at true love gone in one mysterious night."

"Kind of sad, really," Kate mused as she popped a fried pickle in her mouth. "These are really good, by the way."

"Here's a juicy bit. Collin Royce was staying at the beach house when he was murdered. It was under wraps to avoid fans and paparazzi while he focused on the tournament," Nick said.

"*Someone* knew he was there," Kate said.

"The Hayes family," Nick said.

"Or someone connected to the Hayes family," Kate said between bites of pickles.

Nick laughed. Shaking his head, he said, "You are the only person I know who can contemplate murder and heartbreak, yet appreciate a good fried pickle at the very same moment."

Kate shrugged, "I'm hungry. These are really good. Mysteries don't solve themselves."

"No, they don't. Eavesdropping can, though," Nick said. "Before the heart to heart with Sophia, I heard Mark and Sheffield Hayes arguing with another man. It was so tense security had to step in. Their rival, Thomas Hauer, swooped in on their land deal. It seems Sophia might have tipped Hauer off."

"How did she do that?" Kate asked, tossing back another pickle.

"Sophia being Sophia. A heavy pour, a bad day and a shoulder to lean on," Nick said.

"That's devious," Kate said.

"Love and war and billion-dollar land deals, I guess," Nick said. "It sounds like it couldn't come at a worse time. Mark Hayes said their business was really hurting after their last deal. They need a major investment or they are in big trouble."

"The kind of tensions that set people up for murder," Kate said.

"Save your family's legacy or take out the competition," Nick said taking a bite of his burger.

"Where does the reporter fit in to all of this?" Kate asked.

Nick sat his burger down and wiped his hands on a napkin, "He must have gotten close to something. Collin Royce's murderer. Some major legal shenanigans between the Hayes and the Hauers?"

"He's been running in the same circles as we have been," Kate said. "That means we aren't too far from answers ourselves."

"Or danger," Nick said, his expression serious.

Kate's eyes flashed to the fence line where she thought she had seen a figure watching her.

"What about you? What did you find?" Nick asked.

Returning her gaze to Nick, Kate said, "Collin's disappearance was a big deal. The police focused their investigation on the Hayes family and Collin's top rival - Robert Grant. Grant went on to win the tournament and the championship that year. He took top billing as the Hayes' Golf Resort celebrity."

"Well, if that doesn't move him to the top of the list. The police didn't find anything on Grant?" Nick asked.

"According to Professor Granger, a missing persons case with an international playboy with no real evidence of a crime… there was only so much they could do," Kate said.

"Until dead bodies start piling up," Nick said finishing his meal. "We need to learn a lot more about Robert Grant."

Kate nodded as she placed her well-used napkins on top of her plate. "The question is how?"

"He's a fixture at the country club. Mark Hayes gave me the card for his head of operations, Arturo Moreno. I can go back there and see what I can find," Nick shrugged. "You can come with. I'd just as soon keep an eye on you with a killer on the loose."

Kate smirked, "And spoil a chance at another gut spilling run-in with Sophia? I have to imagine she'd be pretty tight-lipped with me around."

"I think I am no longer on the menu," Nick said.

Cocking her head, Kate looked at Nick with curiosity.

"Just a hunch," Nick smiled.

Taking in his words, Kate considered it. "I'm going to do a little research into Hayes Resort poster child Robert Grant."

"Be careful," Nick said.

"I'll be at a public library. I'll be fine. You're the one heading into the hornet's nest," Kate said.

Arturo Moreno was waiting for Nick at the front entrance of the country club. Sitting at the driver's seat of custom golf cart, he called, "Get in."

"Thanks for meeting me," Nick said.

"A friend of the Hayes family is a friend of mine," Arturo said. "Mr. Hayes says you have an interest in southern architecture."

"I do. I like my remodels to embrace the history and evolution of the region," Nick said.

Putting his foot on the accelerator, Arturo said, "Well, you'll find the basic architecture of the resort following a blend of antebellum and Greek revival styles. Large columns, hipped and gabled roofs, cupolas, rounded stairs, evenly spaced windows…"

Nick understood the details that Arturo pointed out on their golf cart tour around the country club grounds. When they stopped for lemonade, he leaned forward for the first time in their journey.

"How long have you worked for the Hayeses?" Nick asked.

"I've been with the Hayes family for a long time. I started as an apprentice on one of their hotels. Mr. Hayes liked the flourishes I suggested and brought me on for bigger jobs, like the building design of the country club," Arturo said.

Nick sipped his lemonade, "Wow. That is quite the nod of approval."

"I owe a lot to Mr. Hayes. Taking a chance on me fresh out of college like that was a big deal. I've been working with him since," Arturo said.

"Do you work on all of their properties?" Nick asked.

"I oversee the design work. Most of it is in the south, so we have tones of Georgian, antebellum, neo-classical, Greek revival… depends on the setting. Like you, we try to make it blend with a bit of elevation that makes it stand out from the rest. If you look at our main building and match it up against the others in the area, like the Hauer property, you'll find a lot of similarities. There are little touches that make the Hayes' resorts a little more elegant," Arturo said.

With a smile, he added, "I have even gotten to play with designs on smaller projects. Coastal cottage, Mediterranean or even plantation style."

"That's a departure from a sprawling country club mansion," Nick said.

"To take something that is rather… ordinary and make it special- it's fun," Arturo said. Nodding for them to continue their journey in the golf cart, he rose from his seat.

Settling back in for their ride, Nick asked, "What about the Hayes' last project? Was that your design, too?"

"It was," Arturo nodded. "Great design. Terrible business plan."

"Oh? How so?" Nick asked.

"Sheffield. Trying so hard to fill his father's shoes. He rushed into it. Didn't take into account environmental restrictions. Native American land rights. The time, additional work and legal fees… as much as I love how it turned out, plug should have been pulled on that one early on," Arturo said.

"Every company has their challenges," Nick said.

Arturo turned toward Nick, "Not ones that threaten to dismantle a family's entire legacy. I'm from an immigrant family. My father got us here. Gave us a chance. I'm lucky to have built something for my kids and their grandkids. The Hayes family, they go back several generations. That's a big gamble."

"There's got to be another project on the horizon. One that makes up for it, right?" Nick asked.

Arturo chewed his lip as he measured his response, "There might be one we've been working on. It would be just what Mr. Hayes needs to right the ship."

"You sound hesitant," Nick observed.

"Let's just say… sometimes ships have rats on them. You need to dispose of the rats or you risk losing the entire ship," Arturo said as he pulled the golf cart up to where their journey had begun.

Climbing out, Nick held out his hand, "Thank you, Arturo. It was a great tour. Very helpful."

"You take care, Nick. Give me a call if you have any more questions," Arturo said.

"I will," Nick nodded as he watched the golf cart scoot away.

He couldn't help but wonder who the rats on the ship were and how exactly they might be disposed of. Climbing into his truck, Nick was excited to share with Kate.

Twenty Four

Kate had become familiar with the library on the university campus. She enjoyed the energy of students as they filtered through the stacks of books. Some gathered at tables or in reserved rooms to work on projects, research papers and study groups.

Finding her spot where she had done research on prior trips, she set her bag down next to a terminal. Settling in, she spread her fingers wide and centered her shoulders before scrolling through search results.

Pulling out her notebook, she went through her checklist of questions. Robert Grant was the focus of her attention. The cursor pulsed in the search bar awaiting her request. Putting in the words "Sophia Hayes" and the year of Collin Royce's death, she was rewarded with dozens of local and national media coverage supported with pages of photographs.

Rifling through the articles and images, most of the Hayes family hosting or attending events. Golf, philanthropic, civic– always polished and poised. Kate clicked on an image of Sophia. She looked young. She looked happy. Not the wicked sideways happy that she wore today. A genuine happy of someone full of life… and love.

Scanning the photos of Sophia, Kate began searching for the love part. The gossip pages were full of copy about Sophia and Collin. There were plenty of photos of the two together. Kate couldn't place it, but something was off in the photos.

Kate scribbled a quick note on her note pad. Changing her search, she input Robert Grant in place of Collin Royce. Again, the gossip pages were filled with sightings and insinuations. In a few of the photos, the pair did look close. Kate tried to discern if the images read romantic.

Clicking on a photo to zoom in on it on her screen, she spied a well-attired man in the background, his attention square on Sophia. Scrolling, she zoomed on another photo. The same impeccably dressed man focused on Sophia. Hitting print on the photos, Kate continued her search.

Removing Sophia from the search, she concentrated on Robert Grant. Grant was a rising golf star along the same timeline as Collin Royce. Collin had a one-year head start in the tournament rankings, but Grant was catching up. Kate admitted that both men were attractive in their own right. Both were congenial with the media and fans. It made the rivalry all the more interesting.

Robert Grant, being a noted friend of the family and Collin Royce the sponsored star, the two were running in a very tight circle. "I wonder how family friend Robert felt about the Hayes granting their sponsorship to Collin instead of him," Kate tapped her pen against her lips as she studied the articles and images.

Hitting print a few more times, she cleared the search, this time keying in Thomas Hauer's name. The search engine exploded with articles on the Hauer family business, politics and over the last decade, golf resorts. The face of the family was young Thomas Hauer. Many of the articles on Hauer included Sheffield Hayes somewhere in the mix. It seemed the pair had squared off since Hauer's entry into the world of golf.

Seeing Collin Royce's name pop in an article title, Kate clicked on it. The golf world rumor mill reported a potential change in endorsement for Collin Royce. Photos of Hauer exiting a private meeting with Collin Royce, looking a bit shell-shocked and unaware of the camera.

Kate noted the date of the meeting. It was during the same tournament weekend that Collin Royce disappeared. Emphatically hitting the print button, Kate leaned back in her seat. "Could all this be over an endorsement deal?"

Scrolling along, she saw a photo that caught her eye. A shot that was clearly taken unbeknownst to the subject—Thomas Hauer and Sophia Hayes, holding hands as they looked at one another. The context was unclear, but Kate scoffed at the ease of coming to a conclusion.

Her head spun with facts and a multitude of angles. Any one of them could have resulted in Collin Royce's death. Getting up from her seat, Kate headed to pick up her printouts.

Frowning as she arrived at the printer, the healthy stack of paper she expected wasn't there. With a sigh, she readied to find paper to refill the tray.

Suddenly, the printer hummed and a single sheet of paper slid into the spot her stack should have been. Curious, she looked at the sheet. In bold print, smack in the middle of the paper, it read, MIND YOUR BUSINESS.

Snatching the paper from the tray, Kate whirled around. Her eyes moved from work station to work station, searching for anyone who might have sent the note and presumably snatched her print outs.

Seeing no one out of sorts and certainly no one that she recognized, she began to return to her workstation. She hoped the search engine retained all of her work and she didn't need to restart it all.

While walking through a row of shelves in a beeline toward her workstation, a book popped off the shelf directly in front of her. Pausing, Kate looked at the book and then up at the shelf it had fallen from. She was surprised to see another book right before her eyes sprang out and dropped onto the floor in front of her. Then another. And another.

Suddenly the entire shelf began to list in her direction. In a sprint, Kate dashed down the row of shelves, diving out of the way just as the one she had paused at slammed to the floor in a loud explosion of books and shelving.

Losing a shoe, buried in the rubble of books, Kate hopped to the end of the row. Seeing a figure dash in the opposite direction, Kate lifted her leg and removed her other shoe. In stocking feet, Kate raced through the library in the direction of the figure. After slamming into the emergency exit, alarms blared as the figure slipped into the blinding midday sun. Kate followed after the figure, ignoring the alarms and calls from library staff. Standing on the lawn behind the library, Kate shielded her eyes from the sun, scanning in all directions for anyone running away from the scene.

Her eyes danced from a couple walking and talking, two boys tossing a football back and forth, and a girl carrying a saxophone case. All she could see were students being students. Shoulders slumping, Kate turned to find several library staff members and a university police officer staring at her in confusion.

"Are you all right, ma'am?" the officer asked.

"I'm a bit wounded by you calling me ma'am, but yes. I'm all right. I think I lost a shoe somewhere," Kate admitted, holding her other shoe dangling from her fingers.

"What happened?" a library staffer asked.

"How did that bookshelf fall like that?" another asked.

The officer held their arm out directing Kate back inside the library, "Come on. Let's make sure you're all right and sort this out."

"Kate Harper. Why am I not surprised to find you amidst all of this chaos?"

Kate turned her head in the study room turned incident command. With a thin smile, she said, "Hello, Detective Nixon."

"Want to tell me your version of what went on?" Detective Nixon asked.

"I was here doing some research…" Kate began.

"What kind of research?" the detective interjected.

Kate studied the detective's expression. It reminded her of her as a child when her mother would be ready to scold her in advance of an explanation. "I was looking up photos of golf tournaments and other events."

"Recent ones?" Nixon crossed her arms.

Kate shuffled in her seat, "From about a decade ago."

"I thought I warned you not to interfere in the investigation," the detective said.

"I was just looking at photos. I didn't really see the harm in that," Kate shrugged.

Glancing out at the clean-up that had begun after the school and the police had taken photos of the incident, Detective Nixon scoffed, "Someone seemed to see harm in that."

"Yeah," Kate nodded meekly.

"Where are these photos?" the detective pressed.

Kate shook her head, "I don't know. They were gone when I got to the printer. While standing there, this was printed."

The detective took the sheet of paper that Kate held out for her. "Cute. To the point. Yet they still felt the need to try and knock a bookshelf over on you."

With a frown, Kate said, "There wasn't anything special. Just photos of golf tournaments, galas, public stuff… and one between Thomas Hauer and Sophia Hayes."

"Our own Romeo and Juliet," Detective Nixon said. Turning to the campus police officer, she asked, "Could you pull footage from the library security cameras? I want to see who was in the library during the attack. I want to see who may have been sitting at the workstation when this note was printed."

"Yeah, we can tap into it from here," the officer pulled out a keyboard and entered her credentials.

Navigating to the security cameras in the library, the officer narrowed in on the time just before the attack. Kate was clearly seen crossing the library and looking confused at the printer. Other than her scanning the library, nothing seemed out of sorts.

When as she began walking back toward her own workstation, a figure with a hood up and sunglasses on crept behind her with their head down. Disappearing between the rows, the figure didn't reshow until an obvious disturbance attracted the attention of all at the library. From the camera's vantage, all they could see was a hooded figure with glasses on streak out of the emergency exit with Kate not far behind.

"Can you get my station a copy? I'd like to see if forensics can get a better image of our hooded culprit," the detective asked, receiving a nod. Turning to Kate, she said, "You're okay?"

Kate nodded.

"I'm sorry this happened to you. You really need to stay as far away from this investigation as possible. I don't want another body on my hands," Detective Nixon said.

Unable to help herself, Kate blurted, "Do you think Dennis Jones' death was related to Collin Royce's murder? He got too close?"

"I don't know, and I do not care to speculate on an on-going investigation, Ms. Harper," Detective Nixon snapped. "If you uncover anything, you don't check it out. You come to me."

A campus police officer appeared in the doorway. Dangling from his fingers was a solitary shoe, "I believe this is yours?"

Kate nodded, happily accepting her shoe.

Detective Nixon observed the exchange almost as if determining whether she should be amused or not. From

Kate's vantage, the verdict must have been "not" because the detective turned on a heel and exited the library without a further word.

"Are you okay?" Nick gasped as Kate shared her story.

"Yeah, I'm fine," Kate nodded, setting her things down on the beach house kitchen counter.

"I'm beginning to think Detective Nixon is right. This is too dangerous. You are following in the footsteps of Dennis Jones. We know how that turned out," Nick said, his concerns clearly painted across his face.

Kate sighed, "I'm fine. It was just someone trying to scare me."

"Any idea who?"

"No. I could barely see them when I ran after them and they were careful to avoid the library's cameras. It could have been anyone," Kate said.

"Who were you looking into at the time?" Nick asked.

Kate laughed, "Everyone. The Hayes family. Thomas Hauer. Robert Grant. Collin Royce."

"Well, there is *one* name we can take off that list," Nick said.

Flashing a look at Nick, Kate said, "There is so much going on in that world. It is all so messy."

"What is at the center of the mess?" Nick asked.

Kate looked up, impressed with Nick's intuition, "Money… and Sophia Hayes."

"No big surprise but greed and passion are the most common motives for murder," Nick said. "What did you find out?"

"There were a lot of media ties placing Sophia and Collin together, romantically," Kate said. With a laugh she added, "And with Thomas Hauer. And with Robert Grant."

"So, nothing new," Nick said.

Kate winced, "I'm not so sure about that. There is something about those old photos, but I can't put my finger on it. I *did* find out that Thomas Hauer had a private meeting with Collin Royce during the tournament. The rumor was Hauer was making a bid for Collin to switch endorsements to the Hauer golf course."

"That would give both Mark and Sheffield Hayes something to be angry about," Nick said.

"And give Robert Grant a huge opportunity," Kate said. Pulling a folder out of her bag, she opened it up for Nick.

"These are the photos you printed. You got them back?" Nick asked.

Kate shook her head, "No. I reprinted them."

"You *stayed*? After all that, Kate?" Nick said, his voice dripping with annoyance.

"What? I figured whoever toppled over that bookcase was long gone and I'm not sure that library had ever been so secure," Kate said. "They even demanded a campus officer escort me to my car."

"Good," Nick said. Pulling out the photos, he sorted them out on the counter. As Kate had suggested, Sophia Hayes was a subject of many of them. Tapping the counter, he looked at Kate, "These pictures of Sophia and Collin… the vibe is off. They seem happy together but, I don't know. I can't put my finger on it."

"I know!" Kate nearly leaped out of her shoes for the second time that day. "I had the same impression."

"Who's that?" Nick picked up a photo and held it closer. "Is that... Thomas Hauer?"

"Gawking at Sophia in several of the photos? Yes. That would be Thomas Hauer taking an immense interest in your lady friend," Kate said.

"She's not my lady friend. I mean, she is friendly, but no," Nick shook Kate's suggestion off. "That poor woman has a lot of baggage to unpack. And I'm hoping she is able to someday."

"Yeah," Kate said softly, leafing through the photos.

Twenty Five

Kate and Nick decided the day had provided enough excitement, and they would instead focus on the beach house. Admittedly, they had let the schedule slip yet again.

Nick tackled the new lighting they had bought, installing fixtures in the hallway now back in its original straight path from the front door to the glass doors on the beach side of the house. The new sconces would cast a soft glow welcoming guests as they were naturally drawn to the sweeping Atlantic views.

Moving from room to room, Kate matched her paint samples with bedding she placed into a shopping cart on her laptop. Finding complementing throws for those evenings when the guests left their windows and doors open to listen to the lullaby of the surf while the cooler coastal air tickled their bodies.

Her phone buzzed. Setting her laptop and paint chips down, Kate answered, "Hello."

"Kate Harper?" a male voice called through the phone.

"Yes, this is Kate Harper," she said, wary of any unknown numbers. She was unsure why she even answered.

"I have information regarding the Collin Royce missing persons, now murder, case," the voice said.

"Who is this? Why are you calling me?" Kate asked.

The phone was silent for a moment.

"If you want answers, meet me at Shepherd's Battery. One half-hour."

The phone went dead. Kate stared at the phone in her hand.

Nick, arms laden with new fixtures for the upstairs bathrooms stood in the doorway and asked, "What's wrong?"

"I, uh. I just received the strangest call. Someone said they had information on the Collin Royce case. Said to meet at Shepherd's Battery at Fort Fisher in half an hour," Kate said, her speech slow as she was trying to make sense of the conversation.

"Did they say who they were? Why were they calling *you*?" Nick asked, setting the fans down on the bed.

"No," Kate shook her head. "What do we do?"

"We keep working and forget about it. Call Detective Nixon. That might be a good idea," Nick said.

Kate's face was wrinkled in contemplation.

"Kate..." Nick started.

"What if they have real information?" Kate asked.

"Call Detective Nixon. Let her sort it out. Your phone should have their number on it, right?" Nick said.

Kate nodded, "Right."

Nick slumped, "But you want to go."

"Kind of, I mean, yeah," Kate said.

"The sun is setting... now," Nick looked outside their window. The coastal sky rapidly moved from Carolina blue to indigo.

"It's a public place," Kate argued.

"It probably closes at sunset, Kate," Nick replied.

The pair stared at each other for a long moment. Nick rolled his eyes. He had been in the losing battle of these conversations enough to know Kate was intent on going.

"All right. I want Detective Nixon on speed dial," Nick said.

"Absolutely," Kate said, already gliding down the steps.

The drive from the beach house to Fort Fisher was a short one. The historic state site, a turning point in the Civil War, remained a testament to the soldiers who fought and died in the land and sea battles. Nick was correct about the site's operational hours. The gate was swung closed and locked. Pulling their car next to the gate, they looked around for another vehicle.

Not seeing one, they looked at each other with shrugs.

Bypassing the Closed sign, they walked briskly toward the site, feeling like the trespassers they were.

"We really shouldn't be here," Nick said, not liking the vibe of this mysterious rendezvous.

"I'm starting to get that feeling, too," Kate said.

They almost held their breath as they walked, taking careful steps, avoiding branches and sticks that might crunch under their feet. The evening sky scattered shadows across their path, deep toughs of black beginning to take shop behind obstacles.

The coastal birds swooped overhead, flying so close you could hear their feathers manipulate the air as they moved to their nighttime perches. Bats replaced the birds in the sky, their erratic flights as they hunted insects.

Kate and Nick preferred the bats and the birds to the quiet stretches. They could swear they could hear their hearts beating as they skulked their way along the desolate trail to their meeting site.

Following the path to the battery and its still functional sea cannons, a figure emerged from the shadows. Stepping forward, he eyed Kate and Nick before speaking, "I'm sorry for the theatrics. One man has already died after closing in on the truth of this case. We can't be too careful, can we, Ms. Harper?"

Kate cocked her head.

"I am aware of the incident at the library. That was a clear warning. Someone feels you are getting close to the truth. Dennis Jones was close to the truth," the man said.

Stepping a shoulder in front of Kate, Nick asked, "Who are you?"

The man nodded, "I don't blame you for being wary- and protective of Ms. Harper. Admirable. I am a reporter. I used to… I used to work with Dennis. When I heard about his death, I came to finish the job. Find out who killed Collin Royce and presumably, who killed Dennis."

Nick remained stoic as the man spoke.

"My name is Andrew Ayres. Dennis and I tackled the Collin Royce disappearance for a decade. To be fair, I worked it for about nine months. Dennis never let up. He stayed on it. Without a trace of Royce, the trail froze over until you two came along and found him in the wall of your beach house. Must have been a dreadful sight, that," Ayres said.

"You said you had information?" Kate asked.

"I do," the reporter nodded. "I was hoping this would be more of… an exchange. Information for information."

Nick's head cocked to the side.

Kate stepped forward, "All right. But you go first. You seem to know more about me and my efforts. I know nothing of yours."

The man laughed in a crooked smirk, "Sure. Okay. Collin Royce was an up-and-comer. But so was Robert Grant. Both were rising stars on the tour. Robert Grant had been a family friend of the Hayeses for most of his life. Yet, Collin had the endorsement contract. That didn't sit well with Grant. But he just stood by and let the chips fall. Royce happened to be one of those chips."

Kate and Nick stood unmoving while the man looked like he had just shared a huge revelation.

Bobbing his head back and forth, Ayres must have realized he needed to share more, "Robert Grant, family friend or not, was mad for Sophia Hayes' affection. In one fail swoop, Grant had a tour win, the endorsement contract and a clear road to Sophia."

The reporter looked proud of himself. Seeing that Kate and Nick were still unfazed, his face fell, "You already knew all that, huh?"

Tapping his lip, the man pondered, "Sheffield Hayes and Collin Royce had a huge shouting match, complete with smashed cocktail glasses the night before Royce disappeared. No one knew what the argument was about. Dennis had some ideas. He felt that was the missing piece of the investigation. He felt something drove Royce away or, well, what we know to be the case today, murdered Collin Royce."

Kate nodded, giving Ayres a boost. With a frown, she asked, "In your… or Dennis' thoughts, how then does Robert Grant fit into Royce's disappearance, or murder as it were, if it hinged on the fight with Sheffield?"

"They were best friends. Sheffield wanted his buddy in the driver's seat, not Royce. Maybe they worked together on the plot to get rid of Royce," the reporter shrugged. "I was hoping Dennis had found out. I'm not sure he did. I couldn't find the link in his notes."

"And you think Collin Royce's and Dennis Jones' murders are connected?" Kate asked.

The reporter nodded, "I have no doubt. Dennis was killed because he was working this case. These are very wealthy, powerful people beyond the veil of lush golf courses and evening galas. Politicians, judges, banks… They all have a lot to gain when things stay quiet and a lot to lose if exposed."

"That makes them dangerous," Nick said.

"It does," the reporter said.

"The timing was just too coincidental," Kate said, confirming her instinct from the start.

"I don't believe in coincidences. Just strings that haven't been aligned yet, the reporter said.

"What is it you want from Kate?" Nick asked, glancing around as the day had given into the moon and stars.

"There's another element to all of this. I think you might have tripped across the answer," Ayres said.

"We're actually pretty much on the same page…" Kate started.

Ayres, affable throughout the conversation snapped, "Don't waste my time, Ms. Harper!"

Nick stepped in front of Kate.

"Information for information. I know you know something. I'm not the only one that thinks so!" Ayres had become irrationally belligerent.

"I think we need to go," Nick said, turning Kate away from the reporter.

Ayres put a hand on Nick's shoulder. Nick twisted, his hand knifing up to where his shoulder was. Grabbing the reporter's wrist, Nick twisted. The searing pain dropped Ayres to his knees. "I'm sorry. I'm sorry. This just… means a lot to me!"

Kate placed a calming hand on Nick, feeling his body relax with her touch.

"It's all right," Kate said softly. "And I did agree to it."

Nick stood firmly in front of Kate as Ayres stood up on his feet.

Pondering which piece of information she wanted to share, she said, "There was something in the photos of Collin Royce and Sophia. Despite being reported sweethearts, and while they seemed friendly… they didn't seem romantically involved. It didn't look like she was in a relationship with Royce. And if that's the case, that takes a big strike away from Robert Grant being led to murder."

Ayres thought about the words for a moment. With a scrutinizing look, he asked, "What makes you think that?"

"The photos. Maybe its woman's intuition or something, but something was off in their photos," Kate said.

"Hmm," Ayres scratched his chin. "He still had millions of reasons to want Royce out of the way."

"Passion, greed… I don't know," Kate shrugged.

A flashlight began knifing through the night sky. The three turned toward the light. By the time Kate and Nick spun back to Ayres, he was gone.

Deciding to face the trouble head on, they walked toward the light.

"Thank goodness!" Kate exclaimed. "I told him we should have left earlier. By the time we found the trailhead it was dark."

The park ranger eyed both of them, shining the flashlight at both of them. "I'm not sure that explains your car on the *outside* of the park entrance, now does it?"

Kate winced. "No. I suppose it doesn't."

"Look, I get it. It's a romantic place. I get the appeal, but you have to respect the historical and ecological sensitivities of the site," the park ranger said. "Follow me. I have your license plate. If I see it here after closing again…"

"Yes, sorry. Thank you," Nick said.

Following the ranger back toward their car, Kate was confused about how Ayres vanished and why they didn't see his car parked in front of the gate.

"If someone were to come by the beach…" Kate began.

"There is the four-wheel drive beach. Still, you aren't supposed to bypass the signs from that direction, either," the ranger said.

"Of course," Kate shook him off.

The ranger stood at the gate, arms crossed watching Kate and Nick scramble into her SUV and drive away.

Nick frowned at Kate.

Glancing from behind the world, Kate offered a sheepish grin, "That was fun, right?"

"Could have gotten arrested for trespassing. Accused of desecrating a historical, ecological and culturally sensitive site. And, we really didn't receive any new groundbreaking information," Nick said. "I don't understand why we had to sneak around a closed state park for that limited exchange."

"I think Ayres was just being careful after what happened to Dennis Jones," Kate said. "And, I'd really like to know more about that fight between Sheffield Hayes and Collin Royce."

"Maybe we should consider being careful moving forward," Nick said, his tone even.

"You surf with sharks," Kate said.

"Sharks won't bother you, most of the time," Nick said.

"Just like meeting with creepy reporters at night in clandestine locations, they're fine, most of the time," Kate teased.

Nick shook his head.

Pulling into the beach house driveway, Kate said, "I think Ayres was there in earnest. But I get the sense there is something he is not telling us. Something burning under the surface."

"He's a bit hot-headed and bitter," Nick nodded.

"Let me tidy up, and we'll figure something out for dinner," Kate said as Nick followed her into the beach house. Pausing at the front door, she said, "That's odd. Did we forget to lock the door when we hurried out?"

"No," Nick said. Inspecting the lock, he pushed ahead of Kate and dashed into the house.

In steady, rapid steps, Nick moved from room to room. Taking in a large sweep and then following up to look into closets and behind furniture. Expecting Kate was on his heels, he was startled when she shrieked, calling from another room. Whirling, Nick raced to her location.

Standing in the room where Kate had assembled her crime wall, she stared at the wall. Nick's eyes followed hers. Everything that had been pinned and connected to the wall had been torn down.

"Someone was worried about what I had uncovered…" Kate said, her mind trying to piece together what clue she had gathered that had someone convinced and concerned she was edging close to the truth. Seeing Nick on his phone, she asked, "What are you doing?"

"I'm calling the police," Nick said. Seeing the concern in Kate's eyes, he was stern, "Someone broke into the beach house, Kate."

With a reluctant nod, Kate allowed him to make the call. Wanting to pilfer the remnants of her own work, she took a step back, "Guess I shouldn't touch anything."

"Come on. I want to check out the rest of the house and I want you at my side this time," Nick said.

Kate wasn't used to the authoritative side of the surfer-handyman coming out very often. Both taken aback and intrigued, she knew it came from a place of caring. Relenting, she followed closely behind Nick as he meticulously searched the house for anywhere a person could possibly hide.

Finding the beach house free from nefarious beings, they relaxed as they waited for the police. Intent on ensuring the intruder was no longer in the house, Nick's eyes began to note other elements out of alignment. His thought was broken by a heavy knock at the front door.

Swinging the door open, they saw a uniformed officer step aside for a stern Detective Nixon to walk through. Her eyes lighting on Nick's and then Kate's, she snapped, "These meetings are beginning to become frequent- a bit too frequent for my taste. How about you tell me what's going on?"

Starting with the front door, they explained that they found it unlatched.

"I noticed the doorjamb had been scraped. Someone probably used a card or piece of plastic to depress the plunger in the lock," Nick said.

Kate scowled, "What about the deadbolt?"

"If it isn't installed correctly and extends all the way into the door, it can be popped open," Nick said. "Kate ordered a new one. It hasn't arrived yet, so we just left it as is."

Detective Nixon leaned closer to the mechanism, "He's right. We see it all the time."

Stepping into the house, the detective scanned the area. "So, was anything taken?"

"Nothing of value," Kate shrugged. "We searched the house. Other than the spare bedroom…"

The detective's eyes lit up, "Show me."

Kate led the detective to the spare bedroom that had been ransacked.

Kate eyed the wall, seeing scratches in the drywall as in haste, the pins that held up her crime clues were ripped out.

"What was here? Why this wall?" Detective Nixon asked.

Kate danced before offering an aloof answer, "Information on the house. Previous owners…"

Spying a torn piece of paper on the floor, the detective bent over and picked it up. Turning it over, she saw partial images of Collin Royce and Sophia Hayes in the ripped photo. "More research like what you were doing at the library?"

The detective's tone reminded Kate of being caught stealing a cookie as a child. Kate merely offered a meek shrug.

Nick's eyes grew wide, "I bet that reporter lured us away and had an accomplice break into the house. We fell for it!".

"Reporter? What reporter?" Detective Nixon asked.

Kate reluctantly told the detective about Andrew Ayres.

"Isn't the park closed at night?" Detective Nixon scrunched her nose.

Nick shot a knowing glare at Kate. Kate nodded, her head drooping.

The detective paced around the room, "A reporter investigating a story who didn't reach out to the police in charge of the case?"

Both Kate and Nick winced at the information.

Studying Kate and Nick, the detective bounced her finger up and down, "I get the feeling you two have a lot more explaining to do. Come down to the station tomorrow. I have some questions for you. In the meantime, are you still staying at the bungalows?"

Kate nodded.

"Good. This will probably fall on deaf ears, but try and stay out of trouble," Detective Nixon said motioning for the police officer who accompanied her to turn and leave. "I'll check for prints on the way out. But unless they are real stupid, I'd assume they wore gloves."

Kate and Nick watched the detective head down the hall.

Kate rubbed her head as she scanned the room, her feet moving in a tight little circle.

"I thought you'd be more upset. All that work… missing," Nick said.

Kate shrugged, a wry smile escaping her lips, "I took pictures of it after the library attack. In case I forgot something, I could zoom in on my phone and remember."

Holding her phone up to where her crime wall had been, she pulled up the photo, "My question is, what about these photos keeps getting people all riled up? They have to be the key."

"It's possible they just want to know what you know. Making a mess of your things and swiping the articles and pictures is just a way to slow you down. Or send a message," Nick said.

"I think I'm close, Nick," Kate said as she studied the photos.

Nick shook his head.

Twenty Six

Like two children heading into the principal's office, Kate and Nick entered the Carolina Beach Police Station with their heads slunk low.

The desk officer looked up, a grim look on their face, "Detective Nixon is expecting you."

Calling back to the detective's office, the officer let Nixon know the pair had arrived. Wincing, he pulled the phone from his ear. Collecting himself he forced a flat smile, "She'll be right out."

It wasn't long before the perma-angry detective marched out to retrieve them. Her even glare swept over them.

Kate held her arms out, a box clenched in her hands. A broad smile dimpling her cheeks, she announced, "We brought you donuts!"

Detective Nixon froze, snarling at Kate, "Do I look like I eat donuts?"

Kate staggered a bit, glancing at Nick, at the desk officer who merely shrugged. "They're Britt's!" Kate stammered, not knowing how else to appease the detective.

"I do. But it means another mile on my run and I don't have time for that right now. I have a murder to solve and I am constantly finding you two underfoot," Nixon snapped. "Set them over there. Maybe they'll be gone by the time I'm done with the two of you."

Kate complied, setting the box down on a table just within the main body of the police station offices.

"Is there maple bacon?" Nixon muttered.

"Uh, yes. I think there is," Kate nodded.

Whirling just short of her office door, the detective growled at the other officers, "There better be maple bacon when I come out."

All heads in the room nodded in unison.

Entering the detective's office, she motioned toward a pair of chairs opposite hers. Closing the door with more force than seemed necessary, the slight but athletic detective slid behind her desk.

Looking at Kate and then Nick and back to Kate again, Detective Nixon stared the pair down as though the stern looks in her eyes would elicit some sort of blurted confession.

Taking a deep breath, the detective said, "What exactly have you two been up to?"

Kate and Nick looked at each other, each mumbling nonsensical words as their expressions feigned as though they had no idea what the detective was talking about.

"You are at the beach house where you just happen to discover bones in the house your company recently purchased. You are at the country club when I'm there to interview the historic owners of the beach house. You are at the university chatting up the Criminal Justice

Department head about cases intrinsic to my investigation. You are off on clandestine meetings, trespassing on treasured historical land, and you have a collection of photos and news articles also directly pertaining to my case pinned to your wall. If I didn't know better, I would say you two are putting yourselves square on top of my suspect board. Yes, Ms. Harper, we professional detectives have those too," Detective Nixon ranted, somehow managing to get all of that out in a single breath.

"I did a little sleuthing myself. You're the ones I read about down in Treasure Island," Detective Nixon said.

"Guilty!" Kate grinned. Her face fell as the detective did not smile at her attempt at humor.

"The arresting officer on the Treasure Island case said I should toss you in jail. He assured me, that no matter what I had to say or how much danger you found yourselves in, you will somehow remain underfoot," the detective said, her expression declaring her displeasure.

Kate's face even further, "You've spoken to Detective Connolly…"

"Here is what I can assure you, Ms. Harper and Mr. Mason. You are most definitely in danger. I am sure your snooping has led you to some conclusion that you and the reporter Dennis Jones were fumbling down the same trail. Dennis Jones is dead. I can further assure you that charming smile and affable wiles will not work on me as they apparently did Detective Connolly in Florida. I *will* put you in jail," Detective Nixon warned. "Moreover, I will escort you to the South Carolina border and expel you from our state. Make you their problem and you can explain to your bosses why you cannot complete their project in Carolina Beach."

Kate shot Nick a glance. Nick looked like his mind was in the distance, waiting for a wave to roll in. He sat still, emotionless and dutifully taking the lashing that Kate had earned for them.

"I understand, Detective Nixon," Kate nodded.

"Somehow, I doubt you do. I'll have these waiting for you," Nixon slammed a pair of handcuffs down on her desk. Her eyes darted from Kate to Nick. "Now, is there anything else you think I should know about *my* case?"

Kate shuffled her fingers in front of her as she sorted through the case, "Thomas Hauer may have a stronger connection to Sophia Hayes than anyone truly understands. Robert Grant was the clear winner in Collin Royce's disappearance…death. The Hayes family is in serious financial trouble with Sheffield Hayes, at the heart of their problems. Sophia Hayes, well, she has a boatload of problems, likely stemming from trauma from *whatever* happened ten years ago. Andrew Ayres seems a bit unhinged when it comes to this case."

Glancing at Nick, he offered a contrite nod, "I think that pretty much sums it up."

Detective Nixon slid deep into her seat staring at Kate and Nick. "Wow, you have been busier than I thought. Maybe I should just put you in cuffs now and save myself a trip," the detective said.

Nick gave a shrug, indicating the detective might be right, promptly receiving a kick in the shin from Kate.

"Look, I get it. This is dangerous, serious stuff. My curiosity was piqued when I found a body in the walls of my company's beach house. You have the case well in hand, and I trust you will get to the bottom of it very quickly and in turn, keep us all safe," Kate said in a single breath.

The detective looked pleased with Kate's assurance.

"I am glad we have an understanding," Detective Nixon swiped the handcuffs off her desk and put them back in her pocket. Pointing toward the door, she said, "You two are free to go. I mean what I said."

Kate and Nick nodded as they got up from their seats. Nick held the door for Kate to walk through. Heading out of the police station, they passed by the box of Britt's donuts which was already nearly empty.

An officer reached in to grab the last donut.

"I wouldn't do that, if I were you," Nick said.

The officer's hand froze, hovering over the maple bacon donut. A curious look at Nick was replaced by a horrified expression when he saw Detective Nixon emerge from her office. The officer quickly pulled his hand away. "I'm good anyway," he wrinkled his nose and backed away from the donut box.

Kate and Nick walked out into the parking lot, heads low after the tongue-lashing they received from the police detective.

"I'm sorry I got you into all that," Kate said.

Nick offered a friendly nod of acceptance, "Well, I guess it's back to work."

"You know, I'm thinking maybe we need a day to regroup," Kate said. "The company has pushed the opening of the beach house off by a whole month. Our schedule is open. We can really concentrate on making it something special. I think we need to experience this area, get the feel for it and then pour it all back into the beach house. What do you say?"

"Okay. I think a refresh from corpses and murder suspects is a great idea. What are you thinking?" Nick asked.

Kate pursed her lips standing outside her driver's door, "How about a day at the beach?"

"Up for surf lesson number two?" Nick asked.

Surprising him, Kate nodded, "Sure, why not?"

Nick laughed, "The surf here on the Atlantic is a little more intense than the shallow Gulf."

Kate looked nervous.

"In many ways, it will actually make it easier. The crashes just can be a bit more spectacular, too," Nick smiled.

With a wary nod, Kate wondered what she had just agreed to as she started her SUV.

Kate followed Nick into the water. Carrying their boards over the breakers, they launched themselves onto their boards, belly-first as they passed the whitewater. Racing the incoming set to reach the swells, they stroked through the water arm over arm. The powerful Atlantic was relentlessly trying to push them backward. Nick reached out, tipping the nose of Kate's board under a wave reminding her to duck dive to avoid being washed back to the beach.

Reaching the rolling swells, they popped up on their boards, legs dangling in the water as they caught their breath. Kate scanned the ocean, vigilant on incoming sets and a natural wariness of creatures they shared the water with.

Taking a deep breath, Kate smiled at Nick, "I forgot how much I loved this part, right here."

"The swells are like a hammock for surfers. A place to relax, rest, hang out…" Nick grinned.

Seeing Kate out of her business attire and on the beach, an innocent, joyful gleam in her eyes, her wet hair hanging over her shoulder, it was a look that Nick thought suited her well.

As their boards rolled up and down with each of the swells passed under them, the ocean became hypnotically relaxing. Nick didn't rush Kate into a ride. He allowed her to completely decompress at the Atlantic's soothing hand.

Nick's eyes drifted to the beach. They entered the water just behind the bungalows, where the waves curled nicely for late morning rides. Just a short walk down the sandy beach was the beach house. His mind suddenly recalled an element of their first night at the beach house. When he opened up the wall, there was sand in the bottom in between the studs. He had to clean it up when forensics let them back in to go back to work.

Imagination drawn in, Nick was transported to the night Collin Royce was killed. Starting at his body being dumped in the wall, he could envision sand cascading to the floor off Royce's sand encrusted body. He was pulled through the house and through the backdoor as Royce was carried under the cover of darkness and according to reports a thunderstorm.

Staring blankly at the beach as his mind played movie projector, he could see Royce dragged up the beach to the beach house after he had been shot. Royce had likely been killed within a couple hundred yards of the beach house on the beach.

"Are you okay? Hello, Nick!" Kate called, placing a hand on his shoulder as they floated atop the swells.

"What? Oh, yeah. Just spacing out. Destressing after everything," Nick said, feeling sheepish that this was Kate's time to clear her head and get away from murders and pools of unscrupulous suspects. Glancing out at an oncoming set, he asked, "Ready for a ride?"

Kate gulped nervously, "Uhm… sure?"

"Come on. You'll be fine. Remember what I taught you, get ahead of the crest, relax your knees, back heel down if you need to pivot and adjust your nose. I'll see you in the wash," Nick said.

Reaching out, he gave Kate's board a little push as she slid to her belly and began paddling. Nick scrambled to catch up, angling to give them a safe distance. Hopping up, he looked over and watched Kate. She didn't look comfortable, but she was up on her board and atop the wave.

Arms wide, knees bent, Kate allowed the ocean to carry her. Like a hand underneath her board scooting her toward the shore, she enjoyed the ride. Watching the shore come closer, the board lost power and sank into the frothy whitewater. Hopping off before she was rudely forced off, she stood waist deep holding her board.

Nick was close behind, pressing his heel. He spun to face the incoming waves as he hopped off. "You did great!"

"Like riding a bike… with no seat, no handles and the power of an ocean trying to kick me off or slam me down," Kate said.

"You make it sound like the rodeo. White knuckles, fighting to stay on top for eight seconds…" Nick laughed. "It shouldn't be a struggle, it should be a dance. The ocean is your partner, and yes, it likes to lead. Feel where it wants you to go, guiding your feet, telling you where to point your board."

Kate looked at Nick, "That is a rather romantic way to look at it."

"It's the love of the ocean. She's a fickle mistress, though. I'll tell you that," Nick said. "These waves are good. They have a nice push to them, not a violent break. A little more power than what we rode on the Gulf coast of Florida."

"I felt that. Made me a little nervous," Kate admitted, pulling her wet hair back over her shoulders.

"You just have to get a feel for where the Atlantic wants to take you today," Nick said.

Kate nodded and with a jump over the breakwater, she leaped back onto her board to paddle out toward the swells.

Nick watched her for a moment. He appreciated her vigor to turn around and try the ocean's hand one more time.

After several rides, Kate and Nick again found themselves standing in the froth. "That was a wild one," Kate exclaimed.

"Yeah, you were a little ahead of the wave's power zone. It decided to break on you," Nick said. "You all right?"

"I'm fine," Kate said. "I'm getting kind of hungry, though."

Nick laughed, "Surfing will do that to you."

"Set our boards back by the bungalows and head to the boardwalk?" Kate asked.

"Sounds good, but I have a better idea," Nick said, tucking his surfboard under his arm and lugging it out of the water.

Boards secured, Kate and Nick sauntered through the warm, white sand.

"It's so nice out here," Kate breathed.

Nick studied her for a moment. It was the first time since they arrived that Kate could fully appreciate the beauty and serenity of the beach town. Despite heading into the heart of activity along the boardwalk, the Carolina Beach strand was relaxing as the coastal breeze brushed by. The waves crashed along the shore providing a soundtrack for them as they walked.

Despite their appetites, Kate and Nick weren't in too much of a hurry. Enjoying the moment was all they needed in that tiny respite of time.

Leisurely pace or not, they found themselves at the beach front restaurant on the boardwalk. Seeing a couple leave their beachside table, they were in luck.

"As soon as we clean that table up, you can sit there," the hostess smiled. "Can we get you anything while you wait?"

"A water would be great!" Kate gasped. Exercise, salt water, sand and breezy heat had her parched.

"Make that two," Nick said.

By the time they had drinks in hand, they were escorted to their table. A waitress was already waiting with a pitcher of ice water to refill their nearly empty glasses.

"Playing in the water, huh?" the waitress smiled.

Their salt and sand caked skin, water and breeze sculpted hair and Kate's flowy swimsuit kimono were more than sufficient clues.

"Yes, and I am starving!" Kate said.

"Well, you came to the right place. You can check out the menus, but after playtime on the beach, I recommend the steam pot, that is if you don't mind working a little for your food," the waitress said.

Kate looked at Nick.

"Seafood boil. Shrimp, corn on the cob, potatoes, usually with other fish or shellfish," Nick said.

"That's right. We toss in some crab legs and clams. Mix in a good heap of Old Bay…" the waitress said.

"Let's do it," Kate nodded.

"Steam pot for two coming up. I'll bring y'all some bread in the meantime. Good to soak up what's left," the waitress said as she walked away with the order.

"Always an adventure with you," Kate said.

Nick smiled, "If we're going to try it, beach clothes instead of work clothes are the way to go."

"How do we live such similar lives yet tackle them so differently?" Kate asked.

"What do you mean?" Nick slanted his brows.

Kate drained her second glass of water, "We visit a variety of coastal towns. You jump into a pair of shorts and hit the water. I find a fitting sun dress and a spot overlooking the water. You find the novel food that epitomizes the area, whatever that may be, and wash it down with a locally brewed concoction. I order a pinot grigio and a salad, fairly consistently. You have taught me a lot about rolling up my sleeves and diving in."

"I'd rather be in it than just watching it. The beach is beautiful, but you become connected with it when your toes are in the sand. The ocean is magnificent, but to feel it embrace you, wrapping around you and moving you, it is an experience, not just a postcard," Nick said.

Kate's face fell, "I have been living a postcard life."

"And that's okay, for some. At least you were there. At least you drank in the views and the culture. Those pictures imprint in your head like photographs. Me, I just happen to have tactile feelings, adventures and a few scars to go with my photographs," Nick said.

"I really need to talk to our marketing team about bringing you on to write our descriptions," Kate said.

"I'm good being the handyman. I'd rather be swinging the hammer than tapping at a keyboard," Nick said.

Kate studied the man across the table from her. Wise, yet childish. Adventurous, yet cautious. Renaissanced, yet rough around the edges. She struggled to completely figure him out. But then, she thought, maybe he was like the ocean. You didn't figure it out, you flowed with it. Like a dance partner.

Her thoughts were broken up when a large metal pot was set in front of them. Kate gave it a curious look.

From across the table, Nick grinned, "You just dive in. Know you're going to get a little messy, but that's why they give you a roll of paper towels."

"I'll bring some lemon water for you as well," the waitress said. Giving Kate a knowing glance, she said, "It will clean your fingers good as new when you're all done."

Following suit, Kate began pulling morsels from the metal pot. "This is really good. Juicy, but good."

"Food can be tasty and fun," Nick said, adeptly cracking into his shellfish.

"And work," Kate said, fighting with her crab leg. All at once, it gave way, a splash of juice hitting Kate in the face making her wince.

Nick reached across the table and dabbed at it with a napkin. Softly, he brought the napkin across her skin. The act was reactionary. It was only when he was mid-swipe that he realized he was crossing a boundary. "I'm sorry, I just…"

"It's okay. I appreciate the attempt," Kate said.

For a moment, they looked at one another. No criminals to chase. No looking over their shoulders. Just a moment where they could sit beside the ocean and relax together.

Lunch turned into a leisurely walk along the boardwalk which folded into early evening fishing behind the bungalows. Catching enough fish for dinner, Nick taught Kate how to fillet as he prepared the rest of the meal.

The pleasant evening eased into a nightcap along the bungalow deck rails.

Glasses of wine in hand, they watched as the moon sprinkled silvery light on the Atlantic Ocean. The froth glowed white as it reached its fingers onto the sand. The calm coastal swells fell into a rhythm gently singing a lullaby to the slightly sunburnt pair silently taking in the view.

"This was a nearly perfect day," Kate said. Holding her glass up to Nick. "Thank you."

"Near perfect?" Nick scoffed, turning to Kate.

"There's always room for something even more special, isn't there?" Kate breathed, yet her lungs burned as though she were holding her breath.

Their eyes locked. Nick's voice was soft, "I can only think of one thing that would make the day any better."

Kate's knees wobbled. They inched close enough that their wine-soaked breath mingled drawing them even closer. They could feel the sunbaked skin of the other radiate onto their own. Their lips tingled with electricity as they neared one another.

Kate closed her eyes and swallowed hard, "Nick… we should… I should go in for the night."

Pulling away, Kate felt as though she were defying herself with the movement. So much of her ached to close the minute gap between them. To once again feel his lips on hers, the idea made her chest swell. Somewhere in the back of her head, the panic button had been pressed and the rest of her reluctantly heeded its call.

She felt like she was in slow motion as she straightened, realizing she had been leaning in. Nick's eyes were a mix of confusion and hope and passion pressing against an imaginary gate.

"I'm sorry. It has been a long, wonderful day. I think the sun and the wine and the time just hit me," Kate said. She knew it wasn't the only thing that had suddenly hit her, but it wasn't the rationale she thought prudent to share.

"I understand, of course. I'm beat, too," Nick nodded cordially.

Kate smiled. Always the gentleman, she thought to herself. "Well, good night, Nick. Thank you, again. For everything."

Turning, Kate walked away. Her eyes were willing her to turn back toward Nick. Her steps were slow as she accepted her reluctance to call the evening to a close. Her heart screamed for her to stop moving. In almost a daze, she trudged dutifully forward until she reached her bungalow. Turning back, she saw Nick abruptly move his gaze to the ocean. With a deep sigh, Kate opened her door and slipped inside.

After a much-needed shower, Kate flopped into bed. She left the curtains and window open allowing the coastal breeze and crashing waves to caress her asleep. Exhausted, she thought she would be overcome by sleep.

It was a *near* perfect day. She thought to herself, she might have deterred the one thing that would have made it perfect.

Closing her eyes, she listened to the ocean. Slowly, her pounding heart fell into its rhythm. Matched like they were in a shared embrace, she fell into a deep sleep.

Twenty Seven

Kate woke with a start. The light coming into her room nearly yanked her out of bed. Glancing at her watch, she realized she had slept in longer than any of the days since she had arrived on Carolina Beach. It wasn't late by any traditional standard, but for Kate, it was unusual.

Sitting on the bed, staring out at the ocean. Her mind reeled. From the fantastic day that she had enjoyed to the abrupt departure when she left Nick standing along the rail overlooking the beach by himself, her mind cataloged the events.

She tried to think about her work to-do list, but was overcome by competing thoughts. Kate almost felt guilty as her mind reeled. She had promised to allow the police to take over the investigation, but the questions of the photos kept popping into her head. Her eyes widened. Along with the plutonic stances of Collin and Sophia, Thomas Hauer lurking in the background had been nagging at her.

Instead of stewing while tossing and turning, she climbed out of bed. Grabbing her notepad, wrapped in a sarong, she sat in a chaise lounge facing the ocean. The surfboard missing from beside his bungalow door and the sound of heavier surf told her where Nick was. A glance down the beach to where the waves consistently rolled, was a figure "dancing with the ocean" letting it lead them on smooth rides to shore. Hopping off one wave, the figure would promptly turn and paddle out to do it all over again.

Flipping her pad to a fresh page, she dictated softly to herself, "What was the story between Hauer and Sophia? What happened to the offer between Hauer and Royce and the seed money?"

Moving to a clean page, she wrote notes on the more recent events. "How did Hauer learn about the Hayes' most recent project? Clearly, Sophia and her saucy libation moments were the likely source. What happened there? Was there more to the modern Sophia and Thomas Hauer story?"

Looking to the ocean as if the answers would roll in with one of the persistent sets of waves it brought to shore, Kate tapped her lip. Thinking about how to learn more about Thomas Hauer, she got up from her seat on the chaise lounge. The bounce returned to her step. Walking away from the case, even for an afternoon gave her mind time to process. Now it was time for answers.

As she neared her bungalow, she ran into Nick. Saltwater glistened on his bare shoulders despite the beach towel that hung around his neck.

"Good morning, Nick," Kate said. She couldn't help but feel like a child handing in a report card she had signed herself.

"Morning, Kate! It was pretty good out there," Nick said setting his board down.

"Looked like it," Kate nodded. "Listen, I've got a couple of errands to run if you don't mind getting started on the house."

"No. I don't mind," Nick said. His mind, too, had wandered. He had his own epiphany that he wasn't ready to share with Kate, though the idea did crease his lips into a grin.

Nick watched as Kate disappeared into her bungalow. He adjusted his board ensuring it was stowed properly and hurriedly showered himself.

The beach house had become less of a work project and more of a challenging puzzle that they returned to as inspiration struck. They would tweak a piece, and another element would develop that halted their progress while another would once again spark an idea.

In the excitement of being dressed down by Nixon, Nick recalled other subtle elements that seemed out of sorts after the break in. He still fumed that the reporter's calling them out to talk at the same time was a bit too coincidental for his taste.

Setting his tools down, Nick repeated the process of searching the house the way he had the night of the break-in. Only this time, he took his time, combing through each room to see the nagging thoughts he had in his head were subtle observations. Vent covers were slightly askew. Molding protruding just perceptibly from the wall. Overlapping cabinet doors misaligned so that they didn't close properly.

Whoever broke into the beach house was looking for something. The discovery of Kate's crime wall was just a convenient happenstance.

Nick scanned the house with a knowing grin. He was on a treasure hunt!

Grabbing his tools, Nick worked the house over. Moving quickly, he wanted to find whatever there was to find before Kate returned. He also needed to get the remodel back on schedule to at least show Kate some progress.

Using a claw hammer and an array of pry bars, Nick scoured the house. With each vent, he removed the cover. Using a handheld otoscope, he peered into each hose, tube, conduit and duct. Carefully popping the molding as the paint crews had already finished their work, Nick searched for even a single sheet of paper that might be stowed behind them or slipped between the drywall.

At each cabinet, he removed the backing to see if anything had been stored behind them. Moving to the major appliances, he kicked himself for not tackling the obvious first. Walking the oven range from its perch nestled tight in the kitchen cabinetry, he shined a light behind it. His shoulder slumped when, other than needing a good cleaning, nothing pertinent was revealed.

Twirling the hammer in his hand, Nick thought about what he might have missed.
"These guys like drywall. Maybe if it's as thin as a piece of paper, I mean that is all a treasure map is…" he considered.

Using a high-tech laser grid, he set it up, shining against every wall. Tiny imperfections would show up as the grid lines would have a hiccup in their even lines. Smoothing his hands over the imperfections he found, he ruled as nothing more than a thicker layer of mudding tape connecting sections of drywall.

Hands on his hips, Nick sighed. Turning in a tight circle, he considered what he might have missed. With inspiration, he muttered to himself, "If I was just a renter, maybe I'd hide a treasure map on the outside of the house. That way I'd have access to it even after my stay was over."

Excited by his new revelation, Nick moved to the outside of the house. Looking for loose pieces of siding, uncapped pipes and even wobbly stepping stones, he came up empty other than finding a few wasp nests that he needed to take care of.

Circling the exterior of the beach house, he pulled out the electrical boxes, an easy place to stow items. Each potential hiding nook came up empty. Repeating the process with the light fixtures, he again found nothing, though it did allow him to address a poorly connected wire in the back patio lights.

The last item he could think of to check was the ornamental sign on the front of the beach house. Setting up a ladder, he scrambled up and carefully removed the sign, inspecting the back of it for an envelope, a letter, a disc–anything. He chuckled as he did find the sign was autographed by the original family who had the house built. It had been painted over several times but the back was left intact with a layer of clear epoxy securing the names for generations. Pulling out his phone, Nick took a quick picture of it to share with Kate.

Putting the sign back, Nick sat atop the ladder, his mind trying to think of anything he might have missed. Before he could think of anything, his phone buzzed. He was suddenly aware of how much time he'd spent on his search. Seeing Kate's name pop up on his screen made his heart race. Other than making a mess, he hadn't accomplished anything on their to-do list.

"Hello…" Nick called meekly into the phone.

Kate recalled when she and Nick were getting the lay of the land and learning more about the Hayes family and their country club, that rival Thomas Hauer's club also held the Cape Fear Golf Museum. In fact, the two courses were in a heated battle at the time pitting their family's money and political favor. A battle that Thomas Hauer had evidently won.

Pulling her SUV into the Hauer Country Club drive, she found the landscape and architecture reminiscent of the Hayes' club. They were so similar, Kate thought that they could be related, almost like cousins. Deep family resemblance with nuances of difference.

Hauer's effort was a bit more ostentatious. The balls of the entry posts were capped with gold. Filigree adorned the entrance columns. The stairs took a different shape, and the buildings were painted in different, creamier shades of white, otherwise they filled a similar footprint and a similar modernized old Southern manor look and feel.

Refusing the insistent calls for her to use the valet, Kate felt better with her transportation under her control. Pulling into a space, she headed into the golf resort.

An expanded wing of the country club held the Cape Fear Golf Museum. Dedicated to the region's evolution of golf, golf courses, tournaments and golf celebrities that called the Wilmington area home, if only for a weekend.

The hall leading to the museum was lined with photographs. Thomas Hauer found himself in nearly every one. Standing alongside politicians, movie stars, golfers… anyone with a name and a recognizable face that Hauer could glean stock and status from.

Passing by the photos, Kate mused that it wasn't that Thomas Hauer's face wasn't attractive. The man exuded confidence. When he spoke, he even had an affable charm to him. What struck Kate was the almost desperate pleas for recognition.

The story unfolded further in the golf museum as each of the area's public and private courses were featured. The sections paralleling the Hayes and Hauer courses painted a clear picture for Kate. Thomas Hauer didn't seek to put forth original ideas, but he was happy to study and recreate -with his own flourishes, someone else's plan. For Kate, Thomas' sudden rise in the golf world following the Hayes' entry onto the world stage was almost more about belonging than competing.

"Interested in the history of golf, ma'am?" a soft-spoken voice called over Kate's shoulder.

Turning, Kate saw a man that would have fit well in a Mark Twain novel. The man's snowy white hair was complemented by a beard tapered into a V-shape. His warm, thick southern accent dripped Cape Fear authenticity a century or two in the making.

Kate shuffled, "More for my guests, I suppose. My company caters to those who might like golf very much."

"I see," the man rocked back and forth on his heels as he grasped at red suspenders that covered his blue and white striped shirt. "You are looking at two of the finest. Those two courses helped revolutionize professional golf tournaments in our corner of North Carolina."

"They are pretty important to golf here?" Kate asked. "Is there room for two courses at this stage in Wilmington?"

The man chuckled, "In a word… no. It depends on what you are after. The hard core golf enthusiasts rather prefer the Hayes course. Those wanting more of a splashy backdrop, well, you are on the right property."

Kate considered the man's words, "The Hauer course isn't considered a tournament course?"

"More of a pro-am. The type of tournament where celebrities are paired with a pro to play a round. A great media spectacle to be sure," the man said.

"But not quite to the level of the pro-tournaments at Hayes," Kate said.

"You could look at it that way. With the right changes in course design and tour endorsement, Hauer could well rise to the main stage," the man nodded. "Let me get you some brochures for your clients. They outline every course in the region as well as discounted admission to the museum."

"Thank you," Kate nodded, stuffing the brochures into her bag.

The museum steward raised a finger as he nodded toward the hallway, "There's Mr. Hauer there."

Kate turned her gaze toward where the man was pointing. Kate saw Thomas Hauer with several other men. In the midst of them, one seemed to have their attention centered on them. Kate looked at the man and then at a photo on the wall. "Is that…?"

"Bruce Montgomery. Expected to be in the running for the PGA championship this year," the steward said.

"The kind of catalyst that could raise a course's stock?" Kate asked.

"The very kind," the man said, taking in the action alongside.

"Mr…" Kate started.

"Hughes. Jamison Hughes, at your service," the museum steward beamed.

"Mr. Hughes, it has been a pleasure. Thank you," Kate said. Her attention was drawn toward the hallway.

She wandered slowly, her ears soaking in the conversation.

"With your presence and your thoughts on course redesign, we *will* have the future home of Wilmington PGA tournaments. I assure you, Bruce," Thomas said, leading the entourage.

"What about Hayes? In truth, it was their course that led me to Wilmington," the professional golfer said.

"And this region will be forever indebted to the Hayes family for shining a light on southeastern North Carolina golf, but Hauer Course and Country Club is in a position to lead into the future," Hauer said.

"I like your confidence, Thomas. How can you be so sure?" the golf star asked.

Thomas stopped the procession to address the group directly, "Their last project overruns have crippled them economically. They can't afford growth. They can't even afford course alterations. Other than moving the flag, you'll be running the exact same course next year and for years to come."

"And you can handle the course changes my team and I would recommend?" the golfer asked.

"Resources are not a problem for us, Bruce," Thomas said. "Besides, when you beat Grant in the rankings, the timing will be perfect to launch forward with the new PGA tournament home for Wilmington, right here at Hauer Golf and Country Club."

"Grant's still popular," Bruce Montgomery argued.

Hauer flashed a wicked grin, "When I win the lawsuit on the new property, that will be the proverbial straw on the camel's back. Grant and anyone else attached to Hayes Golf Resorts will be a joke. He'll be forgotten about as quickly as Collin Royce was. He had an opportunity that he passed on to work with us. Look how that turned out."

Hauer stopped. He was suddenly aware of the guest at the intersection of his office suite and the corridor leading to the museum. Offering a cocky smile toward Kate, he placed a hand on Bruce Montgomery's arm, steering him into the offices and out of incidental earshot.

Kate watched as the door shut.

As Kate listened to Hauer's voice, she knew that was who Mark and Sheffield Hayes were arguing with the day she was caught snooping in their executive suite.

Listening to his comments about Collin Royce sent a shiver down her spine.

Twenty Eight

Kate made her way to the country club parking lot. As soon as she saw her SUV, she knew something was wrong. The driver's side front corner listed slightly. Walking up, she realized very quickly why.

Her tire was nearly completely flat. A note printed in block letters read BACK OFF OR YOU WILL BE NEXT.

Whirling around the parking lot, Kate looked for anyone walking away from the scene or lurking nearby. Aside from an older gentleman stowing his clubs in the trunk of his Mercedes after an early round, she found no one.

With a sigh, she glanced at her watch. She knew if she was that much delayed, Nick was going to worry, especially after the break-in.

"I'll be right there. Go inside the country club or the museum. I'll come find you," Nick said over the phone.

Kate considered Nick's suggestion. Looking at her tire, she was both frustrated and determined not to be made to feel weak and frightened. Instead, she took a cloth used for cleaning her laptop screen from her bag. Pulling her floor mat out from the driver's footwell, she tossed it on the ground. Kneeling, searched the side of the tire, finding a pair of puncture marks.

Opening her trunk, she sighed when she pulled up the carpeted mat to find no spare. Instead, tucked on the side of the trunk wall was an air compressor and sealant. Scanning the directions, she sprayed the sealant into her tire, and then plugging in the air compressor, she proceeded to refill the tire.

Nick arrived, the engine on his pickup truck growling as he wheeled through the parking lot.

Coming to a stop in front of Kate's SUV, he scowled. Climbing out of the truck, he swung the door shut. "I thought you were going to wait inside!" Nick cursed.

"No, you suggested that I wait inside. I decided to fix my tire," Kate said. Eyeing the patch warily, she added, "If temporarily."

"Kate… you received a threat," Nick protested.

"He's right," a voice called from behind Nick.

Detective Nixon circled around the pair as Kate stood up. Smoothing out her dress, Kate picked up her floor mat and tossed it back in her car.

The detective looked at Kate with a new appreciation, "Maybe not so much the damsel in distress after all."

"Detective Nixon, what are you doing here?" Kate asked.

"Mr. Mason called me. He said something about vandalism and a threatening note," Nixon said. "The more pertinent question is, what are *you* doing here?"

"Big golf fan. Big, big golf fan," Kate said.

Detective Nixon did not look amused, "I'll take this threat seriously, but in return, I need you to, Ms. Harper."

Kate nodded, "I came to the golf museum. I wanted to learn more about golf in the area."

Digging into her bag, she produced the pack of brochures given to her by the museum steward.

"Who did you speak to while here? You seem to have a habit of annoying people," the detective asked. "Maybe a disgruntled valet?"

"Just the steward. I mean, Thomas Hauer saw me as he was having a rather interesting conversation with golfer Bruce Montgomery. He didn't seem happy to see me," Kate shrugged.

"I'll go in and speak to Hauer. I'll see if I can get copies of the security camera footage," Detective Nixon said. "We have photos of the exterior punctures. I would like to get shots of the inside of the tire as well with measurements."

"I will ask for that at the tire shop," Kate said. With her fingers wrapped in the cloth, she handed over a small piece of paper, "Here's the note. Also untouched."

The detective received the items and placed them in a baggie.

Looking at Nick, Detective Nixon said, "Why don't you follow her to a tire shop? Those patches don't always hold forever and I don't need to hear a report of a blowout causing more injuries."

Nick nodded.

Walking toward the country club, Nixon paused. Her shoulders slumped as she spun on her heel to face Kate. Her eyes matched her pained voice, "So, what did you hear that was so interesting?"

Kate relayed the conversation she overheard about attempting to sign Bruce Montgomery, Hauer wanting to displace the Hayes family and his callousness about Collin Royce.

"He said Robert Grant and anyone attached to Hayes Golf Resorts would be forgotten about as quickly as Collin Royce was. He said, 'had an opportunity that he passed on to work with Hauer. Look how that turned out,'" Kate shared with the detective.

Detective Nixon looked at Kate after scribbling notes into a pad. Without her expression revealing the tiniest detail of what she felt about the information, she asked, "Anything else?"

Kate's head tilted slightly, expecting more of a response, "No. I think that's pretty much it."

Without as much as a nod, Detective Nixon turned and headed toward the country club.

Kate and Nick looked at each other. With a shrug, Kate said, "I guess we're done here."

Nick watched Kate pace back and forth outside the tire shop. She looked more angry than anything. Chuckling to himself, Nick thought whoever pinned that note to her car tire had only increased her resolve to see the investigation through.

"Unhappy valet?" Kate fumed as she reached the edge of the sidewalk she had to roam. "That was a joke, right?"

Nick looked at Kate, determining whether that was a rhetorical question or not.

"Detective Nixon is mocking me, now," Kate said.

"I think she was starting at a baseline and working her way toward the truth," Nick tried to reason.

Kate calmed long enough for Nick to attempt a rational conversation. "Who do you think it was? Hauer?" he asked.

"Maybe. I mean, I was at *his* country club overhearing *his* conversation," Kate said.

"Pretty quick work to get to your car like that," Nick said.

Kate shrugged, "A quick phone call to his staff. Security... he could. I mean, who else?"

"I don't know," Nick shook his head. "Someone from Hayes? That shifty reporter?"

"Sophia?" Kate asked.

"Not protecting her by any means, but I think you're giving her too much credit," Nick said.

Kate crossed her arms, a testament to the strength of women, regardless of their petite stature.

"Right," Nick acknowledged.

"I mean, she'd have to be sober for long enough," Kate said, her voice dripping with a tone that left Nick trying to ascertain where she was coming from.

"What do you make of Hauer's conversation?" Nick asked, shifting the conversation.

"His callous stance on Collin Royce is pretty telling. He doesn't seem to have a lot of remorse over his loss, especially given the recent developments," Kate said.

"It has been a while," Nick said.

"And his body was just found at a beach house miles from the golf courses. He and Sheffield Hayes were two of the last people to have a conversation with him. In fact, arguing with him," Kate said.

Nick nodded, adding, "Hauer doesn't seem to have any love lost for the Hayeses either."

"It's weird. Kind of an appreciation with a strong desire to put them out of business. One up them at every turn, at the very least," Kate said. "His resort, his business model, is almost a copy of Hayes, just with a bit of embellishment. He is convinced he is going to win the lawsuit between their companies on the new investment property."

"I'm not sure what that means other than there is a lot going on between the two families. Plenty of reasons for murder and mayhem," Nick said.

Kate nodded, looking out at the horizon as she waited for her tire to be replaced.

Twenty Nine

After the excitement of Hauer's country club and emergency tire repairs, pulling into the beach house felt like coming home. Kate was excited to take a moment with the sweeping Atlantic views and allow the ocean's song to help her sort out her massive battery of thoughts.

Nick pulled in after her, a sinking feeling in the pit of his stomach as he hopped out of the truck and watched Kate ascend the steps. Jogging up after her, he had just reached the landing when Kate sprung the door open.

At first, when she walked into the house, her eyes were drawn to the now direct line views to the ocean. After setting her bag down on the kitchen island, her brain began to translate the out of place items strewn throughout the house. Molding pulled from every wall, electrical outlets and switch plates missing, drawers pulled out and stacked a top the counters made Kate do a pirouette taking it all in.

"What... uh, what is happening here?" Kate asked as her eyes swept the room.

Nick squirmed, his eyes following hers as they cataloged the out of place items, "I was trying to get done before you got back, but when you called..."

"Get what done? Tear the beach house apart? Do we have termites? Mold? Tell me we don't have mold," Kate said.

"No, nothing like that," Nick said. "The night of the break-in, I noticed that it wasn't just your crime wall that was disturbed, but I couldn't quite put my finger on it. Then as I was working, I realized little things had been pulled and put back. Things screwed back in place a bit crooked like they were done in haste, like air conditioner registers, the faces on the plugs and switches. Anyway, it seemed like someone was searching for something. Something small and thin that could be folded, slipped or stuffed in a relatively small space, so it dawned on me that I search. Maybe I could be more thorough than a burglar in a rush."

"You didn't tell me?" Kate asked, almost sounding offended.

"I wanted to test the theory. Surprise you if I found anything," Nick offered a sheepish shrug.

"Did you?" Kate asked.

Nick's head fell, "No."

"What were you hoping to find?" Kate asked.

Nick broke into a grin "A... treasure map?"

Kate shook her head. She couldn't help but smile at Nick's boyishness. With a slight frown, she said, "You were about to win points if you said 'clues'."

"Yeah, that probably would have sounded better. Not that clues aren't important, but, come on, a treasure map?" Nick's eyes were wide.

"Well, we need to get this stuff put back in place. We have new appliances being delivered this afternoon." Looking at Nick who seemed a bit dejected, she asked, "Were you done?"

"I don't know. I was pretty thorough…" Nick said.

"What can I do to help?" Kate said, eyeing Nick's toolbox.

His childlike grin returned, "Order lunch?"

"Fine," Kate nodded. "I'll order lunch."

Kate wandered the house, taking note of the remaining projects. Landing in the spare bedroom where her crime wall was in tatters, she got a trash bag and began cleaning it up.

She was grateful that her laptop wasn't left in there for the intruder to destroy or take. Though everything was backed up, it was a hassle she did not want to have to deal with.

As she put the final piece of torn note and photograph in the trash, her mind wandered. She couldn't help but wonder if tearing down the wall was a warning, a distraction or deleting a thread that she was closing in on. A thread that could indicate who the murderer of Collin Royce, Dennis Jones or both was.

With a burst of inspiration, Kate moved her operation to the master bedroom. Clicking on the light in the large master closet, she opened her laptop and began reprinting out everything she had found about the case and the people surrounding it.

Piece by piece, she rebuilt her crime wall in the somewhat hidden confines of the master bedroom walk-in closet. This time, she had additional knowledge on the case serving her as she assembled the large link chart of victims, suspects and articles that tied them together.

Using thin strips of painter's tape, she began making lines between the gallery of subjects. Using sticky notes and a red marker, she highlighted facts that she and Nick had garnered along the way. Stepping back, she looked at the complicated construct she had made of the closet wall.

Shaking her head, Kate mumbled to herself, "One thing's for sure, there were a lot of people between the Hauers and the Hayeses that stood to lose or gain a lot from Collin Royce's murder."

Her eyes landed on the deceased reporter, Dennis Jones. "The question was, who wanted him dead? What did he know that had someone move the target to his back?"

"And is now placing the target on *your* back?" Nick asked.

Kate jumped in the air, her heart pounding as she whirled to face Nick.

"I'm sorry to startle you. The appliance guys are here. I thought you might want to inspect everything," Nick said. Stepping into the closet, he leaned closer to Kate's wall, "So this is where you disappeared to."

Kate glanced at her watch having no idea how long she had been in the master bedroom closet. Her eyes went wide, "Lunch! Nick, I am so sorry. I'll get something right now."

"Don't worry about it. You check with the appliance guys, I'll run down to the Island Grill. I've been wanting to try their honey Siracha shrimp," Nick offered.

"Sounds good. Thank you, Nick," Kate said, pulling herself away from her crime wall.

"No problem," Nick said. As they bound down the steps, he said, "I think this version is tighter. We've learned a lot since we started."

"I don't want to put anything positive on the break-in, but maybe they did us a favor," Kate said.

Nick cast a glance at Kate, "I don't think I'd give them any credit. You would figure things out anyway."

"Everything but lunch," Kate blushed.

"Laser focused. No harm," Nick smiled.

Kate nodded as Nick walked out the door. Staring out after him, she could hear him greeting the delivery crew.

By the time the old appliances had been carted out and the new ones inspected to Kate's liking, Nick had arrived holding up two bags of food gripped in one hand and a beverage tray in the other.

"Honey Siracha shrimp," he called. "How are the appliances?"

"I think they are going to work great," Kate said. "I was afraid of how the new refrigerator would fit, but the delivery guys didn't think it would be a problem."

Nick nodded as he followed Kate to the balcony overlooking the beach, "I was prepared to have to do a little retrofitting."

Sitting at the outdoor table, they sat close together maximizing the little bit of shadow provided by the umbrella that protruded from the center of the table.

Opening her to-go box, Kate let the coastal breeze waft the sweet-spicy blend tease her senses. Her stomach growled. Instinctively, she clapped a hand on her stomach and shot Nick a sheepish look.

"I guess forgetting lunch is taking its toll," Kate looked at the container of shrimp and brown rice in front of her. "You saved the day again."

Nick grinned, "I can do food."

"Yes, you can. I am awaiting your list for the guest book on great Wilmington area beaches food stops," Kate said.

"Another couple of weeks, and I'll have my full recommendations," Nick said.

"Nothing better than fish caught fresh off the beach, though," Kate laughed.

"Nothing better," Nick agreed.

Kate eagerly dug into her food. Normally opposed to sauces painting her lips and fingers, she gave in. Either out of hunger or the allure of the delicate hot pepper and sweet honey note, she didn't care. As her stomach growled again, it was survival.

Glad that Nick was busily squeezing the tails of shrimp to pop the sweet meat into his mouth and not noticing the zeal and wanton devouring of saucy shrimp outlining the shape of her mouth, Kate enjoyed her meal.

Surprised that she outpaced Nick, she used the ample napkins supplied to mop up her mouth and fingers. Returning to her pristine, ladylike form, she placed her items in the bag as Nick finished his lunch.

"That was pretty good," Nick announced.

"Make your list of Carolina Beach must-haves?" Kate asked.

"Maybe. At least for the shrimp," Nick said. "Should we get back to work?"

Kate leaned back in her seat and sipped her iced tea, "The guys will let us know when they are done. Might as well let them finish without being underfoot."

"Works for me," Nick said, following suit in his seat and casting his gaze toward the beach.

For a few minutes, they allowed the surf and breeze to play a sweet melody. As Kate's satiation faded into her puzzle-solving gaze, eyebrows slightly furrowed, she didn't escape Nick's notice.

"Wheels turning. What have you got?" he asked.

Kate's eyes moved from the Atlantic waves to Nick, "No answers. Just a burning question."

Their eyes were locked. Nick's eyebrows raised as if to ask for more.

"I can't help but think the argument between Sheffield Hayes and Collin Royce is key to all this," Kate said. "The timing, everything that was at stake. Royce was staying at Hayes' beach house set up by Sheffield himself. Access, motive, means…" Kate said.

"Means?" Nick asked.

"I mean, he could conceivably kill Royce and wrangle him up into the beach house in the cover of a storm," Kate said.

"Maybe," Nick said. "And stuff him in a wall?"

"When you see a wall stripped to studs, with as much development as the Hayes family does… yeah," Kate nodded.

Nick nodded, considering Kate's theory. Rubbing his chin, he offered his own, "You can't forget about Hauer. He had actual cash handed over for unrequited work. He had as much to gain as the Hayeses had to lose."

"Yes, he did," Kate nodded. "But Sheffield had easy access to the beach house."

"Did the police reports state the condition of the beach house? Had it been broken into?" Nick asked.

"It didn't say in the news reports. Maybe in the police reports, however…" Kate's eyes gleamed. "That would be a nice tidbit of information on this case."

"Only trouble is, you really think Detective Nixon will provide that information? She's been pretty tight-lipped about everything," Nick asked.

Kate's eyes narrowed, "I may not need to ask her directly."

Nick cocked his head questioningly, "Oh?"

"Professor Granger might be able to get his hands on the case files," Kate said, a little bounce in her seat as she typed an email to the Criminal Justice college professor.

Looking up, she beamed at Nick, "He said he would see what he could do."

"Another piece of the puzzle," Nick said. His eyes shifted, "Do you mind if I take a look at your new and improved crime wall? I only gave it a glance earlier."

"Not at all," Kate said.

Gathering their lunch items, they moved back into the house as the appliance crew were shimmying the new double-oven range into place. Ascending the stairs, Kate led Nick into the master bedroom closet. Snapping on the light, she stood back, arms crossed as she proudly let Nick step inside and study her notes.

On one wall, she had Collin Royce's murder. On the other, she had Dennis Jones' murder. In between, she had a host of suspects and their connections to both. With long lines, she connected suspects to both victims and victim to victim.

Kate's eyes narrowed, "Something on this wall got Dennis Jones killed."

"And could just as easily put you in the cross hairs," Nick warned.

Kate shook it off and squinted as she eyed the walls. "Hauer or Hayes…"

"I'm inclined to think that one of us is right," Nick said after several minutes of absorbing the materials that Kate had pasted on her closet walls. "Sheffield, Hauer. Hauer, Sheffield. They both have their fingerprints over all of this."

"They do. So does your friend Sophia. Mark Hayes, the patriarch. And Robert Grant, the Hayes family friend who took over Royce's spot as up-and-coming golden boy on the tournament and the course contract," Kate said.

"So, we're pretty much nowhere," Nick said, taking a step further back.

"Not nowhere, zeroing in from a wide pool of candidates," Kate said.

Nick turned to face Kate, not noticing that she had taken a step closer to her crime wall. Standing toe to toe, his words stumbled as they fell out of his mouth, "You exude confidence. I like that about you."

Kate looked up into Nick's eyes, her chest heaved as her breath deepened, "I, uh, don't know about confidence, I just keep pressing forward… in most things."

"Most things?" Nick asked, the slightest crease of a smile appearing in the corners of his mouth.

"Some things… frighten me more than others," Kate swallowed hard. A tiny bead of sweat tickled her lip. Her tongue subconsciously swept at it.

"Murderers, thieves, angry detectives eager to toss you in a jail cell…?" Nick suggested.

"None of those things," Kate's head dropped as she took a step back.

Nick eyed Kate as her eyes bounced nervously around the closet. Offering a calm smile, he said, "We're all afraid of something."

"Really?" Kate's eyes widened. "What are *you* afraid of?"

Nick smiled. His calm demeanor effusing into the confines of the master bedroom closet. "Losing things that have become important to me," he finally said.

"Things? What sort of things?" Kate blurted in a breathy voice, instantly shaking her head, wishing she could retract her question.

She was relieved when a voice called up the stairs, "Ms. Harper, we're all done. Would you like to inspect everything?"

"I'll be right down!" Kate called. Spinning to look back at Nick, she offered a sheepish curtsy, "I should…"

Nick nodded, "I'll be right behind you."

Kate pushed her lips out before spinning back toward the bedroom and the stairs.

Finding a man with a clip board, he walked Kate through the house and surveyed the appliances. Gleaming in their places, each was an obvious upgrade over the quality but dated pieces they had replaced. With a nod, Kate signed the papers accepting the delivery and thanked the crew.

Nick appeared at the bottom of the steps, "All good?"

"They look great," Kate said. Her eyes glanced off of Nick as though she were guilty of something.

She could feel Nick recognize the look as he shuffled. She appreciated him allowing her to open when she was ready.

Nick made his own sweep through the new appliances, he gave his personal nod of approval after straightening the refrigerator a fraction of a turn.

"Well, I should get back to it. If I focus, I'll get your schedule back on track," Nick said.

"Yeah," Kate said. Her voice was breathy and absent.

"What?" Nick asked.

Kate slumped, "Dennis Jones. What got him killed?"

Nick studied Kate for a moment. The fear of Kate following in Jones' ill-fated footsteps was written all over his face.

"Something tells me you are intent on finding out," Nick said.

Kate's lips pressed tight, "Solve the first murder, and you'll solve the second."

Watching her ascend the stairs toward the master bedroom and her crime closet, Nick muttered, "Oh, boy."

Thirty

Kate slipped out of the house, clutching a notebook she scribbled in from her gazing at the crime closet walls.

"I'll be back in a bit. Let me know if you need anything," Kate sang as she walked out of the house.

"Stay out of trouble!" Nick called back from under the kitchen sink he was installing. Not hearing a reply, he called out, "Kate…!"

With a deep sigh, he hoped his words would be heeded. Grabbing his wrench, he fought his concern for Kate and focused on his work.

Kate pulled her SUV onto the grass shoulder. Through her open window, she stared out at the entrance of Thomas Hauer's golf resort. She studied the entrance and its ornate filigree-adorned columns.

The resort really was in a beautiful setting just inland from the coastal marshes. As if on cue, a bald eagle soared overhead.

The guard station was unmanned, with cameras observing who came in and out. The country club relied on valet and security at the club house to ensure guests were there for the club.

Checking her watch, she pulled out from the side of the road. Barely a mile from the golf course, a blue light flashed in Kate's rearview mirror. Checking her speed, she frowned as she pulled over.

It didn't take long for a woman to step out of her unmarked police cruiser. Even with dark aviator sunglasses on, Kate could tell the woman approaching her side mirror was scowling.

Rolling her window down once more, Kate flashed as pleasant a smile as she could produce, "Detective Nixon. You doing traffic stops now?"

The detective pulled off her sunglasses with one hand and clapped her other on the frame of Kate's SUV.

Leaning in so that she could look Kate directly in her eyes, Detective Nixon said, "Only for those who are snooping into an active investigation."

"I was just looking to see if there were cameras, guards, anything we might have missed. Whoever slashed my tire and left that note must be worried about something I was close to. They might be the killer," Kate said.

"That is precisely why you should mind your own business and let me do my job, Ms. Harper," Nixon said.

Kate huffed for a moment, staring through her windshield, her hands resting on the steering wheel. With a squint, she asked, "The guard station cameras didn't catch anything?"

Nixon took a deep breath, spying on traffic before addressing Kate, "We requested the video feeds. While security at the country club has been helpful, they have protocols they need to follow for their clients' discretion."

"You need a warrant," Kate said.

"And for a minor crime like vehicle vandalism, no judge wants to issue a warrant, no less at a country club they belong to," Nixon shared in a rare moment of openness.

Kate pondered for a moment as she tapped her steering wheel. "Hang on a second," she said. Pulling out her phone she tapped furiously with both thumbs in her search bar.

With a grin, she held her phone out for the detective, "Try this. It's public, no warrant needed."

"What's this?" Nixon snatched the phone to look at it closer. "Well, I'll be…"

Using her finger to scroll on Kate's phone, the detective pushed out to focus in. Shaking her head, she gave the phone back to Kate.

The detective gave Kate a long, hard look before speaking, "Eagle cam, huh?"

"It isn't far from the country club entrance," Kate said.

"Only one turn off between there and the country club. I'll give it a better look at the station," Detective Nixon said.

Kate spied on her phone an image Nixon had focused on. An expensive SUV with surf racks latched to the top. Her eyes went wide, "That's Sheffield Hayes' car!"

"As I said, I will look further into it. In the meantime, you are going to drive away from here and stay far from my investigation," the detective's voice was stern.

"I promise," Kate nodded. Her face fell, "Unless your investigation leads you to the university, then I might be near it."

The detective's head snapped up, "I don't think I want to know. Why do I get the feeling I am going to be called out to campus in about an hour or so?"

"I certainly hope not. I'm just stopping by to pick up something for my historical research," Kate smiled.

Detective Nixon's permanent scowl deepened, her fingers subconsciously draping across the exposed shiny bits of her handcuffs, "I mean it, Ms. Harper."

"I hear you loud and clear, Detective," Kate straightened in her seat.

Nixon tapped on the roof of Kate's SUV and slipped the sunglasses back over her eyes.

Kate swore she heard the detective growl under her breath as she walked back to her cruiser. Through her rearview mirror, Kate watched as the detective pulled out from the side of the road and with a bit of grass flinging from her tires pulled a one hundred and eighty degree turn to head back the way she came.

Starting her own car, Kate pulled away and headed toward the college.

"You're becoming a local around here," the young girl looked up from her desk as Kate walked in.

Kate smiled at the young Criminal Justice student. "I suppose I am."

"Dr. Granger is expecting you," the assistant said.

"Thank you," Kate nodded.

Following the hall, she found the professor's office. Giving a light rap on the door, she heard Granger call, "Come on in."

"Hello, Dr. Granger," Kate said as she pushed her way into the Criminal Justice Department Dean's office.

"Nice to see you again. I see you have held up well after that nasty incident in the library. Some of our classes are using that incident to study investigations and the pros and cons of civilian involvement," Dr. Granger said.

"I see. How is that debate shaping up?" Kate asked.

"The Criminal Justice majors are clearly in the 'con' camp. Some of the others, the political science and certainly the literature majors, lean a bit more to the 'pro' side. I will say, the journalism majors are in favor of a little unofficial sleuthing," the professor said.

"Well, at least there are a few in my camp," Kate said.

Dr. Granger studied Kate and smiled, "Since you continue to seek my help, I assume the police have no interest in encouraging your looking into the case?"

Kate laughed, "I'm more than a little surprised I haven't already been thrown in jail. It has been threatened on more than one occasion."

Reaching onto his desk, the professor picked up a file folder and handed it to Kate, "Interesting case. Might have been different if the body had been found back then. As a missing person's case with no hints at a crime there wasn't much the police could do at the time."

Kate flipped the file folder open and quickly leafed through the copies the professor had placed in there for her. "No signs of forced entry," Kate mumbled. "Points toward someone connected with the house."

"I thought the same. But then again, if someone has the competence to build a wall and neatly blend it in with the rest of the house, they might be able to repair a forced entry as well," the professor said.

Kate flipped through the pages and studied the photos of the front door and back door hardware, "Hard to tell the condition of the locks in these photos."

"I can forward you digital copies, if you like," the professor offered.

"I'd appreciate that," Kate nodded.

"There's one other thing. While our class was digging through the old case notes and news clippings, they found this," the professor handed over another piece of paper.

Kate read the headline as related to Collin Royce and the last tournament that he had played in before he disappeared. The byline made her eyes go wide. "Dennis Jones was the reporter on this article– dated the Saturday that Collin Royce disappeared," Kate said.

"Take it. Read it. I think you will find it interesting," Dr. Granger smiled, a hand held out to escort Kate out of his office. "I'd love to get your take on it, but I have to get to class. Keep me informed on your findings, if you would."

"Of course. Thank you. You have been an amazing help," Kate said following the criminal justice professor out of the faculty office suite.

Kate clutched her documents, excited to give them a closer look. Exiting the building, she was startled to see two people standing beside her SUV.

Once she recognized them, her tensed fight-or-flight muscles relaxed.

"Ms. Harper," the campus security officer nodded. "Dr. Granger said you might be stopping by today. We thought it best to keep an eye out for trouble."

Kate winced, "It does tend to find me."

The officer laughed, "Trouble tends to follow those who stir it up. Break open a bee's nest, prepare to run because they'll soon be chasing you."

Kate studied the officer trying to understand whether the words were a warning or a threat.

"Pursuit of the truth and justice is noble, Ms. Harper. I hope you get your bad guy," the officer said, answering the question in her eyes.

With a nod of thanks, Kate climbed into her SUV and set her papers in the passenger seat.

The officers stayed at their post until she made the turn on College Road and left the University of North Carolina at Wilmington campus.

Thirty One

Kate arrived at the beach house to find Nick pacing in front of the entry. Eyeing him as she walked into the house, she asked, "Everything okay?"

Nick looked surprised at the question, "Yeah, why? I was just, just testing the floorboards. I thought I heard a squeak. No squeak. We're good."

"Squeaks, huh? You weren't wearing lines into the floor because you were concerned about me?" Kate asked.

"Concerned? What? No. Just keeping an eye out, that's all," Nick scoffed.

Kate grinned and leaned a shoulder into him, "So, which is it? Searching for squeaks or keeping an eye out for me?"

Letting out a frustrated breath, Nick said, "You tend to find yourself in trouble… a lot."

"Apparently, I have built a reputation for getting into trouble. Campus security is now alerted when I am at the university. Safety precaution, I guess," Kate said.

"Probably wise," Nick chuckled receiving a disapproving glare from Kate. "Did you get the case files?"

"I did," Kate said. "Dr. Granger is sending digital files so we can zoom in on the photos, I'd like to get your professional take on the entry hardware."

"I can put it on the big screen in the living room," Nick suggested.

Kate checked her phone and forwarded the criminal justice professor's email to Nick, "Would you? That would be great. He gave me something else I'd like to read through while you set that up."

Studying the decade-old article by Dennis Jones, Kate's eyes digested the words. By the time she was finished, Nick had the case file photos displayed on the large television in the beach house living room.

Holding the article up, Kate said, "Dennis Jones was at the tournament when Collin Royce disappeared. He was mostly writing about the tournament, the race between Royce and Robert Grant, and the endorsement deal with Hayes Resorts. At the end of the article, Jones promised a follow-up where he was to get an exclusive with Royce the Monday after the tournament ended where Royce would have 'big news' to share."

Pulling out her old notes, she slapped her leg with a handful of papers, "I never even noticed some of these articles about Royce's disappearance were by none other than Dennis Jones. How could I have missed that?"

"Focused on the facts, not necessarily who was presenting them. It's understandable," Nick said.

Kate shuffled the articles, pulling the ones by Jones aside. Quickly perusing them, she said, "They sing like most of the articles. Royce was in position to win and disappeared. Like many, Jones' article suggested foul play, but with no evidence, he wondered if Royce's mystery would ever be solved."

"Any mention of the 'big exclusive?'" Nick asked.

Kate shook her head, "I'll look again online. Match any articles about Royce to Jones. First, let's see about the house. Dr. Granger says if whoever broke in could make a wall, they could repair a door as well."

"You want me to see if the hardware was replaced," Nick said, turning his attention to the television. Clicking through the photos, he zoomed in on the front and back doors, focusing on the handles.

Taking a step toward the television, Nick inspected the photos. Shaking his head, he turned toward Kate. "Those aren't new. See here and there… spotting from saltwater. They had been in place for a while."

"So, if the hardware wasn't replaced and the police saw no signs of forced entry…" Kate started.

"It's possible whoever murdered Collin Royce had a key to this house," Nick concluded.

"Exactly. The Hayes family," Kate nodded.

"Didn't Robert Grant show up on the rental documents too?" Nick asked.

"He did. So add *him* to the list. Not too difficult to make a key," Kate said. "Both the Hayes family and Thomas Hauer are developers. I couldn't imagine they'd have too tough a time pulling that off," Kate said.

"But Grant? Swinging a golf club is a bit different than swinging a hammer," Nick didn't look convinced with their lineup, "Who could have access long enough and have the skills to do all of this in what? A weekend?"

Kate sighed, "I don't know. How long would it take you?"

"The section of the wall isn't that big. I guess if I had the supplies and I was desperate enough… frankly, I could knock it out in one night. The paint might not be dry, but I could do it," Nick said. "Might be a bit obvious. Doing construction in the middle of the night."

The words struck Kate. Rushing to her stack of papers, she sifted through the police report. Raising a piece of paper triumphantly in the air, she said, "Part of the report is noting the weather conditions. The night Royce disappeared was stormy. Windy and wet conditions. Toss in a little thunder and the killer is cloaked by Mother Nature."

Nick scrolled through his phone, "Yeah. A large band of thunderstorms battered Wilmington and the barrier islands that night."

"So, it is feasible a long night of pounding might not have been heard," Kate shrugged.

Nick looked distant.

"What is it?" Kate asked.

Snapping his fingers, Nick said, "At the bottom of the exposed wall, I found sand. A fair amount of it. It makes sense. Wet sand would stick to whoever walked outside."

"A lot of sand?" Kate asked.

"Quite a bit, yeah. Why?" Nick nodded.

Kate looked out toward the beach, "Collin Royce was killed out on the beach. Shot by a handgun muted by the storm. Maybe in timing with the thunder."

Nick nodded, "Yeah. Could be. Dragging someone through the sand, lugging them up the steps could leave that much sand in the wall."

Kate's face fell, "What was Collin Royce doing out on the beach in the middle of a storm?"

"Being chased by someone," Nick said.

"Someone who came to confront him… or finish a fight they had started," Kate clapped her hands.

"I want more than ever to find out what that argument between Sheffield and Collin Royce was all about," Kate said.

"How do you propose to do that? Walk up and ask him?" Nick asked.

Kate's lips spread into an evil grin, "You could always see if his sister knows."

Nick shook his head, "You are wicked."

"I like to think of it as relentless," Kate said.

"You are that," Nick said.

Kate wiggled her phone, "I even have the perfect way to bump into the southern belle. You may need to put that suit on one more time."

Nick glowered, "Dare I even ask?"

"A little philanthropic work. We are new members of the community,. Why not give back by attending a gala to benefit veterans and their families on the *USS North Carolina* tonight? The top two sponsors– the Hayes family and Thomas Hauer," Kate said.

"It *does* set up for an exciting evening," Nick said.

Thirty Two

Driving up to the *Battleship USS North Carolina* across the Cape Fear River from Wilmington's downtown riverfront was impressive. The hulking ship with its massive sixteen-inch triple turret guns mounted on the bow and mid-stern was a display of engineering brilliance and wildly intimidating.

As Kate parked her SUV and craned her neck toward the ship, she could imagine the fear the ship would have instilled as it patrolled the waters of World War II.

"Wow," Nick said. "If you have to have an event, you might as well do it someplace interesting."

A stream of expensive vehicles filed into the parking lot of the battleship-turned-war memorial.

"Shall we?" Nick held his arm out. Kate accepted the offer, hooking her arm into his.

Making their way across the parking lot and to the long gangway that led up to the ship, they met up with a growing crowd. Up at the top of the gangway under an archway of lights, they could see Thomas Hauer and the Hayes family jockeying for position.

 Mark and Sheffield Hayes stood on one side. Thomas Hauer and his entourage muscled in from the other side. Kate laughed because she noticed certain members of Wilmington society drew a more robust response to lobby for their attention than others. She was sure if one member of the Hayes family, who was conspicuously missing, were there, Nick would have garnered such a response.

 The couple behind them must have been important as Kate and Nick were largely skipped over in favor of lavishing greetings on them. Stepping onto the polished wooden planks of the magnificent battleship was like stepping back in time. Naval soldiers would have stood there at attention watching their home ports slowly drift out of view. Naval balls would have taken place on their decks. Sailors would have scurried to their stations in the face of an imminent attack.

 Now, the sturdy vessel was a monument to her storied history. A walk through time and, unfortunately necessary muscle, to create and maintain peace and freedom for visitors to reflect and imagine.

 On this particular evening, it was a waterfront venue draped in string lights, dotted with wine bars and wait staff offering canapés.

 Guests were gussied up in their finest lightweight suits and flowing dresses perfect for an evening under the stars. Music from the forties was piped throughout the ship, commemorating the era of the ship's launch.

Arm in arm, Kate and Nick slowly meandered the deck of the battleship. Taking note of the attendees, they found nearly everyone with a presumed connection to the case was present. They had already seen Mark and Sheffield Hayes as well as Thomas Hauer. Both were flanked by members of their staff.

Robert Grant was surrounded by a crowd of fans and a group of attentive photographers. Whether standing below the ships' massive guns or leaning on the rail with sunset over the Cape Fear River they didn't miss a shot of Grant's prize-winning smile.

"He certainly has made the most of his position," Nick said.

"If only he was as good at golf as he was smiling for the cameras," a passerby said as they swirled their amber beverage.

Kate shot Nick a look and received a shrug in return. In their brief stroll around the battleship deck, it didn't take them long to realize why Sophia was missing from the Hayes contingent near the gangway.

Her back to the bar, she laughed as a robust man regaled her with a story while he handed her a drink just in time for her to place an emptied one on the counter. Seeing Nick turn the corner, she pushed off away from the bar, waving her glass as a cheers to the man who just purchased her a drink.

Making a beeline toward Nick, she stared with sultry eyes, her vision seemingly seeing right past Kate hooked to his arm. "Buy me a drink?"

Nick was mildly stunned. Kate slipped her arm free, giving Nick a confident press on his back to encourage him to take advantage of the moment.

"It looks like you already have one," Nick said.

Sophia grinned, "Oh, do I?"

In one press of the glass to her lips, she tilted it back and emptied her beverage. Clearing the dew of the drink off her lips with her tongue, she smiled at Nick, "It looks like I'm fresh out."

Nick nodded absently. With a gentle arm around her back, he led her to the bar.

Kate watched as Nick held up two fingers, ordering a pair of whatever Sophia had been drinking. The bartender, seeing the prominent Wilmington figure head her way, was already pouring one of the drinks and added a second glass to her pour.

Nick slapped his credit on the counter as he handed a glass to Sophia. The southern belle grinned as though she had just been handed the grand prize at the county fair. Grabbing his drink and thanking the bartender, Nick shot a glance at Kate who nodded her head toward the stern which was less crowded.

Guiding Sophia away from the bulk of gala attendees, they walked along the taffrail of the battleship. As the rumble of conversations melted away with only the soft wails of forties big band music filling the night air, Nick and Sophia fell into step together.

"Sorry to pull you away from your date. I honestly didn't think you would bite," Sophia admitted, her eyes cast on Nick's.

Nick's look was far from romantic interest.

"You didn't leave your date for me. You just put it on pause," Sophia said.

Shuffling, Nick looked out at the list playing on the water alongside the boat. "I can't help but to wonder what happened to Collin Royce," Nick said.

"And that made you abandon your date?" Sophia asked.

Nick scrunched his nose, "I thought you might be more comfortable just talking to me."

"That might be," Sophia laughed. "That lady friend of yours looks at me like I stole her puppy."

"The night before Collin disappeared… word is he had an argument with Sheffield," Nick said stopping to lean against the rail.

"Probably. Collin and Sheffield cared for each other like brothers and fought like brothers," Sophia said. Her eyes wandered off down the Cape Fear River. "That night, everyone seemed tense. The tournament was in full swing. Thomas was hovering looking to poach whatever, whoever he could. Storms were rolling in. Robbie was making a charge, for once taking a tournament seriously."

"Did he and Collin get a long?" Nick asked.

Sophie took a sip of her drink, "Sure. I mean, Collin was competitive. Robbie, he liked the attention."

"Grant was a family friend. How did he feel about Royce getting a piece of the family business?" Nick pressed.

"Robbie was always going to be involved in some way. He has a laid back, almost surfer like vibe about him," Sophia shouldered Nick. "Collin was always… intense. Like he had something to prove."

"He seemed to be doing well. Why would Sheffield get into an argument the night before the tournament was on the line?" Nick asked.

"I don't know. Like I said, everyone was tense. Thomas was trying to lure Collin away, Sheffield felt like he had given Collin his big break and was ticked there wasn't more loyalty. I never really involved myself with the business of it all. I suppose I was a bit more like Robbie. The fanfare was fun, but the uptight business aspects were a bit of a drag," Sophia said. Suddenly, she turned toward Nick. "You aren't suggesting Sheffield had anything to do with Collin's death, are you?"

"I'm not suggesting anything. I am just trying to sort out the details of that night," Nick said. Changing the direction of his questions, he asked, "What's up with you and Hauer? The tabloids have you paired with Grant. And you… you clearly seem to not be tied to anyone."

Sophia's lips curled into a devious grin, "Why, Nicky, are you trying to see if there is room for us? I assure you I am free to explore. If you are."

Nick absently made more space between them, causing Sophia to sour.

"Robbie and me… what do I say? We make a great media couple. We have fun together. Thomas? He's like tequila. Fun for a night, but you wake up swearing it off and feeling a bit sick to your stomach," Kate said.

Sophia returned her gaze toward the light ripples of the Cape Fear.

Sensing that was all he was going to get from her, Nick's voice was soft, "Thank you for opening up with me."

Sophia turned toward Nick. Her eyes were steely as she surveyed him in the shimmering strong lights for a long moment. "No one misses Collin more than I do. But, to be honest, I wish he had stayed buried in that wall. Opening old wounds isn't doing anyone any good," Sophia dragged a finger across his chest. "I wish I could be more than a source of ancient gossip for you, Nick."

Spinning, she raised her empty glass in the air, "Thanks for the drink."

Nick watched Sophia walk away. He felt sorry for her. Whether her family or Robert Grant or even herself had anything to do with Collin Royce's death, it haunted her. His disappearance and the circumstances surrounding it had given her hell for the better part of a decade. He hoped the pain she was enduring was recoverable. As she was no doubt seeking another suitor at the bar, he had no hope her pain would be eased on this particular evening, regardless of the cocktails she consumed.

With a deep sigh, Nick placed his hand on the rail and looked out at the shimmering water. He felt guilty for using her for information. She was clearly a hurting woman even if dealing with her pain in destructive ways.

Kate gave Nick and Sophia space as they walked toward the stern of the battleship. After watching the pageant of attendees make their way up the gangway, she whirled around to avoid eye contact with Detective Nixon, who received forced friendly greetings from Mark and Sheffield Hayes.

Pulling her hands to her chest to avoid hitting another guest, she found herself face to face with Andrew Ayres.

The reporter's mouth widened into a seedy smile, "Ms. Harper. I'm not sure I expected to see you this evening."

"I'm probably here for the same reason you are," Kate said.

"I suppose you are," Ayres said. "Where's your sidekick?"

"He's off to get us a drink," Kate said.

"Is he? I'm pretty sure I saw him aft with none other than Sophia Hayes. She's a wily one. Most women would have a concern or two with her setting her sights on their beau," the detective said.

Kate's eyes narrowed, "Nick and I aren't… I trust Nick. Regardless of the situation."

"Rather heavy praise. Admirable, really," Ayres said. "Any particular leads you're following on this fine evening?"

"Leads? Just here to support a worthy cause," Kate said.

Ayres scanned the crowd, "A worthy cause, indeed. I doubt most of the people here are all so altruistic."

"How about you?" Kate asked.

Ayres couldn't fight the grin that creased the corners of his lips, "I have something to follow up on. Nothing I'm quite ready to share, but I think this will be quite the exciting evening."

Kate cocked her head, her mouth opened to ask a follow up question, but Ayres looked off into the crowd.

"I'm sorry. Perhaps we'll catch up later in the evening," the reporter said.

Snaking through the crowd and disappearing on the other side of the ship, Ayres was gone.

"Ayres?" Nick's voice asked as he stepped up beside her.

Kate nodded, "He's onto something, but he wasn't in the mood to share."

"About the same as I received from Sophia," Nick said.

"Oh? How was happy hour?" Kate asked.

Shaking off the tease, Nick said, "She said she wished Collin had remained buried in the wall. That him being found wasn't helping anyone."

"Interesting sentiment," Kate said.

"It is," Nick nodded. "She told me that Sheffield and Collin got along like brothers. They cared about each other yet frequently fought with each other."

"So, the night of Collin's disappearance they had just another one of their bouts?" Kate asked.

"According to Sophia," Nick shrugged.

"She say what they fought about?" Kate pressed.

"No. It didn't seem like she knew, honestly," Nick said. "Sheffield might be the only one alive who knows what they were fighting about."

"Convenient that the other one who knew is dead," Kate said.

Her eyes widened. With a hand on Nick's back, she wheeled him around into the heart of the crowd. With a glance over her shoulder, she hissed, "Detective Nixon on our six."

"I see," Nick said, allowing Kate to escort him to the other side of the battleship.

Colliding into a throng, they found themselves on the periphery of an impromptu Robert Grant photo shoot. Sophia was pulled into a few of the shots, Grant's arm draped around her with her hand planted on his stomach.

When the photographers suggested they move to the other side to catch the fading light of sunset, Sophia slipped away.

In the corner of his eye, Nick saw Thomas Hauer spy the Hayes debutant and head in the same direction. Trying to navigate through the crowd, Sheffield Hayes jostled behind them. Mark Hayes appeared to see them line up and began making his way through the crowd as well.

"Well, this can't be good," Nick said. Grasping Kate by the hand, he pulled her toward the developing situation.

Thomas Hauer slapped a bill from his wallet onto the bar and grabbed a bottle of whiskey. Finding Sophia looking out at the water, he slipped in next to her. Waving the bottle in front of her, she looked at him for a second before snatching the bottle and giving it a hearty pull.

As Hauer put an arm around her, Sheffield Hayes closed in. Clapping a hand on Hauer's shoulder, he yanked him away from his sister.

Hauer sneered at Sheffield which seemed to only make him angrier. Rearing back, Sheffield swung a haphazard fist toward Hauer which glanced off the side of his head. Hauer squared up, taking a fistful of Sheffield's suit jacket.

As both men jostled, with Sophia looking perturbed in the background, Mark Sheffield and his entourage arrived. The Hayes patriarch snapped at both men as his operations head, Arturo Moreno stepped between the two men and pulled Sheffield away from Hauer.

Both men, disheveled, straightened their jackets. Sheffield looked obviously angry, while Thomas Hauer almost looked amused by the fracas. Detective Nixon appeared on the edge of the crowd taking intent note of the situation. Mark Sheffield, ever aware, flashed a calm smile and stepped to her, saying the incident was nothing more than excitement over the upcoming tournament. All the while, Arturo continued to hold a heated Sheffield at bay.

"It *is* an exciting evening!" Nick whispered through a grin at Kate.

Kate was less interested in the scuffle than the emotions and history behind it. She studied all of the players intently. She watched as Sophia slipped away to the back of the boat. Arturo escorted Sheffield away from the scene. Thomas Hauer smoothed out his wrinkles and embraced the spotlight as though he won a prize fighter bout.

Andrew Ayres studied the scene in a manner similar to Kate. From the other side of the crowd, he slipped into the shadows as the moment passed.

Kate watched as Mark Hayes patted Arturo Moreno on the shoulder and thanked him for always being there for the family. With that in mind, he requested Arturo find Sheffield to keep an eye on him and out of trouble.

"Now that that's over, I'd kind of like to find our reporter friend Andrew Ayres and see what he knows about the break in at the beach house," Nick said.

Leading Kate in the direction he saw the reporter slip away, they scoured the ship. The back of the battleship was quieter than the bow where the main festivities were taking place. Shadows persisted in the many nooks and crannies of the decommissioned battleship. A figure rushed away as Kate and Nick neared.

Nick stepped in front of Kate, his eyes piercing the darkness to identify who was there. "Ayres! Is that you?" he called as he began to wander the inner section of the ship.

"Uh, Nick. I think I found Ayres," Kate said.

Nick turned to find Kate looking off the steel cable rails of the ship. While rushing to her side, his eyes followed hers. In the lights that shone on the side of the battleship, enough spilled onto the Cape Fear River to reveal a body floating face-down where the ship met the water. A curious alligator slowly swam from the bank to investigate.

"We, uh, we better get some help," Kate said, the color draining from her face.

Pulling Kate's hand, they raced toward where they had last seen Detective Nixon. Flowing through the crowd, they found the detective having a rather civil conversation with Mark Hayes. Her head slumped when she saw Kate and Nick making their way through the crowd.

"I should have known you two would show up," the detective snapped.

"It is a bit worse than that, Detective Nixon. We just found another body," Kate winced.

Nixon's eyes flew open wide, "What?"

"In the water near the back of the boat. I think an alligator is about to make off with the evidence," Kate said.

"Show me!" Detective Nixon snapped, abruptly ending her conversation with the Hayes patriarch.

Following Kate and Nick through the crowd with a large contingent in their wake, they peered over the edge where they had seen the body.

Leaning over the rail, the detective saw what they had. Pulling out her phone, she called it in. Pushing the crowd away, she announced, "This is a crime scene. I need all of you to back off. I also need all of you to stay put until we sort this all out!"

Instinctively, several people moved toward the exit while others leaned over the rails of the ship with their cellphones trying to capture images.

The security detail quickly blocked the entrance to the gangway which would provide an exit from the battleship. As additional police officers arrived, they lined the bank of the Cape Fear River while others boarded the ship and helped Detective Nixon cordon off the top of the battleship closest to the body of Andrew Ayres.

Looking with disdain at Kate and Nick, she pointed, "You two aren't going anywhere."

Thirty Three

It didn't take long before Detective Nixon had the entire battleship locked down. Through irate eyes, she patrolled the anxious gathering of souls haphazardly lined up on deck. Kate's eyes were fixed on her as she tried to interpret what the detective was thinking.

As the detective's eyes did an inventory of the guests, so did Kate's. The slight twitches in Detective Nixon's eyes coincided with the obvious absences that Kate had cataloged.

Sheffield Hayes, Robert Grant, Thomas Hauer and Sophia Hayes were all conspicuously missing from the gathering. Detective Nixon barked orders to officers to comb the ship for any unaccounted for guests.

In close enough ear shot to hear the detective, Mark Hayes played down his son's absence. Claiming he had just been there *after* the reporter's body was found. Nick shot a look at Kate as they both knew that wasn't the case.

Waving to his ground's manager who stood on the periphery of the crowd, Hayes whispered coarse instructions. Arturo nodded and slipped away from the crowd toward where Sheffield had last been tailed by Kate and Nick.

Sophia sauntered up into the midst of the crowd with a cocktail in hand, having helped herself behind the starboard-side bar. Her father's eyes cast a stern glare that was dismissed with a sweet smile and a shrug as Sophia joined his side.

The Hayes patriarch leaned over and offered a lecture into his daughter's ear. Her response said it all as she leaned into her father and looked up with her deep blue eyes. Eschewing her usual alluring appeal for the likeness of an innocent puppy dog, the elder Hayes statesman relented for what must have been the millionth time in the daughter's relationship.

Thomas Hauer strode back into frame in the escort of two police officers who had provided security detail for the event. Hauer smiled as he neared the audience, casually striding with the utmost confidence.

Kate watched as Detective Nixon pressed her radio earpiece into her ear as she received a message from the crew clearing the innards of the battleship. Robert Grant was soon led in front of the detective as he panned the crowd, his eyes momentarily locking on Sophia's. Letting out a broad smile, he winked at an audience member.

Sliding closer to the front where Detective Nixon held command, Kate heard Grant saying he was in a photoshoot when her officers corralled him. Glancing at the crew with lights and cameras on the opposite side of the vessel, she made a note of his assertion.

Finally, Sheffield appeared with Arturo nudging him forward. Sheffield looked angry, which clearly caught the attention of Detective Nixon. Kate could see it was a bad look considering the circumstances, especially with him being the last to appear on deck. His father quickly acknowledged him and nodded his head for Sheffield to hold himself accountable to the police detective.

Detective Nixon didn't waste any time to move her focus to the junior Hayes man. Noting the time on her watch, Nixon scribbled in the pad she pulled from her pocket. With a nod, a pair of officers escorted Sheffield away from the crowd. After he started to protest, his head fell as his father slowly shook his head.

"I've got to try and hear what's being said," Kate whispered to Nick.

"Time for her to make good on her obstruction charge promise," Nick muttered.

Ignoring him, Kate slowly made her way around the crowd. Two officers stood vigil to block off the walkway where Detective Nixon herded Sheffield Hayes.

She could hear the murmur of voices, but they were not clear. She could see shadows cast on the wall with animated gestures that Kate assumed belonged to Sheffield.

Turning on her phone, Kate held the microphone along the side of the battleship as she leaned over as though she were taking in the view of the water down below. She offered a smile to the nearby officer with her phone cupped in her hand.

Nick, realizing what Kate was up to, slid quietly to the rail next to her. Standing shoulder to shoulder, they held vigil at the battleship rail as one by one, any members of the guests that weren't accounted for during the time of Andrew Ayres' disappearance were paraded back to visit with Detective Nixon. As they left her impromptu interrogation room, they were each instructed to stay local as they would be remanded to the station for follow-up questioning.

Kate noted that Sheffield and Thomas Hauer spent the most time with Detective Nixon. Sophia had her freshly poured beverage taken from her as she was escorted back. To Kate's surprise, Robert Grant spent the least amount of time being questioned.

The officers walked up Kate and Nick, motioning for them to each go up individually. Detective Nixon waved them both through together. The detective looked at each in the eye. The pair stood at attention while they were being studied.

"You found the body. What exactly were you doing back there when you saw Andrew Ayres' floating in the Cape Fear?" Nixon asked.

"We saw him disappear to the back of the boat. I thought he might be following Sheffield Hayes after his scuffle with Hauer," Kate said. "And I thought it would be a good time to corral him and see what he knew about the break-in at the beach house."

"Why might he know anything about that? Furthermore, why would it be your job to find out?" the detective asked.

"I just wanted to ensure Kate was safe," Nick stepped in. "Ayres seemed a little shifty. I wanted to give him a chance to prove otherwise."

Detective Nixon's eyes widened, "Oh, so should I be interviewing in a different light? I believe you just gave me motive, I know you had opportunity, and everyone who could lift him over the rail all had means."

Nick paled, "No, I just... we just wanted to talk to him. We didn't get a chance to because we found him over the side."

"I was with Nick the entire time," Kate said.

"Says the accomplice," Detective Nixon snapped.

Kate looked astonished, "How come you let Robert Grant off so easily?"

"What?" the detective's face became angry.

"You spent less time with Grant than any of the other suspects," Kate said.

"You were timing me?" Nixon asked.

Kate looked meek, "I thought it might provide some insight into who was highest on your suspect list."

"Until, now, you two were at the bottom," Detective Nixon fumed. "Along with Grant, not that I owe you an explanation. He was in a photoshoot. Corroborated by the photography crew."

"But, how come they were assembled on one side of the battleship well before he appeared on the opposite side?" Kate asked. "He would have had plenty of time to make that circuit and pass right by the area where Ayres' was likely killed."

The detective's eyes narrowed. With great reluctance, she flipped the page in her notebook and scribbled a comment. Looking up at Kate, she tapped her pen against the notebook. "Anything else I should be aware of?"

Kate looked thoughtful, "There were at least one, if not two, more people down in the back of the ship. We lost track of them when we saw Ayres' body. One of them may have been down there already, the other we trailed."

"And you didn't hear anything? Not a splash?" the detective asked.

"Well, the music was playing, but no," Kate shook her head. "And until we knew what he was up to, we were keeping our distance."

Nick scrunched his nose, "How was Ayres killed?"

"I am not ready to disclose that," Nixon snapped.

"It's just… we didn't hear a gun shot. We didn't hear an altercation, an argument… anything," Nick said.

The detective's eyes bounced from Nick to Kate before she let out a sigh, "It appears as though he were stabbed. We clearly didn't find a weapon on anyone. We have deputies conducting a search of the ship, the river and the marsh."

Kate looked thoughtful, a look that was not lost on the detective.

"It has been a long evening and it is not going to end anytime soon for me. If you would, please join the rest of the guests as they are being released. And since you landed on my suspect board, please stay in town. I may be in touch for further questioning. If you see something, hear something, remember anything, call the station and leave a message directly for me. Do not go anywhere, do not follow anyone into the shadows, do not stick your nose anywhere into my growing number of murder investigations," Detective Nixon said. Darting an arm out for them to follow the officers waiting to escort them, she watched as they followed the crowd off of the battleship.

Glancing over her shoulder, Kate spied the detective, watching the procession as the ship cleared. Bright lights combed the marsh and the river along the edge of the USS North Carolina. Teams worked on rigid hull inflatable boats on the water while others worked in waterproof coveralls.

Kate's eyes trained on the searchers while she listened to the conversations of the guests deboarding the historic ship. The Hayes family was quiet as Mark Hayes and his foreman Arturo stayed shoulder to shoulder with Sheffield. Sophia, almost as though she felt she was being watched, turned her neck. Her eyes met Nick's as she exited the gangway.

Robert Grant followed closely behind having an intense conversation with one of the photography crew.

Feeling satisfied he had gotten his point across, he patted their shoulder as their feet hit the ground.

A healthy buffer was provided for Thomas Hauer to get off the ship. Catching Sophia's eyes after Nick's, Hauer gave a cocky grin and held his thumb and finger between his ear and mouth, annunciating *call me* with his lips. Sophia rolled her eyes and shook her head as she squished between her father and Arturo.

When it was their turn to have their feet once more on solid ground, they peeled away from the crowd as they dispersed toward their cars, Nick leaned in, "We're murder suspects now?"

Kate shot him a mischievous grin, "I'm pretty sure we already were. You're that one who had gone all gallant and regaled the detective with how you wanted to protect me from the shifty-eyed reporter."

Nick's cheeks reddened.

"If it makes you feel better, I don't think she really thinks we did it," Kate said.

"How do you know that?" Nick asked.

"If she did, she wouldn't have interviewed us together. She would have wanted our statements taken separately to see if they corroborated one another," Kate said. Reaching her car, she said, "Come on, I'm excited to get back."

Nick looked surprised as he opened the passenger side door, "I'm surprised you don't want to see if the police find the murder weapon."

"That might take all night- *if* they find it at all. Metal detectors would work well in the water if that's where it is. Won't work so well on a steel ship. Even if they do find it, it probably doesn't have prints," Kate said.

Pulling up to the bungalows, the excitement and chaos of the murder scene on the battleship seemed to have melted away. Replaced with the soul-cleansing sea air and softly crashing surf, the night was blanketed in peacefulness.

"You grab the wine. I'll get the entertainment. Meet me by the lounge chairs," Kate said, excitement ringing in her voice.

Not knowing what she was up to, Nick shrugged and complied.

By the time Nick had corked a bottle of wine and brought them out to the back deck, two acrylic glasses hung upside down from his fingers. He found Kate sitting in a chaise lounge. Another chair was pulled up against hers. She was connecting her phone to her laptop. Holding out a pair of headphones, Kate held one cup to her ear and invited Nick to lean into the second.

"What have you got there?" Nick said, pouring Kate a glass of wine.

"Maybe nothing. Hopefully, Detective Nixon's initial interrogations," Kate said. Hitting play on her laptop, she and Nick leaned in and listened.

Not hearing anything other than muffled voices and a murmur from the crowd, Kate made some adjustments as Nick looked over her shoulder. Suddenly, though faint, they could hear Detective Nixon's voice echoing off the steel sides of the battleship. They especially heard Sheffield Hayes' agitated voice.

"How did you do that?" Nick asked.

"The software we use to make videos of the beach house allows you to adjust the sound or eliminate it altogether," Kate said.

"That's what you were doing with your phone leaning over the railing," Nick said.

"It was a gamble," Kate shrugged.

"A gamble that seems to have paid off," Nick said.

"We'll see. Wanna give it a listen?" Kate asked as she sipped her wine.

Nick nodded, leaning in close to Kate. Their chins grazed each other's as they pressed their ears to the headphones. Pressing play again, Kate played the audio she had captured.

Once more, Sheffield's irritated voice came through the headphones, "I don't even know that guy. I get it if you found Hauer dumped over the side… sorry. That was just a joke. Truth is, as much as we are at each other's throats, we actually get along. We use each other to continually push to improve. I don't mind that he's on a bit of a winning streak. I just don't want the streak to include my sister."

"Andrew Ayres never approached you?" Detective Nixon asked.

"He… he came by the country club. Security caught him snooping outside the executive offices. Said he was looking to talk to me. But I don't know him. I certainly have no reason to dump him over the side of the boat," Sheffield said.

"Ship," Nixon corrected. "What did he want to talk to you about?"

The conversation went silent for a moment before Sheffield responded in a quiet voice, "I don't know."

"How do you not know?" they heard Nixon snap.

"I was on my way to a meeting. I told him if he wanted to have a conversation with me, he would need to make an appointment," Sheffield said. "That's all I have to say. If you want anything else, you can talk to my lawyer."

"I wouldn't make any out of town plans, Mr. Hayes," the detective said.

Kate and Nick looked at each other. Kate's eyes danced in the moonlight. "Let's see what else we got!"

Fast-forwarding through the recording, they listened as Detective Nixon questioned Thomas Hauer. "I wandered the deck like many other guests. I had no idea what was going on back there or who that fellow in the water is. Terrible. Probably want to check with Sheffield Hayes. That ol' boy's got a temper on him. Seems a bit desperate to me."

"Did anyone see you in the stern of the boat?"

"Nah, not that I'm aware of tonight. It was a beautiful night to stroll along a piece of history," Hauer said.

Moving the bar along to the next piece of conversation, they heard Sophia rant about her drink being confiscated. When asked about Ayres, she said, "Yeah. I saw him. He was creeping around the country club. When I had security come to get him, he seemed real excited to talk to Shef."

"Do you know what about?" Detective Nixon asked.

"Something about Collin. Not real sure what he would know about that. Figured another vulture was circling after his body was found. I'm sorry. It makes my stomach sick when I think of poor Collin… stuffed in a wall like that," Sophia said.

Robert Grant seemed to enjoy the attention when it was his turn to be questioned. "Naw, I was in the middle of my shoot. Going to be on the cover of *Golf Courses and Sunsets*. 'Guns under the Guns' they're going to call the spread. On account of me winning the longest drive in the tourney this year."

"You were with the photography group the whole time?" Nixon's voice came over the headset.

"Yeah. Right up to the point when your boys told me it was my turn. You want me to sign something for you?" Grant asked.

"This is just an on-scene witness interview. Official statements will be at the station, if needed," Detective Nixon said.

"No, I mean, like your shirt or a photograph or something?" Grant asked. "This one time, at Palm Beach, this woman had me sign her…"

"That'll be all, Mr. Grant," Nixon snapped.

Kate turned off the recording.

Their ears still sandwiched together with the shared headphones, they swiveled toward one another. Kate's eyes burrowed into Nick's. Her chest heaved a deep breath. "Hi…"

"Hello," Nick smiled, handing the headphones back to Kate.

For a moment, they were lost in each other's eyes.

"I, uh, I should set this down," Kate said.

Pulling herself away, she closed her laptop and set the headphones down.

Settling into their seats, they held their wine glasses in front of them and stared out at the ocean.

"Thanks," Kate finally said.

Nick turned toward Kate, "For what?"

"Just… putting up with me. Nearly getting you thrown into jail. Again," Kate said, her eyes never leaving the white froth of the ocean tide.

Nick laughed, "My pleasure?"

"You are a weird, masochistic man. But I am glad you are along for the ride," Kate said.

"You know what? So am I!" Nick raised his glass.

For another long moment, they refused eye contact. Fixated on the incoming surf, they quietly sipped their wine.

"So… that was a lot to unpack," Kate said.

"Yep," Nick agreed.

"Sheffield lied about knowing Ayres and what Ayres wanted to talk to him about," Kate said. Her gaze never left the rolling waves.

"Robert Grant lied about his whereabouts with the photography crew. He clearly had time after they disbanded to get to Ayres and reappear on the other side of the ship," Nick said.

"Yeah," Kate nodded.

"Hauer?" Nick asked.

"I don't know. He had opportunity," Kate said.

"Where do we go from here?" Nick asked.

"I think… I think I need to go to bed," Kate said abruptly. "Thank you for pouring the wine."

Gathering her things clutched to her chest, Kate hustled to her rented condo. She could feel Nick's eyes looking bewildered as they burrowed into the back of her skull. Standing in front of her bungalow door, she took a deep breath. Heart racing, she turned the key and disappeared inside.

Thirty Four

Kate and Nick arrived at the Carolina Beach police station. The mass of press crews had returned to learn and record as much as they could of the growing pool of murders old and new that were plaguing the coastal town.

Escorted through by uniformed cadets and volunteers, attendees of the prior evening's soiree on the *USS Battleship North Carolina* marched past the photographers and reporters as though they were on a Hollywood red carpet.

Inside the station, the scene was even more chaotic than the press and paparazzi-filled parking lot. Two officers with clip boards greeted each witness. Once checked off the list, they were once more escorted by a cadet to one of two conference rooms. Police Chief Harvey Banks observed the flow of traffic.

Kate was quick to notice the Hayes family and Robert Grant huddled, waiting their turn outside the opposite conference room she and Nick were being led to.

The door to the far conference room opened, revealing a terse Detective Pamela Nixon keeping a close watch on the Hayeses as Thomas Hauer and his contingent of sharply attired attorneys filtered out of the room. The look on Nixon's face declared that the conversation had not been particularly fruitful. As she eyed the battery of lawyers standing with the Hayes', it was clear she didn't have high hopes for that conversation, either.

As the door to the far conference room closed, Kate focused her attention on the gathering she and Nick were included in. Most of the faces were familiar but only from the night before.

Police Chief Banks greeted the attendees, "Thank you all for coming. The events of last night were unfortunate and disturbing. While I'm sure the very thought of what happened shakes many of you, your insight might help bring a murderer to justice. Any details you have to share, no matter how small, might shed light. Our cadets will take your statements. After Detective Nixon has had time to review them, she may reach out for further questions. Again, thank you for your willingness to help out to solve this heinous crime that happened last night at our treasured landmark."

With a nod, the chief slipped out of the room. Kate watched him intently, presuming he was making his way over to join Detective Nixon and the interview with the Hayes family. Their own conference room had been set up almost like a voting station. Lines were formed with five cadets sitting behind desks. A pair of chairs sat opposite while acoustic dividers prevented conversations from interfering with one another.

Kate chewed her lip.

"What?" Nick leaned over in a whisper as they waited their turn.

Eyebrows furrowed, she tapped her foot, "Why are we in *this* room?"

"Hmm?" Nick didn't understand her point.

"The key witnesses and suspects are being interviewed by Detective Nixon. Why aren't we slated to be over there?" Kate asked.

"You want to be included with the suspects?" Nick gasped, his breathy exclamation loud enough to attract the turn of the next couple in line.

"It's just that- Detective Nixon knows we have information… more so than any mere bystander!" Kate said. Smiling at a woman who scowled at Kate's comment.

Nick stifled a laugh, "I'm sure she has her hands full with *actual* murder suspects, not just meddling amateur sleuths."

"Yes, but the original murder took place in *my* house!" Kate pressed.

Her words immediately created a gap between them and the other witnesses in line around them.

"You are the only one I know who would rather be in the conference room being deposed by Detective Nixon. I am sure most of these people would rather not be here at all," Nick said.

Kate nodded, "I don't mean to be callous. I just want answers. I'm not going to get them in this room."

"Probably not. But a good investigator takes in *all* the evidence- even the most mundane. Maybe she did it on purpose knowing you would be in this room to pick up on any clues that she was here herself to pick up on," Nick smiled.

Kate clapped her hand on his arm. Looking up with pursed lips, "You're patronizing me."

"I'm challenging you," Nick grinned. "Come on. Let's be last in line. That way, you can observe the entire room."

Tugging her arm, he excused them as they pulled out of line and found a spot in the back.

Kate's eyes swept the room as she let out a hearty sigh. "Bartenders and wait staff. Robert Grant's photographers. It looks like they brought copies of their footage, that's smart. A few staff members from both golf resorts that I recognize. There's Jamison Hughes from the Cape Fear Golf Museum. Hmm, that's interesting."

"What's that?"

"Professor Granger. I didn't see him last night," Kate said.

"There are probably quite a few university people who attend an event like that," Nick shrugged.

Kate's eyes widened ever so slightly, "And his department assistant."

"You think that is significant?" Nick asked.

"I don't know. Like you said, every piece of information, no matter how mundane…" her words trailed off as she watched the witnesses wait to give their statements. She watched as the department assistant danced in place. Professor Granger leaned over and whispered in her ear. Her feet stopped dancing. Taking a deep breath, she seemed to gather herself before proceeding to the cadet waving at the empty chairs in front of him.

In the adjacent line, a collection of Hayes' management staff pooled around the far desk. One by one, they offered their statements.

When it was Kate and Nick's turn, they took their seats.

"Thank…" the cadet's voice croaked. "Excuse me. Thank you for coming down here today. I will ask you a series of questions and then you can share anything else not covered that you think might be pertinent. Starting with your names."

Starting with their names, their roles at the charity event and their relationship to one another, the cadet read off the sheet in front of her.

"She's my boss!" Nick declared, receiving a glare from Kate.

"We work together, and we're friends," Kate said.

"And how did you come to attend the event last night?" the cadet asked.

"We are wanting to become part of the community. Attending an event that gives back to a worthy cause seemed like an excellent way of beginning that process," Kate said.

The cadet continued down the list, "Where were you, *precisely*, on the ship between nine-twenty and nine-fifty-five?"

Kate and Nick looked at each other, "We were… exploring the stern side of the battleship."

Noting the response, the cadet began to move forward to a different line of questioning on the list. Stopping her, Kate said, "Aren't you going to ask a follow-up?"

The cadet looked over the edge of her paper, "Excuse me?"

"The main activity of the event was on the bow of the ship. The murder took place at the stern. On the port side of the battleship, near where we were," Kate said, receiving a quick kick from Nick.

With her eyes sweeping over Kate and Nick the cadet said slowly, "I will note that. Is there something you would like to confess?"

"Of course not, just being thorough. Details matter in a murder investigation," Kate said.

The cadet stared, dumbfounded at Kate. Looking at the list, she said, "I… I was just told to run through these questions. You are free to add anything you would like at the end."

Setting the paper down and holding her pen lined up to the next line of question, she looked up at an officer who stood by the door. With a nod toward Kate and Nick, her eyes requested assistance.

The officer at the door whispered something into the mic attached to his shoulder and took a couple of steps closer.

Nick could feel the air thicken as he adjusted in his seat. Kate seemed to appreciate the added attention.

"If it's okay, I'm going to continue down the list of questions…" the cadet said.

"Absolutely, I'm sorry," Kate nodded.

After a moment's wary glare, the cadet proceeded through the list of questions on her page. As she asked her last question, she seemed to stammer, reluctantly looking across the desk, "If… you, uh, have anything else to share…"

Kate drew in a big breath, about to unload her thoughts on the prior evening, before a voice cut her off.

"Oh. It's you. I should have known," Detective Nixon approached. With a nod toward the frazzled cadet,

Nixon said, "Thank you, Cadet Wilkins. I'll take it from here. I wasn't getting anywhere in the other room anyway." The cadet eagerly handed the detective the paper with Kate and Nick's responses.

Nixon studied the pair for a moment before saying, "You two come with me."

Glancing over the responses on the questionnaire as they walked, the detective led them to her office. Waving them in, she shut the door behind them.

Plopping into her chair, the typically sturdy detective appeared a bit wilted.

"So, what do you have? It seems you are the only ones in the entire room of witnesses that wanted to add to the report," Detective Nixon said.

"Well, we *were* in the relative area where the murder happened during the time it occurred," Kate said.

Detective Nixon straightened in her chair. Leaning over her desk on her elbows and clasping her fingers together, she asked, "You really want to be a suspect in a murder investigation?"

"That's what *I* said!" Nick blurted, receiving glares from both women.

"It's not that I *want* to be a suspect. I guess I don't want anything to be overlooked, even if it doesn't reflect well on me," Kate said.

"*Us*," Nick corrected.

Kate glanced over, "Sorry, Nick."

Letting out a hearty sigh, Detective Nixon said, "I don't overlook *anything* in an investigation. I also trust my instincts. There are several factors that rule you out. Your college dissertation was on the same day that Collin Royce disappeared. You were several states away with no connection. Your friend there… he was stationed overseas with his Maritime Security Response Team."

With a look of surprise, Kate's head turned toward Nick.

Detective Nixon grinned, enjoying the fact that she knew details about them they themselves didn't know about each other.

"You were in the military?" Kate asked.

Nick shrugged, "We can talk about it later."

"Now, if you want to look at recent events, you were nowhere near Dennis Jones when he was murdered and dumped off of Figure Eight Island. You *were* in the approximate vicinity of Andrew Ayres in the back of the battleship, but you would not have had enough time to kill him," Detective Nixon said.

With a dropped jaw, Nick stammered, "How did…"

"We had a tail," Kate let out an annoyed sigh.

"Details matter, right?" Detective Nixon grinned. "I kept a light eye on you. You didn't have a tail, more of a timestamp. After my talk with Detective Connolly, I thought it best to make sure you weren't trouble. For your benefit, it has kept you out of a cell and the need to call an attorney."

"*I* certainly appreciate that," Nick said.

"So, what is it that you have to add to your official statement?" the detective clicked a pen open.

Kate swallowed hard, "Robert Grant lied to you."

Detective Nixon shook her head, "Excuse me. What?"

"When you questioned him last night on the battleship. He lied to you," Kate said.

"What are you talking about? How would you know that?" the detective snapped.

"The steel ship allowed for vocal echoes. I was able to capture your conversation on my phone by picking up one of those reflections," Kate admitted.

"How do I not have you in a jail cell?" Detective Nixon fumed as she scrambled through her papers and pulled out her handwritten transcript of Grant's deposition. With a shrug, she said, "His deposition is consistent."

"He told you he was with the photography crew the *entire* time. He wasn't. He appeared on the opposite side of the battleship nearly ten minutes after the camera crew showed on deck," Kate said.

"Giving him enough time to circle around the stern and arrive port side," Detective Nixon slammed her pen down.

Gathering her thoughts, she stared at her papers, carefully combing through the golfer's statements. A knock on her office door broke her concentration.

Chief Banks opened the door and peered in, his eyes furrowing as he saw Kate and Nick sitting opposite his detective. "We, uh, we found something. You need to see this," the chief said.

Kate stood up. Glancing at Kate and Nick, she said, "You two go home… to your beach house… your rental… anywhere but here or near my investigation."

Kate and Nick paused for a moment. The detective's follow through made them jump, "Now!"

Spurred to move briskly, they made their way for the door the Carolina Beach Chief of Police held open. Once they had cleared her office, Nixon followed her boss through the station.

"What did they find?" Kate asked in a hoarse whisper.

"Cuffs. Cells. Attorneys," Nick shot back.

"What is downstairs?" Kate asked.

"The evidence cage," a young cadet said as they passed by.

Kate's eyes widened, "What did they find?"

Spinning, Kate turned from the exit and meandered through the police station.

Reluctantly, Nick followed.

Thirty Five

To Nick's great discomfort, he followed Kate as she hovered outside the stairwell door that led to the basement evidence room.

When questioned by an officer, Kate smiled, "Detective Nixon got pulled away from her office when we were in deposition. She told us to stay out of the way. I just wanted to make sure we were cleared to go before we left."

The officer nodded and walked off.

Seeing the look Nick gave her, she shrugged, "She *did* tell us to stay out of the way."

Melting further into the background, they watched as officers suddenly snapped into another gear as they received alerts on their phones and computers.

"Something's up," Nick whispered.

Suddenly, the doors from the stairwell burst open. Detective Nixon, with Chief Banks on her heels, instantly began barking orders. "All right. We have a suspect. He has possibly killed several victims and may be dangerous. Wear your vests and be ready. Nobody moves before I do!"

To Nick's chagrin, Kate left the relative safety of the wall to keep pace with the detective, "What did you find?"

The detective stopped in her tracks. Her head slowly swiveled toward Kate. Her eyes were as narrow as Kate and Nick had ever seen them, "Ms. Harper, this is precisely the time to… no. No, this *is* the time."

In a flash, the detective's hand grazed her hip. In less time than it took for Kate's mouth to open in response, a stainless-steel cuff was snapped on her wrist. With a sweep of her leg, a chair was pulled between them. With her free hand, Nixon pressed down on Kate's shoulder planting her in the chair. In an instant, the other cuff was clicked into place on a steel handle near the seat.

As the detective's eyes locked on Nick's, he found his own chair and sat next to Kate.

Kate pulled up on her wrist, annoyed at being stuck in place as the stainless-steel cuff clanged at its limit.

Nick offered a shrugging grin as he glanced at Kate's shackles, "You're the flight risk."

Without warning, the sound of metal pieces ratcheting into place and cold steel against Nick's wrist, let the air out of his statement.

"Why do *I* need these, Detective?" Nick looked up, his expression as innocent as he could make it.

"Because you are a willing accomplice to anything Ms. Harper sets out to do," Nixon snapped.

Like a child refuting a parent's scolding, Nick mumbled, "I don't know about willing. 'Anything' is a bit broad…"

"Good. I'll see to you two when I get back," the detective said and stormed toward her office.

Kate shot Nick a look that was mixed as apologetic but clearly humored as well.

Nick played with the steel around his wrist.

"Careful, you'll just make it tighter," Kate warned.

"You have more experience being handcuffed in a police station?" Nick snapped.

Kate offered a sheepish grin and a shrug.

Letting out a sigh, Nick stretched out as much as he could in his chair, resigned to be in that state until Detective Nixon saw fit to release them.

Moments later, the detective appeared in a tactical vest checking her service weapon. With a circle of her hand, she commanded, "Let's go!"

The officers fell in line and flowed out of the station.

Kate looked at Nick, "Who are they after? What did they find?"

A junior officer saw Kate's eyes fall on him. She stretched her neck as far as she could to peer over his shoulder. The officer abruptly spun in his chair and focused on the computer screen that he adjusted away from her.

Kate slumped. Scanning the police station, she tried to find anything that would tell her what they found and what suspect the clue led the police after. Police Chief Banks was ushered into the conference room that had been used for the primary interviews. A young woman carrying a box marked *evidence* followed him into the room.

The chief's assistant leaned into the room, "District Attorney Shevin is on line two."

"High profile case, she'll want to be in the loop every step of the way," the chief's voice could be heard. "I'll take it in here."

Kate leaned as far over toward the conference room as she could. As soon as the call was connected, the conference door shut. Once more, Kate slumped in frustration.

Craning her neck, she couldn't hear anything other than the tapping of the officer's fingers on his keyboard. Carefully lifting her chair under her, she crab-walked a few feet. The junior officer paused and glanced over his shoulder. Kate plopped her chair and rotated her neck as though she were stretching. As he got back to work, she again tried to maneuver to catch a view of the room.

Even as she was in direct line of the conference room, she realized it was insulated from sound.

"I, uhm, Officer? I need to use the powder room," Kate said.

The junior officer turned from his desk, "What? Oh, yeah. I was to let you loose as soon as Detective Nixon and her team were out of the parking lot. Sorry. Paperwork is a part of the job. I just never realized how much."

Slipping away from his desk, he opened a drawer and produced a key. Starting with Kate, he released her cuff. Moving to Nick, he repeated the process, freeing both of them.

"You technically aren't under arrest, but Detective Nixon said to ask you to stay away from her and her team while they were making the arrest," the junior officer said. "She thought it might be best if you stayed here and out of trouble. Her words."

"Oh, we aren't going anywhere," Kate said. "Except maybe the rest room. I really do have to use it."

"Sure, second door on the left," the officer pointed Kate in the right direction.

Glancing at Nick who was rubbing his wrist, the junior officer said, "You want some coffee or anything? It's strong, if not particularly great."

"No, I'm fine. Thank you," Nick nodded.

He watched Kate disappear toward the back of the police station. When she made her way back, the door to the conference room opened as the chief's assistant slipped out, leaving it partially open. Kate froze, peering into the conference room. Police Chief Banks stood in front of a screen with a man in a lab coat and the woman who carried the evidence box.

Excitedly, Kate pointed at Nick and then at the junior officer.

With a nod, Nick pulled his chair up to the junior officer's desk. "So, law enforcement. What brought you to this field?"

The officer turned toward Nick, leaving his back to Kate and launched into a conversation that started three generations back.

"This is really the murder weapon?" Banks asked, rubbing his chin.

"It is a match. Had traces of the victim's blood. Fingerprints matching that of the suspect. Even has the suspect's name engraved on it," the woman said.

"True, it is a modest weapon. However, it is surprisingly sharp and easily long enough to sever an artery," the man in the lab coat said.

The chief looked dubious, "Wouldn't opening an artery make a huge mess? None of the suspects at the party had any evidence of blood on them. The battleship was clean with barely a sign of struggle, never mind blood."

The man in the lab coat nodded, "I thought of that. Here, do you mind?"

The chief studied the man for a moment.

"Let me demonstrate," the man in the lab coat moved behind Chief Banks. "Say he was approached from behind or in any event, the suspect maneuvered to be behind the victim. The suspect is athletic and could take one arm to subdue and quiet the victim while preparing to stab him in the neck, precisely into the right common carotid artery while *leaning* the victim over the rail of the ship. As the victim became limp, over the edge he went. Right into the Cape Fear River."

"You are telling me, that a golfer, while charismatic, if not the brightest bulb in the room, could orchestrate such a well-executed attack? That he could precisely hit the artery while managing the flow of blood in a manner that he and the scene are kept immaculately clean from spatter?" Chief Banks asked.

"It would take a bit of knowledge, perhaps a bit of luck," the man in the lab coat nodded.

"The team, scanning with UV light did find traces of the victim's blood on the deck, the rail and the side of the battleship," the woman who delivered the evidence box added.

"All right," Chief Banks nodded. "You have convinced me. Now, we just need to convince the District Attorney and a jury. May I see the weapon again?"

The woman clicked a button on a remote control. A screen in the back of the room was brought to life. In the center of it was an image. Kate couldn't help but take a slight step forward as she studied it.

A metal object with a pair of what looked like sharp fangs with a handle that had none other than Robert Grant's logo on it. Inscribed on one of the fangs was Grant's signature.

Her eyes widened, "That is what punctured my tire!"

The heads in the room turned toward Kate.

"Ms. Harper. Why am I not surprised to see you lurking around my police station," Chief Banks said. With a wave, he added, "You might as well as come in. I'd rather hear what you're thinking than to have you go off on your own. You too, Mr. Mason!"

Kate pressed the door open as Nick scurried across the room to join her. He thanked the junior officer who realized the in-depth conversation about his rich legacy in law enforcement was a ruse to keep him occupied while Kate was able to sneak a peek.

"You say this… tool is what punctured your tire at the Hauer resort?" Chief Banks asked.

"Yes," Kate nodded. Glancing at the woman with the evidence and the man in the lab coat, she asked, "Is that sharp enough to penetrate rubber?"

The man in the lab coat offered a mixed nod and a shrug, "It would be sharp enough."

"We thought her tire had been stabbed twice, for good measure. That does look like it might have been the instrument. One poke and gone. If you think it could have done it," Nick said. He frowned, "What little golf I've played, divot tools are pretty dull and harmless."

"Divot tool?" Kate asked.

"That's what you're looking at. If you swing too low, you chip up the turf. It's golf etiquette to fix the 'divot' before moving on," Nick said.

The chief nodded, "Robert Grant's trademark is the 'Night Slayer'. Slow starts, gets hot toward the latter half of the day. At noon, he might be mid-pack of the leaderboard. By nightfall, he's right up in contention. The fangs are a bit of a gimmick."

"They retract, like a switchblade. So you could carry it in a pocket," the woman said.

The chief scanned the room, "Ms. Kate Harper, Nick Mason, meet Andrea Berkowitz, our chief forensic officer. This gentleman and master of all things macabre is Dr. Jim Herren. You want to get away with anything in this town, you have to get past these two. I don't know anyone who could outwit either of them."

"Robert Grant…" Kate muttered. "That's who Detective Nixon is after."

"It adds up. Your observation was a key to proving opportunity. He had motive. He had means. The murder weapon has his signature, fingerprints and logo on it," Chief Banks said. "He's our man."

The conversation was interrupted as a commotion stirred in the front of the station. Moving out of the conference room, they leaned out to see what was happening.

Officers held reporters at bay while Detective Nixon gripped Robert Grant by the arm, escorting him through the police station.

"Lots of people have that tool. I give them away. It's my calling card!" Grant bellowed.

"Many a murderer has been caught by the arrogance of their calling card, Mr. Grant," Detective Nixon was undeterred. "Yours had your fingerprint on it."

"Of course, it did. Because I gave it away!" Grant argued.

The successful mission couldn't hide a rare grin on the detective's face, until she saw Kate and Nick standing with Chief Banks and the forensics team.

Sitting the handcuffed Grant into a seat while the booking officers made their way over to process the murder suspect, Detective Nixon made her way over to the group observing the scene.

"We got our man, Chief," Detective Nixon announced proudly. With a terse look, she said to Kate, "Ms. Harper, you actually helped. I couldn't establish opportunity without your statement, so… thank you."

"Happy to help," Kate nodded. She was somewhat despondent as she observed Robert Grant. He looked stunned and confused. His complexion was pale. He looked scared for his life.

The detective's eyes followed Kate's, and she said, "Don't let that puppy dog face fool you. It isn't surprise because he is innocent. It is surprise that he got caught."

Kate nodded numbly.

As Grant was escorted to processing, cameras on selfie-sticks tried to capture the scene from their restrained positions in the police station lobby.

Grant winced as he tried to avoid being photographed, ducking between the officers' shoulders.

A man pushed his way through the crowd. Kate recognized him as being part of the Hayes contingent. His perfectly pressed Italian suit and worn leather briefcase told Kate he was part of Hayes' legal team sent to guide Grant.

"My endorsements!" Grant gasped.

"Endorsements?" the attorney gasped. Realizing he had an audience, he smiled, "Any PR is good PR, right?"

Hustling alongside his client, he cursed in a hoarse whisper, "I strongly advise you to be silent, Mr. Grant."

"But I didn't do it!" Grant could be heard as he disappeared into the bowels of the station.

"They always say that. Even when they did it," Detective Nixon said. "Well, I have a lot of work to do and I believe your time here has come to an end, Ms. Harper."

Kate's eyes snapped back from the door where Robert Grant had been taken through. "Yes, of course. Excellent work, Detective."

Detective Nixon looked at Kate, her face softened for a very rare moment, "You know, Ms. Harper. At the risk of encouraging you, your insight was actually, somewhat helpful."

"What the detective is trying to say is good work. Just leave the sleuthing to the professionals," Chief Banks said with a hand extended to a nearby officer, "I believe you are familiar with leaving out the back. I'll have Officer Kantola walk you out."

Kate nodded and accepted the escort. She could hear Chief Banks discuss matching the murder weapon to the sidewall of Kate's car to Detective Nixon.

Successfully avoiding the reporter pool who were intently pressing into the police station lobby, Kate and Nick sat in the SUV. The silence after the excitement in the station was welcoming. For a long moment, they sat.

For Nick, it was a sense of relief that it was all over. "We get to finally enjoy the beach house. Enjoy Carolina Beach."

"Yeah," Kate said, her voice void of conviction. While staring out the windshield, her finger hovered over the "Start" button.

Nick's shoulders morphed from relaxed and relieved to slumped as he recognized the telltale look on Kate's face that had become all too familiar with, "What is it?"

Kate bit her lip and looked at Nick.

"Don't you think it's a little too clean? I mean, using a murder weapon that literally has your signature on it?" Kate asked.

Nick shrugged, "He seems like a nice enough guy, but not the sharpest tool in the shed."

"But sharp enough to carry out a well-executed murder with minimal evidence at the scene. Executing a man with near medical precision? What about Dennis Jones? What about Collin Royce? You really think Grant killed Royce and walled him up in the beach house? To go undetected for a decade?" Kate pressed.

"He had the most to gain," Nick said. "He has earned a ton of money and a ton of accolades in Royce's absence."

"It's just a little too easy," Kate said.

Nick pivoted in his seat to face Kate more directly, "None of this was easy. Maybe Grant uses his affable nature as a ruse. To hide the cunningness he holds inside. To keep his dark secrets… well, secret. The police have their man. It's time to finish the job we were brought here to do and maybe even enjoy ourselves without the fear of a murderer stalking us along the way."

"Yeah," Kate nodded, her voice breathy. "You're right."

Pressing "Start", she brought her SUV to life and pulled away from the police station.

A glance in her rearview mirror displaced a circus of activity in the police parking lot as droves of news crews descended on the small beach town.

Thirty Six

Kate stepped out of her bungalow to a sunrise. Orange and pink spread wide across the faded blue line separating the Atlantic Ocean from the sky. A silhouette emerged rising over the sand dunes. The telltale shape of a surfboard tucked under his arm pulled an unconscious smile to her lips.

"You already heading out?" Nick asked as he approached the bungalows.

"Gonna try a new coffee spot. A little shop owned by a group of friends. They have something called a coffee party pack. Thinking we are going to need it," Kate said.

Nick laughed, "You should just invest in an espresso machine for each beach house. You'd save a ton of money by the time you turn the keys over to vacationers."

"I might," Kate nodded. "It is fun to check out the area hot spots. Support the local economy."

"I'll be right behind you," Nick said, setting his board down.

Kate nodded, pausing as Nick studied her a moment too long. "What?"

"You all right?" he asked.

"Yeah. I didn't sleep much. I honestly thought I was going to, but I just kept tossing and turning," Kate admitted.

"Hence the party pack," Nick said.

Kate shrugged, "Time to focus on the house, right?"

Nick didn't look satisfied with Kate's response, though he looked hesitant to ask, "What was keeping you up?"

"Robert Grant. Sure, he had a lot to gain from Royce being out of the equation. Probably the *most* to gain," Kate said.

"But was it worth killing for?" Nick prodded.

"Exactly. I can't help but to think of those with something to *lose* having a stronger motive that would bring someone to commit a horrible string of deaths," Kate said.

"Thomas Hauer and the Hayeses," Nick said. "What about Dennis Jones and Andrew Ayres?"

"Reporters who got too close to the truth," Kate said, her voice flat. "Like when you tell a lie, the lies after the lie keep building up."

"Pull the string on the sweater, and suddenly it just keeps getting worse," Nick said.

Kate nodded, "I just don't see Robert Grant as that devious of a person. He is opportunistic, sure, but cunning? I don't see it."

"Want to go get coffee and talk about it?" Nick asked.

"No. We need to focus on the house. Detective Nixon is competent. If she has the wrong guy, she'll figure it out," Kate said, shaking her head. "I do need coffee, though. Meet you at the beach house?"

"See you there," Nick nodded.

Watching her as she disappeared down the walkway to the parking lot, he could see the wheels were turning. He had hoped all of the business of murder was finally behind them.

Nick was already working on the house when Kate pushed her way in. A tray full of coffees and a bag of breakfast sandwiches balanced on top were set down on the kitchen island. Following the sounds of progress, she found Nick on a ladder working to remove a noisy and well-patinaed bathroom ceiling fan.

"Breakfast has arrived!" Kate sang.

Wasting no time, Nick set his tools down and hopped off the ladder, "I could eat."

Following Kate to the kitchen, they grabbed their coffee and sandwiches and stole a moment on the back deck to enjoy breakfast while watching the morning surf roll in.

"This is a good sandwich. Thank you," Nick said after taking a bite.

"Avocado toast with caprese. I had them add an extra egg for you," Kate said.

"Coffee isn't bad either," Nick said.

"Worthy of the list?" Kate asked.

Nick nodded, "Yeah, I think it is."

Kate looked at the beach and the sandpipers scurrying along the fingers of waves reaching up onto the sand.

"It's so nice out here," she sighed.

"Bittersweet wrapping up projects, I imagine," Nick said.

Kate looked at him, "It is. You get invested in the community. Embellish the charms of the houses. Become completely enamored with the views. At the same time, the next adventure is exciting to think about as well."

"Eventually, you need to call some place home," Nick said.

"Until then, I get to explore some of the most beautiful locations. I get to discover the people and places that call to me," Kate said.

"The places you've been don't call to you?" Nick asked.

"They do. I'm pulled along like I have some unfinished business that I'm not even aware of. So, I follow along. Until I find it," Kate said, her eyes subconsciously locking with Nick's.

"Yeah, I guess as a hobo surfer, I can understand that," Nick said. Gathering up his breakfast items, he pushed up from his chair, "Right now, I have a bathroom ceiling fan calling to me."

Kate smiled. Watching him get up and walk back into the house, she appreciated his willingness to endure her ramblings. Whether beach gazing and thinking about life or sorting through murder suspects, he was a gentle presence at her side. With a deep sigh, she realized how much she liked that presence.

Shaking off the thought, she glanced at her phone to see her boss had sent a number of messages requesting updates on the beach house's schedule. "Time to focus, Kate!"

For as long as the morning caffeine worked through Kate's system, she remained steadily focused on the beach house. Noting the final items that needed to be done as well as finishing touches in décor she wanted for the completed staging, she was feeling good about how she and Nick were able to pull back in some of the lost time.

Pulling open her laptop to place an order for outdoor furniture, her eyes were pulled to the newsfeed on the computer's browser. A photo of golf pro Robert Grant being led into the police station, a jacket covering his handcuffed wrists. The look on his face was one of bewilderment.

Clicking on the image, she brought up the story. The official press release from the police station was vague, but it pinned all three murders on Robert Grant. Instinctively, she looked over at the foyer hallway where the faux wall had once stood. Shaking her head, she wondered if Robert Grant could have done that. It was seamless. It had to be done quickly.

Her mind wandered, surfing the search bar, she pulled up articles of Robert Grant and Sheffield Hayes. In the stories written about their joint projects, Sheffield often had a tool in his hand. In not a single photograph, did Robert Grant appear to be hands on with any part of the build. Other than a shiny silver shovel wielded for a "breaking ground" photo op, the golfer stood to the side of the work being done, looking impeccable as always.

"Sheffield Hayes…" Kate muttered. Scanning the photographs, she found one of Sheffield patching up drywall after a raucous indoor golf chipping bet went awry. Her finger hovered over the button on her computer. After hitting print, her mind was pulled back into the mystery of the string of dead bodies that started in the beach house.

"Maybe they were working together," a voice over her shoulder called out.

Spinning, she saw Nick carrying the old vent fan to the trash.

Kate studied Nick for a moment.

"Grant certainly has the strength to carry a body. Sheffield the know how to perform basic construction work," Nick said.

"If Sheffield built the interior wall, it would make sense why it was never "discovered". It was his house. If he didn't say anything, who would?" Kate said.

"He still could have done it on his own. The body could have been dragged and not carried. You said who had the most to lose. I think you are looking at him. Right there," Nick said, pointing at the photo of Sheffield kneeling by the drywall patch.

Kate frowned, "Dennis Jones must have found something out about Sheffield that was damning enough to get him killed."

"Andrew Ayres may have found that same piece of evidence," Nick said.

While staring off at the beach, Kate's mind was working at full tilt, "We need to follow their footsteps. Discover what they knew."

"Let me reiterate, whatever they knew, got them both killed," Nick said.

"With the 'case closed', Sheffield might not be as wary," Kate said.

"Where do we begin?" Nick asked.

Kate shot a determined look, "At the beginning. How were Dennis Jones and Andrew Ayres assigned to the Collin Royce story? Who did they work for?"

"Sounds like a plan," Nick nodded.

"Why don't you keep working on the house? I'm going to see what I can find out about these reporters," Kate said. Seeing the concerned look from Nick, she added, "On my laptop from the safety of the beach house."

"Good. It's easier for me to concentrate if… if I know you're safe," Nick said. With the slightest streak of crimson in his cheeks, he spun, giving the old exhaust fan undue attention.

Kate smiled as he walked away. Under her breath, she muttered, "I feel better, too, with you here."

Positioned where she could glance over the edge of her screen and catch glimpses of the ocean, Kate stretched her fingers and went to work. Starting with the article bylines, she looked up Dennis Jones.

Frowning as she searched, she couldn't find any articles from Dennis Jones prior to a few months preceding Collin Royce's disappearance. There was a steady build up with nearly half of his articles about Collin. The rest were about the golfing world, particularly in North Carolina. Most of those articles were pieces on the Hayes family, not all of them flattering.

Kate read articles about the family's clouded history in how they came to claim the land that their flagship course was built on. Mark and Sheffield Hayes' philanthropy was mentioned in an almost mocking manner in some articles. Sophia's improprieties were well documented with great focus on her interactions with Collin Royce in societies in the tabloids.

The library of articles from Dennis Jones continued for several months after Collin's disappearance, nearly all of them centered on the case. Eventually, they dwindled and stopped. His name didn't resurface in a byline until Royce's body was discovered in the beach house.

Sitting back, Kate frowned, trying to make sense of this information.

Fingers dancing above the keyboard, she broadened her search. To her surprise, she uncovered a host of additional articles from Jones, all from the *Newcastle Chronicle*. Digging through her bag, she pulled out a business card from Andrew Ayres. Holding it up to the screen, she matched it as the same news outlet.

Scrolling through the articles, Jones wrote about politics and regional power players. Only in those contexts did he ever write about golf. Biting her lip, she scanned Jones' deep catalog of articles.

Switching gears, she put Andrew Ayres into the same search bar. The Newcastle Chronicle's index remained empty. Studying the card, she made sure she had typed it in correctly. Her search still came up empty.

Tapping the card against the table, she scrolled to the bottom of the page. Dialing the contact number for the paper, she waited for the connection.

"Newcastle upon Tyne Chronicle, how may I connect your call?" the voice said over the line.

"I would like to speak with Andrew Ayres' editor, please," Kate said.

"Andrew Ayres? I'm sorry, ma'am. There is no one at this paper with that name. The only Andrew here is our Circulation Manager, Andrew Jones. He is currently on vacation. Due back… yesterday. Hmm. Is there anything else I can do for you?" the operator asked.

Kate was momentarily lost, her eyes focused on the ocean but not relaying the image to her brain, "Uhm, yes. Would you connect me to Andrew Jones' office, please?"

"Yes, ma'am," the operator said. The line was quiet for several moments before the operator's voice came back on, "I'm sorry, ma'am. Mr. Jones' office line is still switched on his vacation message. Would you like me to connect you with someone else?"

"No, thank you," Kate's voice was breathy while she let the call close. Placing her phone down on the table, she stood up from her seat. In a slow spin, she turned to see Nick coming into the front room. With a squint, she said, "Andrew Ayres is Andrew Jones. He isn't a reporter. He is a circulation manager for the Newcastle Chronicle. Dennis Jones is… was a reporter for the Newcastle Chronicle."

Nick cocked his head, "What does that all mean? Why would Andrew Ay… Jones lie to us? To everyone?"

"To gain access…" Kate wheeled around to her computer. After a few heavily fingered keystrokes, she turned back to Nick, "To gain access to his murdered brother's case here on the Carolina Coast."

Thirty Seven

Nick circled behind Kate as she reviewed her findings on her laptop.

"Here's what's also odd," Kate said, peering over her shoulder as Nick placed his hand on the back of her chair. "Dennis Jones focused on politics and influential people around the Newcastle area. He wasn't a sports reporter."

"That is strange. He was way out of his range. I wonder if the paper sent him," Nick asked.

Kate shook her head. "After I contacted them the first time and learned about Andrew, I collected myself and called back. Dennis wasn't working for the newspaper when he was covering Collin Royce. He was on sabbatical."

"And he only showed up in the U.S. writing about golf when Royce was here," Nick said.

"Before heading back to England not long after Royce disappeared, appearing only again when we discovered the body," Kate said.

"Maybe he had something to do with Collin Royce's death," Nick surmised.

"Maybe. I don't know," Kate shrugged.

Nick frowned, "Where is Royce from?"

Kate turned to her laptop. After a few keystrokes, she said, "Whitely Bay. Right up the coast from Newcastle."

"The Jones brothers have a connection with Collin Royce," Nick said.

With a nod, Kate agreed, "It appears they do… did."

Scratching his chin, Nick asked, "Even if they had something to do with Collin Royce's murder, they certainly didn't kill themselves."

"Maybe someone found out about them and exacted revenge," Kate said.

"Robert Grant?" Nick wrinkled his nose.

Kate looked out at the waves allowing her mind to process. "And who slashed my tires? Toppled the bookcase at the library?"

"Grant is a public figure. How much peace and quiet do you suppose he gets?" Nick asked.

"If he was out somewhere, he was probably recorded and posted on social media," Kate nodded excitedly.

Pulling out a sheet of paper, Kate began putting in time stamps for every incident, starting with Collin Royce's disappearance to Andrew Jones' murder on the *USS North Carolina Battleship*.

Using those times, she did a search for Robert Grant sightings in each form of social media. Every hashtag with "RobertGrantGolf" within those timestamps was captured with source data, time and location.

When she was done, Nick placed a pair of iced coffees in front of them.

Kate tapped her notes, "We cannot account for Robert Grant's whereabouts the evening Collin Royce disappeared. Like a lot of golfers during a tournament, he probably remained low key to maintain his focus. But look, Grant was at Loggerhead Golf Co. for a promotion on their latest virtual golf simulator right before Dennis Jones was killed. From his schedule perspective he *could* have gotten to Dennis Jones. *But*, here is a shot on social media of him leaving the golf shop. Taken by someone next to him stuck in traffic. Look at the time stamp. There is no way he had anything to do with the reporter's death."

Nick looked at Kate, a serious expression on his face, "That means there is still a killer loose somewhere on the Carolina coast."

"Let me see…" Kate spun back to her laptop. "I can't match his location while I was at the library, but, when my tire was stabbed, he was at an ice cream shop in the Cotton Exchange signing someone's visor."

"*If* the same tool used to stab your tire was also the murder weapon that slashed Andrew Jones' throat…" Nick began.

"Someone else was in possession of the murder weapon, *not* Robert Grant!" Kate exclaimed.

"We need to talk to Detective Nixon," Nick said.

Kate nodded, collecting her notes.

Kate and Nick marched into the Carolina Beach Police Station. The reporter pool had dwindled since Robert Grant's arrest. A few stragglers remained looking bored as they waited for updates on the case.

Seeing the pair approach, the desk officer sighed, "I'll ring for Detective Nixon."

The detective appeared in the doorway leading to the police station lobby.

"I was really hoping I was done with you two," Detective Nixon said. Seeing the excitement on Kate's face and the documents she held in her hands, the detective glanced at the reporters who perked up. "Come with me to my office."

Following the detective through the station, she led them into her office and closed the door behind them. Settling into her desk chair, she said, "I'm not sure I even want to know what is in your hands."

Kate's eyes were wide as she held the papers out for Detective Nixon to see, "It is a timeline of incidents mapped to Robert Grant's whereabouts."

The detective's harsh glare melted the pride on Kate's face, "Why am I looking at this and why are you still poking your nose into my investigation?"

"Something felt off to me. Oh, did you know Andrew Ayres is not Andrew Ayres? He is Andrew Jones, Dennis Jones' brother," Kate said.

The detective set the papers down and cast a hard look toward Kate, "We had been having a difficult time tracking him down. Our junior investigator's inquiry to the paper to find family to notify that Ayres was a dead end. I guess we now know why. But what is all of this on Robert Grant?"

"I traced his whereabouts through social media. I figured being a public figure, he couldn't go anywhere without photos being taken and posted," Kate said. "I referenced each post to the time. He couldn't have killed Dennis Jones. He couldn't have punctured my tire."

"And if the tire puncture matched the murder weapon… which I am not saying it did," Detective Nixon rubbed her face. "I have the wrong guy."

"I can't account for his time when Collin Royce disappeared and we know he was unaccounted for during Andrew Ayres', I mean Jones', murder," Kate said.

"Social media posts are terrible courtroom evidence. I will have to chase down each and everyone of these social media accounts to corroborate the time stamps," Detective Nixon sighed.

For a moment, she looked blankly somewhere between Kate and Nick. Her complexion seemed to pale slightly.

Finally, she returned her gaze to Kate, "Anything else I should know? Like, who killed Collin Royce or Dennis Jones? If Robert Grant did in fact, not kill Andrew… Jones, then who did? Or why?"

Kate shook her head slowly, "I'm afraid not."

"I will have this all looked into. Thank you for bringing it to my attention. I fear I am wasting my breath in asking you to stop looking into this case. Can I at least ask that you keep me in the loop from here forward? If I do have the wrong man, the killer is still out there. My guess is the Jones boys got close to the truth. We see how that turned out for them," Detective Nixon offered a stern look at both Kate and Nick.

"I will," Kate nodded eagerly.

The detective's eyes fell onto the sheets of paper that Kate had handed to her. The dejection was impossible for her to hide. Rising from her seat, she said, "I'll see you out. And, let's keep this between us."

While Leading them out of the station, the detective's flat expression had returned and gave the handful of reporters waiting in the lobby a glimmer of hope that some interesting detail had manifested. They were left wanting.

The air in Kate's SUV was unsettled. Her brain was on fire trying to piece the fragments of the case together. She chewed her lip as she flipped through the facts, searching for what she was missing. The link between the Joneses' and Collin Royce. What it all had to do with the Hayes family. Where Thomas Hauer and Robert Grant fit in, if at all.

Crossing over the Snow's Cut Channel and onto Pleasure Island, Kate glanced over at Nick who was caught looking at her. He snapped his head away and fixed his gaze on the approaching island and the swath of blue providing its eastern outline.

"What?" she asked, returning her eyes to the road in front of her.

Nick scoffed, "I didn't say anything."

"No, but you were thinking real hard," Kate said.

Shuffling in his seat, Nick said, "I was just… I was watching you think."

"Watching me think?" Kate pressed.

"Yeah," Nick admitted.

Kate glanced over, "Why would you 'watch me think'?"

Shaking his head, Nick said, "Because… it's impressive. The way you tackle puzzles. Your, almost incessant, search for answers."

"Getting you in trouble all the time," Kate added.

"It's my choice whether I follow you or not," Nick said.

"Why do you?" Kate asked.

Nick was thoughtful for a long minute, "Partially because I think I enjoy trying to solve the puzzle too."

"And the other part?" Kate asked, almost subconsciously as she split her concentration with driving.

"I like to make sure you are safe," Nick said, the answer spilled out immediately.

Kate felt her cheeks glow, "I like having you… making sure that I am safe."

Pulling into the beach house drive, Kate put the SUV in park.

"Well, back to work, I guess. Thanks for coming with me to speak with Detective Nixon," Kate said.

"Always a treat," Nick chuckled.

"Yeah, she's a fun one. I think I am winning her over," Kate grinned.

"I think you are wearing her down," Nick countered.

Kate bobbed her head back and forth, "Yeah, you might be right."

Walking up the steps, Kate pressed her code for the door lock. Suddenly, Nick's arm flashed out, blocking Kate from opening the door.

Her head snapped up, "What…?"

Nick shook his head and put a finger to his lips.

Nodding, Kate frowned and watched Nick cock his head as he studied the house.

Her eyes went wide as she heard it too- footsteps inside the beach house.

In a whisper, he said, "Get in the car and call Detective Nixon."

"What are you going to do?" Kate asked as Nick descended the porch steps and reached into the back of his truck.

Spinning a claw hammer in his hand, he said, "I'm going to see who is in your beach house."

"Oh, no, Nick. We'll just call the police," Kate urged heading toward her SUV.

Not listening, Nick sprinted to the side of the beach house. Running alongside the house, he bound up the wooden steps leading to the back deck.

Kate followed as her thumb hit the line with Detective Nixon's phone number. Her heart thumped loudly in her chest as she tried to keep pace with Nick. Reaching the glass doors, he checked each. Finding them latched and no other clear sign of entry left him bewildered.

Suddenly, his eyes flashed, "The dumbwaiter!"

Sprinting past Kate, he glided down the steps. Racing under the house to the gated dumbwaiter, he found it on the ground floor and open. Whirling, hammer in hand, Nick scanned the area looking for any movement, listening for any crunch of shell and sand underfoot.

Kate caught up to him, eyeing the open dumbwaiter. She asked, "See anything?"

Nick paced toward the driveway and shook his head, "No."

Twirling the hammer angrily in his hand, Nick turned back toward the beach house. Cursing toward himself, he inspected the dumbwaiter, "I replaced all of the locks in the house. I didn't think about the dumbwaiter."

Looking over the lightweight elevator used to make bringing luggage and groceries into the tall beach house easier, Kate placed a hand on Nick's shoulder. "I never thought of it as a point of entry for a person," Kate said.

"Probably not the most comfortable ride, but doable. You still need a key or a code," Nick said.

"So, whoever was here, has been here before," Kate said.

"Like a former owner?" Nick fumed.

"Or at least a guest," Kate shrugged.

Nick began closing up the dumbwaiter, but Kate's hand stopped him.

"Leave it for Detective Nixon," Kate said.

With a nod, Nick wandered away from the contraption. Slipping the hammer into a loop in his pants, he paced.

"It is a good thing you have good ears," Kate said.

"I just wish I was able to catch him," Nick said.

The sound of a vehicle coming to an abrupt stop in front of the beach house driveway captured their attention. Two marked police cars screeched to a halt in line.

The driver's door of the first car opened. Detective Nixon stepped out, whipping off her sunglasses. Her eyes scanned the house before landing on the pair underneath the beach house.

"I can't leave you two alone for a minute!" Detective Nixon snapped. "Are they still in the house?"

Kate shook her head, "I don't think so. We think they used the dumbwaiter as a point of entry and as a getaway."

The detective nodded, "I'd like to sweep the house anyway. Mind unlocking the front door?"

Giving orders to an officer to stay by the dumbwaiter and sending a pair to the rear of the beach house with one on her heels, Detective Nixon followed Kate up the steps of the front porch.

Kate punched in the code for the door lock. Detective Nixon pulled her firearm from its holster. Pressing the lever on the door, she looked over her shoulder, "You two stay outside."

With a nod, the detective disappeared into the house with an officer in tow. Room by room, the detective and officer scanned and announced them "clear" as they went. Kate and Nick stood in the open doorway, listening as the search was completed.

Before long, Detective Nixon met them in the foyer, "There's no one here now. Walk with me. Tell me if there is anything disturbed or missing."

Kate's mind went to her "crime closet", not exactly excited to have the detective find it.

"And yes, I saw your little secret lair," Nixon snapped.

Moving quickly through the house, Kate and Nick scanned for missing items.

Kate saw all of her papers sifted through. Drawers were pulled open.

One of Nick's ladders sat in the living room, and all of the can lights were dangling from the ceiling.

"Someone was definitely searching for something," Nick said.

"That wasn't you?" the detective asked, walking under the lights.

"No," Nick shook his head. His eyes suddenly swept to Kate as a grin began to form.

With a sharp look, Kate deterred him from sharing his thoughts.

"Anything missing?" the detective asked.

"I don't think they were looking for any of our things," Kate said.

Detective Nixon squared with Kate, "Whether they were looking for any of your things or not, they would have certainly found your crime lab. If whoever was in your house is mixed up in the murders, you have put yourself squarely in their crosshairs, Ms. Harper."

Kate looked away as if the Atlantic Ocean held some fitting response.

"Mind if we take a look?" Detective Nixon asked.

With a shrug, Kate couldn't see how the detective reviewing her "crime closet" would cause any more harm at this point.

Giving orders to the officer to secure the front of the beach house, Detective Nixon allowed Kate to lead her up to the master bedroom closet. Clicking on the light, Kate was dejected to find her papers in shambles for the second time.

Gathering her photos, news articles and other items, she began pinning them back to the walls. Detective Nixon watched intently, occasionally jotting a note in a pad she pulled from her pocket.

"From your information provided this morning, Robert Grant is cleared from Dennis Jones' murder. Not necessarily, Collin Royce's or Andrew Jones'," the detective said.

"I think they are tied together," Kate said. "Aside from Grant, the Hayeses and Thomas Hauer had the most to lose or gain, depending on perspective."

The detective frowned, "Why would the Hayeses risk losing everything when they were at their height? They were on the rise when Royce was their poster child. They continued to do well, but not at the same pace after Royce disappeared."

"What was the Jones' connection to Royce? And why did Dennis follow him to North Carolina?" Kate asked.

Detective Nixon tapped on a photo on the wall, "While the Hayes' trajectory leveled off, Thomas Hauer's enterprise took off shortly after. He has no alibi for his whereabouts at the time of Andrew Jones' death. Your tires were slashed at his country club, where his well-outfitted security magically didn't see anything or have operational cameras. I was stonewalled by his very expensive lawyers. I think it's time he and I have a deeper conversation."

"I..." Kate started.

"Thank you, Ms. Harper. I'm once again going to have an officer posted outside of the beach house. Please, and don't let this fall on deaf ears this time, if you uncover anything, let me know. Do not chase it down yourself," Detective Nixon said.

Kate watched the detective leave. Still clutching papers to her chest, Kate looked at Nick who offered a shrug.

Thirty Eight

Detective Nixon drove away, leaving a uniformed officer parked across the street as both overwatch and deterrence.

Kate rolled away from the upstairs window, allowing the blinds she had peeked through to fall back into place.

Nick watched her from the hallway, "We need to be very careful with every move we make. If Detective Nixon releases Robert Grant, the real murderer is going to feel pressured. If they think you are on to them, you're in real danger."

Stepping into the walk-in closet, Kate began reassembling her crime wall, "If they think I solved the case based on what I have on this wall, they clearly see something I don't."

"Let me help you," Nick suggested.

Kate looked over her shoulder, "I was half expecting you to encourage me to throw all this away and hide in my hotel room until the real killer was caught."

"Would you?" Nick asked.

A weak smile leaked from Kate's lips, "No. Probably not."

"Then I'd rather be by your side until the end," Nick said.

Her eyes locked on his, Kate's smile broadened as she offered a slight nod, "I'd like that."

"So, what do we have here?" Nick asked, holding a box of pushpins.

Kate sorted through her papers, "We know Grant didn't slash my tires or kill Dennis Jones or break into the beach house."

"We can't rule him out for killing Collin Royce," Nick said. "Or even Andrew Jones on the battleship."

"No, we can't. But I am convinced Royce's killer is also responsible for the Jones' deaths and most of the associated crimes," Kate said.

"That leaves…" Nick prodded.

"The entire Hayes family and Thomas Hauer," Nick said. "Hauer was already questioned once and stonewalled with his attorney."

"He has some questions to answer. It is only a matter of time and legal pressure before Detective Nixon gets enough to rule him out or in," Kate said.

"So, in the meantime, we focus on the Hayes family," Nick said.

"We do," Kate nodded.

"Start at the top?" Nick suggested.

Kate held up a current photo of Mark Hayes, "He certainly doesn't look like the murdering type. At least not literally. I am sure he is vicious in a boardroom."

"Just the same, ten years ago, he would have had a bit more youth on his side. And he has been around construction for most of his life," Nick said.

"Telling contractors and foremen what to do, but yes, I suppose you would pick up a skill or two here and there. But, do you really think he could overpower a desperate and heartbroken Andrew Jones bent on avenging his brother's death?" Kate asked. "He rarely left the main party on the battleship."

Nick studied the photo before responding, "No. I think he is smart and cunning. Not a hands-dirty killer."

"I think for similar reasons, we can rule out Sophia. She could certainly have her own reasons for wanting Collin dead and silencing the prodding of the Jones boys. But I don't see her lugging a body up the steps from the beach, in the middle of a thunderstorm and building him into a false wall. Or hoisting Andrew Jones over the rail of the *Battleship USS North Carolina*," Kate said.

Nick gave Kate a hard look.

"What?" she frowned.

"Watching you work, I wouldn't question a woman's ability to accomplish *anything* they were determined to accomplish," Nick said.

Kate blushed, "Well, thank you. Still, physical limitations persist. Sophia Hayes *could* have done those things, but it is highly unlikely."

"Fair enough. On the board, just lower down. I have to think Mark Hayes lands in the same category," Nick said.

"That brings us to Sheffield Hayes. Desperate to live up to his father's expectations and public image for being a proper prodigy," Kate said.

"If that is the case, killing the tournament leading golfer that was going to cement your family's legacy seems like an odd choice," Nick said.

"What if there was something... something so damning, Sheffield didn't think he had a choice?" Kate suggested.

"Like jumping ship to the competition?" Nick asked.

Kate shrugged, "Maybe."

"He, like his father, had at least some knowledge of construction. Aside from Sophia, he was the closest to Collin. We know Dennis Jones was in contact with him and could assume Andrew was if he was chasing the same trail," Nick suggested.

"I don't disagree with any of that, but there are a lot of 'assumptions'. His car *was* seen near Hauer's country club when my tires were punctured, which turned out to be done by the murder weapon used to kill Andrew," Kate said.

"As Robert Grant's closest friend, he certainly would have been able to get his hands on Grant's personal divot tool," Nick said.

"I think Sheffield is my guy. I just need to find a way to prove it," Kate said.

Her face fell slightly. Nick noticed and cocked his head.

Offering a sheepish laugh, Kate said, "All while not being able to rule out any of the suspects on this board. At least not completely."

"No one said sleuthing was easy," Nick said. "That is why even pros like Nixon can use some fresh eyes and perspectives. Providing we aren't breaking any rules or getting underfoot."

Kate wrinkled her nose, "Following most of the rules only being a *little* underfoot at times?"

Nick laughed, "I think that is why Detective Nixon fingers her cuffs every time you are around."

"You noticed that, huh?" Kate asked.

Nick nodded. "So, what do we do now?"

"I'm going to run through the facts one more time. I still feel like I am missing something. What did Dennis Jones know? What was so threatening to the Hayeses… or Hauers… to get Collin Royce killed? Want to stay and help me?"

"I am going to search the house one more time. Whoever broke in certainly seems to think this beach house holds a secret," Nick said.

"That's if they haven't found it already," Kate said.

"I don't think so. It sounded like they were still searching when we arrived. I think this house has something to tell us. Something important. Something that leads to…" Nick started.

"The killer!" Kate exclaimed.

"I was going to say pirate's treasure. Think about it, millions in Spanish doubloons and long-lost chalices. Rubies. Emeralds. Gold!" Nick said.

Kate shook her head, "One way or another, it could be vital to solving this case. Good luck."

Nick disappeared with a child-like bounce in his step.

Kate chewed lightly on the back of her pen. Her eyes moved from the photo of Sheffield Hayes to the image of Collin Royce and then to Dennis Jones. She was more and more convinced that the answers were in that triangle.

Pulling out her laptop, she began looking overseas for those answers. Dennis Jones uncovered something that brought him to America. Following Collin Royce to North Carolina, where he was staying in Sheffield Hayes' beach house. Whatever he uncovered, or thought he had, got him killed.

Searching for articles on the Hayeses traveling to Newcastle and, having business ties in England all came up dry. Tapping the pen to her lips as she pondered, Kate flipped through articles and suddenly, she stopped.

Highlighting an image, she magnified it. Taken when the Hayeses were just breaking ground on their flagship golf course, a woman stood next to an at-the-time young adult Sophia. Looking at the write up, she identified the woman as Anne Hayes. Mark Hayes' wife and mother to Sheffield and Sophia.

Isolating the image, Kate whispered to herself, "She was beautiful."

Deleting her previous request in the search bar, Kate typed in Anne Hayes. Sifting through the articles, she paused. Mumbling as she read, "Anne Hayes, formally Anne Clarkson. Born in Tynemouth, *England*. Met real estate mogul Mark Hayes while vacationing in Italy. They were married and had two children, Sheffield and Sophia. Anne passed shortly before the opening of the Hayes Country Club and Golf Resort. The main hall was dubbed Anne Hall in her honor."

Kate tapped her pen against the edge of her laptop, trying to absorb this new information, to determine if it had any impact on the case. The geographic connection between Collin Royce and the Jones brothers was too much to ignore.

Typing in a new search, she pulled up an article on how the Hayes-Royce partnership came to be. Collin Royce was intrigued by the buzz of the Hayes family's entry into the world golf tournament stage. Attaching himself to the new, state of the art golf course coupled with his quick rise up the world rankings, made for a formidable business duo.

"*He* came to the Hayeses…" Kate considered. Pulling out her phone, she scanned through some of the photos she had taken while in the executive offices at the Hayes Country Club. Finding one that struck her, she sent the file to her laptop and hit the print button.

Pulling the image from the printer, she held it up, studying it, she gasped, "Oh my goodness."

Pinning it to the wall, Kate drew a large red circle around the faces in the photograph. Stepping back, she raced out of the closet to find Nick.

Kate followed the sounds of rustling through the house. Cocking an ear, she identified the direction they were coming from. Shouldering the partially open utility room door, she peered inside. The ceiling panel was removed and disturbed dust particles danced in the light as they cascaded through the opening.

"Nick?" she called.

Indiscernible groans and curses from above could be heard making their way across the ceiling until Nick's face appeared upside down through the opening. "Yeah… you need something?"

Kate studied Nick for a second. His forehead had a sheen from sweat working in the attic space. His face was speckled with dirt and dust while his tee shirt had picked up kernels of insulation that stuck to the fabric. The generally affable man wore a distinctly irritated look on his face.

"You okay?" Kate asked.

"It's frustrating. I have been all over this house. Removed nearly everything removable and… nothing. That and this is an admittedly unpleasant environment," Nick said, his voice exasperated.

Kate giggled, and in a sweet voice, she suggested, "Why don't you come down? Take a break. I'll fix up some ice-cold lemonade and show you what I found."

"You found something?" Nick asked, his voice perking up.

"I did," Kate nodded. "I don't know what it means, but, yes."

"Alright. I'm happy to get out of this hot and stuffy pit of scratchy things and spiders," Nick said.

Kate winced at the word "spiders".

"Don't worry. No mean ones, at least that I saw," Nick said. Holding on to the lateral trusses, he curled his legs under him and through the hole. Lowering himself down inch by inch until his feet hit the step stool.

Wiping his forehead against his sleeve, Kate eyed the opening.

Seeing her concern, likely an eerie daymare of spiders descending through the opportunistic access point and taking over the house, he nudged it shut.

"Why don't you splash some cold water on your face? I'll make the lemonade," Kate suggested.

Patting tufts of insulation off his clothes, he nodded.

By the time he had run handfuls of cold water over his face and on the back of his neck, Kate stood in the hallway with two tall glasses of lemonade. Toweling off, Nick happily accepted one.

"Thank you," he said.

"The least I could do. No luck, huh?" Kate asked.

"No treasure map, no decade-old murder weapon, not even an abandoned peg leg," Nick admitted.

"There may just be nothing here," Kate said.

"I'm beginning to think that is the case. Or it has already been found," Nick said. "So, what is it that you found?"

Kate grinned, "Come on, I'll show you."

Leading Nick up the stairs to the master bedroom closet, Kate nodded toward the new sheets she had pinned to the wall.

Taking a sip of his lemonade, Nick leaned forward, "What exactly am I looking at?"

"You are looking at the connection between Dennis and Andrew Jones and the Hayes family," Kate said, her voice triumphant.

"Who's this?" Nick tapped against a new photo of the Hayes family in front of the new property they had purchased for their Wilmington golf course.

"*That* is Anne Hayes," Kate grinned.

"Anne Hayes…"

"Wife of Mark Hayes. Mother of Sheffield and Sophia Hayes. Born and raised a short drive from where Dennis and Andrew Jones called home. The same area Collin Royce started his golf career," Kate said.

Nick's eyes went wide, "Kate! You uncovered the connection."

"Now, to figure out how that connection translates to a string of murders," Kate said.

Nick set his lemonade glass down and took a closer look at the photo of the Hayes family. Pulling the photo of Collin Royce, he held it up. "She was an attractive woman. You know, they kind of look…"

Kate's eyes went wide, "I know, right?"

Nick pondered, struggling to connect the definitive dots that Kate seemed to observe.

"Come on, Nick. There is a distinct family resemblance," Kate said.

"I don't know about distinct… but there *is* some, I mean," Nick shrugged. Suddenly his eyes widened, "You think Mark Hayes had an illegitimate child!"

"Wouldn't be the first millionaire that took part in a little impropriety," Kate said.

"Maybe," Nick said.

"That kind of scandal, just as the family was starting to rise into golf society echelon, would upset the apple cart," Kate said.

Nick frowned, "I don't know. You think the world would have cared that much? It could have gone the other way. A golf world dynasty in the making, even if it was literally born out of imprudence. So, who is the mother, then?"

Kate couldn't hide a wicked grin. Producing another photo, she handed it to Nick.

Nick studied the picture.

"Anne has a sister. Rebecca. Roughly her age, just as pretty…" Kate said.

"Now, *that*, would be scandalous in a way that could tear a family apart," Nick said.

The pair stared at the photos pinned to the wall, absorbing everything they had learned.

Nick's eyes never left the wall, "We need to talk to Detective Nixon."

"Yes, we do," Kate said.

Thirty Nine

The desk officer's head sank when he saw Kate and Nick walk into the police station. Without even asking, he dialed Detective Nixon.

"The detective is very busy right now. Have a seat," they were waved off with the back of the desk sergeant's hand.

Kate nearly vibrated with excitement. Nick observed the reporter pool which had once again grown in size, the reporters busily punching notes into their laptops or creating their news broadcast scripts.

A strangely chipper Detective Nixon showed up at the front desk and waved them in.

"Ms. Harper and Mr. Mason, what brings you in? I am happy to say, I think we have this case nearly sewn up," the detective beamed as she led them to her office. Her face suddenly fell as she eyed the folder in Kate's arms. "Except, you don't think I do."

Kate shook her head, "Not quite, I'm afraid."

With a deep breath and a wary cast around the room, Detective Nixon ushered Kate and Nick into her office and closed the door quickly behind them.

"This really isn't the best time. So, if you are going to waste mine, I am absolutely delighted to escort you down to our holding cells," Nixon snapped.

Kate tapped the folder clutched to her chest, "I have something you need to see."

Handing the folder out for the detective, Nixon snatched it and opened it up. Glancing at the photos, she looked up, "What am I looking at?"

"You are looking at photos of Anne Hayes and Collin Royce, along with photos of the Hayes family and Rebecca Clarkson," Kate said.

Detective Nixon frowned, "Rebecca Clarkson?"

"Anne's sister. The other clippings show that Anne, and Rebecca are from Tynemouth, a town just outside of Newcastle. Newcastle is where Collin Royce, Dennis Jones and Andrew Jones are all from," Kate said.

"So?" Detective Nixon shrugged.

"So, that is the connection that ties this case all together. Tell me you haven't wondered how all of these random people from the U.K. and the U.S. connected to form a decade of murders," Kate said.

The detective sighed, "This is all interesting stuff. But I follow the evidence. Whether these people all partied together, did business together, hate each other, love each other, I don't really care. I care about the evidence that is presented in front of me. Nothing in this file is evidence."

Waving the file at Kate, Nixon abruptly slapped it back to Kate's chest.

"Look at the photos," Kate handed the folder back to the detective.

Shoulders slumped, Nixon reluctantly sifted through the photos, "A rich family, a less rich family, a pro golfer and a couple of newspaper guys… so what?"

"Tell me you don't see the family resemblance between Collin Royce and the Hayes family. Look at Rebecca Clarkson and Mark Hayes and Collin Royce," Kate said.

"There are some similarities, so what?" Nixon asked.

"What if Mark Hayes had an affair with his wife's sister. Their prodigy becomes a world-class golfer and ingratiates himself to the budding North Carolina golf mecca of the Hayes Golf and Country Club?" Kate pressed.

"What if monkeys had wings?" the detective snapped. "That is what you don't get, Ms. Harper. You have a fantastic imagination. You have a drive for answers that, quite frankly, I admire. But imagination and… commendable research does not equate to evidence."

Kate's head fell dejected.

In a rare empathetic voice, Detective Nixon said, "Look, I researched Collin Royce. There are *no* records of his birth. The only documents are his adoption to Mary and Kellen Royce, a, by all accounts, kind family from Newcastle upon Tyne, England. There is no evidence that the Hayeses, outside of signing him to a mutually lucrative contract- have any other connection to him. A contract, by the way, that would have made both parties millions over the course of his career. The Hayes' wanting Collin Royce to disappear had millions, with an 's', in disincentives. Hauer, however, who had means and opportunity, to commit all of the crimes on the board, including threatening you in his own parking lot, had the opposite. As the Hayes family suffered, he gained."

"I'm sorry, Ms. Harper, I have my guy," the detective continued.

Kate blinked at Detective Nixon.

"Look," the detective spun her computer monitor around. "I received this from the *USS Battleship North Carolina*."

The video showed Thomas Hauer striding through the stern of the ship, slipping into the shadows very near where Andrew Jones was killed and thrown overboard.

"The timestamp aligns with minutes of Andrew Jones' death," Nixon said.

"There is another angle," Kate pleaded. "Verify what I just learned and it changes everything."

"Sure, I could do that. I could flush my career down the drain along the way," Detective Nixon snapped. "If everyone stepped up to give DNA samples- including those in England, which is just a bit outside of my jurisdiction, not that the Hayes' attorneys would ever allow it, sure. I could verify your theory as *plausible*. That means nothing in a court of law. Hard, indisputable facts, that is what I offer. That is the difference between a professional detective with schooling, training and years of experience and a… well-intentioned amateur whose beach house happened to be ground zero for a murder investigation."

"But it might *be* evidence," Kate pressed.

"I can't get a subpoena for an affair that took place in another country decades ago. I can get one for a murder suspect where the evidence *directly* presents. I don't have that on Mark Hayes. I *do* have corroborating testimony that absolves him of Andrew Jones' murder," Detective Nixon said.

"What if Sheffield found out about the affair and Collin? He steps into protect the family's name," Kate suggested.

"You have evidence of that?" Nixon countered.

Kate's head fell, "Not yet."

"Ms. Harper," Nixon fingered her cuffs, forcing a strained chuckle from Nick.

Receiving an elbow to the ribs from Kate, Nick straightened up.

"As far as Thomas Hauer goes, just so you will drop this, I have his fingerprint on Robert Grant's divot tool. The one that sliced Andrew Jones' throat and matches the puncture pattern on your tire, at *his* country club," Nixon shared. "I appreciate your instincts. You have sound research skills, but I have this investigation handled, Ms. Harper. Now, if you'll excuse me, I have a meeting with the New Hanover County District Attorney."

Kate and Nick left the police station. Kate was visibly deflated after the conversation.

"I know all of this matters, I just wish Detective Nixon could see it," Kate fumed.

"I think you are on to something. We just need evidence," Nick said.

"How do we get evidence for events that happened decades ago?" Kate snapped.

Nick placed a steady hand on Kate's shoulder, "We find it. Hard evidence that Sheffield Hayes protected his family from the destructive discovery that he had an illegitimate half-brother."

"You make it sound so easy," Kate scoffed.

Nick grinned, "Ask him. His face will tell you everything you need to know."

Kate looked into Nick's eyes, surprised by his direct confrontational strategy.

"Up for a mimosa at a country club?" Kate asked.

Glancing at his watch, Nick said, "It's still before noon. A mimosa sounds great. It *is* a breakfast food, right?"

Nick felt compelled to whisper as they exited Kate's vehicle and headed into the country club, "What is it you expect to learn from coming here again?"

"Honestly, I don't know. I think… I think I just want to observe. See their faces, their mannerisms. See who is beginning to wilt to the pressure," Kate said.

Making their way to the country club dining room and bar, they selected a seat overlooking the course while affording the broadest view inside the clubhouse as well. Nick volunteered to check in with the bartender and order their drinks.

Seeing a familiar face, Nick nodded, "Good morning."

The bartender cocked his head for a moment, "Mr. Mason."

Impressed, Nick smiled, "Wow. You have great recall. I can't remember someone I just met, never mind all the customers you meet on a daily basis."

"Part of the job. You can train yourself to remember names," the bartender smiled as he pulled down some glasses. "The trick is, every time you see that person, you say their name to yourself. No matter what. Each time a customer orders, I repeat the name in my head and then I start saying it out loud. I read somewhere that is where the memory really kicks in. I saw you at the charity event on the battleship. Was great to be on the other side of the bar for once."

Nick held a finger out, "I *did* see you there. Out of context, I didn't make the connection at the time."

"Trust me. It happens every time I go to the grocery store," the bartender laughed. Suddenly, the bartender's eyes flashed up.

Nick noticed. Looking across the bar, he captured Sophia Hayes in a reflection. "And whatever she is having."

The bartender nodded and poured a bourbon mule.

Nick turned to find himself face to face with Sophia. Forcing a suave smile, he said, "Join me?"

Sophia glanced at the bar, seeing two mimosas poured, "If you're double-fisting, I am not sure I could resist. I assume your lady friend is here with you? I'm not sure we've been *properly* introduced. I might rather enjoy meeting her."

Hooking the mimosas in his fingers and carrying Sophia's drink in his other hand, Nick led her to her table.

Watching from her seat at the table, Kate squirmed at the opportunity to learn more about the Hayes family whose history seemed to grow more complex the more she dug into the mystery.

When they arrived at the table, the moment was strangely awkward until Sophia broke the ice with her usual swagger, "The intrepid sleuth. I heard you were helpful in getting poor Robby released. Thank you. None of us could believe he had anything to do with all that nastiness, never mind Collin's murder."

Sitting across from Kate, Sophia looked deep into her eyes as she sipped her drink from a little straw.

"He's not out of the doghouse completely, but I helped the police rule him out of most of the crimes," Kate said. "I… I do have a few questions for you, if you don't mind."

"For the price of another beverage, I'll sing like a bird," Sophia smiled. "Nick, would you be so kind?"

Nick looked at Kate and then nodded, "Sure. I'll be right back."

The moment Nick was out of whisper range, Sophia leaned across the table and hissed, "What's the story with you two? The steaminess between you is palpable."

Fanning her amply displayed cleavage to emphasize the proposed tension, Sophia leaned back in her seat, crossed her arms and waited for a response.

"It's complicated," Kate wrinkled her nose.

"Doesn't look complicated. You're attractive. He's handsome… a bit of a do-right, but has just enough edge to him," Sophia's eye contact with Kate broke as she watched Nick saunter up to the bar.

"He kind of works for me," Kate said.

"So? It sounds like you travel to beautiful, *romantic* beach locations together. What a brilliant match," Sophia said. "Honey, guys like him don't come around that often. Sure, they can be rich, handsome, even know their way around… well, pleasant to be with. But good. Take all of those things and add *genuinely* good… Nick is a catch."

Kate blushed.

Sophia watched as Nick turned from the bar with her drink in hand, "I'm just saying, don't let a good thing pass you by. I did that once, and now look at me– the country club tramp."

"You aren't…"

"Oh, honey. Sometimes the tabloids get the story right," Sophia scoffed.

"You can always change your course," Kate said, her voice soft.

"Yeah," Sophia said, smiling at Nick as he set the glass down in front of her. Taking a sip, she grinned at Kate, "I'll start working on that tomorrow."

"Did I miss anything?" Nick asked, taking his seat next to Kate.

"Just girl talk," Sophia said. "So, you had some questions for me?"

Kate nodded, "I heard there was a big argument between Sheffield and Collin the night… the night…"

"The night he was killed. Yeah. They argued. It seemed to be a growing thing between those two. Collin looked up to Sheffield even though I always thought it should have been the other way around. For whatever reason, Collin idolized my brother. When he didn't get the affirmation he sought after, he would be dejected, like a scolded puppy. I think that is what started the defection to Thomas' sponsorship. I think it was just Collin shaking things up, getting Sheffield's attention," Sophia said.

"Did it work?" Kate asked.

"Probably too well. That led to the big blow up. Sheffield was furious. My family is big on loyalty. My dad modeled that brutally in his business dealings, Sheffield watched and learned from him. I didn't see Collin's ploy as such a big deal. Collin never even cashed Thomas' check. He wasn't going anywhere. But he did, I guess. Horrible," Sophia's head sunk to her chest.

"I'm sorry. It must have been so hard, not knowing and now…" Kate started.

Sophia nodded, "It was. Losing Collin was like losing a family member."

Shifting gears to not lose Sophia to sour emotions, Kate asked, "Were you guys close to your mother's family?"

Sophia reeled slightly at the abrupt change in direction, "We used to be. We used to vacation together all the time. My mom would visit for months at a time, especially when my father was busy on a project. At some point, Mom and Aunt Rebecca had a falling out. I never did know why. I just know we never went back to England after that. That was years ago. Why do you ask?"

"Collin was from England, wasn't he?" Kate asked.

"He was. Not too far from where my aunt lived, actually. When his agent was looking for sponsorship deals, he said that connection was a factor that made partnering with Hayes Golf that much more appealing. Hometown connection, even if across the Atlantic, I suppose," Sophia said.

Sophia sat back and sighed, "We all loved Collin. I didn't love him in the manner the media wanted me to. He was handsome and charming." Her eyes flash to Nick before her lips erupted into a mischievous grin, "But there was just something where we just didn't click romantically. I mean, I had a reputation to uphold so we made the most out of photo ops."

Kate smiled at Sophia. There was something likable about the woman despite all of her brokenness and wild behavior.

Draining her mule, Sophia set the glass firmly on the table, "This romp down memory lane has been fun, but I really need to get going."

Standing up out of her seat she looked at Kate, "Don't let things pass you by, Kate. Nick, always a pleasure."

Slipping on a pair of sunglasses, Sophia made a beeline for the doors leading to a patio overlooking the course, the nearest exit.

Nick played with his half-drunk mimosa, "So, Sherlock, what is your takeaway from all that?"

"I think Sheffield is a pot that constantly hovers near a boil. I think there is more to the argument he had with Collin. I think it was he who punctured my tire which would place him with the murder weapon that killed Andrew Jones. He owned the beach house that Collin's body was encased in following his murder. He has construction knowledge and is physically fit enough to have carried out the murders. Now, I just have to prove it," Kate said, her voice defiant.

Forty

Kate walked through the Hayes Country Club doors with purpose. With a steady walk and confident smile, she strode past the staff and up the stairs to the executive offices. Nick followed in tow, his eyes failing to deliver the same air as he offered apologetic smiles.

Pushing through the office doors, they were quickly stopped by the executive assistant, "May I help you?"

The assistant studied Kate and Nick, her eyes glinting with recognition.

Kate smiled, "I am here to see Sheffield."

"Do you have an appointment?" the assistant asked.

"No, I do not, but…" Kate began.

"Then, you are *not* here to see Mr. Hayes," the assistant snapped.

Kate started to speak, but she was interrupted as her mouth opened.

"It's all right," Sophia Hayes' voice said softly. "Ms. Harper and Mr. Nixon, I was just heading out. Walk with me?"

"Sure," Kate nodded.

Nick offered a friendly smile.

The assistant pursed her lips, her eyes narrowing as she reluctantly backed away from the conversation.

Kate and Nick followed as Sophia pushed the door open.

"You *really* think Sheffield had something to do with Collin and those reporters," Sophia said.

"Unfortunately, I do," Kate said, her voice even.

Sophia was unmoved by the steadfast comment, "Well, perhaps he can clear things up for you once and for all. I get the feeling you aren't going to stop poking around until you are satisfied."

"Thank you. I appreciate your openness," Kate said.

"My brother can be a bit of a shark in the business world, but in life, he's a puppy dog. There is no way he had a hand in killing Collin or anyone else," Sophia said. Stopping in front of the clubhouse, she said, "Sheffield and everyone else who is deemed Wilmington aristocracy are heading to Airlie Gardens for an oyster roast. It is a bit of an annual tradition."

"I've heard of that," Kate nodded.

"You heard of the public one. This is a prequel so the money players can enjoy it without mingling with the riff raff. I'll ensure you have a pass," Sophia said.

Both wore curious expressions. Nick finally said, "Why… are you being so helpful?"

Sophia looked at Nick. Her usual playful, sultry look was wiped clean from her face. Instead, she was stone serious, "Because, I am looking forward to a long, painful chapter being put to a close. Once and for all."

True to Sophia's word, Kate and Nick were waved through by the park security detail that had been installed for the event. Much like the country clubs, the garden's parking lot was filled with expensive vehicles. Among them was the luxury sports car with surfboards tied down to a rack.

Seeing the vehicle just reinforced Kate's suspicions because Sheffield's car was easily identifiable and clearly the one the cameras picked up outside of the Hauer Country Club the day her tires were slashed.

Navigating their way through the crowd, sampling an array of wine and cocktails paired with plates piled high with oysters, Kate and Nick sorted through the Who's Who of Wilmington and the region's islands. Thomas Hauer, the Hayes family and Robert Grant mixed in with Cape Fear region elite.

Spying Sheffield, who was working the crowd with the aplomb of a politician, Kate led the charge.

"Mr. Hayes…" Kate called out.

Sheffield spun on his heel, hand extended to greet whoever called him. Seeing Kate, he was reticent, "I remember you. You were in our offices… and on the *USS North Carolina*. It seems trouble for my family seems to percolate when you are around."

"If it makes you feel any better, it isn't just your family," Nick quipped, receiving a sharp look from Kate.

"I just have a few questions about you and your relationship with Collin Royce," Kate said.

"*I* have questions about Collin. I guess you're the ones working on the beach house," Sheffield said..

"We are," Kate nodded. "There was information that you learned about Collin that led to a fight right before his death."

"Wow, you get right to the point, don't you?" Sheffield said, his face turning stony. Glancing around, he nodded, "It's true. Collin had a moment of not feeling as appreciated by the Hayes family as he would have liked. He felt he was a big part of our growth. He wasn't wrong, but the success and rewards that came with it were mutual. We disagreed on the proportions. It happens in business. Doesn't mean I killed him. I still loved him like a brother. Brothers fight. His disappearance was a blow to me financially and personally."

Kate's eyes surveyed Sheffield's as he spoke. "Dennis Jones followed Collin Royce over. I believe he had information that you may have wanted to keep quiet," Kate pressed.

"The reporter? That weasel was always angling for something. Always hanging out with the sports reporters but never really covering golf. Always pressing about my family. He's the one who started the rumors between my sister and Collin. The entertainment world loved it, so they just went with it," Sheffield said.

"Went with it?" Kate asked.

Sheffield shared a terse look with Kate, "Sophia always had a thing for Thomas Hauer. A total Romeo and Juliet thing. To be honest, I had always hoped things would work out with her and Robert. But after Collin, she just got... a little twisted."

"Look, this isn't really the place," Sheffield glanced around, offering a smile across the lawn to the Wilmington councilman. "I get that you have questions. If I found a body stashed in the walls of a house I had just bought, I probably would too. Doesn't make it better that I happened to own that house at the time the body was placed in there, but I had nothing to do with it. Collin and I scuffled from time to time, we are… were both highly competitive. I wouldn't kill him, though."

"One last thing, why were you at Hauer's country club last Wednesday?" Kate asked.

Sheffield squinted, looking away as if to search some mental appointment book. Turning back to Kate, he said, "I wasn't. I have only ever been there for a golf tournament or for a museum event. Last Wednesday, I spent the whole day checking new hole placements."

"Your car was seen driving by just before noon," Kate said.

"Just before noon, I was on the back nine of the south course. I had the second nine to check and the entire north course after that," Sheffield said. His tone snapped, "I really have to go. Excuse me."

Brushing past, Sheffield hurried up the walk, waving at an attendee of the event. His entourage, including recently released Robert Grant, his father Mark and sister Sophia were looking on at the discussion.

Nick looked at Kate, "What do you make of all that?"

"Let's walk and talk," Kate suggested. Swatting away a bug, she glanced at the concessions near the main building, "After I get us some waters."

"I'll get it," Nick said.

"Thank you, I'll wait for you out on the pier," Kate said.

With a nod, Nick jogged to the Garden Services Building. Kate wandered past the Airlie Oak, a massive five-hundred-year-old tree. "That fella has some stories to tell," Kate muttered. Stepping out onto the Bradley Creek Pier, she glanced over where a gathering of people had been watching something in the water below. Leaning against the pier rail, she realized what had caught their attention. A twelve-foot alligator floated with his front feet and head just at the surface of the water.

The group moved further down the pier allowing Kate to get a closer look while she waited for Nick. The dangerous creature looked so docile as it floated, seemingly as curious about the crowd as they were of it. A second pair of eyes shone in the lights that lined the pier railing as if trying to catch a glimpse of what caught the first alligator's attention.

Leaning against the rail, Kate appreciated the bit of coastal breeze that started to play in off the water as the sun was setting. In her peripheral vision, Kate thought she saw another group passing by. To her surprise, a pair of hands grabbed her at the waist and in one fluid motion, heaved her over the side.

Kate's mind was in pure panic. Salty water filled her lungs. Expelling as much water as she could, she lost what little oxygen she had. None of that weighed on her mind as much as her two reptilian friends whom she now shared the water with.

Desperately trying to get her bearings, she used the light glow from the railing lights to lead her to the surface. Her heart raced as she knew it was those lights that revealed the alligators' very presence.

After taking in a gaping lungful of air, Kate's eyes scanned the surface of the water. To her horror, the alligators were making a beeline for her. With strokes smooth as her terrified body could make, she broke for the shore. Congested with marsh grass and cottontails, she knew that even if she could out swim the alligators to shore, she was afraid they would catch up to her as she picked her way on to shore.

Head down, she did the only thing she could do, keep swimming.

Nick looked up as he heard the shriek. Glancing toward the pier, he saw a mass of people huddled around one side as a hooded figure ran on shore and streaked for the shadows. He didn't wait for confirmation of who or what was going on. He knew Kate was there.

Dropping his newly purchased drinks, Nick sprinted toward the pier. As he ran, he heard frantic voices shouting "in the water", "alligator" and "woman".

Without needing another word, Nick ran onto the pier, glanced into water and leaped over the rail. Knifing into the water, Nick split Kate from the curious alligators. The sudden dive bomb into the water gave the instinctive creatures a moment of pause, enough time for Kate to reach shore.

Met with a growing crowd of park workers and security, Kate was pulled to safety. Nick was on her heels as one of the alligators closed in. With both on shore, the alligator stopped, its eyes locked on its would-be prey mere feet from the water's edge.

Nick's hands reached out for Kate's shoulders, looking her in the eyes as she coughed, "Are you okay?"

Kate nodded in between gasps of air, "I'm fine… I'm fine. I can't believe you just jumped in there after me."

"I can't believe you doubted that I would," Nick said, his eyes locked on hers.

Exasperation turned into gratefulness as she moved in to hug him. Her arms wrapped around his waist as she pressed her head into his chest, "Thank you."

Nick's response came as a return hug.

With her safe, Nick's eyes scanned the crowd and the direction that he saw the hooded figure run off to. He didn't imagine he would see anyone, but he was hoping others may have seen them as well.

"Let's get you guys some place to dry off," one of the security guards said, nudging their shoulders with an assertive hand.

Letting go of their embrace, they nodded, allowing the security guards to take them away from the scene. One remained posted at the pier.

"What happened, ma'am? How'd you fall in?" the guard asked.

"I didn't fall in. I was *thrown* in," Kate said.

"Maybe someone brushed by?" the guard suggested.

Kate stopped, her head turning toward the guard, "Then I would have bumped against the rail, not over it."

"I saw someone wearing a hoodie run off the pier and into those trees over there," Nick pointed.

The guard looked incredulous at the accounts. Turning to one of the other guards trailing them, he said, "Grab Murray and see what you guys can see. I'll take these two to the volunteer room and get them some towels."

With a nod, the trailing guard spoke into his walkie talkie and broke toward the treed area.

"So, why would someone want to push you into the water?" the guard asked.

"I would assume because I'm getting close to solving a murder," Kate said.

The guard's head whipped to Kate, "You… what?"

'It's a long story," Nick shrugged. "You might want to call Detective Nixon with the Carolina Beach Police Department."

The guard just shook his head as he led them inside a conference room being used as a hospitality suite for the staff and volunteers. "You two make yourselves comfortable. Help yourself. I'll hunt down some towels for you," the security guard said.

"You sure you're okay?" Nick asked when they were alone.

Kate shot Nick a lopsided smile, "Because I was dumped into the marsh and nearly eaten by alligators?"

"It would be enough to shake most people," Nick said. As the fear had completely dissipated, angry determination replaced it on Kate's face. "I know, you are not most people."

"I'm a bit shaken up," Kate admitted.

"Have an idea who did it?" Nick asked.

"Sheffield is the obvious candidate," Kate shrugged.

Nick frowned, "He seems too smart to be obvious."

"I know," Kate nodded. "I need to talk to him."

"You won't get your chance if you're dead, Ms. Harper," a voice snapped from the hallway. "Here, the head of the security detail found these in lost and found."

Detective Nixon handed Kate and Nick beach towels, which they readily accepted.

The angry and annoyed version of Detective Nixon returned. "What are you two up to, now?"

Kate offered a sheepish grin, "Just an evening swim."

"I heard alligators were involved," Nixon snapped.

"I'm pretty sure whoever did it- knew that," Kate said.

"And you know who that was?" Nixon pressed.

"No," Kate shook her head. "The sun was just going down, and they were mixed in the crowd on the pier."

"I saw someone in a hoody run from the pier and into a stand of trees," Nick said.

"You couldn't see who it was?" Nixon asked.

"They kept their head away, and with the hood on, it was nothing but shadow," Nick shrugged. "My focus was on helping Kate."

"Which you did by jumping into alligator-infested Bradley Creek," the detective spoke of the inlet that knifed inland from the Intracoastal Waterway and Wrightsville Beach.

"Seemed like the thing to do at the time," Nick said.

"I imagine," Nixon eyed him with her non-emotive face. Turning to Kate, she asked, "What was it you were chasing down this time?"

"I wanted to talk to Sheffield Hayes," Kate said.

The detective sighed, "This is an exclusive event for Wilmington's elite. I imagine questioning him among his peers would make him angry. How did you even get in here?"

"Sophia got us in," Kate said.

"Did she know why you were here?" Nixon asked.

Kate nodded, "She did."

The detective leaned back and mulled the situation, "I have been berated and dressed down by Thomas Hauer's attorneys all day. I am not in the mood to spool up the Hayeses and their onslaught of legal advisors."

"I'm sure that isn't a good idea. I'm not even sure it was Sheffield who did it anyway. It could have been… it could have been anyone here. Including Thomas Hauer as a way to cast suspicion on Sheffield," Kate said.

"Or Sophia, since she gave you access to this soiree," Detective Nixon said.

Nick frowned, "The figure running from the pier looked like a male, but she could be working with someone," Nick said.

The detective looked directly at Kate, "I can't stop you from attending events that you have been invited to or public places. But I can ask that you call me if you wish to question anyone or poke your nose into *anything* to do with this case moving forward. Will you do that?"

Kate nodded, "Yes. I can do that."

"Thank you," Detective Nixon said. "You two go back to your hotel. Get yourselves dried up. I will see if the security team comes up with anything. In the meantime, stay away from the Hayes family and Thomas Hauer… for all of our sakes."

Kate nodded, getting up from her seat. Placing the towel over the back, she looked at Nick, "Dry clothes and dinner sound pretty good."

Forty One

Kate got out of the shower and toweled off. After her adventure in the water of Bradley Creek, she was happy to get cleaned up. Staring at her clothes, she fretted over what to wear. Nick said he would take care of dinner provided she had an open mind and wore clothes worthy of a seaside adventure.

He had showered quickly and raced off in his truck for "supplies". By the time she rounded the bungalows to the parking lot, he was pulling in with his truck. A glance at the truck's rack gave Kate furrowed brows.

"I can't help but notice that's not a surfboard up there," Kate said, reluctantly climbing in as Nick held onto the door waiting for her.

"No, that is not a surfboard," Nick said as he slid into his own seat. He turned and grinned, "That is a kayak."

"Those are generally used on the water. It's nighttime," Kate frowned.

"Not ideal for a waterway crossing but it'll be worth it," Nick said.

Kate looked dubious.

"It's a full moon tonight. It will be fabulous. I promise," Nick said. "I got a tandem, so if you just want to sit there, I can do all the paddling. Like one of those romantic movies."

"Or horror movies. I've seen that plenty of times as well," Kate muttered.

Undeterred, Nick put his tuck in gear and started down the road. Driving to the north end of Carolina Beach, he put his camping pass on his dash and carefully drove along the compacted sand to his designated spot. Passing other campers, Kate shot Nick a look, "What's the kayak for?"

Nick grinned, "This isn't where we are camping."

Kate shook her head, her lips forming a stressful pout.

"Come on," Nick encouraged hopping out of the cab of his truck.

Undoing several latches on the rack that covered his truck bed, he scooted the kayak along the edge until he could loft it over his head.

"You need help?" Kate asked, dancing behind him, unsure of how she could slip between him and the kayak to help him offload it.

"No, I've got it. You just enjoy the moon playing off the waves. I'll have us underway in no time," Nick assured.

Laying the kayak down, he placed a metal disc, a bundle of wood and a cooler into the kayak. Handing Kate a life jacket, he said, "Here. Put this on. We've had enough close calls for one day."

Kate looked at the kayak and then at the ocean, "We're going out there. At night?"

"Yeah," Nick nodded.

Kate shook her head, "I'm beginning to think you tried to feed me to the alligators. When that didn't work, you're trying your hand at feeding me to the sharks."

"I don't think that will happen. The idea is to stay *in* the boat. We'll be fine. I think," Nick said.

Kate wasn't satisfied with Nick's response but followed alongside as he pulled the kayak through the sand.

"I thought maybe we'd do something special after everything we've been through," Nick said.

"Special," Kate muttered as she stared at the kayak.

"Come on, you get the front seat. Paddling is optional," Nick said.

Kate screwed her face, "I think I'll paddle. That means I have some control over my last ever journey on earth."

"I'll get you back safe. I promise," Nick said.

Kate stuck a foot into the kayak before sliding into the seat.

"There we go," Nick said. Running along the back of the kayak like a bobsledder launching into a race, he hopped in his own seat as the kayak was fully buoyant.

With several quick strokes, he pointed the bow to slice through the waves. "It's a calm night. Should be an easy paddle," he said.

"I can't believe how well I can see… except… down in the water. It's pitch black, and frankly, horrifying," Kate said.

"Stay in the boat, you'll be fine," Nick assured.

Joining him, Kate put her paddle in the water, making smooth strokes with the blade, propelling the tiny vessel past the surf and into the calmer swells. From there, Nick pivoted the boat and crossed from Carolina Beach Inlet at the northern point of Carolina Beach to the tip of a dark, uninhabited island.

"That's where we're going. Masonboro Island!" Nick said.

Kate stared at the black land mass, "We're going *there?*"

"There is some of the most amazing stretch of beach that for a night can be like your own private island," Nick said.

"We can do that?" Kate gasped.

"Certain times of the year. That's why I brought a fire disc. It will help us limit any impact on the island. Leave it as unspoiled as we came," Nick said.

Finding a spot that he liked, he once more dug hard on the side of the kayak, pivoting it toward shore. With a few heavy strokes he leaned back, "You can put your paddle down. The waves will bring us in the rest of the way."

As he said that, the kayak lifted up and rolled toward the shore. Once the nose of the boat found friction with the sand, Nick hopped out and waded alongside the kayak. Keeping it steady, he pushed the boat all the way to shore. Holding out his hand, he helped Kate out of her seat and onto the sand.

Pulling the boat up a few more feet to ensure it was secure, Nick started gathering his things.

Kate stood with her hands on her hips, looking out at the ocean, "It's so quiet here."

"I know," Nick nodded, his hands laden with firewood and the campfire disc.

"You aren't going to kill me out here, are you?" Kate asked.

"No," Nick shook his head. "I think I have made myself pretty clear that I like you very much on the alive side of the equation."

"Good," Kate breathed. "How can I help?"

"I have a beach blanket next to the cooler. Would you mind spreading that out?" Nick asked.

"I'm on it, Captain," Kate saluted and retrieved the blanket from the kayak. "Is here good?" Kate asked, finding a spot that was out of reach of the wave's fingers stretching up on shore.

"Perfect," Nick said. He had already managed a small flame in the portable fire pit.

"You work fast. Were you a boy scout or something?" Kate asked.

"Or something," Nick winked in the moonlight.

"Detective Nixon mentioned your served in the military," Kate said.

Nick paused for a second and looked at Kate. His expression was even, "A story for another day. Tonight, it is all about peace and calm."

Hauling the cooler out of the kayak, he set it on a corner of the blanket. He produced two acrylic wine glasses and a bottle of wine.

Kate tried to peer over his shoulder.

"You open the wine. I'll get dinner going," Nick said.

Checking the fire, Nick held his hand over the flames to test the heat. With a spare log, he tamped at the bits of wood and turned the flames to a smolder. Reaching into the cooler, he set two bundles against the edge of the fire ring. Satisfied those were cooking, he produced two skewers stacked with shrimp.

Turning, he found Kate eyeing him, two glasses of wine held out in her hands. "Watcha got going on there?"

Nick grinned, "Barbecue shrimp and Lau Lau Mahi."

"Lau Lau?" Kate craned her neck.

"Wrapped in ti leaves, brushed with a little coconut oil," Nick said.

Kate shook her head, "You never cease to impress me."

Nick accepted the glass of wine and held it up to the moonlight, "Salud!"

"Salut!" Kate brought her glass to his. "Okay. Now that we are here. And I did not get eaten by a shark, this… this is amazing."

"I thought that you would like it," Nick said. Leaning over, he rotated. the shrimp skewers. "The first course is almost ready."

"You know, swimming for my life and being shanghaied along a moonlight adventure has made me quite hungry," Kate said.

"Then, I should solve that for you," Nick said. Pulling the skewers from the fire pit, he placed them on an acrylic plate. "Dinner is served."

"The finest restaurant in town," Kate said, sitting cross-legged on the blanket.

Gingerly nudging a freshly barbecued shrimp off the skewer, she brought it to her mouth. Slicing into it with her teeth, she took a bite. Her eyes widened, "This is good!"

"Nothing like shrimp on the beach cooked over a fire," Nick said.

"You are telling me," Kate said, reaching for a second shrimp.

Nick wandered to the fire. Poking one of the ti leaf wrapped fish, he pulled it onto a plate where he could open it and check it. "I think the second course is done!"

Pulling the other wrapped piece of fish, he placed it on a plate and brought it to the blanket. Pulling a set of chopsticks from his pocket, he handed them to Kate.

Grasping them, she looked up at Nick who was silhouetted with the moon behind him. "Chopsticks?"

"Sure. Easy to carry in your pocket as opposed to a knife and fork," Nick said.

"You're impossible," Kate said as Nick sat next to her on the blanket and straddled his own plate of fish.

"What do you think?"

"It is another winner!" Kate said, gingerly squeezing a morsel between the tips of her chopsticks.

When they were finished, Nick took their plates to the water and rinsed them off in the waves. With a shrug, he said, "The little crabs and fish love this stuff!"

"You're too much," Kate said.

"I was going for juuust enough!" Nick teased as he tossed a new log on the fire, bringing it back to life.

Kate leaned back on one elbow as her other arm supported her wine glass, "Have you always been this way?"

"What way?" Nick asked.

"A man-child. Competent. Strong. Yet an impetuous child," Kate said.

"I like the middle ones…" Nick said, his voice low.

"I'm serious. You are so full of life, carefree... I don't get it," Kate pressed.

Nick faced her, leaning on an elbow, "Not always, no. There was a time when life was a bit more complicated. Very serious. *Too* serious."

"When was that?" Kate asked.

"Before I retired," Nick shrugged. "I wasn't always a carefree surfer. I had obligations."

"And then?" Kate asked.

"And then I didn't," Nick replied.

His distant look told Kate that was all he wanted to share. She didn't care. She liked this Nick.

For a long silence, they watched the moon sparkle off the incoming waves. Nick's newly prodded fire added ambiance to the night. No matter where they looked, there was peace and quiet. Not another soul around. Kate found the idea that they were the only two humans in existence on that island both frightening and titillating.

Setting her glass down, Kate looked at Nick. His face glowed in the flicker of the flames. His eyes glistened in the shimmering moonlight. Kate found her breath uneven as she was overwhelmed by the moment.

"Thank you," Kate rasped. "Thank you for being you."

Nick's eyes left the moon dancing on the breaking waves, "That's all I know how to be."

"Hmm," Kate murmured, drunk in the symphony of crashing waves, the seclusion of the uninhabited island and the light play of the moon and firelight.

Nick could see the quandary in her eyes. Relieving her of the burden, he dropped on his back and looked up at the night sky. He made the moment about the experience and not about them.

Forty Two

Kate had never slept so peacefully. The crashing waves drowned out her thoughts and worries. The cool coastal breeze coming in off the Atlantic chased away the heat of the day. Knowing Nick was close made her feel safe, whether she wanted to admit it or not.

She was almost surprised to wake up in her bed in the bungalow. The open window was a first for her since she didn't feel safe in an accessible level guest room. Fatigue, Nick's assurance and a midnight island adventure left her to sleep without a care in the world.

With enough wood to cook their meal and an hour's ambiance, Nick paddled them back to Carolina Beach and drove them home when the firelight died.

Kate sat up in a start. Glancing at the clock, she realized she had slept later than she had in years. Throwing on a robe, she walked out of the bungalow and shielded her eyes from the morning sun as she scanned the horizon for a surfer bobbing in the swells. Not seeing one, she turned back to her bungalow. She saw a note taped to her door.

Snatching it, she read, "You seemed exhausted. Let you sleep. Will have coffee waiting for you at the beach house."

Studying the note as though it were a beautiful poem, Kate retreated to her bungalow. Hurriedly showering and getting dressed, she got ready for the day.

Arriving at the beach house, she wandered the interior, searching for Nick. Seeing open electronic fixtures scattered throughout the house, she followed the trail to the master bedroom where he was unboxing a new ceiling fan.

"You're hard at it, I see," Kate said as she glanced over to a coffee cup with her name written on it.

"Sleeping Beauty, you found your coffee!" Nick exclaimed.

"I did, thank you. It's almost as good as that deserted beach dinner I had last night," Kate said.

"If only I had packed s'mores, it would have been perfect," Nick said.

"It pretty much was perfect, but I think you are right. S'mores would have taken it to a whole new level," Kate said.

"Next time," Nick said as he lined out the parts for the ceiling fan.

"There is going to be a next time on an uninhabited island?" Kate asked.

Nick shrugged, "You never know."

"I guess not," Kate smiled. Looking at the array of parts strewn about she asked, "What are you doing? I found similar crop circles throughout the house."

"Making sure I have everything I need. Lining everything out. That way, once I get started, I can hammer through the entire house and get everything installed quickly and efficiently," Nick said.

"Spoken like a true professional," Kate said.

"You mean a handyman-surfer?" Nick scoffed.

Kate shook her head, "I love the thoughtfulness and the strategy."

"Earning my salary, boss!" Nick quipped.

Kate rolled her eyes, "I will let you get to it. I have lots to catch up on myself."

Nick cocked his head, "No tracking down Sheffield Hayes? Running down clues? Investigating the gardens and the mysterious alligator chummer?"

Kate flashed a smile, "I have a message into Sheffield's assistant. I have spoken to Detective Nixon. She said that if I keep my nose clean, she will let me know about any developments from her side."

"I will give you a prize if you manage to hold to that promise," Nick said.

Kate leaned forward with her finger laced under her chin, "A prize? What kind of prize?"

"I will go on any ride at the boardwalk as often as you want," Nick said.

"You're on!" Kate grinned. "Speaking of prizes or at least surprises… last night… that was amazing."

"I'm glad you enjoyed it," Nick said. His face displayed an unusual tension, and he turned away.

"Right, I said I would let you get back to work," Kate said.

Nick nodded and quickly focused on setting out the pieces of the ceiling fan he needed to install.

Kate was busy enough through the day that she was able to stave off the compulsions to march right back into Sheffield Hayes' office and demand answers. A lunch break with Nick was all the interaction they had had. A playful reminder that their bet was in play as they parted.

It was only when the sun began to set, that Kate's phone received a message.

Reading it, she traced Nick's completed installations and found him laboring over the last ceiling fan. Drenched in sweat from frequent forays into the attic and crawlspaces to update electrical connections, he peered through a small hole in the ceiling at Kate.

"You just gave me a new thing to be creeped out by in the middle of the night. I just got a message from Sheffield. He is willing to meet. Wants it to be private," Kate said.

"O…kay…" Nick expressed his reservation. "How private?"

"The Carolina Beach Boardwalk. It says to meet at the pavilion. Semi-private, semi-public. Could be worse," Kate shrugged.

"Could have been another pier adventure," Nick said. The sound of tools being set down and shuffling overhead paused as Nick said, "I have a couple of wires I need to cap to leave this safely…".

"No, no. Safety first. I didn't need to take you away from your work," Kate said. "Besides, I am going to make good on my promise. I am going to go down to the station to take Detective Nixon with me."

"Wow, that is very un-Kate-like," Nick laughed. "Still, I'd feel better if I was there with you."

"It's all right. And, you are going to join me for an evening of rides at the amusement park," Kate said.

"Kate…" Nick started.

Kate was already bouncing out of the room, "I've got to go. I'll be careful and call you as soon as I know anything!"

As she left, she could hear muffled curses from the attic.

Kate sped into the police station, oblivious to the reporter pool drinking coffee waiting for news to break.

The desk officer looked up, "I know, you need to speak to Detective Nixon. She is in a meeting with the mayor. It should wrap up any moment."

Kate danced back and forth, glancing at her watch. She said, "Let her know I am meeting with a suspect at the Boardwalk Pavilion. She needs to get it. The moment she is free."

"I'll be sure she gets it," the desk officer drawled.

Kate didn't have time to make a more fervent impression. Racing out the door, she hopped into her SUV and drove to the Carolina Beach Boardwalk.

Slipping out of the driver's seat and into the night, she found the area was eerily quiet. The rides were shut down, and the music was silent. Most lights were off for "Turtle Hours". The nearly full moon cast plenty of light for Kate to easily make her way to the pavilion. It also cast a myriad of haunting shadows across the beachfront landscape.

As Kate approached the pavilion, a figure leaned against the rail overlooking the Atlantic Ocean. "Sheffield?" Kate called.

She saw the figure's shoulder shudder as though they were laughing. The figure's voice was muted by the crashing ocean waves, "You aren't nearly as smart as you think you are, are you Ms. Harper?"

Nick scrambled to complete the ceiling fan installation as fast as possible. Having to replace each of the electrical boxes made the project that much more arduous and doubled the installation time. His effort was made only the more challenging as his mind was nowhere on electrical boxes and ceiling fans. It was on Kate. He wanted to be by her side as fast as possible. The idea that Detective Nixon would be with her was the only factor that allowed him to focus at all.

In his rush, Nick didn't tighten the head on his cordless driver well enough, sending the attached bit flying through the attic under the soft blanket of blown-in insulation. The shiny metal bit flashed in the glow of his work light before it splashed down in a drift of insulation.

Scrambling across the rafters on all fours, he made it to where he saw the bit fall. With one hand supporting him on a rafter, the other pawed at the insulation. Digging through, he concentrated on the bottom layer, where the bit would have touched down. His fingers danced along the ceiling board of the room below desperately seeking the bit so he could finish his job.

About to give up and head back downstairs to his toolbox to get another bit, his finger hit something. It was decidedly not a bit. It was leather-like. Finding the edge, Nick grasped it in his fingertips and pulled it through the insulation. Brushing it off, he found it was an old leather pouch. He had enough light to see what he was doing, but not enough to properly review the contents.

Reversing his journey to where he was working, he unzipped the pouch. It held only a few pages. To his excitement, the paper was of heavier quality. His fingers grazed over an embossing. As he held it to the light, Nick was disappointed. The documents in his hands were not ancient parchment leading to a secret pirate stash, but they were in a way, a treasure in themselves.

Stuffing the papers back into their protective pouch, Nick hurriedly capped off the exposed wires. "What I should have done in the first place!" Nick cursed to himself. Patting the document pouch against his hand he added, "But, I guess I wouldn't have found this."

Finding the attic stairs, Nick descended down to the upstairs hallway. Grateful he didn't have to shut off the air conditioning to do his work, he splashed water on his face and toweled dry.

Pulling out his phone, he dialed Kate. Receiving her voicemail, he quickly hung up and dialed Detective Nixon. Leaving a hasty message, he raced down the steps to go find Kate at the boardwalk.

Kate studied the figure by the rail. Taking several strides forward to confront them, she froze. The figure, dressed as smartly as Sheffield, began to turn. As they did, their fingers slowly lowered a mask over their face, just in time to obscure their identity from the sliver of moonlight that shot through ominous clouds.

A gun was pointed directly at Kate, motioning for her to move out of the pavilion. As she complied, she slipped her hand into her pocket.

"Lose the phone, or I will kill you right here," the figure said.

Kate froze. The last thing she wanted to do was relinquish her last lifeline. Pulling the phone out, she held it for the gunman to see. As they reached out for it, Kate tossed it in a nearby garbage can.

"Move. Toward the beach," the gunman growled. Glancing at the trash can as they walked by, he mumbled a curse deciding to remain focused on Kate.

Off the coast, flashes of lightning lit up the sky. A tremble of thunder rippled through the air. Suddenly, Kate's heart was in her stomach. She was prodded along the beach in the same manner Collin Royce was a decade before her.

Her eyes glanced toward the Carolina Beach Boardwalk. She hoped headlights or flashlights would cut through the night sky. The next flash of lightning that danced through the sky was the only light she could see as the clouds swallowed up the last trace of the moon.

Fat raindrops began to speckle the sand and pepper them as they walked. Kate's window for escape was about to be consumed by the storm, just as the moon was.

"Hey!" a voice cut through the night in between the thunderclaps.

The gunman looked toward the southern strip of the boardwalk. A man sprinted toward them. "Stop!" the man yelled.

"Nick!" Kate gasped under her breath.

The gunman swiveled his aim from Kate to Nick. As lightning flashed, the trigger was pulled, the report of the pistol obscured by the roar of thunder that followed.

Kate took advantage of the distraction and ran in the opposite direction.

The gunman spun, waiting for an opportunity to pair another shot in concert with the storm. As Kate ran, Nick sprinted to cover closer to the beach's edge. The gunman moved his aim from Kate to Nick from Nick to Kate.

Deciding to take aim at Kate, the gunman steadied and waited for his next opportunity. Lightning flashed, a hammer ripped through the night, hitting the gunman just as he squeezed the trigger.

Kate was unaware of the bullet that sailed past her and embedded into a sand dune. She found steps on the north end of the boardwalk and ran up them faster than she had ever run in her life. She wanted desperately to get to Nick but she knew between them, was a man with a gun.

Streaking past the boardwalk and through the beach front shops, Kate rolled into a shadowy alley as lightning lit up the sky. Pressing her back against the wall, she held her breath as she could hear footsteps approach.

Driving rain and a gust of wind scattered sand into tiny tornadoes as another loud thunder cracked. A bolt of lightning turned the sky into daylight. A silhouette stood in the alley where Kate took refuge.

Slowly, an arm raised up. The glint of a handgun muzzle flashed in a splash of lightning, "I'm sorry, Ms. Harper. It didn't have to be this way."

The thunder rolled right on top of the flashes. Kate knew the next bolt would come with a ball of hot steel. She winced as lightning struck so close it had to be in the park. To her surprise, she was alive to hear the thunder crash rumble so heavily it shook the ground at her feet.

At the end of the alley, the gunman was in a bear hug as strong arms wrapped around him. The shot that was intended for Kate ricocheted off the cement at the base of a shop.

The gun fell to the ground as the gunman slammed his shoulder and his attacker into the wall of the shop. For a moment, his attacker broke their grip allowing the gunman to spin producing a wicked looking blade from his belt. With slashing movements, he backed his attacker up.

A flash of lightning revealed a soaking wet Nick Mason ready to parry the next strike from the gunman.

"Run, Kate!" Nick yelled.

When the gunman took a swipe at Nick with the blade, Kate dove to the ground. As she rolled and popped up on her feet, she appeared in the following flash of lightning with the gun in her hands. "Hold it right, there!"

"You won't shoot me," the knife-wielding figure snarled.

"Before you shot at me and Nick, I might have agreed with you. I'm a bit cranky and over that right at this moment," Kate snapped. "It's over for you, Arturo Moreno."

"So, you know who I am," Arturo said.

"And I know you killed Collin Royce. I know you did it for Mark Hayes," Kate said.

"I didn't do it for Mark," Arturo snapped. He kept the blade brandished within striking distance of Nick.

"You did it for Sophia," Nick said. "I found her birth certificate. The one that Collin Royce brought with him to prove who she really was."

"Collin was an opportunist. He just didn't know how to take advantage of it," Arturo said.

Kate stepped forward, "But, *you* did."

"I was fulfilling the dying wish of the woman that I loved," Arturo said.

"Anne Hayes," Kate said.

"Mark didn't deserve her. But with Sheffield born. She was reconciling with Mark after a tiff. It broke my heart, but it kept hers intact," Arturo said. His voice dropped and his shoulders drooped.

In a flash, he spun, striking Kate in the wrist. Nick launched himself forward but was stopped as Arturo held the blade in front of Kate's face. "Where is the certificate?"

"I, uh, it's at the beach house," Nick said.

"Pretty Ms. Harper will accompany me there. If I find it where you say I will, I will let her live. If you are lying to me…" Arturo warned.

Nick dropped his head and held his hands out to sway Arturo into not harming Kate, "It's in my truck, in the bed-mounted toolbox."

Arturo turned toward Nick with a savage grin. Waving the knife back and forth, he said, "That is your only chance to toy with me and not pay the price."

Bending down, Arturo felt for the handgun. As his fingers swept the ground searching for it, Kate's toe slowly slid it further and further out of his reach. In frustration, Arturo took his eye off Nick to spy the gun.

Nick kicked at Arturo and pulling Kate by the shoulders, led her away just as Arturo recovered and fired a shot that slammed into a nearby souvenir stand.

Holding her wrist, Kate tried to keep pace with Nick who ran with his arm around her. Another shot sailed by, smashing a window that was directly in front of them.

Turning, Nick broke the line of sight with Arturo. Ducking, they crept along the base of the giant gondola wheel ride. Taking a moment, Nick ripped a piece of his shirt and hastily tied it around Kate's wrist. Looking at his chest, Kate said, "You're cut, too!"

"Well, then let's get out of here so we can get patched up," Nick said.

Lightning flashed, revealing their location to an enraged Arturo Moreno. Firing a shot in their direction, they were again on the run. They could hear sirens approaching. Red and blue lights joined the brilliant flashes of yellow and white lightning.

Kate and Nick wanted to run toward the police cars, but instead, they were forced to move further away as Arturo pressed forward. No longer concerned with marrying his shots with the cover of thunder, he squeezed the trigger with little regard.

Slipping into an alley, they found themselves blocked. Using flashes of lightning, they searched for a way to escape. Seeing Arturo lit up at the end of the alley, they were trapped. The barrel of his gun took careful aim.

Forty Three

Nick shouldered his way into a locked door pulling Kate in with him just as Arturo squeezed the trigger. Their heads spinning, they found themselves in the arcade. The light glow from the machines, even in their sleep state, gave them a source of eerie light to navigate through.

Sliding a pinball machine in front of the doorway would do little to slow Arturo down, but Nick and Kate hoped that it would provide them a few seconds to find a hiding spot. They hoped that Arturo's increasingly aggressive use of his firearms would alert the police to their location.

Scanning the arcade, they found each machine provided some degree of cover, and there was a sea of shadows for them to dive into. Nowhere provided any level of safety that made them feel secure.

To their horror, some machines came to life on their own. A screen lit up, beckoning them to combat zombies another revved an engine as a race car waited at a starting line.

"We must have tripped a sensor," Nick said.

Staying in the center of the walkways, they could hear Arturo crawl out from under the pinball machine. He strode with purpose. As he did so, he tripped a sensor. An animated clown sprang out at him, laughing a maniacal giggle. Arturo reacted with a shot that shattered the plastic clown's head.

Nick and Kate hunched down in the prize room. Nick had shoved a chair up against the door handle. Kate slithered into a giant bin of stuffed animals. Nick kneeled under a desk as they heard Arturo try the prize room door. When the handle turned but the door didn't budge, Arturo kicked it open with enough force to break the door and shatter the top rail of the chair, freeing it from its place.

As Arturo stepped over the bramble, Nick pounced. Placing all of his focus on the gun hand, Nick forced Arturo into an errant shot. With both hands wrapped around Arturo's arm, he focused on the gunman's wrist, slamming it into the doorjamb. He kept repeating the action until Arturo howled in pain and dropped the pistol.

Staggering, Arturo slashed out with his knife, catching Nick in the arm. As Nick wheeled around to prepare for a follow-up strike, he tripped over shrapnel from the chair landing on his back.

Leaping, Arturo landed on top of Nick, blade in hand, he prepared to strike. Kate burst through the blanket of teddy bears and jumped on Arturo's back. The stronger man cast Kate off with ease, readying another strike on Nick when beams of light sliced through the dark arcade.

"We're in here!" Kate called as Nick used both hands to try and protect himself from Arturo's blade and superior position.

"Freeze!" a voice yelled. Detective Nixon was flanked by several officers.

Arturo glared at Nick, intent on completing his strike before his muscles softened. Nick kicked him off to the side and scooted back away from the man.

Detective Nixon strode forward. Kicking the blade aside, she motioned for an officer to put Arturo in handcuffs.

Glancing at Kate who recovered from Arturo hurling her off of him, the detective asked, "Are you two okay?"

"A couple of cuts, but we're fine," Kate said, her hand gingerly placing pressure on her wrist.

"We'll see that you two get medical attention. And then we are going to get to the bottom of this, but I suspect you already have," Detective Nixon said. "Is there anyone else we should be looking for, victim or otherwise?"

"No. It's just us," Kate said.

Nick stood next to her. They both looked the worse for wear.

"Let's get you two out to the medics. The storm has finally passed over," Nixon said.

Under the red flashing lights of the ambulance, Kate and Nick were checked over, their cuts and slashes properly bandaged. The medic said, "I recommend you both go to the ER and see if you need stitches."

They nodded as the EMT walked away. Detective Nixon had been watching and waiting for them to be cleared. She stood in front of Kate and Nick, who sat on the ambulance tailgate.

"I figured I should talk to you before I even try and question Mr. Moreno," the detective said.

"First, I came by to talk to you before coming here," Kate said defensively.

"I know. My desk sergeant told me. When I got your call and got no response from you, I knew something was wrong. I couldn't be sure, but I thought I heard a gunshot between thunderclaps," Detective Nixon said. "Oh, one of my officers found this in the garbage can."

"Arturo wanted it. I thought getting some kind of message to you and tossing it in the trash was a better idea," Kate said.

"It was a good one. I thought you were here to meet Sheffield Hayes," the detective said.

"I thought I was, too. He was even dressed like Sheffield," Kate said. "I should have put it together sooner."

"Put what together?" Detective Nixon asked.

"Arturo Moreno was the killer. When he pulled the mask down I caught a glimpse of his sly smile. It reminded me of someone. It wasn't until Nick confirmed it with evidence he found in the attic of the beach house. Sophia Hayes is Arturo Moreno's daughter, not Mark Hayes'," Kate said.

Detective Nixon's jaw dropped, "What?"

Nick nodded, "It's true. I found the birth certificate. Arturo Moreno and Anne Hayes, though on the birth certificate, she used her maiden name, Clarkson."

"I don't understand," the detective said.

"I don't have all the pieces, but I believe Arturo and Anne had an affair in England when she was on one of her trips abroad. It sounds as though she was going through a rough patch in her relationship. When Mark wanted to reconcile, Anne was pregnant. Everyone thought it was with Mark's second child, but two people, and maybe a lab somewhere, knew the truth. A truth they were willing to protect at all costs," Kate said.

"Why wouldn't Arturo just fess up and claim Sophia after Anne passed?" Detective Nixon asked.

"It was in honor of Anne's dying wish," Kate said.

"And Collin… the reporters?" Nixon pressed.

"Being from the same area, they somehow found out. Came here trying to find a way to leverage the Hayes family… as one of them. Except, he asked too many questions and said too many things that made Arturo afraid the secret would get out. Collin must have let it slip that he had proof. A fatal mistake," Kate continued.

"And the reporters Dennis and Andrew Jones?" Nixon asked.

"I assume they were on the trail. They went to school with Collin. Dennis came to make a name for himself on the national stage. When Collin disappeared, the trail went cold. He went back to England," Kate said.

"Until we found Collin Royce in the wall of the beach house," Nick said.

"Exactly. His quest for news fame was once more on the table. His poking around the Hayes family triggered Arturo to make sure whatever Dennis Jones knew, the world would never see it in print or hear of it," Kate said.

"And his poor brother followed Dennis right into the same fate," Detective Nixon nodded. With a sigh, she asked, "Is there anything else I should know?"

Kate shook her head, "Aside from what we learned tonight about Arturo and Sophia, everything else is just theory."

The detective put away her notebook, "Well, you two should follow the medic's advice and get properly checked out at the ER. I have a long, long night ahead of me with Arturo Moreno."

"Good luck. Thanks for coming to our rescue," Kate said, her voice meek.

Detective Nixon turned to face Kate, "Ms. Harper, you have good instincts. Without training, those instincts are liable to get you killed- and your friend, Nick, too."

As the detective walked away, Kate looked up at Nick, "She's right. I'm sorry I got you into all this. I was so worried you were going to get hurt."

"I don't know that you can help it. But I told you, I have your back. Wherever that places me," Nick said.

Kate leaned into him, her head on his shoulder.

Forty Four

Kate expected to have to catch the remaining details of the case from the news. She was surprised when she found Detective Nixon on the beach house doorstep.

"May I?" the detective nodded towards the interior of the house as she whipped her sunglasses off.

"Of course. Come on in," Kate said, waving her arm toward the hall and shutting the door behind them.

"I hope you are both okay. I know once the adrenaline goes away a lot more bumps and bruises seem to come to the surface," the detective said.

"Glad to be alive. That kind of trumps everything else," Kate said.

Nick came bounding down the steps, "The last light fixture is installed. No more trips to the attic… Oh, hello, Detective."

"Mr. Mason," Detective Nixon nodded. "No more work in the attic? What if I told you I learned from Arturo

Moreno that there is a pirate treasure map hidden somewhere in this house?"

Nick's eyes widened.

Kate shot the detective a questioning look. Nixon just grinned and shook her head.

"That is so mean!" Kate hissed.

Nixon laughed, "I thought you two might like to hear how my conversation with Arturo Moreno went. I felt you *deserved* to know."

"Thank you," Kate said, leaning forward.

"It turns out, most of your assertions were correct. With Nick's evidence, we could corroborate that Sophia is indeed the child of Arturo and Anne Hayes. He admitted that Collin, who is a distant cousin of the Hayeses, tripped across the information while trying to learn more about *his* family. He didn't know what he wanted to do with the information, but Arturo thinks he was trying to profit from it. When Arturo learned about Collin and learned that he had proof that would break his promise to Anne, he killed him under cover of the storm and stuffed him in the wall," Detective Nixon said.

Nick slapped himself on the forehead, "And he had the knowledge and the skills to build him into a wall in the beach house."

"You didn't think Sheffield could do that, did you?" the detective asked. Both Kate and Nick shrugged.

The detective laughed, "I always thought he… or Thomas Hauer or maybe even Mark Hayes just paid somebody. Arturo had inside information that made it easy to plant confusing clues."

"Like getting ahold of Sheffield's car keys to drive over to the Hauer course and puncture my tires," Kate said.

"And Robert Grant's custom golf tool," Nick added.

"He didn't care if the blame got pinned on Grant or Hauer, but Anne wanted her family left intact," Detective Nixon said.

"That must have driven Arturo crazy," Kate exclaimed.

The detective's jaw dropped, and she stared at Kate, "You think? I believe he killed three men and chased you around an amusement park trying to kill you."

"Yeah," Kate bobbed her head around.

"Kind of an odd romance to it. A man risking everything. Resorting to terrible acts to preserve the promise to the one woman he ever loved," Nick said.

Both women turned their heads to Nick. He shrugged, "What? I'm not saying it was sane. It was like a Shakespearian tragedy, but with gunfights."

"Sure. I hope your chest wound heals without issue," Detective Nixon snapped.

"What about the bookcase and throwing me in the water at Airlie Gardens?" Kate asked.

"He said he was the one at Airlie. He had hoped you would stop investigating. He was really frustrated you wouldn't. It was the first and only time he and I had anything in common during his interrogation," Detective Nixon said. "As for the bookcase, he said it wasn't him. He was tailing Andrew that day. He thinks they were trying to scare you off."

"And breaking into the house?" Nick asked.

"That was Arturo. He knew his way around. Knew he could enter through the dumb waiter. Not finding the documents was another source of frustration for him," Detective Nixon said.

"What happens now?" Kate asked.

"He made a full confession. The district attorney may still ask for a deposition, so please check in before you guys head home," the detective said. Glancing around, she said, "The place looks great, by the way."

"Thank you, Detective Nixon. For everything. And sorry for being such a pain," Kate said.

The detective leaned in close and smiled, "You're welcome. And if you ever come into my town and stick your nose into one of my investigations again, I won't hesitate to toss you in a cell until the proper authorities close it."

Without another word, the detective spun and left the two standing in front of the massive oceanfront windows, absorbing everything they had learned and everything they had been through.

Kate looked at Nick, and the mischievous look returned, "I do believe you owe me on our wager."

"I'm not sure that I do. As I recall, you went out by yourself, got shot at, got me shot at, both of us sliced up in a knife fight…" Nick protested.

"Yes, but I went to the station first. And then I got Detective Nixon on the line and my phone led them to the rescue. So…" Kate said.

"I don't think that is winning," Nick scowled.

"Come on," Kate pleaded, tugging at Nick's arm.

"Fine. Let's get this over with," Nick said. "Do I at least get a post-ride hot dog?"

"Oh no. We aren't going to the boardwalk," Kate said.

"We aren't?" Nick looked confused.

"You promised me a ride. I have something else in mind," Kate grinned.

Forty Five

Kate bubbled with excitement, "Come on. We have a schedule to keep!"

"Schedule? I thought adventuring was time piece and compass be-damned! Well, maybe not the compass. Those are useful," Nick said.

"This adventure very much runs on a schedule," Kate said.

"Are we taking a train?" Nick asked.

"Something like that," Kate teased.

Climbing into her SUV, she headed south on the island. Passing the Fort Fisher State Historic Park and Monument, Nick let out a sigh of relief, "Good. I'm pretty sure we are banned from there. But I don't think there is much on the island after this."

Kate pulled the SUV into the Fort Fisher Ferry Terminal, "We're going for a ride. Like I said."

"A ferry ride. Nice. I like boats way better than Ferris wheels and roller coasters," Nick said.

Driving onto the ferry and parking, they got out and walked up to the outdoor observation deck. As the ferry's horn blew, it pulled out of the terminal and pushed into the Cape Fear River.

Leaning against the rail, they watched the water spill by as the big diesel engines of the ferry churned. A breeze whipped across their faces, gently blowing Kate's hair in the wind.

"I love this. It feels great to be on the water. And not at night. Not in a tiny boat smaller than the creatures that might like to eat me," Kate said.

"You know I am all about the water," Nick said. "Those critters might nibble, but they'll spit you out. You're not their food. Besides, bad humans that you have a tendency to chase after are far, far more dangerous. But, yes. It is great being out here."

For a few minutes, they rode in silence.

Kate leaned far out over the rail, catching the full force of the breeze as the Cape Fear River met the confluence of the Atlantic Ocean. Suddenly, she shrieked and pointed, "A sea turtle!"

"A Loggerhead. She's a big one, too," Nick said.

"How do you know it is a 'she'?" Kate asked.

Nick pointed, "Smaller tail, narrower head, slightly more domed upper shell. That, is a lady Loggerhead."

"Is there anything on the water you don't know about?" Kate spun from the rail to face Nick.

Nick swallowed, "I have no idea what the female of the human species thinks while out on the water… or anywhere, for that matter."

Kate's lips folded under her teeth as she thought of her response, "Yeah, that one's a mystery for me too."

Spinning to once more face the water, Kate said, "I am thinking… I would like to take this one step at a time."

"This?" Nick asked.

"Us. You and me," Kate turned back to Nick and smiled. "The job, after all, is done. You are no longer on the clock."

Kate pressed up on her toes toward Nick.

He smiled and met her, their lips connecting with a spark that made both of their chests swell.

When they parted, Nick cocked his head, "I'm not on the clock, but the company is still paying my way home, right?"

Kate swatted him on the chest, Nick reeled as she struck right where he had met with Arturo's blade. Pulling her hand to her mouth, she gasped, "I am so sorry."

Nick drooped his head, "There is one thing you can do to make it feel better…"

"Oh, yeah?" Kate grinned.

Pulling her close, Nick leaned in to kiss her.

"You're making me want to do that again," she giggled.

"No, no. You are free to kiss me as often as you want," Nick said.

"This doesn't make us boyfriend and girlfriend, you know," Kate said, watching

Southport's shore and ferry terminal come into view.

"Call it what you want. I just enjoy spending time with you," Nick said.

Kate grinned, wrapping her arm around him, "I do, too."

"Where are we going, anyway," Nick asked.

"Southport. It is this *charming* southern, coastal town," Kate beamed.

"Your company have properties there?" Nick asked.

"Not *yet*," Kate said, a twinkle in her eye. "You never know."

Nick pulled her tight, "You never know."

About the Author

Seth Sjostrom is a serial entrepreneur, adventurer and author. His novels include the thrillers *Blood in the Snow*, *Blood in the Water*, *Blood in the Sand*, *Penance*, *Penance: Unredeemable*, *Penance: Absolution*, *Patriot X*, *Patriot X: Insurrection*, *Dark Chase* and *Dark Chase: Dead Run* as well as the romances *Back to Carolina*, *Finding Christmas*, *The Tree Farm*, *Letters from Santa*, *The Nativity* and *The Toy Store*. He recently released the first of his Beach House Mysteries series *Trouble on Treasure Island*. Seth partners with Hire Heroes USA with proceeds and volunteer hours dedicated with sales of his Patriot X series. Sales of *The Christmas Café* help to support Jen Lilley and Ale Boggiano's "Christmas is Not Cancelled" charity fundraising for foster children. Seth has also shares a portion of author proceeds of his Penance Series with the Mel Greene Institute to Stop Human Trafficking.

www.SethSjostrom.com
Twitter: @SethSjostrom
Facebook: @authorSethSjostrom
Instagram: @SethSjostrom

More Books by Seth

Christmas Titles
Finding Christmas
The Tree Farm
The Nativity
The Toy Store
The Christmas Café
Love at The Christmas Con

Beach House Mysteries
Trouble on Treasure Island
A Caper on Carolina Beach
Peril on Palm Beach

Other Titles
Back to Carolina
Penance
Penance: Unredeemable
Penance: Absolution
Dark Chase
Dark Chase: Dead Run
Patriot X
Patriot X: Insurrection
Blood in the Snow
Blood in the Water
Blood in the Sand

Children's Books
Letters from Santa
The Hollow
Cryptid Rangers: The Secret of the Skunk Ape
The Heart of a Reindeer
The(Too) Helpful Little Angel
A Puppy Whisperer Christmas